THE SWING

WHERE TRUE LOVE HANGS IN THE BALANCE

LIFE CHANGING FICTION SERIES
BOOK 1

J A CRAWSHAW

XYLEM
Publishing

MY PERSONAL MEMOIR

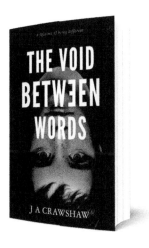

*Available on all platforms and bookshops. Hardback
Paperback Ebook and Audiobook*

The inspirational true story of how I overcame dyslexia and
50yr fear of words to write this novel.

https://books2read.com/u/bMX5Vk

CONTENTS

1

1979 OXFORDSHIRE

The smug, menacing face of the Grim Reaper wielding his sickle was now ingrained like a tattoo on the inside of Charlotte's brain. The Death card was the last one she wanted to pull from the deck.

The Fool

Was she the fool? Was life meant to be full of rejection and self-doubt? Was there more to her feeble existence?

Love

Charlotte had never experienced the feeling of being in love. She was too young. Fairy-tale weddings and handsome knights on horseback were confined to storybooks, as far as she was concerned.

Death

It was true, Charlotte felt empty and neglected, and sometimes very lonely. She'd contemplated it a few times before. You know. Ending it all. Maybe now was the time?

She took one last, lingering look at all three cards before stuffing them into the back pocket of her jeans. She then proceeded to hide the rest of the pack in their usual hiding place, within the lining of an upholstered chair in her bedroom. If her father knew about them, they would be confiscated, and she would be punished.

She crept out of her room and made her way along the secret passage to her father's office where, with all the stealth of a cat burglar, she slid open the top drawer of his stout wooden writing desk. Without hesitation, she grabbed his prized hunting knife, with its leather sheath embossed with the family coat of arms. She let her finger momentarily trace the outline of the gold lettering and thought of her father's arrogant and stern face. Then she retraced her steps and sprinted down the hall, leaping over the well-known squeaky floorboards, which could easily have given away her intentions to Mother or the house staff.

On leaving the house, she dashed across the lawn, through the trees and down towards the river. She didn't care about getting her feet wet as she ran along the water's edge. She jumped from rock to rock, enjoying the risk of potentially falling into the fast-flowing torrent, and gathered pace. What did it matter, anyway? No one cared.

Her heavy heart pounded as she occasionally dipped her foot into the cold water and soaked her sneakers. At the age of eleven, Charlotte wasn't allowed down by the river alone. Her father forbade it and would often tell her the story of a young poacher who had plummeted to his death trying to jump the ferocious weir. But Charlotte respected the poacher's valiant effort and often thought about what it must feel like to end your life in such a way.

The early morning air was chilly, and the sun's spear-like rays pierced the mist rising through the woodland canopy. Charlotte was heading to her special place. It had been on her mind for weeks as the end of term at boarding-school approached, and she was desperate to cast off the starchy rules and restrictions of the classroom and be free.

She checked the contents of her back pocket with one hand and gripped the knife tightly in the other, slowing down as she proceeded along the woodland edge to jump over a series of badger holes.

'Hello, badgers,' she whispered. Normally she'd shout at the top of her voice, hoping they'd hear her, deep below her feet. Today was different, though. Her greeting was a mere formality; it was more important not to give away her whereabouts.

She proceeded with purpose and, after a while, reached a fallen tree. Its rigid straight stem and fissured bark offered precarious access over the river to the woodland on the opposite side, and was the swiftest and most direct route to her final destination. Holding her nerve, and balancing with arms outstretched, Charlotte negotiated the sturdy trunk and finally jumped onto the steep bank. She checked her back pocket once again and glanced at the protruding handle of the knife as she gripped it in her fist. The bank was strewn with the serpent-like silvery-grey roots of abundant beech trees. Charlotte grabbed hold of one, and perched her knee on another. With all her strength, she hauled herself up the gnarly root staircase, the hole in her jeans ripping even more, allowing her knee to poke through completely, giving her maximum leverage for her clamber to the top.

Once there and out of breath, she paused, hands on knees, to gather herself, and suddenly became aware of something moving in the dense undergrowth ahead. She crouched down further and listened intently. Her heart was thumping so much, she could sense it in her temples. She was intrigued, but also apprehensive. Whatever it was that was lurking, it was moving slowly, brushing through the tall bracken, advancing towards her. She tentatively rose onto her tip toes in an attempt to see, then heard a twig snap, followed immediately by another. Her heart still racing, she glanced back at the river. It would be an undignified descent and there was a serious risk of plunging into the deep water, but at least she had an escape route. She re focused on the bracken fronds still moving before her and stood her ground. Suddenly, out of the vegetation, the long and unmistakeable double-barrel of a shotgun appeared, and out stepped a man with a ferret-like moustache, clad in camouflage and a green hat with a single pheasant's tail feather sticking up on one side.

He pointed the gun away from her. 'Miss Charlotte! What are you doing down here?'

'Erm... I was just out for a walk and I followed one of the badger tracks, which led me here.'

The gamekeeper adjusted the peak of his hat and looked at her inquisitively. 'You'd better make sure your father doesn't find out you're out in the woods alone.'

'Please don't say anything, will you?' The nervousness in her voice made it go an octave higher as she hid her hands behind her back.

'You really should go straight back to the house. It's dangerous down here. I thought you were a deer. I could have shot you. A gamekeeper's job isn't shooting young girls. Especially the boss's daughter.'

'I will, I promise. I'm so sorry.' Charlotte was shaking and she turned to make her escape.

'What's that?' he said, raising his voice.

'Oh, erm... nothing,' she said, trying to cover the knife with her hand.

'It doesn't look like nothing to me.'

Charlotte shook her head and took a couple of steps back.

'Is that what I think it is?'

With that, she made a dash for the top of the bank and, without stopping, jumped and began to slide on her bottom, jarring herself on the rocks and roots, until she landed with a thump beside the river, bruising her back and legs.

'Ouch!' she said out loud. She glanced up to see if she'd been pursued, but the gamekeeper was nowhere to be seen. She lay on the ground, gasping for air, and took a minute or so to recover. Thankfully, nothing was broken. Just a few bruises and a cut on her knee. She picked herself up—and realised it had gone. The knife! She'd lost it in the fall.

Desperately, she sank to her hands and knees and scoured the undergrowth among the reeds on the water's edge, pulling frantically at the leaves and moss. A wave of relief hit her as she saw a reflection of light, a twinkling of metal, and she caught her breath. The knife's handle, carved from a fallow-deer antler from the estate, and its razor-sharp blade, now separated from the leather sheath, were shining in the sunlight. Her father's hunting knife was one of his most trea-sured possessions and one Charlotte was never supposed to touch.

She had a decision to make: assume the gamekeeper would report her and so head straight back home, or carry on with the mission. She looked up at the bank once more. The coast was clear, so she dusted herself off and slotted the knife back into its sheath. Her father was away on business, after all.

With the gamekeeper lurking, attempting to climb the bank again was out of the question. It was the shortest and easiest route, but there was another option. It meant following the river through the dense woodland and crossing the weir at the very end. She'd never attempted it before, but she had no choice.

The riverbank soon became densely overgrown, and Charlotte tussled with the bramble and the Medusa-like stems of the hazel that impeded each stride. At one point, she had to scramble along a tricky ledge way above the river, the plummeting stones hitting the water sounding unnerving as her feet slipped on the shaley ground. Eventually, she arrived at the top of the vertical weir. Her eyes traced the river as it flowed eerily until it was funnelled into a fast-flowing, deep channel, and then she glanced at the powerful cascade itself, spouting over the top of the weir and down into the lake below. The noise of the water was loud and powerful. Her temples thumped so hard, she felt dizzy.

The lip of the weir was covered in green moss and looked slippery. Charlotte ground her shoe into the slime to assume better purchase. A decent enough run-up and a leap of faith and she would be over.

She paused and scanned the lakeside, searching for her special place in the distance. It was there beside the tiny pebbly beach, the familiar shape of the mature oak tree, with its sturdy, unbalanced branches lit up in the sun, just visible through the mist and spray of the turbulent water. Charlotte placed one foot on the slippery slab, ground it in again and focused her eyes on the endpoint. Stepping carefully, but purposefully, one foot at a time, and not letting the force of the water intimidate her, she made her way to the edge.

2

1979 YORKSHIRE

Peter jumped up onto the lock gate. The canal below was black and filthy from the leaking engine oil of the barges shunting coal from the colliery. The air was thick and damp with the smell of sulphur, and it was difficult to see what lay beyond. With arms stretched out beside him, he traversed the thin solid-wood rail, not daring to look at the grimy water some fifteen or twenty feet below him. He reached the end and leaped onto the stony ground. The white cotton strands of the hole in his jeans snapped, exposing almost his entire knee.

At eleven years old, Peter was starting to venture further from home and discover new places. Six weeks of summer holidays meant time to explore, and he wasn't going to waste a minute.

He picked up a perfectly flat and rounded stone and skimmed it across the water. It skipped delicately on the surface, creating a series of oily ripples, before hitting the solid wood of the lock gate and sinking into the murky depths. He looked up to observe an enormous barge loaded with coal chugging towards the lock. Peter waved at the driver in anticipation. The boatman, in his hefty black coat and grubby white miner's helmet, signalled from the stern for him to come close.

'You going to help out lad?' he said, in his broad Yorkshire accent.

'Yes, please.' Peter nodded eagerly.

'It'll save me having to get off if you open the sluice and push the gate.'

'I know what to do. I've done it before.'

'OK, then. Wait until I give you the signal, then turn the wheel and open the sluice, give it a few seconds, then push as hard as you can on the gate. You got that, lad?'

Peter gave a thumbs up and ran up to the gate. The barge pulled into position and, right on cue, he received a raised arm from the boatman. Peter, using both hands, gradually wound the large iron handle. It was stiff and took all his strength, but he didn't want to give in. Then, suddenly, the sound of rushing water gave him confidence. The sluice was opening. A gradual release of pressure meant he could put his back to the solid oak beam of the lock gate and begin to push back with his feet. The pressure of the thousands of gallons of water behind the gate made progress extremely slow, but bit by bit, the gate started to move until, with everything he could muster, Peter opened it fully, and the gigantic boat, piled high with jet black coal, entered the lock. The boatman gave him a nod of approval, and he felt proud to have helped. He smiled back and gave a cheerful wave.

Peter didn't stick around to see the boat progress on its passage. Instead, he sprinted off, following the perimeter fence of the coal mine and along the foot of the slag heap. The acrid air caught the back of his throat as he picked his way through items of discarded waste from the mine. Timber, bricks, other random masonry and broken chairs and tables, all dumped along the fence line, made progress slow, but Peter had somewhere to go. His place. His secret place and his sanctuary. A place tucked away from the booms and crashes of heavy industry, where he could observe the wildlife moving around below, among the trees and gorse.

He slithered down the sludgy bank and stopped dead to marvel at the ancient oak tree. It formed the centrepiece of a dell and was instantly recognisable by its gnarly, twisted trunk and wide-spreading branches.

Peter placed his hands on the solid stem. 'Hello, tree,' he said, securing his foot onto a small branch stub, ready to climb her. He scrambled his way up through the complex structure of sturdy branches, twigs and extensive vivid green leaves. His perch, halfway up the tree, was as if it were made for him. A stout branch, thicker than his body, left the trunk in a sweeping, open U-shape, forming the perfect bucket seat, where Peter could sit with his back up against the trunk and dangle his feet in mid-air.

Once in position, he adjusted his head to catch the sun on his face. The tree canopy moved effortlessly in the warm breeze, intercepting the sun's rays and making him feel safe. He closed his eyes, feeling the sun warm his eye-sockets and heightening all his senses. He couldn't get away from the stench of sulphurous coal, but the smell of the gorse and wild garlic below cut through in drifts on the breeze.

Every few minutes he heard the shunting of the coal from the railway onto the barges ready to take the cargo to the power station. When the rumble of coal subsided for a moment, there came a faint buzzing. Intermittent and frantic, it seemed to be close by. Peter stood up on the branch and tried to locate the source of the sound. He climbed higher, using the branches like a ladder, until the noise became louder. On the rough bark of the trunk, and just below a decayed scar where an old branch had dislodged, he could see what looked like a dragonfly, trapped in a spider's web. Its dazzling red body and almost translucent wings were desperately trying to break free.

Peter hooked his leg around a branch to steady himself and was thus able to reach out with both hands, carefully sever the web and bring it towards him for a closer look. He'd never been so close to such a beautiful creature; it felt incredibly delicate and vulnerable in his hands. He could see that the web completely bound its wings, which looked as delicate as the web itself. He began to meticulously and carefully pick away at the gossamer strands in the hope he wasn't damaging the insect. It wasn't easy. With every pull at the web, the wings were flexing. What seemed amazing to Peter was that the animal didn't appear to be scared or try to beat its wings. That would have made the operation much more difficult. Instead, Peter felt it trusted him to set it free, and with an enormous sense of purpose, he painstakingly removed the tangled web until its wings were loose. He held his hand out, so the insect could fly to freedom, and its wings slowly started to beat, getting faster and faster... but it didn't leave! It remained on his fingertip, and Peter marvelled once again at the detail and colour of this fascinating creature. It dipped its body many times, as if to thank him. Peter wished it well and offered his arm, outstretched again. The dragonfly bowed a couple more times and then its wings beat so fast, they could only be seen moving by the flickering sunlight upon them. And suddenly it was gone.

Peter smiled. 'See ya,' he said, straining to catch a glimpse of it beyond the tree.

He could have stayed up in the oak for the rest of the day and night, but he knew his mum would start to get worried, so he climbed down and thanked the tree for... well, just thanked it, before rushing off back along the fence line and, once again, carefully picking his way through the piles of dumped waste. He paused momentarily, his eye drawn to a bright orange plastic seat, which no longer had any legs. It was similar to the chairs they had in the dining hall at school, and the perfect size. Peter pulled it from the pile and carried it on his head like an oversized motorbike helmet as he tentatively retraced his steps.

As he approached the canal, he made the noise of a motorbike, racing and screeching to a halt. He climbed over the lock gate and back up the hill towards home, then cut through the snicket along the back of the houses and out onto the cobbled alley which continued down to the shop and the corner of his street. Most of the main streets had been covered over with tarmac, but the shared alleys of the back-to-back terraces were still paved with ankle-twisting cobbles. Dashing from high point to high point was the skill, while simultaneously dodging the numerous garments and bedding hung out to dry on the lines overhead.

Peter's house was mid-terrace and easily recognisable by the rotten wooden gate attached solely by the top hinge, and only openable if you hoisted it off the ground. Instead of using the gate, Peter always jumped up and over the concrete coal bunker, vaulted into the side path and then made his way to the back door. He opened the shed door as he passed and carefully placed the seat on top of a pile of timber and other oddments he'd purposely assembled. He shut the shed and smiled.

'Another five minutes and I was going to call the police,' his mum said as he entered the kitchen.

Peter shrugged. 'I had to rescue a dragonfly.'

'Sounds important. Did you manage it?'

'Yep.'

'You're a good lad. Come and give your mum a hug.'

'Love you, Mum.' Peter squeezed her tight.

'Love you too, son.'

Peter rested his head on her chest while she ran her fingers through his thick hair.

'Mum.'

'Yes?'

'Don't stop. Will you?'

3

THE LAKESIDE

S tep by step, the powerful flow of the water forced
Charlotte's legs towards the top of the weir. She was
beginning to lose the feeling in her feet as the cold water filled
her shoes, but she was at the point of no return. Her mind was
focused on getting to the other side and she was eying up the
fast torrent, and whether she could make the all-important
jump. She recalled the words of her father and the story of the
young poacher who had died attempting exactly the same. She
gulped and clenched her fist tight around the knife. If she
misjudged the distance, the water would sweep her off the top
and down into the swirling plunge pool and rocks below. This
wasn't the time to get nervous, but suddenly she stumbled off
balance. She fell to her knees and, with one hand still gripping
the knife, grabbed with the other at the slippery green stone
surface, in an attempt to cling on.

She was shaking with fear. Should she turn back or go for
the jump? The painstaking deliberation made her dizzy and
unstable, yet at the same time, the sound of the powerful water

cascading over the weir made her feel strangely exhilarated and free.

She focused her eyes on the channel of water and, on closer inspection, it didn't appear so wide. It was no longer to jump over than the eight squeaky floorboards in the house. One leap and that was it. Just a run-up, and a leap.

Her feet, legs and hands virtually numb, she stood and stretched out her arms towards the gap.

'I can do this,' she told herself. 'I will do this.'

She twisted her foot on the wet slab and, with her eyes fixed on the landing point, began her run-up. One, two, three... Both feet left the ground, the force of the water and the air above it seemed to lift her and then, suddenly... splash! Her feet landed on the other side. She'd made it.

'Yes!' she said.

After clambering up the bank and onto a grassy knoll, she looked back at the weir for a moment before breaking into a run. She ran hard, her legs and feet tingling as she gathered pace, faster and faster along the shoreline, leaping over rocks and fallen tree branches. Nearing a small stony beach, she stumbled on a protruding tree root and dropped to her knees. She looked up. It was there, her place. She collapsed onto her stomach, her breathing rapid and her heart thumping. She was exhausted, but she had made it.

Her eyes followed the gnarly exposed root, tracing its twists and turns, and then she focused on the mighty trunk—solid, sturdy and dependable, anchored strongly within the bank. It was exactly as she remembered—old, yet graceful, with a huge spreading canopy, thick with leaves. She'd tried on a previous visit to work out how old the tree was, by using her hands like a compass around the girth. One inch was about one year.

She'd read this somewhere and worked out its age to be around 290 years.

She slotted the knife down the back of her jeans and clambered up to the trunk, placing her hands on it.

'Hello, Mr Tree,' she said, hugging him tight. Instinctively, her eye was caught by the huge branch which spread out towards the lake. To Charlotte, it was the most important branch of the whole tree. Long, twice as thick as her entire body, and solid. It had to be, as suspended from it was Charlotte's swing. No ordinary swing: this was her swing, and her secret sanctuary. She'd constructed it herself, after fashioning it from two lengths of stout, twisted hemp rope, which she'd found in one of the estate workshops, and a weathered piece of driftwood she'd encountered floating on the lake. It wasn't anything fancy; the holes were cut rustically with the knife and there were bold knots to secure the seat, but it was all Charlotte's and had been worn smooth with her love.

Taking to her feet, she grabbed the ropes and positioned herself on the seat, then pushed her legs back and began to swing backwards and forwards in silence. Her long brown hair flowed freely as she tilted her head backwards. She looked up into the vast spreading canopy and speculated on what it would be like to climb to the top, look out over the family estate and ride the branches swaying in the wind. She appreciated the wisdom of the tree. Often, she would give it a hug, as she'd just done, and talk to it as if it were some great authority, telling it all her secrets. Sometimes she heard it speak back through its creaks and groans, and it always seemed to understand.

Kicking with her legs, she swung as high as she could before jumping off at the last minute, landing in a sprawl on the dirty ground. She felt the knife release from the leather sheath and heard it land with a clatter. She stared at it, her breathing shallow and rapid.

'It has the potential to do anything, that knife,' she said to herself. 'Anything.'

Still fixated on the blade, she drew out the cards from her pocket and fanned them out.

Love

She loved her tree and swing, she knew that, but she questioned whether she loved herself.

The Fool

Freedom, recklessness, and new beginnings. She understood the traits, but was this her?

Death

Symbolising endings, transformation and release. Ultimate release. She let her mind became strangely empty, like a vast cavern, dark and cold, as she stared at the Reaper.

Then she threw the cards on the ground and watched them tumble on the light breeze—one becoming wedged between two jagged stones, one taking off to blow along the beach, flipping constantly as the air carried it, and the other straight into the water, where it slowly started to sink.

Charlotte picked up the knife and examined its broad, shiny blade before running her finger along its sharp length. It sliced her skin, and she winced as she dropped it. Blood dripped fast from the cut; she pushed it into her mouth and tried to stem the flow with her tongue. It tasted metallic and uniquely savoury, yet sweet. There was a release, like absolute freedom, and she smiled.

She continued to taste the blood oozing from the wound as she stared at the motionless blade. Her blood stained the metalwork and, on its own, it lay helpless. She kicked it with her outstretched foot. She was in control of it. It would do whatever she wanted it to do. It was her choice. It could set her free—free from the agonising stretches at boarding school; free from the misery of loneliness; free from worry and the anxiety of high expectations, and free from the pain of wanting to be loved. The knife was the answer to all that. Swift and painless, immediate and final.

Charlotte's arms and legs began to shake, and an intense wave of self-doubt consumed her. Was she able to be happy? She shook her head. It was all too overwhelming. So many pressures. She just wanted to be free—immersed in nature, swinging and laughing, without a care. But that wasn't reality. She knew that, deep down, and the time was right to escape.

She tentatively touched the handle of the knife and began to toy with it, nudging it in the dirt. Then she grasped it tight and brought the menacing blade close to her. She wiped the soil and blood off on her jeans, making the sharp metal shine again, and then brushed the blade up and down her forearm, softly singing the words of a lullaby she remembered. Forcing down on the blade, she sliced into her skin. It felt effortless and tingly, rather than painful. She sliced again and watched with interest how the blood oozed down towards her hand. The colour was like nothing else: unique, deep red, but almost crimson, too. A tear fell from her eye and pooled with the blood in her hand.

Charlotte imagined her parents' faces when they found her lying there. Would they be angry that she'd made them late for an engagement or that she'd brought her father back early from a business trip? Would they care?

Raising her hand high, she stabbed the knife, then pulled it out and stabbed it again brutally, and again and again, repeatedly stabbing it, until it was stuck firm. She let go of the handle and stared at it, her whole body shaking.

'Sorry!' she shouted. She shook her head in disgust, grabbed the handle and tried to pull. It wouldn't move. It was stuck firm, having passed right through the bark of the mighty oak and into the wood beneath.

'I'm so sorry,' she said. She spread her arms around the tree trunk, pushing her body hard against it and mixing her blood with the exuding sap. 'I'm sorry.' Leaving the knife protruding from the tree, she sobbed, wiping her eyes from time to time with her blood stained T-shirt. She was disappointed in herself that she was unable to go through with it, angry that she had come to this point and scared about how to explain the blood and her wound.

Pulling on the knife with all her might, she finally managed to release it. She immediately pushed it into the bark once more and, prising off a chunk, followed by another and another, she began carefully carving letters into what she considered to be the tree's skin. The blade cut into her hand as she engraved her ownership on the mighty beast. She worked tirelessly, gouging and slicing, until she dug out the final letter and stood back to view her work.

Charlie, it read, the letters painstakingly created in cursive script, as though written in fountain pen.

'Charlie,' she said out loud to herself. 'I'm Charlie.'

4

BIRTHDAY SURPRISE

The summer holidays passed as quickly as they'd arrived, and it was time to return to school. Peter trudged down the street, scuffing his new black leather shoes along the pavement. Coming from a single-parent family, he qualified for free school uniform and shoes. The trousers felt like steel scouring-pads as they chafed his legs, and the shoes looked old-fashioned; within the first few strides, they'd started to rub a blister on his heel.

His heart sank as he entered the austere wrought-iron gates. The joy and freedom of the summer vanished immediately as he crossed the yard and went into the building, with its instantly recognisable municipal smell of cleaning fluid, floor polish and chalk dust. The only thing keeping Peter going was the thought of his birthday at the end of the week. With this in mind, he gritted his teeth, kicked open the classroom door and took his place at his desk.

'Four more days to go,' he kept saying to himself, as the day dragged along. When the last bell rang, he endured the pain of the perfectly formed blisters all the way back home, leaped over the coal bunker and let himself in. His mum worked as a seamstress at a little dress repair shop and was usually home an hour after him. This gave Peter time to get to work in the shed, and the basic toolkit Grandad had set up for them made anything possible. A rusty-headed hammer, an assortment of screws and nails and a saw were enough to enable Peter to work on his 'special project', something he'd been secretly working on for some time. But first, he set about trying to repair the broken gate. He'd found a piece of wood on the canal-side which he thought he could nail to the gate and thus reattach the bottom hinge. His aim was to mend it ready for his mum's arrival, when he planned to push it wide as if she were the Queen arriving at a grand opening.

He swiftly set to work and, using the floor as a workbench, sawed the wood to length and proceeded to nail the hinge in place. He finally lifted the gate onto the hinges and gleefully pushed it open. He stood back to admire his handiwork. 'Rustic' was probably the best way to describe it, but it worked.

He just had enough time before his mum's arrival to make some crucial adjustments to his project and he disappeared into the shed. Before long, he heard her car pull up outside. He downed his tools and, with great gusto, pushed open the shed door, ran and jumped over the coal bunker and opened the car door with a nod of his head, as he'd seen the Queen's driver do on TV.

'You alright?' his mum said.

'Will ma'am follow me into the palace?' He gestured towards the gate, then promptly stood with his hand on the top of it, looking proud. As his mum approached, he pushed it open and bowed.

'Have you done this? It's perfect. Well, those protruding

nails might need filing down, but it's an entrance fit for a queen. You're my hero.'

Peter smiled.

'Cheese and pickle sandwiches for tea?' she said, grinning from ear to ear.

'In the drawing room?' he replied in a posh accent.

'How about sitting on the back step with a glass of milk?' she said with a giggle.

As they passed the shed, his mum's eye was caught by the orange plastic seat through the open door. 'What's that?'

'Oh, it's my special project. A bobsleigh.'

'Of course it is.' She laughed. 'I guess it's what every eleven-year-old has in his shed.'

'I saw them on TV. The Olympics. Zooming around those corners. It looks amazing, Mum.'

'Where are you planning on using it?'

'I'm going to build a bobsleigh track off the coal bunker,' he said enthusiastically.

She nodded and smiled. 'Of course!'

'It's nearly complete. All I need is to fit the seat and the number on the front. Number one.'

'What do you mean, the number?'

'They all have numbers in the Olympics. Can I have one for my birthday?'

She raised both eyebrows.

'I've seen them in town at the hardware shop. Stickers with numbers. It's all I need to finish it. Please, Mum.'

She shook her head, then put her arm around him and gave him a squeeze. 'Is that what you really want? A little sticker? Wouldn't you like a new football or a skateboard like the other boys?'

Peter looked down at the ground. 'You have to have good

runners and a sturdy seat if you're going to hit those corners right, Mum. But the number is just as important.'

'I see. I've been saving a while and Grandma and Grandad gave you some money too, so you can have the sticker and something else as well.'

'Oh, thanks, Mum. It's going to be the best bobsleigh. Maybe I'll get to the Olympics one day.'

'There's just one thing.'

'Yes?'

'Make sure you file down any protruding nails.'

'OK, Mum.'

They both laughed, then his mum stepped into the house while Peter entered the shed, where he began marking the position on the bobsleigh for the finishing touch.

After a few minutes, she called him in for his sandwiches: sliced Cheddar cheese and tangy pickle between two thick slices of white bread, and a tall glass of cold milk. Peter perched on the concrete step and, as he devoured his tea, his mum sat beside him and put her arm around his shoulders.

'You are the best son any mum could ask for. Do you know that?'

Peter just shrugged and smiled. He knew alright. His small feet more than filled the shoes of the man of the house. He helped his mum by being head map-reader on car journeys, chief shed cleaner-outer, odd-job man, and often best friend. He helped her through bouts of loneliness too, nursed her when she was ill and, in his mind, kept her safe, especially when the local eligible bachelors came a-knocking.

On the day of Peter's long-awaited twelfth birthday, he rushed home from school and eagerly awaited his mum's return from work. She'd promised to take him into town to buy the number for his bobsleigh, a metal file, and also the seven-inch single of 'Eton Rifles'.

Peter waited impatiently at the window and, in between alternately looking up the road and watching the clock, visualised himself holding his nerve as he boldly took each corner of the world's fastest bobsleigh run at speed, while listening to the rebellious beat of The Jam.

Peter's mum never came home that day. A drunk driver in an Aston Martin crossed the white line and hit her full-on, doing twice the speed limit. The police pronounced her dead at the scene.

Peter only found out some hours later, when his grandparents woke him from his slumped position in the window after hours of waiting. A note scrunched in his hand read, 'Love you to the moon and back, Mum. Love P xx'

5

SELF-DEFENCE

The Bentley purred through the imposing gates and stopped by the enormous front door. The heavy oak and rusted metalwork made Charlotte shudder as she stepped out, clutching her brown leather satchel close to her chest. She looked up at the prison-like windows and high, dark stone walls of the convent school and let out a tiny whimper, which she tried to contain but couldn't.

Slowly, she moved her legs, hoping the walk up the steps would last forever. Turning only her head, she watched the car reverse around and leave. Her mind filled with the comforts of home, all her things and her swing. A cold shiver started in her toes and moved quickly, as if it were running through the core of each and every bone in her body.

Inside the convent, dour oil paintings of previous headmistresses and past head girls adorned the walls, and symbolic religious artefacts, constant reminders of the faith, gave an eerie and foreboding air. Charlotte looked at the paintings and saw her mother and grandmother both staring back at her. Their faces brimmed with pride. Knowing both had attended the school and reached head-girl status added to Charlotte's overwhelming feeling that she had no choice other than to follow tradition and endure her internal pain.

That evening was dark and cold. The wind was powerful as it whistled through the gaps in the rickety sash windows and rattled the glass in her dormitory. Mandy and Cynthia, two girls for whom Charlotte had little regard, were being particularly hateful. They pulled hard on Charlotte's long hair and taunted her by dangling her new shoes out of the window. She hadn't even had a chance to wear them. They were immaculate, with a delicate, shiny buckle and a small heel. She pleaded for the shoes not to be dropped into the muddy flower bed below, but Cynthia's indignant look only stalled the inevitable. She dangled them on the tips of her fingers and then released them with a sickening smile. Mandy tugged Charlotte's hair harder and laughed.

Charlotte crouched in the corner of the room next to a large wooden locker with her hands over her head, trying not to show she was upset.

Suddenly, she heard her father's voice down the hall, calling for her. She instantly knew it was him from the deep, booming and commanding voice. Thank God! He'd come to rescue her. He'd be cross about the shoes, but she wouldn't tell him straightaway, and hopefully she could pick them up on her way out.

'Charlotte! Charlotte!' he called. Discreetly wiping away the tear on her cheek, she stood up. The other girls were still laughing at her. She didn't acknowledge them, but walked tentatively to the door, placed her hand on the ice-cold brass knob and twisted it.

'Are you running away from us? Are you scared?' the bullies taunted.

Charlotte plucked up the courage to look them straight in the eye. 'My father is here. I'm going to tell him about the shoes, and he won't be happy. You'll get into trouble and you'll be sorry.'

Hearing his booming voice again, she pulled open the dormitory door and skipped into the hallway with the hugest of smiley smiles.

Charlotte's father wasn't a huggy kind of dad, and there wouldn't be any kind of physical contact, but boy, would she be pleased to see him, and he couldn't have come at a better time. A rescue mission on the first day was superb. Maybe he would take her out of school the following day and take her to the zoo to see the elephants, a trip they'd had to put back from the summer because of his work. Wouldn't that be the best thing in the whole world ever? Relief and joy filled Charlotte's whole body. She could defy anyone with her new-found excitement, and she raced down the hall looking for him.

'Daddy!' she shouted. 'Daddy!'

But the hall was empty. Where had he gone? She listened intently for his voice and slowed to a walk so she could hear him again. 'Daddy, I'm here.' But there was nothing—a great gaping void of nothing.

Charlotte stopped and looked around. All she could hear was the boom made by the icy wind that blew down the deserted hall and in between the double doors which opened onto the top of the bleak stone stairway outside.

'Daddy! Daddy!'

There was no answer.

She ran to the entrance. He just *had* to be there. She struggled to push the mighty wooden doors open against the strength of the gale. A forceful blast made her stumble as she scanned the desolate stairs.

'Daddy!' she cried. 'Daddy, where are you?' She slumped into a desperate heap against the cold tiled wall, the wind freezing her tiny feet. At the other end of the hall, huddled in a tight clump, the other girls were laughing and pointing.

Where was he? What about the zoo? Charlotte's stomach felt wretched, her veins drained to a trickle and her heart was so very empty. She wished she were dead.

Deflated and feeling imprisoned, Charlotte took to her bed. She tried to busy herself and picked up a notebook and pencil from her bedside drawer.

Day 1

Ways to deal with the bullies

Show strength and not weakness

Learn self-defence

Take the moral high ground

Itching powder in their beds and clothes is sweet revenge.

Try not to think about home—parents are designed to let you down

'*I miss home*,' she wrote. '*But I'm confused. When I'm there, my parents are often too busy to bother playing games or to explore in the grounds, so why do I miss it so much? I feel lonely. Maybe one day, yes, one day I will see the elephants.*'

Over the following weeks, she managed to gather allies—other girls who were also resentful of being bullied. Mira, Sam and Jojo were all on-side and, together, they gradually became tougher. Trying not to think about home and family was always the best way to keep strong, although Charlotte craved them every single day. She joined the self-defence classes on

Saturday mornings and learned how to disarm someone quickly with an elbow in the stomach and a swift twist of a wrist. Rose hips were abundant in the sisters' garden too, and could easily be crushed to form a devilish itching powder, and stored ready for a revenge attack.

Day 86

Show strength and not weakness
Restrain school bullies using self-defence techniques
Maintain moral high ground
Try not to think about home
Collect more rose hips

'I miss home more and more,' she wrote. *'I long for my freedom and to swing without a care.'*

Day 512

Resilience is my true strength, but I still have moments of insecurity
My mind is my self-defence now
I miss home less and less
I'd really like a puppy
I tell myself sadness makes people weak
I've been relieved of my gardening duties!

Being awarded the accolade of head girl in her final year was not only a rite of passage for Charlotte—a family tradition and something that was expected—it was also exhausting. To attain the coveted title, her track record had to be impeccable; she had to show she'd never put a foot wrong and was continually at the beck and call of the teachers and head. Luckily, the itching powder charge was dismissed and forgotten after her father funded the new roof on the music block.

Charlotte wrote in her journal. *'My resilience has helped me cope, although I still feel lonely every day. Fulfilling my parents' dream of becoming head girl feels like a hollow victory. It feels like it was for them and not for myself. I miss home, yet when I am there, I crave a simple life, where all I need is my tree and swing. But I'm resourceful and my resourcefulness has kept me strong.'*

'Mira, Sam, Jojo, I need your help tonight. Huddle up and I'll tell you the plan.'

The girls congregated on Charlotte's bed in the upper dorm.

'I have a rendezvous with a boy from the village and he's taking me to the cinema. I can sneak out when Sister is on her rounds in the lower school, but I need you to cover for me if anything comes up or she suspects I'm out.'

'What do you want us to do?' Jojo said, enjoying the drama.

'Make sure miserable Mandy doesn't get a whiff of my manoeuvres. She's not happy playing second fiddle and is looking for any opportunity to step into my shoes. Tell her I'm in the sick bay, period problems, or whatever comes to mind.'

'That'll be tricky, but we'll do our best.'

'Thanks, Jojo, I know I can rely on you. Mira, Sam, do the usual trick and place a bag under my sheets, and if Sister asks, I'm not feeling too well and have taken an early night. Got it?'

'Yes. But what if she becomes suspicious?'

'You'll have to think on your feet. Give her the runaround, cause a distraction in the lower dorm or something. I need this one. He's really cute and apparently he has two mates, one for each of you, and a Frankie "Relax" T-shirt he said he'd give me.'

'Really? OK, we'll do it for you, but we're not taking the rap if you get caught,' Sam said, making her feelings perfectly clear.

'You have a brilliant time and get the names of the other boys.' Mira giggled.

Charlotte put her jeans and T-shirt on under her uniform and rolled up the legs. Her plan was to hide the uniform, once out of the door, and then collect it on her return. She waited impatiently for 7.30pm when Sister would be starting her lower-dorm rounds, but the clock above the door seemed not to progress beyond twenty-five past.

Finally she hitched up her dress and stuffed her lipstick and mascara into the back pocket of her jeans. 'Ready, girls?'

'Go for it, Charlotte. Have a fabulous time and tell us if you get a kiss.' Sam jovially puckered her lips.

'I'm coming next time,' Mira said, pushing her out of the door.

Charlotte looked left, and Mira, right. 'All clear,' they said simultaneously. Charlotte crept along the hall and tiptoed down the stone steps. She paused before opening the door at the bottom. She anticipated it squeaking and was undecided whether to push it slowly, in the hope it would be so quiet no one would notice, or go for the fast, obvious, but over quickly option. With a silent wince she pushed the door slowly and, right on cue, the hinge gave a slow whining tone... which would have woken the dead! She poked her head around the door. The coast was clear.

Just the back door to freedom now, but that was opposite Sister Margaret's room. Charlotte's heart raced and her legs were wobbling like jelly, but she persevered along the corridor. Placing each foot quietly on the floor was a painstaking process. Eventually, she had her hand on the stout iron bolt at the top of the door. '*Clank,*' it went, as she slid it back. She scrunched her eyes up, anticipating her capture and wishing everything was not so large, metallic and clunky. She turned the huge handle and optimistically pushed at the door.

'So far so good,' she thought. 'Once outside, it should be a breeze. Walk calmly over the yard, uniform off and hide under the bench by the back gate. Up and over the wall and then a Frankie T-shirt, kissing and two fingers back at the school. Easy.'

Stealthily, she opened the door halfway and slid out. She closed the door with the softest and smoothest action.

'So. What's going on here?' a voice said in front of her. Charlotte froze. 'Not planning an escape, were we?' The gravelly, deep, and almost manly voice of Sister Margaret made Charlotte's heart sink.

'I was just taking some fresh air.' She made out Sister Margaret's silhouette, arms folded and leaning with her back to the wall in the dim light.

'Lift up your dress.'

'Why?'

'Lift up your dress,' Sister insisted.

Charlotte reluctantly lifted it.

'Jeans! Nice. Lipstick as well, I suspect?'

Charlotte reached into her back pocket to retrieve the contraband.

'I don't need to see it,' Sister said. 'So where were you heading?'

'Just into the village.'

'To meet someone?'

'Well… kind of,' Charlotte reluctantly confessed.

'I don't have to tell you that this is not the behaviour of the head girl, is it, Charlotte?'

'No, Sister.'

'So how about I do a deal with you?'

'What do you mean?'

'You get me two packets of Woodbine and a small bottle of Scotch, and I don't say anything to anyone.'

'Gosh. That's quite an ask.'

'Here, take this.' Sister Margaret thrust some rolled-up notes into Charlotte's hand. 'Is it a deal?'

Charlotte took a moment to think about it.

'Any Scotch, I'm not fussy,' Sister Margaret added with a smile.

'OK. I'll knock on your door when I'm back and drop it off.'

'I do like a head girl with common sense.'

Charlotte stuffed the cash into her pocket, ran across the yard, hid the dress under the bench as planned, and scaled the wall. She jumped into the street, rolled her jeans down and ran past the church and into the village. Around the corner by the cinema, Billy was leaning against a lamp post.

'Hi,' Charlotte said, gathering her breath.

'Hi. I thought you weren't coming.'

'I was held up on the way out. Will you help me get some things from the shop?'

'What?'

'Two packets of Woodbine and a small bottle of Scotch. Any Scotch.'

'Blimey! You convent girls really are hardcore. But I like it.' Billy smirked. Charlotte rolled her eyes and handed over the cash. 'Alright, alright. You want me to get you some dope too, while I'm in there?'

'Funny.' Charlotte shoved him towards the shop door. 'And get everything in a brown paper bag.'

The film started and the pair took their seats in the dark. Charlotte felt Billy's hand creep over the armrest and plonk itself on her leg. She promptly ejected it. She wanted him to touch her, but not use the full hand-on-the-leg manoeuvre so early on. He placed it back on her leg and squeezed her thigh. Charlotte glared at him and removed it once again.

Billy leaned over and whispered, 'I thought you convent girls were always up for it. When are you uncorking the Scotch?'

'I'm not that kind of girl. I expected a gentleman, not a grubby letch.'

'I know when a girl is playing hard to get. How about we bypass the film and head out the back? I have something for you.'

'Is it the T-shirt?'

'What T-shirt?'

'You mean you didn't even bring that?'

'Ssshh,' came from someone in the row behind.

'I want to leave.'

'Fab, there's a little back alley I know well. We can get to know each other a bit better down there.'

'No. I want to leave. Right now.' Charlotte grabbed the paper bag and stood up. They both headed to the door and, once outside, Billy took her by the hand and dragged her around the corner.

'What are you doing?'

'I've got something to show you,' Billy said, with a sinister glint in his eye. 'You'll like it.'

'I told you I'm not that kind of girl. I'm leaving.'

Billy refused to listen and kept on pulling her into the alley. He pushed her up against the wall and started groping her. 'Nice tits. A bit small for my liking, but they'll do.'

'Stop that, you're scaring me.'

'All I want is a kiss. You won't deny me that, after I paid for the cinema?'

'I don't come that cheap and get your hands off me.'

Billy didn't reply. He took his hand and forced it up her T-shirt, then pressed his mouth against hers. Charlotte tried pushing him away, but he was too strong.

'I told you, you'd like it,' he said, forcing his hand into her bra.

'Stop it, stop it! Let me go!' she screamed.

Billy thrust his mouth onto hers once more. He was pressing hard, and he was hurting her. He squeezed her breast, and then, with one single blow, she hit him over the head with the bag containing the bottle. He released her to put his head in his hands. Charlotte immediately pushed him out of the way, dropped the bottle, and started to run.

'Hey!' Billy shouted, but she was gone. She ran and she ran until she arrived at the school gate. Out of breath, she started to sob.

The gate suddenly opened. 'No need to climb over. I was keeping an eye out for you.' Sister Margaret met her with a knowing smile and ushered her into the yard, locking the gate behind her. Charlotte handed her the fags, which were crumpled within the bag.

'And the Scotch?' the nun asked.

'I had to use it in self-defence.'

'That's a shame. I was looking forward to a wee dram before bed. Is he alright?'

'I hope not. He's a vile boy.' She sobbed again.

Sister Margaret put her arm around her and escorted her inside. 'A good lesson learned, maybe. God has a funny way of showing us good from bad sometimes. Did you get two packets of fags?'

6

BIRTHDAY BLUES

A rustic fruit cake topped in blue icing awaited Peter when he returned from school. The sixteen candles illuminated the entire room. He ditched his bag on the floor and grinned at his gran, who was frantically summoning his grandad to the kitchen table.

She gestured to an envelope in front of the cake. 'Go on,' she said, with a nod of approval.

Peter smiled and tore the envelope open to reveal a card showing a boy riding a bobsled in the snow. The caption read, '*Many Happy Returns, Son*'. His gran always got him one with 'Son' on it.

Grandad entered and put his arm around Gran and they both watched as Peter stood the card up by the cake.

'Thanks,' he said, smiling the biggest smile at both of them. He thought about saying something about maybe being too old for blue icing now, but he thought better of it and thanked them again.

'Go on, blow out your candles,' said Grandad. Peter's face

lit up with a golden glow as he crouched down. He took a deep breath and blew with all his might. Only half the candles were extinguished, so he took a deeper breath and attempted to finish them off. As he did so, all the candles burst back to life. He gave an almighty blow and managed to extinguish two-thirds of them, before once again, to his complete surprise, they reignited.

'You two jokers. Honestly!'

'It was your grandad's idea. He saw them at the newsagent's,' his gran said, as they all tried to blow them out. They all shared a chuckle, then Gran and Grandad flung their arms around Peter and hugged him tight.

Grandad reached into his pocket. 'Here you go,' he said, holding out a modest and faded-looking red velvet box.

'What is it?'

'Open it,' Gran said eagerly.

Peter tentatively lifted the hinged lid to reveal a shiny but slightly tarnished gold watch. Slim and delicate, yet manly, with an immaculate white face.

'Every man needs a good watch. It was my father's, and now it's yours. It's old, but it still works and probably worth a bob or two?' Grandad said, with a crack of emotion in his voice.

Peter lifted his gaze and nodded. He didn't have any words.

'Look after it,' Grandad said proudly.

On the day Peter went into school to get his final results, he knew he hadn't done well. His mind had been far from focused on schoolwork. He preferred to escape to the woods or down to the canal, where he felt solace among the wildlife. His commitment to school had waned.

As he expected, his results were poor. Peter barely stopped to peruse the details before heading for the last time to the school gate. Suddenly, he came face to face with Scott Moorfield, otherwise known as the school bully, and his entourage of scrawny scumbags. Scott's thin, bony face, skinhead hairdo and menacing eyes always scared Peter, and although Peter was no pushover, he had had run-ins with Scott before and always come off worse.

As Peter walked towards him, Scott stood square on, blocking the gate, flanked by his two heavies. They looked at him like three hyenas about to make a kill. Peter kept his head high and brushed past them, knocking Scott's shoulder.

'You taking your results home to your mummy?' The words came out of Scott's mouth like poison. 'She'll be proud of you, Mummy's boy.'

Peter stopped in his tracks. He felt an emptiness inside, a hollowness that froze him to the spot.

'Is there no one to help you, Mummy's boy, all alone now?' Scott smirked, then laughed out loud with the other two.

Scalding anger rose from Peter's feet. He sensed the blood pumping in his legs, up through his body and down into his arms as he clenched his fists and turned around to face them. He looked Scott straight in the eye. 'She'd be proud of me,' he said, without flinching.

There was an evil expression on Scott's face. 'I heard she was a prostitute. Everyone knows it.'

Peter, without hesitation, sprang onto his toes, launched himself at Scott and punched him clean on the jaw. His henchmen could only stand back and stare in shock as Peter, in a complete rage, hit Scott again on the side of the head and then once again, directly below the eye. Scott staggered, bleeding from his nose, looking dazed.

The headmaster was shouting at the top of his voice as he ran towards them, but Peter, with gritted teeth, grabbed Scott by the scruff of the neck. 'My mum was a decent person, not like you, dickhead.' The first drops of heavy rain began to fall on them as, filled with hatred, Peter thumped Scott on the nose again. The bully fell to the ground with a thud.

The headmaster shouted louder and louder, but Peter ignored him. He was the Yorkshire schools' cross-country champion, so he could run. He abandoned his bloodstained results in the dirt, the anger still pumping inside him, and began to run and run, occasionally slipping on the rain-soaked cobbles as he headed towards the village.

He turned the corner by the bakery and narrowly avoided knocking an old gentleman to the floor. He ran past the Post Office and started the climb up the hill. The last shop on the right was the florist's. It had a display of plants on a bench out front and, without stopping, he grabbed a potted white rose and pulled it close to his chest, then proceeded to charge in front of a car, causing it to screech to a halt. He carried on running. There was only one place he was heading.

It was a long climb up the hill to the church and the graveyard beyond, but Peter ran all the way without stopping. He ran fast, the fastest he'd ever done it. Careful not to drop the earthenware pot, he held it in both hands as if it were the most important thing in the world. On passing the church, he saw the vicar in the doorway putting on his coat. They acknowledged each other with a nod. The rain was torrential by now, and Peter slipped on the sodden grass and fell to his knees. He heard the distant shriek of the local policeman's piercing whistle and knew he was in trouble. But he didn't care. He looked at the neatly manicured grave and modest headstone. He came up every day to say hello to his mum, and to pull out any weeds and polish the headstone. His knees pressing hard into the wet ground, he offered the rose to her and put the pot in the centre of the grave. The rain was soaking his thick black hair and streaming down his face, and his knees sank deeper into the sodden, muddy ground.

'Where *are* you when I need you, Mum?' He tried to hold back his tears and then shouted at the top of his voice. 'I hate you, Mum. Why did you leave me?'

He wiped the rain from his face and, once again, heard a sharp blow from the whistle, followed by another, even closer.

'Why, Mum...? Why?' The tears rolled down his face and mixed with the rain as the droplets fell onto her grave. The next whistle was close. He looked around. The policeman's helmet was bobbing along behind the churchyard wall. Peter stood up and staggered backwards, his despair making him numb. He fell back against the broad trunk of an ancient yew tree overhanging the grave. He pushed his back hard against the bark and felt it dig into his skin through his shirt, which was thoroughly soaked from the monsoon-like rain now bouncing off the ground. The mighty tree offered some cover as he spread out his arms behind him, and he gripped the bark as if asking it for protection.

The whistle sounded again as the policeman came through the gate and began stomping through the puddles between the graves. Peter hung on to the tree, his body steaming as the adrenaline continued to circulate in his core. He felt himself swirling, dizzy with despair, the tree taking him around and around like an out-of-control carousel. He wished it would take him away from this painful agony, back to his mum, back to what they had had before.

PC Dodds stood beyond the tree's far-reaching canopy, and in a breathless but calm voice he said, 'Come on, Peter. Let's get you out of this rain. Come on, now.'

Peter looked out of the corner of his eye at a gap in the wall where the coping stones were missing, then at PC Dodds, who had his hands on his knees and was still panting, and then again at the wall. Loosening his grip on the tree, he shifted his weight to his toes, then pushed himself away and started a run for his escape.

No sooner had he found his stride than a hand grabbed his shoulder from behind and pulled him to the ground. PC Briggs, the assistant constable, had silently come up behind him. The two policemen grappled with him, the three of them in a skirmish on the muddy, wet ground. Peter broke free and started to crawl, then tried to stand and run, but when he got to his feet, PC Dodds made a grab for his leg and pulled hard, bringing him back down. Peter kicked out at him, trying to get some purchase in the mud, but as he did so, the policeman's feet knocked Peter's mum's headstone.

Peter stopped kicking and watched helplessly as the head-stone crashed flat onto the sodden ground. He wiped the dirt from his eyes and lashed out at the mud-covered police officers with his feet, kicking off one of their helmets and injuring his shoulder.

'Peter, don't be stupid now,' cried Dodds. 'Come on, let's talk about this.'

Peter stood in a daze, looking at the devastation of his mum's boggy grave and the flattened headstone. There was no escape. The tears ran down his face. Dodds and Briggs looked at each other and eased back, giving him some space.

'It's alright, Peter. It's going to be alright,' Dodds said, with kind authority.

Peter fell to his knees, put his head in his hands, pulled his hair, and shouted as loudly as he could.

'I hate you, Mum. I hate you!'

7

BIRTHDAY CELEBRATION

The impressive arched front door of Charlotte's home, topped by two castellated turrets, was the entrance to the palace that unfolded beyond it. In the centre of the building was a courtyard, with a lawn and impressive magnolia tree, with extensive east and west wings sprawling out to either side. Turrets, arches, gargoyles and hundreds of ornate chimneys added to the splendour of a residence that had belonged to the family for generations.

Set in 230 acres of mature Capability Brown parkland—where herds of fallow deer, reminiscent of those of a Renaissance hunting lodge, gathered nervously in groups—the veteran oak, beech and cedar trees added to the overall impression of grandeur. There was also a meandering river, and a further 148 acres of woodland and lower lake.

The parched lower croquet lawn was the quintessential setting for Charlotte's sixteenth birthday party. The pristine white marquee that had been erected centre stage appeared starchy and incongruous against the yellow-brown sandstone of the house. Inside the marquee, numerous staff were creating elaborate table displays with fresh flowers; ice sculptors chiselled masterpieces and a string quartet had begun setting up their stage.

The sky was blue and the air warm, and as Charlotte observed the busy activity below through her open bedroom window, she pondered what the day might have in store.

'Miss Charlotte, isn't it time you were dressed?' came the kind voice of Mrs Hathersage, the housekeeper. 'I've laid out your dress in your dressing room.'

'Wait a minute,' Charlotte said. 'I can hear a commotion on the lawn. Daddy's talking to Cartwright about something, but he's shouting. And now Cartwright is storming away. What's going on?'

'I think there's an issue about some silverware. I don't really know the facts.'

Charlotte scrunched her eyebrows. 'It all looks very strange.'

'I wouldn't worry yourself about all that. I think your father has had a little too much to drink already today. You need to get dressed.'

'Thank you, Mrs Hathersage. Which dress is it?'

'The one your father bought you for your birthday.'

Charlotte carried on watching the hustle and bustle below and sighed. 'I'd rather wear my jeans and just go to my sw—' She stopped. 'My place, I mean.'

'I don't think your father would approve, do you?' Mrs Hathersage lifted the lid from a huge box. 'Here are the shoes, too. Red, your favourite colour.'

Charlotte looked over. 'I love them. Would look fabulous with my jeans.'

A frail yet commanding voice spoke from the doorway. 'Are those my shoes?'

'Mother!'

'I thought I'd lost those shoes. What day is it today?'

Charlotte's mother clung to the edge of the door, looking pale. She didn't venture outside much and spent days and days in her room.

'It's my birthday, Mother. My sixteenth birthday.'

'No, it isn't.' She scowled. 'It's my daughter's birthday.'

'I am your daughter. I'm Charlotte.' Charlotte paused. 'Mother, are you alright?'

'I'm perfectly fine. Once I find my daughter. She must be lost. She's only a baby.'

'Mother, it's me, Charlotte.' She took her mother by the hand.

'Get off me. I don't allow the staff to touch me. Where's my daughter?'

Mrs Hathersage intervened. 'Come with me, Lady Winterbourne. I'm sure we can find her. I'll bring your shoes.'

She escorted Charlotte's mother into the hall, acknowledging Charlotte with an understanding smile, and began to lead her back to her room.

Charlotte felt her stomach cramp and a tear ran down her cheek. She was losing her mother. Her onset of dementia had come way too early in Charlotte's mind. She didn't know anyone else in their mid-fifties like this. Some days, her mother was normal. They would sit together and sew and chat about her childhood, but increasingly, she was becoming forgetful and confused and it scared Charlotte.

The string quartet made way for a more upbeat jazz band— Charlotte's father's favourite music. Champagne corks popped and the waiting staff paraded with platters filled with elegant canapés of king prawns, pitted olives and caviar. The younger children played croquet and Charlotte's school friends huddled in a group, sipping colourful mocktails, flirting with the boys and giggling uncontrollably. Charlotte did what was expected. She floated from one family group to another, exchanging pleasantries and collecting cards and exquisitely wrapped gifts.

Eventually, everyone took their seats for lunch within the marquee—Charlotte in the centre of the head table, flanked on either side by her parents. Her father, in a pinstripe suit, immaculate white shirt and blue tie with the family crest, was engrossed in talk about offshore investments and property. Her mother, in a mint green dress and contrasting bright red shoes, chatted to her cousin beside her. Charlotte put her hand on her mother's knee. Her mother swiftly removed it and carried on chatting, without acknowledging her. Charlotte sighed and stared out into the room filled with guests. Her heart felt empty, despite seeing so many friends and family before her. She looked again at her father. He was gesturing forcefully with the hand that was clutching a large sherry glass, while puffing from a fat Havana cigar.

'Father, what happened with Cartwright earlier?' Charlotte demanded.

'I sacked him. You can't trust anyone these days.'

'Why? What's he done?'

'It's not your concern right now,' he said indignantly. 'We can get another butler. They're ten-a-penny these days.'

The waiting staff filled the champagne flutes, ready for a toast. Charlotte's father stubbed out his cigar and, straightening his jacket, stood to address the gathering.

'Ladies and gentlemen. When Charlotte was born, it made me the happiest man alive. Her mischievous smile, one she's had from a very early age, has never changed, and it says a great deal of her character. I'm also pleased to announce that Charlotte has been awarded the position of head girl at St Cuthbert's, which has made us all very proud. This has prompted me to reaffirm our family commitment to the school, and not only have I paid for a new roof on the music block, I will be funding the creation of a new science facility to allow the school to continue to prosper. It will be called the Sir Henry Winterbourne Wing.'

Charlotte rolled her eyes secretly and sighed.

'Anyway, enough about me.' Her father chuckled to himself and then coughed. 'I stand here today as a very proud father. We are all immensely proud of you, Charlotte,' he said, taking a large swig of sherry and loosening his tie. He stumbled slightly and leaned ungracefully on the back of the chair, looking a little confused. Then he mopped his brow with his sleeve before regaining his composure and continuing, 'The years have simply flown by, and in that time we have seen Charlotte become a beautiful, intelligent and capable young woman.' He bent over, supporting himself on the table with his outstretched arm. He looked pale, and his forehead was beaded with sweat. Charlotte handed him a napkin, and he gratefully dabbed his brow. 'I'd like you to raise a glass with me to our fabulous daughter, Charlotte.' He looked over at Charlotte's mother, who was rummaging in her bag and not paying attention.

'Charlotte!' everyone said, clinking and raising their glasses.

Charlotte smiled a wide smile and thanked everyone, and then turned to watch as her father dramatically stumbled sideways and crumpled onto the table, violently knocking over glasses before sliding to the floor.

'Father! *Father!*'

Everyone gasped as Charlotte dashed over and placed her hand on his cheek. His face was white, and his skin cold.

A commanding voice instructed everyone to step back. 'I'm a doctor. Please let me through and someone call an ambulance immediately.'

The doctor began to attempt to resuscitate, pounding down on her father's chest and breathing into his mouth. Charlotte collapsed onto a chair and watched in disbelief. She knew he was dead. She'd felt his face and sensed no breath.

The ambulance crew eventually arrived and, after sterling attempts to restore his life, they pronounced Charlotte's father dead.

Charlotte's mother took to her room and stayed there for many days. No one seemed to know what they were doing. Especially Charlotte. She was empty, and the emptiness seemed to squeeze out any attempt to pull herself together. The pain from the cramping of her heart and stomach was so traumatic, she felt sick. The staff tried to continue as normal, but with no clear leader, they, too, felt disjointed and insecure. Losing Cartwright hadn't helped, either. Mrs Hathersage tried to hold the ship together and made sure Charlotte had everything she needed.

After many days of battling with the loss, Charlotte ventured out. She knew exactly where to go. 'I'm going for a walk, Mrs Hathersage. I'll be back, but I need some thinking time.'

'Where will you be going, madam?'

'I can't tell you. Not far, just somewhere private where I can breathe and think about Daddy.'

'Right you are. I'll lay the table for tea, for when you return.'

Charlotte ran and ran and sobbed as she did. She crossed the fallen tree, raced up the bank and down through the woodland to the lakeside. There it was. Solid and reliable, majestic and dependable, its leaves fluttering in the breeze, and her swing moving effortlessly back and forth, as if offering her the opportunity to ride. She grabbed the ropes and plonked herself on the seat, and it started to move of its own accord. She took a deep breath. She felt alone. More alone than ever before, but the tree, with its welcoming branches, offered her protection, hugging her, making her feel safe. She pushed her legs out in front of her and leaned back, arms straight, forcing the swing to move higher.

How was she going to cope?

The following day, a man arrived at the house wearing a black suit and clutching a leather briefcase. Other members of the wider family and Charlotte's father's solicitor followed him. Charlotte instructed Mrs Hathersage to fetch Mother and everyone seated themselves in the grand drawing room.

'Are we having lunch? Why are there so many guests?'

'No, Mother, the man is here to read Father's will.'

'Where is your father? I've been expecting him back from his so-called business trip. He said he wouldn't be long.'

Charlotte placed her hand on her mother's and smiled. She wanted to cry, but she beat it back, so as not to cause a scene in front of everyone. Opposite her sat Uncle David, his face calm, occasionally smiling as someone new entered the room. David was Charlotte's father's brother. Next to him was Cecil, a thin gentleman with wisps of grey hair. He was her father's cousin, and next to him were her father's lawyer, his investment banker, his closest friend Sir Bernard Botherington and next to him, Charlotte's mother's doctor. And that completed the seating plan.

Charlotte observed them glancing at each other and making uncomfortable small talk about how fabulous her father was. She, however, kept silent. She wasn't really interested in what was to be disclosed. She just wanted to move on as quickly as possible, complete her schooling in peace, let the beneficiaries slice up the cake and let life resume some normality.

The lawyer opened his briefcase and produced a document with a red wax seal clearly visible on the front.

'I call upon the people here present to witness the reading of the last will and testament of the deceased, Sir Henry Charles Bartholomew Winterbourne.' He peered over his wire-rimmed spectacles and then continued to read.

'"My dearest and loving wife. You have been at my side through thick and thin and fathered me the most precious gift. Thank you. I am truly sorry to leave you. A statement will be read by Dr Sanderson, but you have my promise that you will be cared for in the manner to which you have become accustomed for the rest of your life."' The lawyer shuffled his papers. '"David, I leave to you my collection of vintage cars and Grouse Lodge in Scotland, including the lairdship and full hunting rights."'

David nodded.

'"Cecil, I leave to you any three paintings from my collection, excluding the Picasso, the Reubens and anything currently hanging on the walls of the house."'

Cecil nodded.

'"I wish to leave £200,000 to the Polo Club and ten million pounds split equally between my chosen charities. All current house staff, grounds managers, gardeners, gamekeepers, etc., to be given a personal gift of ten per cent of their annual salary to spend on whatever they please, and a day off each and every year on the anniversary of my death. Thank you for your fault- less service and commitment to the household. I would also like a cedar tree to be planted in my honour in the garden. A tall, worthy specimen, in better health than mine. (Shouldn't be difficult.)"' The lawyer cleared his throat. "'Last, but by no means least, my darling Charlotte, I give everything else to you: the family crest, the family house and contents, the London house, the villa in Corsica, the Alpenblick Palace and the balance of my entire wealth—all the investment funds and current property portfolios, and any monies in my private bank accounts.'" The lawyer looked at Charlotte. 'The private accounts alone are worth around £200 million.'

Charlotte shook her head; she had no understanding of what all this actually meant. She felt dizzy and steadied herself with her arm on the table. Then she noticed her mother leave her seat.

'Did he say he was coming home soon? He promised to take me to the ballet,' she said. She made a pirouette and exited through the open French windows.

8

CLOSE CALL

'Stop! *Stop!*'

From his position high in the mature cedar tree, Peter heard the muffled shout below as he released the trigger of the chainsaw. He looked down to see his groundsman, Chris, waving both arms and jumping up and down.

'What is it?' Peter cried.

'You were about to cut the branch you're secured to, you idiot.'

Peter shook his head. He knew what he was doing; he'd done it hundreds of times. He studied the bright orange climbing rope, which was bearing his entire weight. His eyes tracked from the secure karabiner on his harness up and around the sturdy branch right in front of him, which was the one he was about to cut.

'You're right,' Peter called. 'I don't know what I was thinking. I was about to cut the wrong piece.'

'Yeah, I know!' Chris replied, gesturing for Peter to descend. Once he was on safe ground, Chris shook his arm. 'What the hell happened up there? You scared me, man.'

'I have no idea. My mind must have wandered for a second.'

'You could be dead, you idiot. If you want to continue being a tree surgeon, twenty-three is no age to die.'

'I know. Thanks. I mean, thanks for looking out for me.'

'It's not like you, Pete. What's on your mind?'

'I don't know. My mind's been foggy for a few days. I've been thinking a lot about my mum and whether one day I might actually move on. You know, emotionally and all that?'

'I understand, mate, but there's a time and a place for that. Look, let's call it a day and come back to this with fresh eyes tomorrow. I said I wouldn't be home too late anyway, as Amanda's out with the girls tonight.'

Peter put his hand on Chris's shoulder. 'Sorry, mate. I know I shouldn't let my mind wander. You'd better not let Amanda down. Let's get moving. She's a good woman. You did well to find her.'

Chris reciprocated with a slap on the back and smiled. 'I know it's none of my business, but... your mum... it's been ten years, hasn't it?'

'Yes.'

'Do you think you need to get some help?'

'You mean, like a shrink?'

Chris shrugged and raised an eyebrow. 'Maybe? Someone who can really help. Not a crazy lumberjack, like me. What do I know?'

'I'm not seeing a shrink. I'm not mad.'

'Sorry, Pete, I didn't mean to pry. Maybe you just need a good woman in your life. Look what Amanda did for me. Turned me all... grown up.'

'Well, maybe. I'm not ready for growing up just yet, though. I can't see me being in a relationship.'

Peter got the impression Chris wanted to mention the shrink thing again, but then his friend seemed to hold back. 'Come on,' he said instead. 'Let's get a move on.'

Peter's phone woke him with a start.

'Pete? Is that you?'

'Of course it is. Who else would it be?'

'If you're coming, can you bring one of those energy-saving lightbulbs? We've had one blow in the kitchen.'

'Don't worry, I'll be there shortly.' He laughed. 'Give me twenty minutes. I'm still in bed.' He placed the phone on the floor and lay on his back, looking up at the brown stain in the corner of the ceiling which seemed to be getting bigger. A drop of water ran across the skylight, gathering momentum as it swelled in size. It ran down the edge of the glass, squeezed through the botched seal in the corner and fell as if in slow motion, missing the dented saucepan which had been collecting water all night, and instead, landing with a splat on Peter's hairy chest.

His toned, naked body, only partially covered by a corner of the blue-and-white checked duvet, jerked with the cold impact. He wiped the droplet from his chest with the duvet and looked up in despair at the skylight. The landlord had been promising to fix it for weeks, but nothing had happened.

The saucepan, now a permanent fixture, was balanced precariously on a pile of books: *The Art and Science of Tree Management*, *The Power of Now*, *How Parents F***k You Up* and *15-Minute Meals*. His rented flat was small—a studio with a kitchen, bed and everything else in one room. It was cold in the winter and cold in the summer; it smelled of damp and whatever he'd cooked for dinner the previous evening.

Peter reached over, switched on the kettle and grabbed his jeans and lumberjack shirt from the back of the old leather chair which had been his mum's. His chest was broad and strong from years working as a tree surgeon. He buttoned his shirt with his capable hands, tightened his belt, dropped a Yorkshire teabag into the brown-stained mug and topped it up with boiling water.

He ran his hand once through his hair and then across his stubbly chin to check it hadn't become a full-size beard. Then he brushed his teeth with one hand while slipping on his shoes with the other. He gulped his tea, put on his jacket and hurried down the stairs, bulb in hand. He had two very important people to see.

Peter rushed up the garden path and opened the door to the little council bungalow.

'Peter, is that you?' a voice came from the sitting room.

'No, it's the milkman,' Peter said, in his broadest Yorkshire accent.

'Oh, it *is* you.' His grandmother gave a sigh of relief. 'It's Peter, Albert. Peter's here.' She tugged on the sleeve of his grandfather's dressing gown.

'Has he brought the lightbulb?' his grandfather muttered.

'Don't worry, I have the bulb. How are you two today?'

His grandparents were sitting in their small lounge, which had green walls and the same green-and-gold carpet they'd had when Peter lived there.

'It's like the Bahamas in here with three bars on the fire.'

Peter removed his coat. He went over to each of them and gave them a hug, and his grandmother a kiss on her wrinkled cheek.

'You alright?' Peter looked his gran directly in the eyes.

'All the better for seeing you, love. I've had a bit of a fall, but I'm fine—just a bruise. Tripped over the rug in the kitchen. Couldn't see a thing. The bulb's gone in the big light.'

Peter shook his head. 'Why the hell do you have those rugs in there? I trip over the damn things every time I go in there, so what chance do you have?'

His grandfather cleared his throat. 'The floor's too cold without them,' he said, struggling to push himself out of his chair with his frail arms. 'Can you sort the bulb out, Peter?'

Apparently Gran, frustratingly, wasn't prepared to let him go standing on chairs to reach the bulb. Peter leaned over and took his grandfather's hand in a tight grip with both of his.

'I'll sort the bulb out for you, don't worry.'

Grandad was eighty-three years old and Gran eighty-one. They were proud folk and rejected any kind of outside help, but clearly things were getting on top of them. Gran had been fit for many years, helping out at village events and the Women's Guild, but had declined rapidly after a succession of falls and a cataract. Grandad had been declining steadily for years—nothing wrong with him, just old age catching up. He'd been a fit man, had fought in Germany during the war and had liberated one of the concentration camps and seen some dreadful sights. He rarely spoke about those times, but Peter could sense he'd been affected by it. After the war, his grandfather had worked as an engineer at a power station. He understood a wiring diagram inside out, invented crazy gadgets and had been an avid walker, sculptor and cyclist, well into his eighties.

'I'll come and help you,' his grandfather said. 'If it wasn't for your gran, I'd have jumped up on the table and had that done by now.' He began hobbling with his stick into the kitchen.

'Yeah, right,' Peter said with a smile.

'What was that?'

'I said yes, of course. Come and steady the chair for me.'

His grandad's sight and hearing were rapidly fading, but his inquisitive mind was as sharp as ever.

'You didn't have a bulb, though?' Peter asked him.

'I've three boxes of "old-style" bulbs in the shed, but apparently we have to have these new-fangled ones now. Perfectly good, the old ones,' Grandad muttered.

Peter replaced the bulb, while his grandad supported the chair.

'It's done. Should make it easier to see what you're doing in here now.'

As Peter stepped down, he noticed some spilt soup which was now encrusted on the floor.

'Are you two coping? Are you managing?' But his concerned voice didn't seem to register with their selective hearing. 'Did you hear that?' he shouted to his gran.

'We're OK, Peter,' she said. 'Your grandad won't have anyone in to look after us. You know what he's like.'

'Mmm.' Peter looked lovingly at both of them. 'I'll try to get in to see you as much as possible, and don't go tripping over those damn rugs.'

'What about you? It's been a tough few years for you. You liking your job?'

'Beggars can't be choosers with a criminal record, can they? I like it, though. Especially working with a great guy. I'm getting there.' He gave a little chuckle. He was saving every penny for a deposit on a place and didn't want to burden his grandparents with the detail.

'You're a good lad, Peter. Maybe a good woman in your life would help.'

Peter sighed and shook his head. 'Not you as well. Why is everyone obsessed with that? I'll call in and make tea for you one evening this week. Keep safe. I've gotta go.'

Gran grabbed his arm. 'Here, have this.' She placed a £20 note in his hand.

'Gran! You keep your money, I'm fine. Love you.' He squeezed her hand and gave her the note back before dashing out of the door.

9

THE SHRINK

'Do you love me?'

'Of course I do.'

'You never say it.'

'Yeah, but you know I do, that's why I don't.'

Charlotte looked at Sebastian and sighed. Her stomach was turning. She didn't like the way he ignored her and how he was always so dismissive when she questioned him.

Getting married at twenty-three had felt like the right thing at the time, but she was becoming increasingly disillusioned. She'd graduated from Cambridge in Classics and Modern Languages and married Sebastian, her boyfriend of two years and a fellow student. Many suitors had come along, but she'd never really known who to trust, especially if they had wind of her inheritance. She'd made mistakes and sometimes attracted the wrong kind of attention, but Sebastian fitted the mould. He was the son of an investment banker and already part of a wealthy dynasty. A year after they'd married, Charlotte gave birth to Lucy, a thriving redhead with boundless energy and the same naughty grin as her mother.

'Sebastian, is that your phone again? You'll be disturbing Lucy. Your phone is constantly beeping. What is it?'

'It's just business. Foreign investors, you know, they're in a different time zone to us.'

'Well, can you tell them to email or call the office?'

'Of course, I'll try,' he said, looking at his message and replying speedily.

'Are you around this weekend?' Charlotte asked.

'Erm... why?'

'I've agreed to visit the Wallbridges with Lucy and stay the night. And you, of course, if you have some spare time?'

'I'm working. There's an important deal coming in and I need to be one step ahead of everyone else. You go. I'm sure Mrs Wallbridge isn't interested in seeing me.'

'It would be nice to go as a family. They were very supportive after father went.'

'I'll leave you to it, if that's OK?'

Charlotte dropped her head and sighed.

The Wallbridges were delighted to see Charlotte. They'd been family friends for many years and were always keen to see how Lucy was getting on, especially since she would be starting school soon.

'Are you alright, Charlotte?' probed Mrs Wallbridge.

'To be honest, I am a little unsettled.'

'I thought so. You seem to be thinking about something. Not that I want to pry.'

Charlotte squirmed in her seat. 'Did you always know that Mr Wallbridge was the man for you?'

Mrs Wallbridge raised her eyebrows. 'Not always. I guess

it's something that grows between you. I know he loves me, though.'

'Really? How can you be sure?' Charlotte took a sip of tea and noticed her hand was shaking.

'Well, I wouldn't say this to anyone else, but the way he looks at me, and our kisses are... you know... special. Do you know what I mean?'

'I'm not sure I do.'

There was a pause, interrupted by Lucy entering and flopping onto Charlotte's lap. 'Can we go now? I'm tired,' she said, her eyes filled with boredom.

'I guess so. We were meant to stay the night, but I can see it might be better to go home. Say goodbye to Mrs Wallbridge and thank her for the delightful hairclips.'

The drive back to the house was done in silence. Lucy fell asleep almost instantly, and Charlotte thought about what Mrs Wallbridge had said. By the time they entered the estate, it was dark. On reaching the house, Charlotte parked next to Sebastian's car and carried Lucy into the house, taking her straight upstairs to bed. At the top of the stairs, she entered the east wing corridor and noticed a light was on in the guest bedroom at the end. That room hadn't been used since the Harcourt-Baileys had visited from South Africa three years earlier. Charlotte put Lucy in a fresh nightie and gave her a glass of water to sip.

'I'll be back in a moment,' she said, trying not to sound agitated. She quietly proceeded down the long hallway and approached the bedroom door, which was slightly ajar. The yellowy light of the bedside lamp enabled her to see part-way into the room, but she would have to lean in and stick her head around the door to see it entirely.

She heard grotesque groaning and stopped to listen. There

seemed to be two people inside. She placed her hand on the edge of the door and tentatively peered inside. Then she froze. The sight of her husband's bare bottom writhing between a pair of stocking-clad legs and the red-painted nails scratching down his back almost made her retch.

'Get out of my house. Get out of my house!' she screamed.

Her husband immediately rolled aside and grabbed the sheets to hide himself, but in doing so, he revealed the bleached blonde hair, smeared lipstick and enhanced breasts of the barmaid from the Ferret and Whistle pub in the village.

'Get out of my house, I said. Both of you!'

The London house was large and grand and, once inside, didn't disappoint visitors. It had once been the Gambian ambassador's residence as well as a hospital in World War Two, and Charlotte had bought it from a family who were moving to America. It had a luxurious Portland stone exterior with immaculate topiary to the front and, inside, solid wood flooring and impressive chandeliers. It was a good base for London, and only a short walk across the park to Mr Shorofski's office.

It never mattered what time of day it was, the light through the shuttered windows in his office always looked the same, and so did Mr Shorofski. Perpetually in beige and stiff black shoes which contrasted with his brown socks. Style was not his forte, but he had a worldly knowledge about him. He was highly respected within his profession and his fee reflected that.

Today Charlotte chose the cream leather chair instead of

the couch. Mr Shorofski sat back in the opposite chair and looked at her over the top of his wire-rimmed spectacles.

'How are you today?' he asked, in his usual calm, liquid voice.

Charlotte adjusted her skirt neatly over her knees and sat up straight. 'It's been a while since I last saw you. Life doesn't always pan out like you expect it to, does it?'

Mr Shorofski said nothing; he just seemed to open his face, while tilting his head to one side.

'I'm losing my trust in people and I don't like it. Nothing seems to be going right. I thought I'd married a man I could trust. Mother is increasingly unwell, and I just don't feel I have the support around me that I would like. As a child I was lonely, and I never wanted to feel like that again.'

Thumb on chin, Mr Shorofski gently rubbed his lips with the back of his index finger and again said nothing.

'I'm worried I won't be able to trust anyone. Father abandoned me, my husband cheated on me, and I'm concerned I might never find love again.'

Her counsellor nodded. 'If you have love in your heart, you will find it. Maybe it's best not to feel under pressure to do so.'

Charlotte came straight back without a pause. 'That's the other problem. I'm frightened I might make a huge mistake and lose the house, or Lucy. Everything!'

'You're a bright woman. Try to think positively and I'm sure that won't happen.'

'Can I talk about Lucy?'

'Of course. You can talk to me about anything,' he said calmly.

'Well, I just don't feel like I'm being a good mother, either. She has everything, obviously, and maybe that's the problem. She seems to take everything and everyone for granted, with no respect. It's been hard for all of us, especially after her father left us for that tramp. She sees him now and again and they have holidays, but she feels he neglects her and I know how that hurts. And seeing Mother like she is confuses her. It does me too, especially when she's up in the middle of the night, throwing things around her room and accusing us of imprisoning her.'

'What makes you feel like you're failing as a mother?' Mr Shorofski said, sitting slightly forward in his chair.

'I often don't feel like I'm in control.'

He raised an eyebrow. 'Of Lucy, or anything else?'

'Everything, Mr Shorofski. Up to Father's death, I had no real concept of the family wealth and the responsibility that goes with it. I'm constantly worried I might make a wrong decision and lose it all, or someone might take it from us. As well as making all the household decisions, I shoulder the responsibility for Lucy's future and the family name all on my own. I miss my father dearly, but I'm increasingly beginning to despise him, and that scares me.'

'And what about Lucy?'

'I feel like I give her too much, because I shoulder the guilt for her father running off with that... woman, and for her losing her grandfather, too. She has no male role model. There's no "man of the house" anymore. I'm aware I rushed into marriage, but that's because I was scared to go it alone. I send Lucy off to boarding school, because it's a family tradition and everyone talks about how fantastic it is and how well I did, but I hated it there, and I know Lucy feels the same. I'm riddled with guilt.'

'I see,' he said. 'In our last session, you talked about taking your own life and how sometimes it's impossible to get that out of your mind. Has that changed at all? Did you see your doctor, as I suggested?'

'Life wasn't worth living after Father died—it was a low point. I've thought about it many times since, and I've been close, very close, but my responsibilities prevent me from taking things any further.'

'And your doctor?'

'I take the pills he's given me.'

Mr Shorofski leaned back in his chair. 'Mmm. These are difficult times for you, but running away from your fears is not always the answer. Some things are out of our control. We have to take time to reflect and you're doing the right thing. A problem shared is indeed often a problem halved. Is there anyone else you can talk to?'

'Maybe I do get lonely, but I can't see myself getting into another relationship.'

'I didn't necessarily mean that.'

Charlotte squirmed in her seat. 'I know what you meant, and... sorry, no disrespect, but my faith in men is at an all-time low. I don't know if I can ever trust again.'

'It sounds like you have many different issues going on. Is Lucy well? Is she thriving at the school?'

'Well... yes. She says she hates it, and it's cold there in the winter. The showers are freezing and you can rarely find any privacy. But the staff are superb, as are their results.'

'And what is Lucy like when she's home with you?'

'She's a handful sometimes. Rebellious and emotional. I guess I was like that too, but I had that knocked out of me. I have duties and responsibilities now. I'd like to spend more time with Lucy, but there are often issues, too, to resolve on the estate, or a charity event or dinner. When we're in the house, she is either glued to my side or creating havoc with the staff.'

Mr Shorofski smiled a very thin smile and nodded, without really nodding. It gave him a strange air of arrogance, yet compassion.

'My advice would be to take one step at a time. Deal with one aspect in earnest, perhaps, rather than becoming bogged down with everything together.'

Charlotte took to her feet. 'Thank you for your time, as always. I will settle your invoice immediately.'

Mr Shorofski nodded and reached for the door.

'Thank you again.'

'Perhaps see your doctor again and don't lose faith in yourself. You're a capable woman.'

'Is that you, Pete?'

'Of course it is. Who else would it be?'

'Pete, I have some tree-surveying work for you, if you're interested? In London.'

Peter held the phone closer to his ear. 'What is it?'

'You'd be helping me out, to be honest. It's work I haven't time to look at. It's the usual rate, plus a bit extra for travel.'

'Appreciate that, Chris. I'm always looking for more work.'

'I thought you might be. There's one other thing too.'

'What is it?'

'Can you babysit for Anna tomorrow evening? We can't find anyone at this short notice and, you know... a favour for a favour and all that.'

Peter laughed. 'You know I'd drop everything to play dolls with a seven-year-old girl, but sadly, I'm busy tomorrow night.'

'Are you sure?' Chris said.

'Honestly mate. It's Gran's eighty-second birthday. I can't miss that.'

Chris huffed. 'OK, I understand. I'll send through the survey details. It's a Ms Percival, somewhere in Notting Hill.'

Ms Percival was concerned about the safety of a twenty-metre-high plane tree towering over her conservatory. At the door, Peter was greeted by a woman in her early fifties in a black skirt and white blouse. Peter noticed the skirt was a little too tight, and his attention was also drawn to a prominent wart on her face and her attempt to cover it with thick make-up. Ms Percival had a pleasant smile and welcomed him into the house.

'I work from home when I can,' she said. 'And I like to sit and contemplate the garden while doing so.' She showed him into a modern glass-and-timber conservatory and then out into the rear garden, where the imposing tree stood. Peter rolled his sleeves up and gave the tree a thorough examination. He was able to reassure Ms Percival that it was, in fact, safe, but because it was such a large specimen and overhanging the house, he suggested it may be prudent to raise the crown by removing some heavier, lower branches, and take out a couple of pieces of dead wood which were dangling precariously. This would also allow more light in. Ms Percival agreed and thanked him for his advice and for saving her a lot of money. She'd thought she would have to get someone in to remove the whole tree.

'Sometimes you just have to have peace of mind,' Peter said. 'It's a beautiful garden.' He looked at the paperwork scattered all over the desk. 'What work is it you do, if you don't mind me asking?'

'I run a bespoke dating agency. We match people on our books for dates, and hopefully longer-term relationships.'

Peter raised his eyebrows and said with a chuckle, 'I didn't know that sort of thing existed.'

'Very much so, and I'm always on the lookout for eligible bachelors,' she answered with a smile.

'I'm not really looking for anything like that.'

'Really?' Ms Percival looked him up and down demurely. 'Are you single?'

Peter looked up. 'Yes. I've been single for a while now, but I'm not considering a dating agency.'

Ms Percival walked over to a thick pile of papers on the top shelf of an in-tray and rifled through them. 'There's a real shortage of men on the books at the moment. Well, there usually is, to be honest. We put out some ads now and again and we get interest, but we're down to an eight-to-one ratio of women to men.'

'Well, maybe they can't afford it, like me.' Peter shrugged and laughed. 'I'd best be off now. Let me know if you need any more advice regarding the tree.'

'OK, I will.' She paused. 'Erm... would you reconsider? I mean, about joining the agency. We could do with a few more men like you on board. Interesting and eligible and... handsome.' She looked at him with a hopeful smile.

Peter stared back. He didn't know what to say and touched his face in an awkward gesture. He couldn't afford anything like the service she was offering, but there was something deeper holding him back, too. His mind switched to an image of his mum, with an overwhelming feeling of how close they'd been and how relationships had proven difficult since her death.

'Look, Ms Percival, with all due respect...'

'Why don't you give it a try?' she said. 'If I can show more men on the books, it may help to attract both men and women. You'd be helping me out, really. There's no cost to you. It would be my thank you for saving me so much with the tree.' She gave a reassuring nod.

Peter thought for a minute. 'As I said, that's generous, but I'm not looking for anything at the moment, thanks.'

'I'll level with you, Peter. To be honest, I'm rather desperate. What if I paid you?'

'You'll pay me? No... No thanks. That's like some kind of gigolo.'

Ms Percival looked at the floor and then directly at him. 'I can see how that looks, but I'm about to launch an advertising campaign and women will only be interested if I can show I have a variety of men on the books. Call it expenses, or travel costs. Please.'

'I can't believe I'm even thinking about this. Can you reassure me I wouldn't have to go on a date? I'll just help you get the numbers up, that's all.'

'Yes, of course. Just that. Why don't you stop by the office next week sometime and I'll get you on the system. It won't take long. A few questions and a photograph or two.'

Peter sighed. 'I can't believe I'm doing this. You promise?'

'Absolutely. Here's my card. The address is on the back. One Berkeley Circus. Thanks, Peter, it's greatly appreciated. It really is.'

The appointment was set for Wednesday of the following week.

Later that day, as Peter was pulling up back at his flat, his phone vibrated in his pocket.

'Mate, it's Chris. Amanda has pains in her stomach, bad ones. I need to get her to hospital. She said I should call you.'

'Shit, sorry to hear that. I'm not a doctor, though!'

'I need to get her to the hospital right now. Can you look after Anna? Please?'

'You're asking the wrong guy here, mate.'

'Please, Pete. Amanda wants you to do it.'

'You're kidding. I don't know what to do with a seven-year-old.'

'We're desperate.'

Peter turned the key in the ignition again. 'Jeez! Everyone's so desperate at the moment. OK, I'll come straight over. Is she going to be OK?'

'I hope so. Hurry.'

Not long afterwards, Peter arrived to find Chris panicking at the door. Amanda was already in the car.

'Good to see you, mate. I don't know how long we'll be. Help yourself to anything. Anna is fed and should be in bed by eight. Give her a glass of milk before.'

Peter pushed him out of the door. 'Go on.' Then he shouted to Amanda, 'Hope you're going to be OK.'

Amanda gave him a smile, and the car sped off at high speed.

Peter turned and looked at Anna, who was playing on the floor. 'Hi,' he said nervously. 'Do you remember me from your birthday party?'

'Of course I do. Some of my friends had to go early, because you threw juice all over them.'

'Well, I didn't know the cat was going to trip me up, did I?'

Anna rolled her eyes as if she were going on thirteen. 'Do you want to play dolls?'

Peter paused. 'Sure. What are their names?'

'This one is Rosie, and this one is Jemima. You can have Jemima.'

'Thanks.'

'They're going out, so we need to dress them.'

'Where are they going?'

'On an adventure, silly.'

Peter laughed. 'I wouldn't expect anything less from a tree surgeon's daughter. Got any camo gear?'

Anna rummaged in a box and produced some black boots, camouflage trousers and tops, followed by an off-road buggy, a rocket launcher and some hand grenades.

'I never thought playing dolls was going to be so much fun.'

Anna laughed and threw him a matching hang-glider.

'It's going to be some adventure,' he said, with a big smile.

Chris and Amanda returned late in the evening. A suspected rumbling appendix was the diagnosis. They opened the door to find Anna and Peter both fast asleep, Anna wrapped in her duvet on the sofa, surrounded by dolls, teddy bears, squirrels, badgers and a rocket launcher, and wearing a sparkly plastic tiara. Peter was on the floor with his head on a giant pink unicorn and Jemima, in full ski gear, in his hand.

Amanda and Chris looked at each other and smiled, put a blanket over Peter, and headed for bed.

10

THE DYING SWAN

Charlotte sauntered around the walled garden, plucking ripe raspberries, savouring the taste of late summer as the juice made her lips tingle. She admired the figs forming on the trees pruned tight to the south-facing wall and stopped occasionally to listen to the water splashing in the fountain. The fountain formed the central point for the pathways that divided the plentiful vegetable plots of the walled garden. As she listened, she sought the warm sun on her face, and smiled.

The flowering cherry tree Charlotte's father had planted for her when she was born was thick with cherries, but they were often too sour to eat. By the side of it was the cedar and Victoria plum trees she'd planted recently in his memory. She liked that they were side by side and recalled how her father always savoured a sweet, juicy plum.

She peered up at the window of the west wing, which overlooked the garden. Her mother was staring out, her palm on the glass. Charlotte waved, but there was no reaction. Her dementia was stealing her away from normality more and more. It didn't seem fair that her mother was losing her mind.

It felt to Charlotte like she'd lost both parents, and the burden of being the head of the family bore down heavily upon her shoulders.

Usually, Mrs Hathersage or a member of the junior staff would choose the flowers for the table, but today was special. Charlotte wanted to pick and arrange them herself. She wanted the centrepiece to be lively and fun, in line with tradition, and occupying her mind with it helped to brighten her thoughts. Fragrance and form were equally important for her, but this time she chose bright purples, reds, blues and white, offset with young fronds of eucalyptus and contorted willow.

As she entered through the solid oak door which led to the large utility room, known as the pantry, Mrs Hathersage confronted her.

'Miss Charlotte, I would have chosen the flowers for you this morning. You have enough to think about.'

Charlotte smiled and laid the flowers on the side. 'Thank you, but I wanted to select them personally.'

The housekeeper began to gather cutlery. 'Shall I prepare the table, with Lucy at the head?'

'Yes, please, and settings for eight: Mother, Uncle Henry and Silvia, Cousin Emily, myself and the Wallbridges, excluding their eldest son.'

Charlotte arranged the flowers in an antique vase, tweaking and pricking each flower into place, while singing softly to herself the words to a tune she was making up in the moment. 'Sweet peas and humming honeybees…'

Her song was suddenly halted when Lucy came crashing in, still brushing her hair.

'Are we going to make cupcakes? You promised we would make cupcakes. Can we do them now?'

'Have you had breakfast yet?' Charlotte asked with calm authority.

'I don't want breakfast. I don't want stupid breakfast, especially when there will be a huge lunch in my honour.' She spun round the terracotta tiled floor, flailing her arms like an out-of-control, conceited thirteen-year-old ballet dancer.

The ingredients were already laid out on the marble worktop and the Aga eagerly awaited with its radiant heat.

'I want to do black icing, seeing as I'm the dying swan.' Lucy continued her twirling until she crumpled in a mess on the floor.

'We'll do pink icing or blue or both,' Charlotte insisted.

'I want to do black. Black is for death! I'd rather die than go back to that horrible school.' Lucy lay outstretched on the floor, pretending to choke.

Charlotte rolled her eyes. 'Please don't talk about death. I want the day to be light and optimistic. Maybe purple. There isn't a black die. Anyway, the sending-off lunch is a tradition which has been passed down from my mother to me from her mother, and her mother before, so no radical changes. Also, we don't want any hints of early demise and we need to wear our smiles boldly for Mrs Wallbridge. She's just been diagnosed with breast cancer, so high spirits are required. High spirits, did you hear?'

Lucy was still flailing around on the floor. 'Yeah, yeah, yeah, poor old Mrs Whalebridge.'

'Lucy! Show some respect. It's Wallbridge. She's been very kind to us over the years. OK, hands washed, let's crack these eggs.'

They'd made cupcakes together before and always enjoyed mucking in with each other, while Charlotte would tell tales of when she was a girl. Now Lucy beat the eggs and Charlotte poured in the sugar.

'I really don't want to go,' Lucy said, without looking up.

'What do you mean?'

'I don't want to go back to that school. I hate it there. All the girls are so bitchy... and...' She paused.

'Yes?' Charlotte probed.

'I... get lonely sometimes, especially when they're so cruel to me.'

Charlotte sighed. 'I do understand. I found it hard sometimes, too, but it's a fantastic school, with an excellent reputation, and it's a tradition. Your grandmother, and her mother before her, and I all gained Head Girl, not to mention Daddy's legacy, so there's no letting the side down. OK?'

'Do you mean the Sir Henry Winterbourne Wing?' Lucy asked, throwing her hands down onto the counter.

'It was your grandfather's wish. Don't you think I'm as much embarrassed by it as you?'

'And there are no boys.'

'Oh! Is that what this is all about?'

Lucy remained silent and carried on whisking.

'If that's what this little tantrum is all about, then you seriously need to think about who you're representing here. We have a social standing to keep.'

Lucy's whisking became slow and lacklustre, and she dragged her nail-bitten finger through the mixture and sucked it. 'Don't make me go back there. I truly hate it and they hate me. I can do my schooling from home and spend more time with you. Please.'

Charlotte reached behind her for the flour and as she did, her mind wandered to when she'd asked the same question of her mother. A cold shiver shot through her core and she felt numb, as though her heart had stopped beating for a second or two. An overwhelming and uncomfortable feeling of déjà vu rendered her motionless. She pictured herself being taunted by the other girls in her dorm.

Mrs Hathersage broke the painful silence. 'The table is set, Miss Charlotte. Will you be having wine or just water?'

'Wine! Yes, wine. Select a vintage white with hints of summer fruits,' Charlotte replied with a false smile, wiping away her tear. 'And Lucy can have some, too.'

Mrs Hathersage hurried out, and Lucy and Charlotte looked at each other.

'Let's get these cakes finished and you'll feel much better when you finally have something to eat,' Charlotte said. 'You know, school will be the making of you. Look at me,' she added, biting her lip.

Lunch was the traditional sending-off party after the summer holidays, the day before returning to school. The females in the succession had kept it going, while the males historically would have gone out hunting within the grounds and brought back pheasant and quail for the table, or even, sometimes, a deer. But the male succession had taken a hit. There would be no male heir and Charlotte, at forty-five years old, knew this was unlikely to change. Besides, she detested the hunting scene and any form of animal cruelty. Landscape watercolours, pencil sketches and pressed flower pictures now replaced the stag and boar that once adorned walls.

The lunch went as well as expected. Charlotte kept her spirits high, and Mrs Wallbridge appreciated some uplifting conversation and a change of scenery. Lucy didn't speak much. She shuffled the food around her plate and then disappeared to her room early, complaining of a migraine, taking a cupcake with her for later, much to Charlotte's silent disappointment.

The following morning, the Bentley stood elegantly on the gravel, ready to take Lucy to school.

Charlotte spoke to a portly gentleman by the car. 'It's wonderful to have you back, Cartwright.'

'It's good to be back, madam.'

'I'm sorry about what happened between you and Father, but I've always trusted you and we need you here now.'

Cartwright had explained that her father had got it wrong all those years ago—he'd placed the silverware in the car to be taken for polishing. Charlotte nodded and smiled. 'An easy mistake.'

Replying with his usual graceful nod he opened the door, ready for Lucy. In the years he'd been away from the house, he'd worked for a member of the Royal Family and had gained an impeccable reputation.

'Are you alright with the additional driving duties?'

'Absolutely, madam. I'll take good care of her.'

Charlotte had tied her hair into a ponytail. Her hair had a natural wave and sometimes it was easier to tie it up rather than try to tame it. Lucy, by complete contrast, had a striking head of auburn hair in a short bob. She'd cut it herself at the start of the holidays, in a rage about freedom and right of expression. Charlotte had shown her disapproval by withholding the new pair of shoes she'd promised for the summer, but secretly, she'd wished she could do the same.

'Come on, Lucy,' she shouted up the grand staircase. 'Cartwright is waiting in the car.'

The car was laden with bags, books and straw boater, and Lucy's moth-eaten teddy bear lay on the parcel shelf. Cartwright stood patiently with the rear door half-open, in the expectation of leaving on time.

'Lucy! Come on now.'

Lucy appeared at the top of the stairs, dragging her feet and sobbing, occasionally wiping her eyes with a tissue. She hesitated on each step, hoping that at some point she might get a reprieve.

Charlotte walked partway up the sweeping stairs and gently took hold of her hand. 'I understand how you feel. It's hard for anyone to go back to school after the holidays, but once you're back, it will be like you never left. Here, I have a gift for you.'

Lucy gave a little smile as she opened the box to reveal the lovely open-toed shoes.

'I have something else for you too.' Charlotte produced a mother-of-pearl locket her grandmother had given her. Lucy took it and, on opening, revealed a photo of Charlotte and herself laughing in ballgowns, taken at a party earlier that year. 'This will keep you safe,' Charlotte said as she led her to the door.

Lucy tried to smile again, but was too distraught. She held on to her mother's hand all the way to the car and then clung on even tighter as Cartwright opened the door fully. She wiped the tears from her nose. 'I'll miss you so dearly.'

'And I will miss you, too. It won't be long until half-term. You must go, or you'll be late.'

Cartwright closed the door and Lucy waved through the window as they drove steadily away and along the drive, through the parkland and over the arched bridge, before disappearing into the trees and to the gatehouse.

Charlotte stood on the gravel expanse, trying to control her tears. She understood that wretched feeling so well.

After a few minutes, Mrs Hathersage appeared at the door. 'There's tea and toast ready in the breakfast room, Miss Charlotte.'

Charlotte slowly made her way to sit in the window seat,

where she looked out across the extensive parkland towards the upper pond and the trees beyond. She placed a cushion behind her and, tucking her legs up, pulled her knees tight into her chest as if to cuddle herself, and rested her chin.

Lucy needed a firm structure to her schooling. She did have a tendency to go off the rails, and it would give her a sturdy backbone to her life, exactly as it had done for Charlotte. The connections there were exceptional too, and the chances of her going to Oxford or Cambridge afterwards were high.

Charlotte closed her eyes, and her mind flashed back to her first days back at school after the holidays and how she missed home and her swing. She questioned whether she was being a good mother, and whether Lucy would resent her. And she thought about how the people around her made it almost impossible to change generations of family history.

'Would you like more tea?' Mrs Hathersage ended Charlotte's stark and unnerving delve back into her youth.

'No... No, thank you,' she said.

The housekeeper nodded and busied herself folding a tablecloth.

'Mrs Hathersage, I am a good mother, aren't I?'

'Of course you are. Don't you worry about the school. It didn't do you any harm, did it? And look at you now.'

Charlotte didn't reply. She just tucked her knees up tighter into her chest and rocked backwards and forwards gently in the window seat.

That afternoon, Charlotte was gazing out of the window again, watching the droplets of rain run slowly down the glass and merge into a pool on the sill. She was contemplating doing nothing with the rest of her day when Mrs Hathersage came in.

'Miss Charlotte, it appears you have visitors.'

Charlotte looked over in dismay. 'Tell them kindly to come back another day, if you would.'

'It's the girls, madam.'

At that point, three heads appeared around the door and then eagerly barged in, throwing their coats on a chair, before producing a bottle of Prosecco.

'We thought you needed cheering up,' said Jojo.

Charlotte was speechless.

'We thought you'd become a recluse or, worse still, a nun,' said Sam.

'Haha. Funnily enough, I was contemplating it,' Charlotte said with a smile, dropping her guard.

'Fizz, darling?' Mira began searching for glasses.

'In the cupboard above the ice-machine,' Charlotte replied. 'So, what's this all about?'

'It's about friends looking after each other. Mira said she was missing you. I haven't seen you since we last went skiing and Sam has just split up with her man, so we thought, let's drop in on Charlotte.'

'So sorry to hear that, Sam,' Charlotte said, as the cork popped and Mira poured the fizz.

'He was a bastard, just like all the others. Said one thing and did the complete opposite.'

'She's not bitter.' Jojo laughed. 'Cheers.'

They all raised their glasses and Charlotte asked Mrs Hathersage to bring in some pastries.

'Anyway, I have some news,' Jojo said, taking a large gulp of fizz, which made her sneeze. 'I'm getting married. Look.' She showed off her diamond solitaire ring, which sparkled as it caught the light from above.

Charlotte's ears pricked up. 'It's beautiful. A man of taste, I can see. Who is it?'

'Do you remember spotty Harrison from the boys' school choir?'

They all laughed.

'Yes!'

'Turns out he really could sing and he's now the lead singer in the Tribe. They're just about to release their fourth album.'

'I love the Tribe,' Charlotte said excitedly. 'Never knew that was spotty Harrison.'

'Jake. And his spots have made way for broad shoulders and an impressive stage presence.'

'I bet. Sounds like he gives an excellent performance.' Charlotte gave an exaggerated wink, which sent the girls laughing uncontrollably.

'This calls for champagne. Have you set the date?'

'No, not yet. He's on tour at the moment, but we're in no rush.'

'I wouldn't hang about,' said Mira, looking stern.

Cartwright appeared shortly afterwards with a bottle of Dom Perignon which he poured into fresh glasses.

'Just to let you know Miss Lucy got to school fine, madam.'

'Thank you, Cartwright.'

'Cheers again,' said Jojo, raising her glass. 'Anyway, we have something else to tell you.'

Charlotte stopped drinking and looked at her. 'What?'

'Well, it's like this,' she said, hiccupping. 'We thought it would be a good idea to enrol Sam with a dating agency. She needs a bit of fun, nothing serious after her split, so we did it last weekend. She has three dates lined up already.'

'Wow, you don't hang about. Who are they?'

'All interesting guys by the sound of it. One's an explorer, one's a cricketer and the other a radio DJ.'

'Sounds good. Are you sure you're ready for it, Sam?'

'Not really. But I guess it won't do any harm.'

Charlotte smiled. 'I guess not.'

Sam topped up Charlotte's glass. 'Anyway, we enquired on your behalf, and they have vacancies.'

Charlotte spluttered on her champagne. 'I'm not interested in that at all, thank you.'

'We thought it would be good for you to get out and stop moping around the house. You know, let your hair down and have some fun.'

'I didn't think that,' said Mira, still looking stern.

'Come on, Charlotte, you and me. It will make me feel better about it,' Sam said, fluttering her eyelashes.

'No way. No. This is ridiculous. You can't just gate crash in here and sign me up to a cattle market.'

There was a silence and Sam poured everyone more champagne. 'Erm... well... we kind of have already.'

'You have to be kidding!'

'No. The lady offered us a two-for-one if both of us go on three dates each, so we paid. Go on, it'll be a laugh.'

'For you, but not for me.'

Sam leaned forward. 'Go on, Charlotte. It would be a support for me, and we could share our experiences. I'm a little nervous, and knowing you were there doing the same thing would make it easier.'

'I'm not happy, girls.'

'So that's a yes, then? It's just three dates. It won't kill you and I'm not talking out of school, but you really do need to let your hair down a little. We all agree that.'

'Just don't forget your real friends,' Mira said, guzzling back her champagne.

Charlotte thought for a moment. 'I can't believe I'm going along with this.'

'*Salut*,' said Sam and Jojo, clinking their glasses.

11

THE TIP

Charlotte's car drew up on a street in Mayfair.

'Pick me up in ninety minutes if you would, Cartwright.'

'Certainly, madam. I'll pick up the food hamper and give the Bentley a wash in the meantime. Call if you need more time.'

Charlotte floated from the car into the boutique and was met by the owner, Chester.

'Charlotte, how delightful.' *Mwah, mwah.* 'Champagne, darling?'

'Perfect, thank you, Chester.'

'And what are we looking for today?'

Chester was flamboyant, with a completely bald head—and body too, probably. He knew how to dress a lady and he knew how to flatter them, as well as run a very successful and exclusive fashion boutique, specialising in one-off outfits for his many aristocratic and famous clients. His reputation was wide, and it gave him a sense of importance and arrogance.

'I'm looking for something sophisticated for a charity event

I have coming up. Oh, and with shoes to match? I thought a little retail therapy might cheer me up, too.'

'Well, you've come to the right place. Cin-cin.' They gestured with their glasses of champagne as he looked her up and down. 'Mmm, I'm guessing a size 8?'

'Thanks, Chester, I'm a 12 and you know it.'

He smiled. 'Whatever, darling, you're gorgeous anyway, but keep up the hot yoga, or 12 might be knocking at your door.' He gave a toss of his head. 'How about blue? Mmm? Or red? Bear with while I rummage in my bowels, darling.'

He disappeared behind a purple velvet curtain into the back of the boutique, where no client ever ventured.

While waiting, Charlotte browsed casually through several items on a rail by the door while simultaneously trying to call Lucy, to see how things were back at school. There was no answer. She decided she would call the principal later to make sure everything was OK.

While the phone was in her hand it rang, so she answered it. 'Martin, yes, I hadn't forgotten. At the rescue centre, yes. I'm almost on my way. See you shortly. Bye-bye.'

Charlotte had grown fond of supporting the local animal rescue shelter and had bought some equipment for the unit and also funded a new veterinary wing.

Chester appeared through the curtain. 'How about this?' He held up a blue lace dress.

Charlotte held it up against her body. 'It's not quite as summery as I was hoping.'

Chester whisked the item away and once again disappeared into the bowels of the shop to reappear shortly afterwards waving a floral sleeveless dress.

'Mmm, I'm not sure.' Charlotte was thumbing a cream linen item displayed on a mannequin. 'What about this?'

'I thought you said sophisticated.' He shook his head and pirouetted back through the curtain, while Charlotte checked her phone and took a sip of champagne.

'You're gonna love this little number, darling.' Chester sashayed through the velvet curtain towards her. 'This is the one,' he said, pursing his lips. 'Teal, darling. Understated chic. You'll be the belle of the ball.'

'And the shoes?' Charlotte said impatiently. She had her appointment waiting.

'How about these open-toed high heels? They'll go fabulously.'

'I had my eyes on those.'

She quickly tried on the calf-length dress and shoes and felt the bodice hugging her figure perfectly, which made her twirl and smile.

'They're perfect, Chester, I knew I could rely on you.'

Chester carefully wrapped the items in crisp wrapping paper and slipped them into a huge boutique-style bag.

'Darling, it's been a pleasure.' He made the shape of a woman with his hands as he looked over the top of his glasses. 'Next time we go for something a little more daring, sexy lady!'

Cartwright was standing by the open door of the car and Charlotte glided inside, feeling very pleased with herself.

'Cartwright, straight to the animal rescue centre, please. I have a quick meeting and then I want you to take me to Berkeley Circus—number one.'

'Certainly, madam.' Cartwright sped off down the road. Charlotte immediately took her phone from her bag. There was still no message from Lucy, so she called the principal, Mrs

Hardcastle. She had a name that suited her. Not a soft and warm-hearted kind of person, and her immaculately vertical posture, thin, pale face and tweed suits reinforced her position of authority.

'I wanted to check that Lucy had settled in OK. I've heard nothing from her and she left home under not the best of circumstances.'

'Lucy is absolutely fine. They've been busy settling themselves in the new dorm, and there are a couple of new girls. I've made Lucy their chaperone, so she's been rather busy with all that. I wouldn't worry.'

Charlotte took comfort from her answer and smiled. 'That's good. Would you ask her to call me when she has a minute?'

No sooner had she finished her conversation than they arrived at the animal shelter. Charlotte couldn't resist looking at each and every one of the lost or abandoned puppies and cats, all eagerly awaiting a new owner and a new life. The centre also took in rescued wildlife too, and there were badgers, foxes, owls and even an otter in residence. Her benevolence towards the charity was greatly received, and they always welcomed Charlotte with open arms. She was there to discuss their latest fundraising event, but on her way in, Charlotte was struck by a cute little fella in the end kennel, and went back for a second look.

'What's his name?' she asked.

'He doesn't have a name,' the vet replied. 'We found him abandoned by the old meat factory about a month ago and he wasn't in good shape.'

'What breed is he?'

'He's a West Highland Terrier cross. Not that you would have recognised that, the shape he was in when we found him.'

The puppy jumped around and put his front paws up on

the mesh door. His ears were pricked high, and he had a longing look in his eye that caught Charlotte off guard. She couldn't help noticing that he had the top part of one ear missing. At that moment, Martin Groome, the head of the facility, came through the door and greeted Charlotte with a firm handshake and a kiss on both cheeks. Charlotte always had a little chuckle to herself at the fact he was called Groome, and often thought maybe he was born to rescue dogs. Anyway, she liked him. He was friendly and compassionate, and she was keen to offer all the support she could for the centre to thrive.

The London streets were shaded both by tall plane trees and by the buildings, five and six storeys high. They were grand buildings of pristine Portland stone with marble columns and black-painted railings. Peter turned the corner and entered a circular parade of luxury houses, all with shutters and wrought-iron balconies filled with clipped topiary, some with blue plaques displaying the names of famous historical inhabitants. A little garden with a single mulberry tree in full leaf formed the centrepiece to the Georgian splendour. He scanned around to find the street name and spotted it high up on the end-house wall.

Berkeley Circus.

Peter fumbled for the business card in his pocket. 'What number was it?' he mumbled to himself. 'Here it is... Number one.'

A robust, black, gloss-painted front door with a brass lion's head knocker faced him; to the left was a polished brass intercom. He pressed the button that said 'Berkeley Introductions'.

There was a beep and a pause, and then a female voice said, 'Yes?'

'It's Peter.'

'Come on up, Peter. I'm on the first floor,' came the husky and slightly schoolteacher-ish voice of Ms Percival.

Peter walked up the sweeping staircase. He didn't take time to dwell on the walls filled with sullen-faced portraits and hunting scenes. As he reached the top, he could see Ms Percival standing in an open doorway. She was instantly recognisable by the rosy red wart on her right cheek and the slightly overdone blue eyeshadow.

'Please come through. How lovely to see you again, Peter.'

'And you, Ms P—'

'Please... call me Augusta,' she said, running her hand through her blonde hair. 'Please take a seat.'

She gestured to a chair by a large mahogany-and-leather writing desk. As she did so, Peter noticed that her grey tweed suit jacket was buttoned unevenly, as if she'd dressed in a hurry. Her white blouse was also buttoned low, and Peter noticed the lace of her red bra and her ample cleavage as she took her chair. There was the smell of beeswax, and a vase of white lilies on the desk gave the room a slightly melancholy air.

'As I said, we are really rather short of eligible men at the agency, especially handsome ones.' She looked him straight in the eye and smiled. 'I'm hopeful we can find love for you, Peter. What do you normally look for in a lady, may I ask?' She projected her lacy bosom towards him, invading his personal space.

'Blondes... er brunettes,' Peter said with an awkward swallow, not knowing what to say.

'I wouldn't narrow your view, Peter.' Her voice grew deeper.

'Blondes can be so much fun.' She laughed and touched his arm. There was an awkward silence.

'Anyway, I'm not looking for love. Just to help you out, you said.'

'Yes, of course,' Ms Percival replied, while appearing not to listen. 'I'll take some pics of you right now for the site and some Instamatic, if that's OK?'

Peter reluctantly posed in front of a bare section of wall.

'Great. I just need to ask you a few personal questions and get some measurements.' Ms Percival took notes and explained in some detail the matching process and how she personally checked all the credentials to find the perfect partner.

'It will take me a few days to get all the information on the system and match it to potential suitors,' she explained.

'Remember, I'm not really looking for any suitors. Just happy to help you out. Please don't put me forward for any dates.'

Peter thanked her with a polite handshake, which she held onto for slightly too long. Relieved to be leaving, he made his way down the grand stairs towards the front door. Halfway down, he noticed a gigantic gold-framed oil painting of a very large lady with blonde hair reclining on a rock in a garden, eating a mouthful of grapes. Rolls of fat spilled out over the rock. Two hunting dogs in the foreground were gorging on a fox, with bloodied tongues and a tormented sky above them. Peter felt a shudder go through him; he detested fox hunting, and there was something about the lady that made him most uncomfortable. Next to the painting was a window. Rain was trickling down the pane. It was pouring outside. He looked to see how wet it was and noticed a Bentley pulling up, tight to the pavement. When he reached the bottom of the stairs, he opened the large imposing door, and was surprised to see a lady dashing towards him with great vigour.

'Thank you, Cartwright,' the woman called over her shoulder to the driver of the Bentley. She then headed up the steps and across the threshold. Peter stood back to let her in. The woman shrugged droplets of rain from her coat. He could see she was eager to get into the dry and, as she barged past, she put her hand into her pocket and thrust a £20 note at him, thanking him for seeing that she was 'in peril from the awful rain!' And 'What a great idea it was, having a doorman to greet clients.' She dashed up the grand staircase to the office, leaving Peter in a daze and £20 richer.

He closed the door behind him and headed out into the street, giving a friendly nod to her driver. Then he paced across the Circus to reach the cover of the trees, still clutching the £20 note. He looked at it and shook his head. How patronising was that? What a strange woman! He put the note in his pocket and scuffed his shoe through a puddle. Around the next corner there was a homeless man huddled in a moth-eaten sleeping bag. His face was dirty and thin. Beside him, a forlorn-looking whippet caught Peter's attention.

'There's £10 for you and £10 for the dog. OK?' He placed the note in the man's hand.

'Thank you, sir.' The man's meagre smile showed his blackened and missing teeth.

Charlotte headed through the open office door and was greeted by Ms Percival, who was just making a filter coffee.

'Charlotte, how are you?' *Mwah, mwah.*

'I'm delightful, despite this dreadful weather. And you?'

'I'm always rushing around, but I'm fine. I have some splendid matches for you today. Have a seat.' Ms Percival gestured towards the writing desk while taking Charlotte's coat. 'Coffee?'

'Oh, yes, please. I'm parched. Just had a meeting at the animal rescue centre and wasn't offered a single drop.'

Ms Percival looked up with raised eyebrows. 'Not even a doggie bowl?'

'Haha, no. I'm holding a fundraising event for them and they've asked me to say a few words. It's the least I can do.'

'I'm sure!' Ms Percival sighed and then, with a hopeful smile, declared, 'I've searched very hard to find you a match and I'm pleased to say there are three gorgeous men on the books who meet your criteria.'

Charlotte sat up straight and gave her an indignant look. 'As I said, my friends persuaded me to sign up to this. I'm not entirely sure this is my kind of thing.'

'Totally understandable, Charlotte. I have other people on the books who came to me in exactly the same way. This is a new way to meet someone, and most people are a little apprehensive at the start.'

'Well, to be honest, I'm here so I don't insult my friends, not because I'm desperate. I promised to do three dates, and that's it.'

'Don't worry, Charlotte. It could be fun. Let's see if we can find you a fabulous man.'

Charlotte rolled her eyes.

'OK, well, here's the first one. Simon. He's forty-eight years old, a merchant banker, divorced, but no children, and looking for something long-term. He enjoys Asian food, art and fast cars. He has a yacht and spends his weekends between London and Monaco. Here's his photo. What do you think?'

Charlotte stared at a blonde man with a kind face and a lovely smile. He was sitting at the helm of a boat beside a gleaming brass wheel, with neatly arranged ropes on the deck and the glistening emerald sea behind him.

'He's quite a catch, isn't he?' Ms Percival said.

'And who's the next one?'

'Erm... yes, of course. The next one is Donald, a forty-five-year-old... He only joined a few days ago. He's a lawyer and very successful, by the sounds of it. He's never been married. Enjoys reading the classics, fine dining and collecting rare Eastern European stamps. He sounds interesting, doesn't he?'

'And the next?' Charlotte asked hastily.

'Ah, yes... Bernhard. He's originally from Austria. He's forty-two and currently living with his mother. Some complication with a house move, he said. Oh, and he's a film director! And, interestingly, an arachnophile. I nearly dated him myself.' Ms Percival laughed out loud in an encouraging way.

Charlotte took a minute to compose herself and said, 'They don't really sound like my type.'

'They match all your criteria. Things are always different when you meet in person.'

Charlotte smiled nervously. 'OK, I guess I have little choice. Let's start with number one.'

'Great!' Ms Percival jumped right in. 'I'll get the ball rolling with Simon, and I'll be in touch regarding a mutually convenient time for a date. I would suggest a coffee rather than committing to dinner, and then you can see if you'd like to take it further. With coffee, you can always get away for that "nail appointment" you'd forgotten, if you know what I mean.'

They both laughed and Charlotte stood up to leave.

'I'll be in touch with the exciting news.' As Ms Percival helped Charlotte with her coat, her sleeve brushed the desk, flipping over a photo of a dark-haired, rugged-looking man who appeared vaguely familiar. Charlotte stopped to take a closer look.

'Who's that?' she asked.

'Oh, that's Peter. I haven't put him on the system yet. He's super new, but I don't think he fits your criteria at all.' Ms Percival frowned and shook her head.

'Oh, I see, yes, absolutely. He does look a little rugged. I look forward to meeting Simon. Not!'

'What was that?' Ms Percival thrust her jaw and ear toward Charlotte.

'Nothing. Keep me informed.'

Charlotte floated down the stairs in her usual way, stopping briefly with disgust at the sight of the grotesque painting by the window. On reaching the bottom, she had to use all her might to open the imposing door.

'Where is the doorman?' she grumbled to herself.

12

USUAL CIRCLE

The date was set. Coffee at Simon's private members' club. It was predominantly a men's club, but women were tolerated in certain areas.

Cartwright pulled the car up outside the club and was met by a doorman in a black suit and top hat. He opened the door and Charlotte stepped out onto the steps to the main entrance. Dressed in black trousers, a pink cashmere jumper and kitten heels, and holding a Gucci clutch bag, she felt confident and assured. The doorman led her into a grand hall with a black-and-white tiled floor, Roman-style columns, and an array of large, closed and secretive-looking oak doors. She took off her sunglasses to see an overweight gentleman coming towards her. He came closer and offered his hand.

'Hello. Charlotte? Pleased to meet you. I'm Simon. Please come through to the ladies' lounge.'

A naturally lit room unfolded in front of them, with regimented tables and chairs, floral cushions and coat-stands. There was a stale smell in the air, a faint hint of cigar smoke mixed with perfume. Charlotte smiled as Simon showed her to a table sandwiched between two austere wooden chairs. She was sure no woman had had anything to do with the décor, and she was right. Simon told her it had been a men's private members' club for hundreds of years, and although there had been pressure in recent times to accommodate women, this hadn't come naturally or easily. However, they had tried, and Simon was comfortable there.

Simon seemed well known and commanded an air of presence and importance, and Charlotte took comfort that she was in good hands.

'Coffee or something a little stronger?' he said, giving Charlotte a little wink.

Charlotte shuddered. There was one thing she hated, and that was a winking man. 'A coffee will be fine, thank you, with milk.'

Simon clicked his fingers, and the waiter came over. 'Good afternoon, sir, madam. What can I get you?'

'A coffee with milk and my usual, on the rocks.' Simon's booming voice could be heard above everyone else's.

'Certainly, sir.'

Simon looked straight at Charlotte, who was sitting in the upright chair as if in a job interview. 'So, I hear you like to travel? I have a fifty-foot yacht. It's berthed out in Monaco. I have the staff preparing it for a trip I'm making to Corsica next week. Do you know Corsica?'

Charlotte nodded. 'I know it well. It's a lovely place.' She didn't want him to know she had a place out there.

'I'll keep the boat until next year, and then I'm looking for something much bigger to tour the Mediterranean. Could do with a pretty filly on board to keep things shipshape,' he boomed, with yet another wink.

Charlotte looked at her watch in despair. 'Do you have the captain's hat too?' she asked with a wry smile.

Simon carried on booming, clicking and winking for the next half an hour. Finally, Charlotte told him she'd like to visit the bathroom. Once inside, she didn't hesitate to get out her phone and send the SOS.

'*Cartwright, car, 5 mins.*'

'*Certainly, madam.*'

She returned to the table and, without sitting down, asked Simon for her coat. 'I have another appointment now. It's been wonderful. Thank you for the coffee,' she said politely.

Simon looked surprised 'You're going so soon! Let's do it again sometime.'

Charlotte smiled and turned to the door. Cartwright appeared right on cue, and the escape plan worked like clockwork as she hurried down the steps. With a friendly wave, they were off, leaving a bemused Simon behind.

The following day, Ms Percival rang to get an update. She told Charlotte that Simon was very keen and felt the date had gone fabulously well, and that 'You seemed enthralled about his upcoming Mediterranean trip.' Charlotte spared nothing when explaining to Ms Percival that he was a bore, and an arrogant bore at that. He had financial stability and could hold court, which she admired, but he really wasn't the man for her.

Number two was scheduled, and Charlotte felt as though she were trapped in some sort of inevitable machine, which left her quite anxious. She had no trouble meeting men—or women, for that matter. In fact, both found her attractive, and she had had a little flirtatious episode with a girl at university. They'd had rooms nearby in halls for a term, and one evening Charlotte and Claire had come back from a party after drinking far too many cocktails. As Charlotte rummaged in her bag for her key, Claire came close and kissed her on the lips. Charlotte liked it, and they kissed gently in the doorway before crashing into the room, where they kissed passionately. Claire put her hand into Charlotte's blouse and teased her nipple through her lace bra. Then she took it further and gently sucked on it and teased it with her tongue. Charlotte didn't stop her. She liked it. It felt good.

At the exact moment Charlotte's nipple was between Claire's lips, her roommate came home. As they heard her putting the key in the door, they quickly got themselves together, and when the door opened, Claire left rapidly, flustered and confused.

They never returned to that moment again, although Claire suggested it frequently. Charlotte knew she preferred men. There was something about their smell, their strong, muscular arms and shoulders and the way they took control that made her go weak at the knees.

The morning of the date with Number Two, Charlotte lay in bed thinking about how she would prefer to meet someone through the conventional routes, if at all. She'd promised, though, and, although reluctant, she felt duty bound to see it through as quickly as possible.

Out of the corner of her eye, she kept noticing her tarot cards on the little table standing below the large sash window that overlooked the garden and the glorious chestnut tree in the property beyond. She observed the large leaves blowing gently in the breeze. She adored the way the dappled sun picked out the colouring of each leaf. A sense of calm filled her mind and her breathing became deep and centred as she changed position. Again, she caught a glimpse of the cards on the table, concealed in their inviting box. Should she just take a look and see what they had to say? She sat up straight and stared intently at the pack. Should she?

It wasn't the right moment; she could feel it. The cards were not calling. Not this time. She didn't want to know, anyway. She stood up, walked over to the table and glanced one more time at the cards. No. Not this time.

A piece of paper with the details of her date lay beside them. 'Donald, age forty-five,' it said.

Donald. She hated that name. She had a second cousin once removed called Donald. A fat, waddling layabout who inevitably reminded her of the duck. She sighed and looked out of the window. 'You don't have to go,' she said out loud.

There was a polite knock on the door. 'Breakfast is served, madam,' Cartwright announced from the other side.

'I'll have it in the conservatory, Cartwright.'

Charlotte headed into her dressing room to choose clothes for her date, which was at 12.30 in the café in the Victoria and Albert Museum. She was a patron of the museum and always loved an impromptu visit. It was a good choice of venue by Donald, which she held onto as a positive sign.

Cartwright dropped Charlotte right at the door of the V&A. He came around to open the car door and Charlotte walked gracefully up the cascade of stone steps and in through the grand entrance. Not only was she a patron of the museum, but she also had a small exhibition of paintings on loan too—her father's collection of Impressionist artists, which collectively were worth several million. She, of course, knew many people there, and if she were recognised, she would be escorted to the director's office and given the VIP treatment. On this occasion, she wanted to slip in unnoticed and just be Charlotte. She wore a headscarf in an attempt to disguise herself. The truth was that she could in no way disguise her way of floating into a room with great poise and presence. The headscarf made her stand out even more from the hundreds of tourists and art appreciation societies milling around the halls in their jeans, trainers and dowdy coats.

She turned the corner into the café and was immediately confronted by a tall man in a double-breasted three-piece pinstripe suit, his huge hand reaching out in greeting. 'You must be Charlotte,' he said briskly. They shook hands, and he escorted her to a table. 'I took the liberty of ordering tea.' He sat down opposite her.

'Yes, tea, that's lovely,' Charlotte replied uneasily. She was almost glad that there was no food on offer. She was happy to keep things simple.

Donald sat in a bolt upright position, a very serious man, immaculately presented; his hair looked as if he had it trimmed every day and he was cleanly shaven to the bone. Charlotte hadn't totally forgotten her tomboy childhood, but she'd been taught to respect order and that a smart appearance was important. Donald was very assured, and Charlotte noticed he had a pocket watch, much like her father used to wear.

When she asked him about it, he looked down at the gold chain streaming out of his breast pocket.

'It was my grandfather's. It keeps perfect time. It's Swiss. I take it to Switzerland every year to be serviced. Do you like it?' he asked, producing it from the pocket and laying it on the palm of his hand.

'It's beautiful. It reminds me of my late father's watch. He wore it every day.' Charlotte gulped, a slight lump in her throat. 'It had a damaged link, which I remember him trying to fix with a lump hammer in the study one evening, and I remember how proud he was that it was "unique" and "had his personal stamp".'

'Do you still have it?' Donald enquired with interest.

'Yes, indeed. I keep it together with his other personal items. My father was a very punctual man and never kept anyone waiting. I like that,' she replied, comparing Donald to her father. There was something about him which reassured her.

'On that note, the tea is getting cold. I'll pour.' Donald reached for the china teapot, and with a straight face and arm, poured the tea. 'Thank you for agreeing to meet me,' he added, in a businesslike manner.

Charlotte immediately thought of all three of the men she'd been lined up to meet and nearly said, *You were the best of a bad bunch*, but stopped herself and said instead, 'It's my pleasure. Have you been single long?'

Donald looked her straight in the eye. 'I've never really been in a relationship. Not for any significant length of time. There was a girl when I was younger, but she moved away and, to be quite frank, I've concentrated on my career. I find my work to be most satisfying and rewarding. Do you always get straight to the point on your dates? You really put me on the spot there.'

'No, not usually. I'm sorry I put you in that position.' Charlotte felt guilty for asking and quickly changed the subject. 'So, I hear you collect rare stamps?' Her tone was upbeat as she tried to lift the atmosphere. Donald's face seemed to open up.

'Yes, indeed. I've recently returned from Latvia in search of a rare 1950s stamp I've been on the lookout for.'

Charlotte's eyes started to glaze over as Donald spent the next twenty minutes talking in detail about his vast collection of rare Eastern European stamps and showing her a huge number of photos on his phone.

'I wouldn't know one end of a stamp from the other,' she said eventually, trying to lighten the one-sided conversation.

'I'd love to show you my collection, if you're really interested?' he said with enthusiasm.

'I really need to powder my nose. If you'd excuse me.' Charlotte picked up her bag and headed for the bathroom.

'*Cartwright, car, 5 mins.*'

'*Certainly, madam.*'

Never had the V&A been so tedious!

Charlotte heard her phone ringing in her bag. It was Ms Percival, calling for an update.

'He wasn't for me, Ms Percival. In fact, can I come in to see you? None of this is really for me.'

'What about number three, Bernhard the Spiderman? He's quite eager,' Ms Percival replied.

A silence, which seemed to go on for five minutes, was broken by Charlotte's calm but slightly annoyed response. 'I'm coming right now. My driver will drop me off at the office in ten minutes. I really need to talk to you.'

Ms Percival could do nothing but agree. Not long afterwards, Charlotte buzzed the intercom and came bursting into the room.

'Charlotte, how lovely.' *Mwah, mwah.* 'Coffee?' Ms Percival pointed to the gurgling machine.

'No, thank you. I really did want to see you in person. You see, this is actually making me quite stressed.'

'It's completely natural.' Ms Percival stopped her in her tracks. 'Most of my clients feel the same until they settle in a bit. Here, have this.' She passed Charlotte an espresso. 'Please have a seat.'

Charlotte sat down at the large wooden desk and sipped her coffee. A photo of the man she'd seen on her previous visit caught her gaze. He was in an open-necked plain blue shirt, his rolled-up sleeves revealing his hairy forearms.

'Who's that? I saw him before, didn't I?' she asked, transfixed by the gentleman's smile. It was the kind of smile that seemed to pull you in by the scruff of your neck. His eyes appeared to be looking straight at her, and only her.

'Oh, yes, that's Peter. As I mentioned before, I don't think he's the man for you. He's... well... how can I put it? Not from your usual circle. I haven't finished putting him on the system yet, but from what I know, he wouldn't match any of your criteria.'

Charlotte looked up curiously. 'Oh, I see.' She took another look at his masculine jaw and the slight glimpse of hairy chest through his unbuttoned shirt. 'OK, well, I think we've come to a natural end. As I said, I knew this wasn't for me.'

She reached for her phone and sent a quick text for the car, then stood up and straightened her skirt.

'You did promise you would do three dates?'

Charlotte lifted her head and looked Ms Percival in the eye. 'Regrettably, yes.'

Ms Percival picked up the photo from the desk. 'What if I arrange a meeting with Peter?'

'You said we would have nothing in common?'

'Well, yes, but I did get a message from Sam saying not to take no for an answer or you'd be letting her down. She's booked for her second date this evening.'

'Yes, I know.' Charlotte gritted her teeth.

A short while later, Cartwright greeted Charlotte at the steps and ushered her into the car. She didn't notice the lack of a doorman this time.

She sat quietly for a few minutes as they negotiated the streets of west London.

'I want to go home, Cartwright. I'll call ahead and get Mrs Hathersage to prepare for our arrival. I need to rest from all of this. Can you arrange for chef to cook some of my favourite salmon tonight? With asparagus and salad.'

'Certainly, madam.'

'Thank you. And one more thing. Can we stop by the rescue centre? There's someone I need to pick up.'

The car entered the grand stone gateway to the estate, with its family crest high above the centre arch, above the name Loxley House. The drive took them up through a woodland of beech, ash, hazel, crab-apple and holly, with wild roses. In the spring there would be a mass of bluebells. Although it was autumn, the dappled sunlight streaming through the tree canopy appeared to be nature's own artistry. Charlotte settled back into her seat. She was home and able to relax here. Contact with the nature that proliferated was sometimes all she needed to stem a downward turn in her feelings and get her head back on track and into a positive gear. She also had someone with her.

Someone new to the house; someone she knew would enjoy the abundant space as much as she did.

Mrs Hathersage was waiting patiently in her pristine white apron, carrying a handful of flowers. Cartwright opened the car door and before Mrs Hathersage had a moment to think, she was greeted by a very excited ball of wiry hair, with a wagging tail and dirty paws that instantly soiled her apron.

'Oh, my! I didn't expect a puppy. What's his name?'

Charlotte smiled. 'He doesn't have one yet. He's Lucy's birthday present. Do you think she'll like him?'

Mrs Hathersage dusted down her apron. 'Well, I hope Miss Lucy will be looking after him, too. All those muddy paw prints everywhere!'

Charlotte spent the entire week at the house. She invited various guests over for lunch and dinner, for which food was brought in from the kitchen on silver platters, along with large bowls spilling over with colourful fresh fruit. Being at home was the perfect tonic. The dog was starting to settle in, and she found him a welcome new companion.

She decided to extend her stay by another week and arranged for the head gardener to walk around the walled vegetable garden with her to discuss the condition of the produce, and any new varieties she might want to introduce. Charlotte loved picking the ripe tomatoes, or else cutting open a melon from the greenhouse, and she was actively involved in the day-to-day running of the place. The vegetable garden always seemed to be busy, as did the estate yard, but there were quiet areas too, and none more special than her oak tree and her swing.

She wrapped up warmly in a corduroy dress, tights, boots, a thick wool jumper and a scarf, and headed down through the maze of mown paths towards the river, closely followed by the dog, his 'torn' ear, as always, slightly droopier than the other.

The oak tree's character was different every time she visited. Its ever-changing appearance was a product of the seasons and Charlotte always thought the tree was at its best in the autumn, when the leaves turned greenish-brown and the acorns fat and ripe.

On approaching the tree, she put her hand on one of the dangling ropes of the swing. She used her fingers to examine the intricate weave of fibres and then moved them onto the weathered wooden seat. There was a strangely deformed acorn sitting right in the middle of the seat—dark green, but slightly reddish and gnarly, and weird-looking. Charlotte examined it with great interest and placed it in her pocket for later.

She walked around the trunk of the tree, striding over the prominent exposed roots, and running her hand along the rough bark until she happened upon a familiar indent—the first letter of her name. She pushed her finger into the groove of each letter one by one, so that she could feel the warmth of the tree. Without looking, she traced every scar with precision.

Charlie was home.

When Charlotte eventually returned to the house, she took the odd-shaped acorn out of her pocket, placed it on the table and scrutinised it closely. It was a strange-looking thing, and even Mrs Hathersage didn't have a clue what it was.

Later, sitting in her favourite seat in the window, she looked out across the rear garden and up to the large Henry Moore sculpture which she'd positioned at the end of a pleached-pear avenue. The shape reminded her of when she was pregnant with Lucy: that profound, rounded bump, full of expectation and love.

When Mrs Hathersage came to discuss the arrangements for dinner, she told Charlotte there was a message for her to call a Ms Percival in London—rather urgent. Charlotte explained she would dine alone and would have no wine, just water. She didn't want her day spoiled by the thoughts of some fat, bald, egotistical bore checking her out, and so she busied herself arranging some flowers she'd picked on her walk through the rose garden. Afterwards, she sat in the window and read an article in *The Times* about bespoke dating agencies and how that was the new way to find a partner.

She had a snooze and was woken by the sound of preparations for dinner.

'Sorry, madam. I tried to be as quiet as possible.' Cartwright spoke in a soft and comforting voice. 'Dinner will be in ten minutes. Would you like me to postpone if you're running a little late?'

'No, no, I'm fine, thank you, Cartwright. Ten minutes is just perfect. I'm really rather hungry.'

'Not a problem, madam. Do you want me to do anything with this?' He held the deformed acorn between his fingers.

'Yes—can you put it on the shelf by the Aga? It looks interesting.'

Cartwright took the object in his hand. 'Oh, yes, madam, did you receive the message from London—Ms Percival, I think it was?'

Cartwright was always sure of the facts; he had an eye for detail and had built up a reputation for reliability and diplomacy, and was becoming the closest person to Charlotte regarding her everyday life. She relied on him more and more and trusted him implicitly.

'Thank you, Cartwright. I had forgotten about the message. I'll call now and put the whole thing to bed.'

'Certainly, madam. It is a little late, though. It's after eight.'

'I'll try. The least I can do is leave a message.' Charlotte shook her head. She'd thought she'd dealt with the matter and wasn't happy about being disturbed.

'It's a gall, by the way, madam,' Cartwright said, pointing to the odd-shaped acorn, then turned and left the room, closing the door quietly behind him.

Charlotte called Ms Percival.

'Hello?'

'Hello, Ms Percival. It's Charlotte here. I think you left me a message to call?'

'Yes. Thank you for calling back. It's just—'

Charlotte interjected impatiently, 'I don't mean to be rude, Ms Percival, and I know I promised, but I don't want to continue and—'

Ms Percival stopped her in her tracks. 'I've arranged things with Peter. It would help my reputation if I can deliver what I promised. I'm judged on my results.'

'Ms Percival, this isn't sitting well with me at all.'

'Think of it as a last-ditch attempt.'

Charlotte closed her eyes and sighed. 'Very well. I don't know how I've got myself into this ridiculous situation.'

13

CUCUMBER SANDWICHES

The fact that the tarot cards appeared to fall at Charlotte's feet from a perfectly sturdy table was no reason to want to look at the pack. No, they were there for special times, to consult when it mattered. She trusted them implicitly and many times before they'd turned out to be accurate. But this wasn't the time and it was certainly not a sign.

She picked up the deck and placed it back on the table, but then noticed the flap was open and a single card was protruding slightly, its face not visible, yet somehow offering itself to her. Charlotte placed her finger on top of the card, but was distracted by her phone ringing.

'Sam, hi.'

'Charlotte, I'm on my way to the salon to have my hair done before my date. I'm feeling quite optimistic about this one.'

'I wish I could say the same for myself, but I'm glad for you, Sam.'

'Honestly, I know it's silly, but knowing you're doing the same is a support. Sorry it hasn't been going so well for you.'

'Well, they were bores. It's made me realise there probably isn't a man out there for me. Anyway, not that I'm looking.'

Sam chuckled. 'Darling, there will be someone. You just have to open your heart and find your adventurous side again. Remember all those times you sneaked out of school?'

'I was young and carefree. Things have changed.'

'Well, thanks anyway. Good luck this afternoon. You're going to Brown's for your date, aren't you? I wish we were; we could have adjacent tables and swap stories.' Sam giggled even more.

'Wouldn't that have been fun?'

'Ciao, darling.' Sam ended with an enthusiastic kiss and Charlotte threw her phone onto the bed and took a deep breath.

Her eye was drawn once again to the pack of tarot cards with the lid open, but she resisted temptation and headed to the shower. The water was warm, and she enjoyed washing her hair and feeling clean. She left feeling invigorated and stood blow-drying and brushing her hair before applying her make-up for the day. Simple but elegant was her style.

In the mirror, she could see into her bedroom. Her attention was drawn again to the purple-and-gold packaging of her tarot pack. Why was it catching her eye? She brushed her hair twice more and then headed straight over. Holding it in her hand, she tentatively pulled at the protruding card. She exposed the corner and then pushed it partially back in. This wasn't her usual technique for reading the cards and she felt uneasy. She had a ritual. To sit in complete silence: no negative energy and no crossed arms or legs as she shuffled the cards with a clear and open mind.

She put her finger on it again... and then proceeded to pull it out.

. . .

Soulmate

The picture showed a couple sitting close together, hesitating just before a passionate kiss. At the bottom were the words: 'Yes, this is your soulmate.'

Charlotte gasped and could do nothing else but stare at it. She sat in silence for a couple of minutes. It meant nothing. It wasn't her usual way.

There was a faint tap on the door. 'Breakfast is served, madam,' Cartwright announced quietly but reassuringly from the other side.

'I'll be down in five minutes,' Charlotte said calmly.

Once again, the rain poured onto the streets of London. Peter wasn't the sort of man to carry an umbrella. Instead, he dashed from one door to another with his jacket partially hunched up over his head. An inconsiderate pedestrian forced him to step into a puddle and he felt the water fill his shoe; his foot got wetter and wetter as he progressed. The rain soaked through his shirt where his jacket was raised.

A phone call from Chris prompted Peter to find shelter under the canopy of a stall selling umbrellas and street-maps of London.

'Mate, how's it going?' Peter asked.

'We all wanted to wish you all the best for your date.'

Peter raised his hand to his forehead. 'Jeez, man. It's not even a date. It's a formality, a joke.'

'Someone wants to talk to you,' said Chris, with a smile in his voice.

Anna snatched the phone from her dad. 'Uncle Peter! I thought you might need some proper advice for your date.'

Peter relaxed and smiled. 'Hi Anna. What is it?'

'Well, don't go throwing juice on anyone, wear clean socks —matching ones—and call her by her first name. Oh, and don't talk about trees.'

Peter chuckled to himself, moving out beyond the canopy to feel the light rain on his face. 'Thanks, Anna, I don't know what I'd do without you. Can you put your dad back on?' He sighed as Chris returned. 'What the hell is going on here? I have the whole world checking in on me and I'm receiving dating advice from a seven-year-old. It's not even a date!'

'Good luck, Pete, you're going to need it.'

Peter shook his head and ended the call.

He eventually arrived at the grand entrance.

'Good afternoon, sir,' the doorman greeted him. Peter entered, leaving a trail of wet footmarks up the steps and into the lobby.

Brown's quintessentially English and tastefully decadent interior stopped Peter in his tracks. He'd overheard two ladies on the Tube discussing their fabulous afternoon tea, and he'd gone ahead and booked a table for two. Now he marvelled at the impressive chandelier, the floral arrangements and the smartly dressed staff hurriedly going about their business. He introduced himself to the lady at the little desk and she took him to a beautifully laid table: white linen, silver cutlery and impeccably polished glassware, and a single red rose as a centrepiece.

He was seated in the middle of the room, surrounded by many other tables, all occupied by elegantly dressed people chatting and laughing.

Peter began to feel a little uneasy. He was there as a favour, but he didn't want the whole room knowing his business. He looked around and spied a vacant table over by the window, a round one in a corner position, with a comfy sofa-type seat curving around two-thirds of its circumference.

'Excuse me,' he said to a passing waitress. 'Do you think I could move to the other table over there?'

'I'm afraid that's reserved, sir,' the waitress replied politely.

Peter beckoned her nearer and spoke firmly. 'I'm here on a first date, and I think it might be a bit loud here in the centre to talk. I'd really like to take that table if at all possible.'

The waitress glanced around and said, 'Bear with me, sir,' before walking over to the little desk.

Peter checked the large antique clock above the fireplace and noticed it was 1.30pm. It was time. He looked around to see if she was coming in... No sign.

The waitress approached. 'You can have the table in the corner, sir, but I will need it at 3:30,' she said firmly.

'Thank you so much. Thank you.'

She smiled, and Peter took his position on the sofa. Shortly afterwards, the waitress approached again, with a woman beside her. This must be Charlotte. She handed her coat to the waitress. Underneath she wore a cream knitted jumper, a black skirt with a large red crocheted flower just above the knee, black tights, and boots.

Peter stood up and welcomed her with a kiss on the cheek. Charlotte gestured for a second kiss on the other cheek, which Peter hadn't anticipated, and there was an awkward rocking of heads. He attempted the kiss, but the moment had passed.

'It's foul out there, isn't it?' he said calmly.

Charlotte immediately picked up on his accent. 'Where are you from?'

'I'm from Yorkshire. It rains a lot there, too.' He laughed. 'Have you been?'

She nodded. 'I've been to the Hepworth Gallery and to see the Henry Moore sculptures. I think that was in Yorkshire.'

'Yes, you're right,' Peter said excitedly. 'In fact, not too far from where I grew up. The Yorkshire Sculpture Park.'

Charlotte didn't respond, and there was an uneasy silence. He was caught out by her high society voice and quiet demeanour—and she was beautiful. He wondered if she disliked the Yorkshire accent.

'Shall we order afternoon tea?' he suggested, in a mild panic that seemed to bring out his broadest accent.

Charlotte gave a little smile. 'That would be lovely.'

The Brown's speciality tea, a selection of crust-off sandwiches and some tiny scones, arrived on a cascade of china plates and doilies. It looked fabulous, and Peter was starving.

'Tea?' he offered.

'Yes, please,' replied Charlotte, and Peter took charge and filled their cups.

'Sandwich?' He gestured to the copious array.

'I'm OK just now, thank you. To be honest, I don't have a great deal of time, as I have another appointment later.'

'Oh, yes, me too,' he replied, thinking her comment was rather rude. He felt his stomach aching with hunger. 'Anyway, it's good to meet you. This dating is a funny old thing, isn't it?' he blurted out, desperately trying to get the conversation flowing. 'Arranging to meet from someone else's recommendation and a photo.'

Charlotte took a sip of tea. 'I'm not sure the agency thing is quite my cup of tea,' she said, with an ironic smile. 'How long have you been with them?'

'Not long. You're my first date. What about you?'

'Oh! Erm... like you, not long. I've had a couple of dates. Ms Percival said you worked in the environmental field. Environment means so many things these days.'

Peter chuckled. 'Yes, you're right. It seems everyone is jumping on the environmental bandwagon, but essentially, I work with trees. Specialising in saving trees on development sites, disease management, and basically trying to solve the issues posed when trees and humans conflict with each other. I'm passionate about trees and animals. Aren't you going to have a sandwich?'

'I'm not feeling very hungry, but you have some.'

'No, no, I won't if you're not,' Peter answered. He felt it impolite to stuff his face with food without her.

'Do you work with elephants?' asked Charlotte.

'No... it's a little outside my expertise. But I do love elephants.' Peter felt confused at her questioning and uncomfortable, a feeling that was further exacerbated by his itchy leg as his wet clothes stuck to his skin. He squirmed and tried to scratch.

'Are you alright?' she asked.

'Yes, I'm fine. My trousers got a little wet in the rain.'

She looked puzzled. 'Didn't you get a cab?'

'No. I... er... decided to take in the sights on my way.' He couldn't afford a cab as well as everything else. His shirt was also sticking to him and making it hard to move. He wanted to remove his jacket, but he was worried about any potential steam which was building up. He also wanted to speak, but he couldn't find any more words. There was a desperate silence between the two of them and he began to become even more agitated.

'So, erm... She's a bit of a strange woman, Ms Percival, isn't she?' No sooner had the words come out of his mouth, than he wished they hadn't.

'What do you mean?'

'Well, I mean the whole place is a bit strange, not specifically Ms Percival.' He tried to backtrack. 'There's that grotesque painting with the hunting dogs on the staircase, for one.'

There was another agonising pause.

'Yes. I saw that. I hate fox hunting.'

'Me, too. I don't like the thought of a poor defenceless animal being hounded like that.'

'It's barbaric. I come from a family with a long history of hunting, but I've stopped it now.'

'Good for you. The world needs more people like you.'

Charlotte blushed. 'Do you think so?'

'Yes, absolutely. Someone to stand up for the rights of the animals and put a stop to it.'

'I'd like to think I can offer more than that, too.'

'Well, yes, absolutely. You're an attractive woman.' Why had he said that? Of all the intelligent things he could have said, he came out with that!

'Oh!' Charlotte replied, looking a little embarrassed.

'I mean, I like that you like animals and that makes you attractive.' Phew! Perhaps he'd managed to turn things around slightly.

'Well, I'll take that as a compliment. You have lovely eyes.'

There was another uncomfortable silence, and then Charlotte placed her pristine white napkin on the table and stood.

'Please excuse me.' She made her way across the room, heading for the bathroom. Peter watched her walk away in her elegant manner. In complete desperation, he grabbed a couple of salmon-and-cucumber sandwich triangles and rammed them into his mouth, and as he did, he wondered why they'd removed the crusts. They were the best bit of a sandwich. He eyed up a slice of Battenburg, but then thought while she was gone, he should take the opportunity of calling Chris. He was the only person who knew he was on a date.

'Hey mate, how's it going?' Chris said.

'She's in the loo, so I might not have long. I'm struggling to work her out. We don't really have a lot in common. She likes animals, thank God, but there's been some humdinger silences, so I'm racking my brain to keep things going. And she's posh. Like her dad's a bank manager or something.'

'Does she like you?'

Peter pursed his lips. 'I don't know. I don't think so.'

'Has she touched you? You know, a little tap on the shoulder or arm?'

'She hasn't been near me, mate.'

'Best leave it then, that would be my advice. A girl will give you a signal if she likes you.' Chris sounded like he'd learned the hard way.

'There's something about her, though, that I like. I didn't expect that. The way she flicks her hair, and her smile.'

Chris paused for a second. 'Well, despite only doing this for a favour, I'd go for it, mate. What have you got to lose?'

'Oh, great. Now I'm even more confused. Anyway, she's coming. See ya.'

He watched her return. She had a refined poise and her walk was super confident. He was trying to process what Chris had said and knew he had to get the conversation flowing again.

When Charlotte returned to the table, as she perched on the edge of the seat she put her hand on Peter's arm. 'It's been lovely, but I do have another appointment.'

Peter nodded. 'Yes, of course, er... me, too. Yes, absolutely, me too. Oh! Is that the time?' He looked at his watch. 'I'll get the bill.'

Ninety-five pounds for a pot of tea and sandwiches she never touched! Peter was shocked, but he gallantly settled in full. The waitress brought Charlotte's coat and Peter escorted her to the door in a gentlemanly fashion, trying to keep his head and his dignity held high.

'I'll walk you to where you need to be,' he offered.

Charlotte replied instantly, 'I'll hail a cab. It's a ride from here.'

Peter looked up the street. 'There's one.' He stuck out his hand, and the taxi indicated to pull in. 'It's been lovely.' He didn't know what else to say.

'Yes,' she said, as she turned to look at him. Their eyes met. There was a pause in time, a split second in reality, and the whole world seemed to stand still. Peter lifted his hand, put it on her cheek, and then kissed her gently on the lips. She tugged at his jacket to pull him closer and the kiss continued. It was passionate, and entirely unexpected. The taxi pulled up. They said their goodbyes and, before he could register it, she was gone.

Peter put his face into his hands and started to punish himself for embarrassing himself in such a stupid way, pouncing on her like that, especially when he'd sensed she wasn't interested.

At home, he headed straight for the shower and let the warm water drown his entire body.

'Damn, damn, *damn*.' He slapped his hand hard against the wall. She hadn't liked him. That was obvious—the conversation was stilted, and he couldn't even remember what they'd talked about, apart from him doing most of it. He'd been on some weird dates, but this was a candidate for the top prize. She was way out of his league—posh, sophisticated, intelligent and worldly.

He scrubbed his hairy chest with soap to get a good lather, washed himself down as if to clean himself of the disaster, and made the decision that he wouldn't make contact with her again. Just confine the event to the dating disaster waste bin, save the embarrassment and move on.

14

RIDICULOUS

The London house had an air of organised chaos as Charlotte entered. She observed the florist busily installing a new display. A stunning arrangement of green foliage and impressive petals of white, pink and blue filled the large wood-panelled entrance hall. The stained-glass window let in the intermittent afternoon sun, which warmed the air and highlighted the magnificent marble staircase.

Charlotte escaped to the dimly lit library and collapsed into her favourite seat in the room, an old upholstered winged armchair which used to be her grandmother's. It was her 'thinking chair': comfortable, safe, and quiet.

A call from Sam cut through the anxious silence.

'Sam, how are you?'

'I'm good, thanks, but more importantly, how are you? How was the date? Was he handsome?'

'He was an arrogant, brusque, opinionated Yorkshireman. That's about as good as it gets.'

'But did you like him?'

'No. Well, not really.'

'Not really. What does that mean?'

'Well... he kissed me.'

'Oh, yes, one of those types. That's despicable.'

Charlotte could almost see Sam pursing her lips and shaking her head.

She paused for a moment. 'No... It was gentle, yet passionate. I don't know, it's ridiculous.'

'Sounds like you do like him?'

'Don't be so silly. Of course not.'

'I'll drop by later and you can tell me the full story. I'm pleased for you.'

'For goodness' sake, there's nothing to tell.'

The call ended with Sam chuckling as she rang off.

'Ridiculous,' Charlotte murmured as she eased back into the chair. She certainly wasn't expecting a kiss, especially on a first date. That was rude and arrogant. But the way he came close, looked deep into her eyes, and purposefully but delicately pressed his lips to hers, was like nothing she had ever experienced. Sheer, exquisite freedom. A man who knew how to take control, but with the naivety of a schoolboy.

'Tea, Miss Charlotte, or something a little stronger?' Cartwright said, slicing through her thoughts. 'A tonic, maybe?'

He knew her very well.

The following morning, Mira dropped in unannounced for a catch-up.

Mira always wore a real fur coat in winter, and often in the summer too. She struggled with her weight. Yoyo dieting and the latest eating fad played leading roles in her life, and she felt comfortable hiding behind coats and large bags. She'd told Charlotte the coat was fake, but it had been bought for her by her father on a trip to Russia. Charlotte knew that but chose to keep it secret.

'So?'

'Hello, Mira, why don't you come in?'

'Hello, darling.' *Mwah*, *mwah*. 'I don't need to ask, but hopefully you've concluded this silly dating charade and now realised there are no decent men out there. I thought Nobu or Annabel's, perhaps? Come on, let's hit the town.'

'Well... I don't really know what to say. It wasn't the date I was expecting. He was rugged, not like my other dates, and then...'

'What?'

'He... He kissed me.'

Mira scowled so much, Charlotte knew even her toes were scowling. 'On a first date? And you didn't even want to be there.'

'I know. I'm confused.'

Mira gave a fake smile. 'He sounds a bit desperate.'

'I guess so.' Charlotte bit her lip. 'I'll wait for him to contact me.'

'I think you're wasting your time. He sounds like a loser. The type of guy who'll drag you down and take all your money.'

'Mira!'

Three days went by, and Charlotte busied herself with her full social diary and, of course, dinner with Mira at Nobu. In many ways, her foray into reluctant dating had confused her, but had also encouraged her to embrace her social commitments again. She sat at the large table in the kitchen. It could comfortably seat eight people, but her chair was wearing more than any of the others.

She hadn't checked her phone to see if he'd contacted her. Well, not obsessively. Three or four times an hour, that's all.

She wouldn't contact him, naturally, but the feel of his kiss, still present on her lips after three days, one hour and thirty-seven seconds, acted as a constant reminder. It was almost impossible to stop biting her bottom lip gently and thinking about his stubbly chin against her.

'Ridiculous!' she said to herself out loud. The girls were right—men were all the same. And why would she want to spend valuable time even thinking about it?

15

STEPHENSON'S ROCKET

The earthy smell of green moss and tree bark filled the air as Peter clipped the final karabiner into his climbing harness and started his ascent of a hundred-foot Douglas fir tree. A full week had gone by since his date with Charlotte. He cast the whole episode aside, not caring to think about it. He fancied her, he knew that, but it felt forced and unnatural. He was, after all, just helping out.

Douglas fir was one of his favourites to climb, high and challenging; he'd have to use pretty much every muscle in his body to ascend it. He remembered learning at college that this species was the tallest tree in the UK, with the biggest ever recorded being 217 feet. To climb the enormous trunk, with its rough bark, was no easy task. He used the body-thrust technique to climb a rope he'd suspended over a high branch. Weight in the harness and feet against the tree, he thrust his body upwards and pulled down on the rope, using every muscle for this thrusting and pulling until he reached the first branch.

The tree was set within a proposed development site. The

area was due to be cleared to make way for a new luxury car showroom, but the tree was suspected of being a potential bat roost. Bats being a protected species in the UK, the presence of them was possibly enough to halt the entire scheme. A couple of woodpecker holes in the trunk at sixty feet were likely roost points, and Peter had to get a close look in each hole. He thrust up and anchored his rope at around seventy feet. Next he would need to descend below each hole carrying his endoscope. A camera on a flexible wire was the best way to peer inside without too much disturbance.

Peter was out of breath by the time he reached the first hole. He'd cut his arm on a broken branch and blood was dripping onto the ground. Using both hands to secure himself tightly to the tree, he could do nothing but let the cut clot naturally. He installed his second safety line to pull him close to the hole, reached with his hand to find the endoscope dangling from his harness, pressed the 'on' switch and carefully pushed the camera inside. Sensitivity was vital, as he didn't want to scare any residents within. The digital screen indicated a tight cavity and that, inside, the wood was smooth.

Something had been using the hole. A woodpecker had first carved out the cavity, exploiting some rot where an old branch had fallen off, and the likelihood was that the bird was still resident. But as Peter probed further up into the cavity, he was in for a surprise.

A little brown hairy face came into view. A roosting bat with a white front and longish ears stared at him, and there was a second one close behind. Bechstein's bat. He recognised it immediately. They were rare, and he'd only ever seen just the one before, on one of his training courses. Bechsteins were definitely tree-dwellers, commonly in woodland, but it was clearly also possible that they could come to rest within this magnificent tree. A snapshot of the bats from the endoscope camera would be enough to prove their presence and give the tree and the bats full protection from the proposed development.

Peter smiled and started his descent, moving fast, abseiling down the rope; his cut was still bleeding, but some resin from the tree had stuck the hairs on his arm over the wound, helping to stem the flow.

On reaching the ground, he cleaned up the blood with his mouth and wrapped a spare T-shirt he had in his bag around it. The developer would not be happy at his news, but he felt warm and fulfilled at the thought of giving nature a helping hand.

He coiled the rope back into the bag and checked his phone. There was a text from Chris.

'*Mate, charity dinner tonight. The missus laid up in bed with a bug. Need a plus 1. You up for it? Suit and tie job, pick you up 7.15. How'd it go the other day? Call me.*'

Peter pressed the button to dial. 'Chris, it's Pete. I'm skint, mate. You know I'm putting all my money into a deposit for a flat. I just don't have the funds to get involved in buying rounds of drinks, let alone contributing to charities.'

'Don't be daft, it's all paid for. Slap-up dinner and drinks, and a free taxi there and back. Anyway, I need you by my side, mate. You know how boring those old boys can be, wittering on about false hips and which cruise they've recently been on. Come on. It's a deal.'

'That sounds like a great laugh. Not!'

'I'll take that as a yes, then?'

Peter sat on his rope bag and sighed. 'I'm not in the mood at all, especially after that horrific date last week.'

'I thought you said it wasn't a date?'

'Ha, funny. You know what I mean.'

'She wasn't so cute, then?'

'No. She was cute. Very. She was posh and educated. I didn't understand most of what she was on about, and anyway, my head's not ready for dating.'

'Well, tonight will be the perfect tonic, then. No excuses. Pick you up at 7.15.'

Chris's dad was in the local Freemasons and he was often invited to business dinners and charity nights, where the prizes were auctioned for ridiculous amounts of money but all for good causes.

'You scrub up well for a tree-climber,' Chris said as they raced each other up the red-carpeted steps into the charity gala venue. 'Where did you get the suit? Saville Scarecrow?'

'At least I don't resemble an egg in a straitjacket, fatso!' Peter replied.

'Are you going to make it to the top, old boy, or do I need to call an ambulance?' Chris panted. 'Anyway, I can't help being bald.'

They both entered the room with big smiles on their faces.

A waitress guided them through the maze of huge round tables draped in white linen, where people stood chatting and blocking the route. Chris instantly noticed a friend from the golf club who Peter didn't know. There were big handshakes and much slapping of backs, so Peter filed off, still following the waitress, and found his seat at the neatly laid table. He noted the name card next to him. *Sir Henry Stephenson.* He wondered if he was a pompous politician with a dodgy hip.

Other people began to fill their seats and Peter introduced

himself to each one with a firm handshake and a smile. Chris eventually arrived and started hamfistedly sloshing red wine into Peter's glass.

'Red alright for you, you old wino?' He seemed drunk already.

Sir Henry turned out to be the great-great-great-grandson of George Stephenson, the inventor of the 'Rocket' no less. Peter was in awe, and while the speeches were in full flow he whispered in Chris's ear to explain who his neighbour was, gesturing with his eyes to Sir Henry.

'I knew there would be some big names here, mate. We're mixing with the top brass.'

'No shit.'

Chris indicated the table in front of them. 'Apparently on that table there's some bobsleigh champion or other.'

'You're kidding me. Shit, I need to find out who.'

Chris nodded, smiled, and sloshed more wine into Peter's glass.

With the solid thump of the auctioneer's gavel, the bidding was underway. Chris bid on a golfing weekend with Rory McIlroy, but stopped bidding at £500, which was just as well, as the winning bid came in at a staggering £25,000. Peter just kept his head down, and everything else for that matter, in the fear he might inadvertently bid on something. A set of Muhammad Ali's boxing gloves reached £1.5 million from an undisclosed bidder, and a scruffy old writing desk went for a quarter of a million.

Peter came close to Chris's ear. 'Jeez mate, are there any "normal" prizes, like a bottle of aftershave or a knitted toilet-roll cover?'

'Don't look now,' said Chris. 'But there's someone behind you who hasn't taken her eyes off me all night.'

'How do you mean, "don't look now" How can I not look now?'

'It's a brunette in a red dress and seriously, mate, she hasn't stopped looking over. I knew I could pull off a suit and I've lost a few pounds this month, but she's a stunner.'

'You're married, you idiot,' Peter replied with contempt. 'Is it anyone we know?'

The music, now uncomfortably loud, made it difficult to hear.

'What?'

'Is it anyone we know?' Peter replied.

'She doesn't look familiar; you'd better have a look.'

'You said don't look. Is she looking?'

'Hang on.' Chris glanced over and must have caught her eye, because he smiled and looked away.

'Yes. I'll tell you when she isn't.'

'This is ridiculous,' Peter said, turning his head instantly and fixing his eyes straight into her gaze.

'Shit. It's her.'

'Who?'

'The girl from that horrendous date.'

'What! Looking at me?'

Peter shook his head and rolled his eyes. 'Is she still looking over?'

'No, she's gone.'

'Great. The last thing I want is to have to talk to her.'

'Jeez, mate. She's a cracker, and she's minted, you said.'

'Probably minted. Honestly. What are you like? There's more to life than money, you know.'

Chris raised an eyebrow and shrugged.

'I'm off for a pee,' Peter said, rising from his seat.

When he came out of the gents, the contrast between the

lighted bathroom and the dark venue made it difficult to adjust his vision. He stood for a moment, trying to locate his seat among the myriad of tables.

'Hi,' a demure voice said.

'Hi,' Peter replied, still gaining his bearings.

'I didn't expect to see you here,' the voice said again.

'Charlotte,' Peter cried. 'No, me neither. I mean, you, not me. What are you doing here?'

'I like to support various charities. I'm here with my friend Mira.'

'Yes, me too,' Peter said with a polite smile. 'Well, my friend Chris, not Mira.'

They both laughed, and Peter shuffled his feet uncomfortably. 'Has anything caught your eye?'

'I bought a writing desk.'

He stopped shuffling. 'Really?'

'Yes, it's beautiful. In antique oak. It used to be T. S. Eliot's, apparently.'

'Wow.' He gave a bold laugh. 'Couldn't you afford a new one?'

Charlotte looked at the floor and an awkward silence followed.

'I hope the tree didn't suffer,' Peter went on, back-pedalling.

Charlotte raised her gaze. 'Suffer?'

'Yes. The oak tree that made the desk.'

'Are you saying trees can feel things?'

Peter scrunched his lips and nodded. 'Of course. They're living things. When you chop off a limb, they grow one back. They feel the wind and grow strong roots to compensate. They can feel when they're under attack from insects and they send poisons to their leaves. And when you cut a tree, they bleed. Have you ever seen that?'

'Yes,' Charlotte said, with eyes open wide. 'Yes, I have.'

'Look, sorry. I get a bit geeky when it comes to trees.'

Charlotte paused for a moment and put her hand on Peter's chest. 'Can you just steady me while I adjust this strap on my shoe?' she said, lifting her leg and resting her weight against him. 'It's been irritating me all evening.'

Peter nodded and watched her tussle with the delicate buckle, while admiring her slender calf.

'I like that about you,' Charlotte went on. 'What you know about trees. They're incredibly grounded. Like you too, perhaps? And they're wise.' She lingered with her hand on his chest and giggled. 'Thanks for helping a damsel in distress.'

Peter nodded again. 'No problem. Enjoy the desk. Anyway, good to see you again.'

'And you too, Peter,' she said, as he walked away.

16

LUCY'S BIRTHDAY

The London house was again in complete chaos. There was barely room to manoeuvre in the vast entrance hall for bouquets of flowers and presents wrapped in dazzling gold, silver and pink, and bows, ribbons, and sparkly confetti. Charlotte was in chief organiser mode and the staff moved swiftly and with purpose. Lucy was expected any minute, and the place had to be ready and immaculate and, most important of all, they had to make sure the puppy, who had been an incredibly difficult secret to keep, had:

a) no access to the presents and gifts before Lucy, or there would be gift-wrapping carnage

b) been out for his daily constitutional and

c) been cleaned, brushed and made ready to meet his new owner.

The taxi pulled up outside and everyone took their places. Chef was busy in the kitchen preparing the lunch, the housekeepers were squirrelled away in the rooms below and Cartwright was on high alert to receive Lucy and her bags before moving on to serving canapés and drinks. Charlotte was hiding with the puppy in the sitting room and bursting for a wee in anticipation. She spied through the keyhole and as soon as Lucy stepped through the front door, she carefully came out, leaving the puppy behind, and went to greet her. They flung their arms around each other, and Lucy squeezed her mother.

'Happy birthday, my love. I can't believe you're thirteen. Anyway, we have lunch set and friends and family arriving later. But first, there's something I want to show you.'

'What is it?'

Charlotte opened the door and out bounded an excited bundle of hair, wagging tail and busy paws. He ran straight to Lucy and, as she crouched to stroke him, he licked her face and wagged his tail uncontrollably. He dashed to Charlotte and then back to Lucy.

'Happy birthday, darling.'

'I really don't believe it. I've dreamed about getting a puppy. Can I take him for a walk? What's his name? Can he sleep in my bed tonight?'

Charlotte was delighted to see Lucy so happy, and the puppy seemed to love her, too, as he excitedly dashed away, before quickly returning for more fussing.

'He has a poorly ear,' Lucy said, concerned.

'He's from the rescue centre. We have no clue to his full history, but he was obviously neglected and has probably been in a fight with another dog. He must have felt abandoned and lonely, but he's yours now.'

'I want to call him Vincent.'

'That's a strange name to call a dog.'

'Not if you've lost part of your ear.'

Instantly inseparable, Lucy and Vincent opened all her gifts together, most of which seemed to be for Vincent. Collars with studs, collars with LED lights, even a collar with diamonds and a matching lead.

Before lunch, Lucy and Charlotte took Vincent into the park and threw his new ball for him, and he gladly chased it down and retrieved it. At one point he had to be put on the lead when he became distracted by a precocious labradoodle in a little coat and pink bow.

Vincent ran around in circles, and Lucy followed. They were such a joyful sight to see, and Charlotte smiled contentedly. 'It's a cheerful house, at last. It's a sunny house,' she said.

The vibration of her phone in her pocket became impossible to ignore after the third time.

'Yes?' Her heart sank as she took in the news. 'That sounds serious. How much did he take? Where is he?'

When she put her phone away, Lucy asked her what was wrong.

'It's nothing to worry about right now. Some money has gone missing. I have to meet with Mr Scrivener and the police later.'

Lucy looked a little scared. 'Are we going to be homeless?'

'No, darling.' The sum mentioned had been frighteningly large, but seeing Lucy's anxious expression, Charlotte put on a brave face. 'It's just some investments. Right, where's that ball?'

When they got home, they gave Vincent some water and food from his new, gleaming stainless-steel bowls, and Lucy made sure everything was perfect for him, organising his bed and arranging his toys on the table.

'Vincent, we can go to the park every day if you want,' Lucy said, squeezing the ball until it squeaked. Vincent spun around in circles, in pure delight.

The birthday party was a great success, and it was difficult to tell who was the centre of attention, Lucy or Vincent. In the late afternoon, people began to depart. Vincent escorted each and every one of them to the door before collapsing on his bed. When the final stragglers had eventually gone, Charlotte and Lucy collapsed, too, on the sofa, with Lucy snuggled tight into Charlotte.

'What a day,' they both said simultaneously, and then laughed.

Charlotte's phone began to vibrate on the coffee table in front of them.

'Mr Scrivener. Yes. It's not ideal, but I understand the urgency,' Charlotte said, trying to keep the anxiety out of her voice.

'What is it, Mummy?'

'Lucy, I have to meet with Mr Scrivener and possibly the police. It's very important.'

'Don't leave me, Mummy. It's my birthday.'

'Darling, it's the last thing I want to do, believe me, but that's the trouble with being a mother and head of household. I have to protect us. That's you and me. OK? The housekeepers are here and Cartwright, of course. I should be back before your bedtime.'

'Don't go, Mummy. I want you to stay. Please stay. It's my birthday, don't leave me alone.'

'Lucy, pull yourself together. It's something I have to do. I have no choice. You have Vincent now and I'm sure Cartwright will be more than happy to accompany you to the park.'

'I don't want to go with boring old Cartwright. Anyway, he's already told me that dogs shouldn't be allowed to mess up a house. "Those hairs get everywhere," he said.'

'I won't be long. Finish opening your presents and I'll be back before bedtime.'

Vincent followed Charlotte lethargically to the door, while Lucy sighed and punched a balloon.

Charlotte's meeting was important. Vitally important. One of her portfolio advisors had disappeared with a substantial amount of money. The police advised her to divert and amend other funds, to protect them, or she could lose a lot more.

'Is there anything else I need to do, Mr Scrivener? This is all very disconcerting. Thank you for alerting me as quickly as you did.'

'The police will follow up as they need to and I'm sure they'll come back for more from you if they require it.'

'This is where I need Father. He would know exactly what to do. I'm flustered and scared. Will everything be alright?'

Mr Scrivener closed his diary and gave a reassuring nod. 'Yes, the police are sure they can resolve this. You can relax.'

'Thanks again. It's Lucy's birthday and I'm trying to be the best mum in the world, and not succeeding. I feel guilty having to leave her, but what else can we do when there are such untrustworthy people around?'

'It's all in hand, Charlotte,' Mr Scrivener reassured her once more.

The next day, Charlotte woke abruptly. Her face was being enthusiastically licked by a slavering tongue and there were paws on her arm.

Lucy stood in the doorway. 'Morning, Mummy. Can we take Vincent to the park today?'

Charlotte manoeuvred Vincent to one side and yawned. 'Yes, of course we can. Sorry about last night.'

'It's OK,' Lucy replied, but there was a forlorn look about her. 'Promise me we can go to the park.'

'I said yes, didn't I? Let's have breakfast first. And I do have a meeting with the gardener at 10am to discuss a new water feature I want by the pergola. We'll go after that.'

Lucy smiled and skipped off joyfully. 'Vincent, come on,' she shouted.

The gardener at the London house was a plump man with wild, unkempt hair. He spoke with a West Country accent and had earned Charlotte's respect for numerous projects, both at the Loxley estate and here in the city, with his eye for detail and consummate knowledge.

'The installation of the main feature should be fairly easy, madam. I'm a little concerned about the pipework, though. We might have to cut through a few roots on the lime tree to get it in.'

'Is it not possible to install the pipe without harming the tree?'

The gardener shook his head. 'I don't think so, madam, but to be sure, I asked a tree expert to come along this morning to advise us. He may have a solution.'

Charlotte looked up into the dense green canopy. 'I do hope so. I'm looking at trees in a very different way these days, for some reason. When is he coming?'

'Should be here any minute.'

'Fine. I'm going to the park with Lucy and Vincent. Ask him if the tree will recover if we have to chop the roots, and whether there is a solution in any way?'

'Of course, madam. Did you want to see him yourself?'

'No, no, not at all. I'll leave it all in your capable hands.' With that, Charlotte hurried off to find Lucy.

A short while later, as Lucy and Vincent ran around the park, shouting and laughing, Charlotte was able to look on her daughter with a warmth in her heart she hadn't felt for a while. Maybe she wasn't such a bad mum, after all.

When they returned to the house, Charlotte heard muffled male voices. Vincent bounded up to the front gate and proceeded to jump enthusiastically at the gardener, who was with another gentleman.

'I'm so sorry. Get down, Vincent,' she cried. 'Lucy, will you control him, please?'

'Don't worry, it's fine. I like dogs,' the man said, with a friendly smile.

The gardener turned immediately. 'Please, let me introduce the tree expert.'

'No need.' Charlotte shook Peter's hand and tried not to show a slight weakness she felt in her legs.

'You know each other?'

'He gave me some advice on an old piece of oak recently.'

Peter smiled. 'And a very beautiful one at that,' he said.

Charlotte gave a coy smile and played with her hair.

'I must be going. Here's my card. Call me if you need any further advice.'

17

GROUNDED

Charlotte positioned herself in a booth dimly lit by the soft greens, yellows, blues and reds of a Tiffany lamp. Inconspicuous, yet with a good view of the door, it was the perfect place to observe people coming in.

The bar was warm, so she removed her cashmere shawl and adjusted her skirt.

'Can I get you anything?' the barman asked politely.

'A bottle of champagne and two glasses, please, and some water.'

The door opened. Peter had his shirtsleeves rolled up, exposing his muscly forearms. Her heart gave a little jump as he walked straight towards her.

'Hi,' he said.

'Hi.'

'Can I get you a drink?'

'I took the liberty of ordering champagne. Is that OK?' she said.

'Yes, of course, champagne is fine. I am driving, though. I'll just have a glass and you can keep going without me if you want. So, what are we celebrating? The Best First Date Ever award?'

Charlotte laughed. 'I'm glad you gave me your number. I feel I do need some more advice.'

'It was a bit cheeky, and a long shot.'

'I liked it,' she said.

Peter sat down beside her. 'Look, I'm sorry about what happened before. On our first date. It was inappropriate. I let myself down. Can we draw a line under it and move on?'

Charlotte toyed with her hair. 'You mean start where we left off?'

Peter said nothing and looked at her intently. They began to move imperceptibly closer.

'Your champagne, madam,' the waiter announced. Peter and Charlotte laughed as he filled their glasses.

'Great timing,' Charlotte said, smiling.

Peter smiled back. 'What are you looking at?' he asked.

'That... just that. I like your smile. It reminds me a little of my father.'

'Really? Is he a nice guy?'

'He's sadly no longer with us. He died many years ago.'

'I'm sorry to hear that. What about your mum?'

'She's not well. I have to care for her.'

'Must be tough.'

'Indeed. Anyway, what about your parents?'

Peter's eyes closed, and he seemed to struggle to respond. 'I lost my mum when I was young,' he said eventually, 'and never knew my dad.'

'Gosh. I know how you feel. I mean, I don't know exactly, but I kind of do.'

Peter nodded. 'We were both loved. That's what we have to remember.'

Charlotte could hardly take her gaze from his deep blue eyes. They were pure blue, a blue that changed with the light, azure like the Mediterranean Sea and then turning midnight blue as he looked at her.

Something impelled her to confide in him. 'I have an oak tree, which I love dearly. It's a beautiful tree. I climbed it once. Well, to the first branch to install my swing. I nearly killed myself.'

Peter laughed. 'The hardest bit is getting down again, isn't it?'

She laughed with him.

'I used to visit an old oak tree when I was a boy,' Peter went on. 'I haven't been there for many years. It was a good friend.'

Charlotte put her hand on his broad shoulder. 'Mine is a great friend. It sounds stupid, but I talk to it.'

'That's not stupid. Doesn't everyone talk to trees?'

'I've never discussed it with anyone before.'

'They talk back, too. Does yours?'

Charlotte couldn't answer quick enough. 'Yes, it talks to me, reassures me and gives me energy.'

'Of course. They're very wise and feel everything. Not like us.' He touched the delicate skin on her face with his thumb. 'You have a smudge on your cheek.'

He dropped his hand, and picked up his glass.

Charlotte looked at him curiously. 'You seem grounded and in touch with nature. I like that.'

Peter shrugged. 'If you're not in touch with nature, you're not in touch with yourself.'

'You know, I think you're right. Are you in touch with yourself?'

'All I know, lass, is life is full of surprises.'

'Lass! What am I, some kind of sheep dog?'

Peter broke into a laugh at that. Something shifted between them, and he leaned back on the bench, the faint hint of awkwardness leaving him. They talked all evening, until the lights eventually flickered, and the barman politely asked them to leave. Charlotte put on her shawl and headed for the door.

'I'll walk with you. I want you to be safe.'

'No, no, it's quite alright,' she said.

'I'll walk you over the road, at least.' They crossed the road, her arm in his as though they were Victorians promenading along the seafront. They turned the corner by a sushi restaurant and walked a little further.

'I'll be alright here,' Charlotte said. 'It's just up there. Well, you know.'

Peter looked up the tree-lined road flanked by large, detached residences of Portland stone, manicured hedges and stately cars. 'No, lass, I'll make sure you're home safe.'

Charlotte smiled and tightened their locked arms together. On reaching the front gate, she heard Vincent barking inside.

'It's been a fabulous evening,' Peter said. He gently placed his hand on her chin, lifting her head slightly. There was a pause and then their lips seemed to meet like they'd always known each other, delicately touching in a brief kiss before Peter gently pulled away. His hand moved to her cheek and their eyes met, as if reaching into each other's souls.

Their noses touched point to point. 'I'd better go,' Peter said softly.

'Yes, you better had,' Charlotte said, not wanting him to leave.

Peter took her hands in his and held them tightly. 'Bye, then.'

'Drive carefully.'

She turned and walked a few paces before turning her head. Peter gave a little wave and she continued into the house, wearing a huge smile.

18

DOUBT

'Ouch!' Peter took the skin off his knuckles for the fourth time while trying to undo a large nut with an adjustable wrench. The landlord had once again promised to fix the leaking sink and was, as usual, uncontactable. The flat really was becoming unbearable, and Peter was begrudgingly taking matters into his own hands.

He somehow had his head, body and one leg in the kitchen unit, his arm twisted backwards behind the U-bend and the other leg up against the fridge door. Blood was dripping from his knuckles and dirty water was running down his arm.

He tightened and reassembled the pipe unit and shook off the smelly dirty water, hairs and food waste which had been blocking it. 'Mr Blue Sky' was playing on the radio and, still wedged under the sink, he began to sing along—'Sun is shining in the sky, there ain't a cloud in sight.' He laughed. What a funny position to be in! He was glad no one was there to see or smell him. And it was pointless getting annoyed. There would be someone somewhere worse off, for sure. 'And don't you know, it's a beautiful new day, hey, hey, hey.'

Still singing along to the radio, Peter tore off his clothes and threw them in a pile on the floor, stepped into the shower, turned on the tap and found the shower head came off in his hand. He stood for a moment in total disbelief. Could it get any worse? He stood there, naked and cold, trying to put the head back into the socket and screw it in tight.

Charlotte's hair was done—a touch of colour to 'help' with the rogue grey areas, and extra curls, which always accentuated her youthful looks. She was anxious she was ageing too fast and thought she was carrying a bit too much weight and too much cellulite. She wanted to look fabulous for her third date with Peter, though, and she knew exactly what she would wear. A summery little cream dress and matching cream lace underwear which she'd bought especially. She wanted to feel feminine and confident without being too obvious.

She'd taken the shortcut through the park. The smell of late summer was in the air, but there were families still picnicking among the tall grass. Her dress blew gently in the breeze and the warm evening sun made her smile.

After turning the corner by the Victorian bandstand, Charlotte did a little pirouette, her arms wide. It seemed just the right moment, and no one was looking. Then an unmistakable, fast-paced figure came into view, dressed in a fur coat.

'Mira. What are you doing in the park? And don't you have a lighter jacket? It's so warm this evening.'

'It was chilly earlier.' *Mwah, mwah.* 'Anyway, I could ask the same of you, all dressed up like a nymph. Going anywhere nice?'

'Yes, just for drinks. Where are you heading?'

Mira shuffled uncomfortably. 'I was hoping to give you a surprise visit and plan a girlie shopping trip sometime. We haven't done that for a while.'

'Oh! Yes, well I've been busy, you know, birthday parties and the like.'

'Are you meeting up with that tree hugger?'

'Mira, please don't say that.' Charlotte was beginning to wish she'd never mentioned anything about Peter.

'Look, Charlotte, someone has to say it. I'm just worried he's after your money and you're blind to it. I mean, he's like a gardener, for goodness, sake. What kind of future can he offer you?'

'Well, I like that he hugs trees. Maybe, just maybe, there are things you don't know about me.'

Mira stood firm. 'Just ask yourself what your father would have thought.'

'That's not fair, Mira. You know I can't ask him.'

'Just saying. That's all.'

Charlotte started walking away. 'I really do have to dash. You've upset me. You really have.'

When she finally reached the bar, Charlotte positioned herself in the same booth as last time. She put her little bag beside her, took out her pocket mirror and made a few minor adjustments to her make-up, the Tiffany lamp giving her face a healthy glow.

She continued to ponder what Mira had said. She was consumed by a wave of insecurity and felt nervous and unsettled. What if he wasn't what she remembered? She knew, of course, that he wasn't from her usual social circle and immediately started comparing him with her father.

Maybe Mira was right. What was she doing? A man from a different class—she didn't even know where he lived or whether he knew which knife and fork to use. Surely this was a big mistake?

She fully understood that these bouts of insecurity, which were becoming more frequent in her life, could be very destructive, but she also had to listen to her red flags. Clutching her bag tightly in her shaking hand, she straightened her shawl and decided to leave discreetly.

'Anyway, how could I ever take him home to meet everyone?' she thought. 'He's a tradesman, after all, rather than a potential partner.' Yes, it was out of the question, and he was late anyway. Another trait Charlotte hated. She waited another couple of seconds and, without drawing attention to herself, stood up and walked calmly to the door.

She stepped onto the street and, as she did so, was overwhelmed by an enormous sense of relief. Her heart was pounding and her legs like jelly, but she'd done the right thing. She had things to do at home, anyway, a few letters to sign and her perfumes to rearrange. She was turning the corner when, without warning, a cyclist came speeding by.

'Get out of the way,' he shouted. Charlotte flew back in fright, taking a step backwards, and twisted over on her kitten heel. A sharp pain shot through her ankle.

'Damn cyclist,' she blurted out as she tried to regain her composure. She tentatively put some weight onto her foot and her leg buckled under her.

A strong arm came from nowhere to steady her, and a deep voice said, 'Are you OK? That was close.' Someone was holding her tightly against his body. 'Charlotte! Are you alright?'

She recognised the voice. 'Peter... I don't know. My ankle is hurting. That damn cyclist nearly ran me over. They should be more careful.'

She turned and faced him. He looked concerned. 'Come on,

let's get you inside and get a drink to calm your nerves. Sorry I'm a bit late. Looks like you are, too. Were you just arriving?'

Peter helped her in through the door, his arm around her waist, supporting her weight.

'Here, let's get you sat down, and I'll have a look at that ankle.' He helped her into the booth, the same one they'd had previously.

'I'll order tea—mint for you and green for me.' He laughed. 'No champagne this time. You'd never get home.'

Charlotte nodded and smiled. 'Thanks, Peter. There's no one at home to come and pick me up. I gave the housekeeper and the butler the evening off.'

'It's alright, lass. I'm here now. Get your leg up here and let me have a look.'

Charlotte lifted her leg and rested it on Peter's. His hands were warm and had a roughness to them—hands that were capable, she thought; the sort of hands that did hard work, and the sort of hands that could build a romantic log cabin in the woods and chop logs for a cosy fire. But they had a gentle touch too.

He took off her shoe and supported her foot. The swelling was starting to bruise.

'I'm sure it will be fine, Peter. I've twisted my ankle once before, running by my lake, but it didn't swell up like this.'

'Your lake?' Peter gave her a comical look. 'We need to get some ice on it,' he went on firmly. 'It doesn't appear broken, but ice will help. I'll ask the barman for some.'

'No. Not in here, Peter. I don't want to draw attention to us. Let me have a minute to rest and have some tea. I'll feel better in a short while.'

Peter nodded.

'Thank you.'

'Don't worry, you've already thanked me.'

'No, I mean, thanks,' she said, scrunching up her lips.

Peter looked at her in bewilderment. 'Can you wiggle your toes?' he asked. 'That's good. It doesn't look any worse than a slight sprain.' He held her leg in his hand firmly and massaged her calf. 'Does that help?'

She smiled and sensed a tingling inside. A wonderful tingling. 'You're a lovely guy. You know that?'

'Well, some people might disagree.'

'What do you mean?'

'I've had my moments.'

'No, seriously. Before you arrived, I had a little panic attack that you might not be the person I thought you were.' She didn't want to tell him what she really thought, but she needed to let him know she felt insecure.

'Don't worry. What you see is what you get with me.'

'Don't stop. It's really helping.' She giggled. 'Do you have healing hands?'

'Ha, well, I don't know about that. Look, the tea's here.' The barman unloaded the tea and cups onto the table. Peter chuckled. 'You pour while I carry on with some more healing. I'll have you dancing around in no time, lass.'

Charlotte felt a shudder go through her body. 'That's the second time you've called me lass.'

Peter looked up and smiled. 'It's a term of endearment up north. Consider it a compliment.'

He brought her foot to rest on his thigh, and her heel was almost in his groin, which she kept looking at and then pretending not to. He used both hands to move up and down her leg, massaging gently. Her short, summery dress was barely enough to cover the tops of her thighs.

'Thank God I wore the new underwear, and thank God I decided not to stay,' she thought to herself with a smile.

She felt comfortable and relaxed in his hands, although she did nearly drop the teapot as he ran his hand up above her knee. He looked her deep in the eyes and said firmly, 'Just making sure nowhere else is broken.'

She quivered with excitement and desperately tried to disguise it. She instinctively bit her lip. 'It might be... I can definitely feel something,' she said, flirting with him.

'You have amazing skin.' Peter moved his hand around to her inner thigh. 'Can you lift your leg?' He slowly raised it. Luckily the table was hiding most of the action, because her dress rode up further.

'Oh my God, what is he doing?' Charlotte thought. He could see straight up her dress. Quite without warning, her pelvis was flooded with warmth.

Peter gently put her leg down and reached for his tea. 'Seriously, we need to get some ice on that, or it'll swell right up like a balloon.'

Charlotte laughed at the way he said 'balloon'. He seemed a gentleman, she liked that, but he seemed to have a naughty streak too, and she loved that even more. They finished their tea, and she asked if there was any possibility that he could walk her home. She had ice in the kitchen and, after putting some weight on her foot, felt she was able to try and walk.

She managed, with Peter's help, to hobble back towards the house. Halfway there, Peter bent down and scooped her up into his arms.

'What are you doing? I'm far too heavy.'

'No you're not. I can't bear to see you struggling. I'll carry you to the door. It's the least I can do.'

She didn't protest and flung her arm around his shoulders.

They arrived at the house, where Peter carried her through the gate and up the Italian marble pathway to her immaculate red front door, with its brass knocker. Charlotte fiddled in her bag for her key.

'Shall I drop you here?' he said.

'No, would you be so kind as to carry me in? As I said, there's no one here, and if you could get the ice for me, that would be most helpful.' She unlocked the door and, on entering the hallway, instructed Peter to take the door to the right, into the sitting room. He pushed it open with his foot and they entered the dimly lit room with its leather chairs and sofa. The window overlooked the garden, where a few up-lighters gave enough light to make out the marble sculpture.

'Am I too heavy for you?' Charlotte felt like a damsel in distress in his arms, and although her ankle was probably good enough to hobble, she loved Peter's chivalry. It was turning her on.

Peter positioned her on the sofa, where he could get a closer look at her ankle.

'No, you're as light as a feather.' He held his back and pretended to be in pain.

'You're very strong.' Charlotte put her hand on the bulging muscle of his upper arm.

'I'd carry you a hundred miles if I had to, lass,' he said.

Charlotte smiled as he leaned in close to her. He brushed her face with his thumb, gently pulled her to him, and kissed her on the cheek. She gasped and pressed her hand on his arm. He kissed the corner of her mouth with the corner of his, and then brushed her lips with his, teasing her. She tried to kiss him, but he held her back and playfully gave a shake of his head. She was going crazy; she wanted to feel his lips fully on hers, but he was in control. He kissed her again on the other corner of her mouth and then it came: a glorious connection of delicate lips. He kissed with such passion, but with a lovely sensual sensitivity. Charlotte put her hand on the back of his head and pulled him in tighter as she revelled in the delightful embrace, her heart popping with pleasure.

Peter broke away. Charlotte's dress had ridden up around her thighs, exposing her slender, bare legs. He sat beside her and carefully stroked her lower leg. 'I'm just checking for any other breaks,' he said with a devilish look.

'It's quite painful higher up,' she said.

He took his hand and ran it up her inner thigh. 'Do you mean here?' He smiled, and she nodded. 'And here?' He ran his hand up inside her dress. She nodded again and slightly opened her legs.

He massaged her thigh, cheekily moving further and further up, but without rush.

'Your skin is incredibly soft.' His tone made her go weak and, instead of replying, she gave out a little squeal and bit her lip again. He looked deep into her eyes before dropping his head to kiss her leg just above the knee. His lips tickled her skin. 'Really soft,' he murmured.

She said nothing as he pushed her legs apart with his hand. Every stroke of his tongue made her quiver. She put her hand on his head to stop him from going any higher; he took her arm, pushed it against the back of the couch and kissed her on the lips.

'I should go now,' he said.

Charlotte paused for a moment. 'Yes, you probably should. I liked that, though.'

'I don't want to overstep the mark.'

Charlotte bit her thumb and nodded. She liked the fact he

hadn't rushed in too fast; he was gentlemanly and gallant—yet rough and naughty.

'Maybe I'll have one last kiss,' he said, lowering his head. He confidently pushed her legs apart and ran his tongue from her knee to just short of the top of her leg. She opened her legs further, and he kissed her right on her panties. She juddered with surprise as he started licking and gently kissing and nibbling her. When she thrust herself into his mouth, as a sign that she wanted more, he put his finger into her panties and pulled them to one side. She was wet, and as his tongue made contact, it glided smoothly, with ease.

His tongue was gentle and somehow reassuring, and it was exploring with confidence. He was teasing her. Not charging straight to the point, like so many others, but teasing around and around and ever so close and down and up, his whole tongue enjoying her readiness. She loved the gentle sensation, and Peter seemed to realise it. The teasing began to send her wild with anticipation... and then there he was, right on cue, tasting her and pleasing her. Charlotte writhed and shuddered in complete ecstasy. He pushed her legs further apart and quickened his pace, but still gently, his tongue running up and down and almost, very nearly, actually, yes entirely running over her clit. The feeling was exquisite; his timing was perfect. There was no going back. Charlotte relaxed fully into her reclining position and, with one hand, ran her fingers through his hair. She teased her nipple with the other. The sensation began building; tiny shudders of pleasure and pangs of intensity filled her body, and then suddenly it came, the quickest orgasm she had ever had, like a bullet train straight to her heart.

Peter held off while she squealed and juddered, and let her ride it out. He pulled her dress back down and kissed her on the forehead and then her lips, which were dry. When they kissed, it was the most beautiful kiss.

'I really had better go now,' Peter said. 'You need to get some ice on that ankle, too.'

'I'd forgotten all about it. You're the greatest painkiller.' She laughed and said, still out of breath, 'There's some ice in the kitchen, through the other door.'

Peter returned with the ice, wrapped in a tea towel, scooped Charlotte up in his arms and carried her into the great hall. 'I'll tuck you up in bed and you can have the ice for when you need it in the night. Where's your room?'

Charlotte grinned from ear to ear.

The sweeping marble staircase led up to the first floor, and right in front of them was the passage to her room, with its chandelier dangling in the centre and a large queen-size bed with lots of cushions. Peter placed her under the covers, tucked her in, put the ice just by her ankle and said in a soft voice, 'Will you be OK?'

'I'll be just fine now, thank you. Take the key and lock the door behind you—and post the key back through the door, if you don't mind.'

'Of course I will. Sleep tight.' He gave her a kiss on the forehead and headed down the grand stairs. Charlotte heard him lock the door and the key fall on the marble floor before he headed out into the dark.

19

ETON RIFLES

'Peter, you are a complete gentleman, and I can only thank you for your gallant efforts to make sure I was safe and secure and... taken care of. Thank you from the bottom of my heart. I would very much like to see you again. Cx.'

Peter smiled, stopped what he was doing, and contemplated the text. A rush of excitement filled him. What was it he liked so much about her? He didn't know. That was the honest answer. She was quirky and not from his world, but that made him even more interested.

He replied. 'Charlotte, I don't know what you would have done without me! You certainly seemed to respond well to my treatment. Oh, and how's the ankle? Px.'

She replied without hesitation. 'Well, let's just say your bedside manner, Doctor P, was very encouraging! Ankle doing well btw. Cxx.'

Peter laughed and replied, 'Glad to hear it. I was thinking, if your ankle is up to it, how about a picnic in the park, just you and me in the long grass, maybe take a look at that ankle again? ;-)'

'*That would be lovely, but can we make it Sunday afternoon when Lucy has returned to school?*'

'*Perfect Sunday afternoon. Call for you 3.30pm? I'll provide the food, you provide the blanket. Pxx.*'

∽

Peter knocked on the door and then, not sure if he should use one or the other, also pressed the intercom. Within five seconds, the door opened.

'Good afternoon, sir. Please come in. Madam will be down shortly.'

Peter replied nervously, 'Erm, I won't, if that's OK. I have the bikes.' He pointed at the two bikes leaning against the wall.

'Don't worry, sir, I will deal with those.'

'Please, let me help,' he said, as the butler struggled to bring in the bikes. He couldn't bear to see anyone made subordinate to him. In his eyes, everyone was equal.

'Don't worry, sir, I can manage.'

Peter entered and waited uncomfortably in the hallway. After an agonising minute or two, Charlotte appeared, dressed in cute three-quarter-length blue trousers, a blouse and a small white jacket.

Peter's eyes lit up. 'Hi.'

'Hi,' said Charlotte. 'Oh! Bikes! I haven't been on one for many years.'

'Don't worry, we can take it easy. I thought it might be easier than walking. You look lovely, by the way. How's the ankle?'

'It's a little sore, but it will be fine. It's really good to see you.'

'I couldn't wait. It seems ages.'

She laughed. 'It's only been a couple of days.'

'I know, but... you know?' Just then the bounding dynamo, which was Vincent, came scurrying to greet him. Peter fussed over him and scratched him behind his ears.

'So, this is who was making all the noise the other night,' he said.

Peter had made a picnic of continental meats, cheeses, sun-dried tomatoes in olive oil, hummus dip, French bread and baby vegetable dippers and ripe English strawberries for pud. He'd hoped it would be posh enough as he'd bundled it into a rucksack and hired two Boris bikes. The bike-hire scheme lent itself well to an impromptu adventure. Rented by the hour or the day, and with a basket on the front to carry the Prosecco and two glasses, the bikes were ideal.

'Is there somewhere for the blanket and my jacket?' Charlotte asked.

Peter took the items from her and put them in one of the baskets.

'I'll adjust that seat for you,' he said. 'Just sit on it for me... That's right, and now, up.' He gave her a slight tap on the bottom.

'You're a naughty boy,' she said, laughing as she looked around. He kissed her and said nothing, just concentrated on tightening the seat screw. 'It's great to see you again,' she added with a smile.

'Come on then, follow me,' he said. They negotiated the road, which led to a little path into the park. It was a warm day, with a gentle breeze and the clearest of blue skies. The long grass in the park was brown and parched. Peter let Charlotte go in front so he could check she was OK on the bike with her ankle. She sped up and pulled away. He watched her for a little while with delight, then pulled alongside her. Her smile was huge, and she began laughing as her hair blew in the wind and whipped around her face. She lifted both legs off the pedals high into the air.

'Wahey!' she shouted.

Peter soaked up her enthusiasm and spirit and felt a warm, joyful excitement in his stomach, as well as relief that the bike idea had paid off. 'We're free, like dragonflies, beating our wings,' he said.

Charlotte peddled faster. 'Wahey, yes! Like cycling dragonflies.'

They sped around the various paths in the park, narrowly missing pedestrians and dogs, racing each other without a care.

'Follow me,' shouted Peter, taking a small path away from the main area towards some twisted and gnarly sweet chestnut trees which cast welcome shade over the long grass. He located the perfect spot for their picnic and pointed.

'Let's stop here. Are you ready for a little nibble?' He looked back. She was still grinning the biggest grin. He rested his bike against one of the chestnuts and helped Charlotte with hers. 'How is the seat position?' he asked.

'Perfectly adjusted, thank you, sir.' She raised an eyebrow and smiled.

Peter laid out the blanket and arranged the food he'd lovingly prepared. They sat side by side. 'You know, you nearly knocked that old lady with the little Shih Tzu flying, you were going so fast,' he said jokingly.

'Oh! Did I? Gosh, I didn't realise I was such a daredevil.'

Peter touched her lips with his fingers. 'Your smile is so beautiful.'

'Thanks for organising the bikes, Peter. I haven't had this much fun in years.'

'Me neither.' He lay down, putting his hands behind his head, and stared up into the vast sky.

'Do you ever think she's looking down on you?' Charlotte said suddenly. 'Your mum?'

Peter sighed. 'Yes, all the time. I couldn't manage if I thought any different. It's been a long time without her, but I constantly have a pain in my heart. I used to feel let down and abandoned, but now I just feel like there's this empty gap, which will never be filled.'

'I feel that, too. Although I never saw much of my father when I was a girl, I miss him. I guess I'm still waiting for him to take me to the zoo.'

'Why the zoo?'

'I mean, spend quality time with me, instead of dashing to business meetings or travelling abroad. I would ask him to play and he'd always say "In a minute," or, "Maybe tomorrow."'

Peter nodded, and she lay down beside him to stare up into the sky.

'As long as you were loved, then there's hope for us.'

Charlotte remained silent and, after a few moments, put her hand on Peter's chest. 'Well, that might be my problem.'

Peter lowered his arm and cuddled her so that her head was resting on him. 'What do you mean?'

'I'm just being silly. I know I was loved... but somehow, I never really felt it deep down. I mean, I had everything I wanted and an excellent education... but sometimes all you need is a hug and to see the elephants.'

Peter squeezed her tight. 'Elephants! Now you're going mad. What about your mum?'

Charlotte said nothing and then took a deep breath. 'She's cold. Simple as that. Wrapped up in her own world, she never had time for me. The house, the parties... somehow I felt invisible.'

'I'm sorry to hear that.'

'I think she's been ill for a long time. Depression and mental health issues, you know. Dementia. She probably longed for my father's love, too.'

'Do you think you can be loved?'

'What kind of question is that?'

'Well, I wonder whether the pain in my heart is so strong, I wouldn't be able to let someone in.'

Charlotte pushed herself away from his chest. 'Are you saying that you're cold, too?'

He looked at her. 'No. I mean, I've never met anyone I could let into that gap in my heart. I've always known it would have to be someone pretty special.'

'I suppose we both think we might get let down again.' Then she nudged him, the sombre mood broken. 'But what do I know? Talking rubbish with a Yorkshire tree hugger!'

'Well, as you said. Hugs are the best thing and, anyway, trees don't need no mortar board and cape to be wise.'

Charlotte laughed, met Peter's gaze and smiled. 'I like that you like the simple things in life.'

'My mum used to say it's not what you have, but the things you've done and the people you've done it with.'

'Yes, but money buys you options.'

'You can't buy happiness.'

'Tell me about the dragonfly.'

'Oh, that! Well—' Peter was interrupted by Charlotte's phone vibrating. 'Had you better answer that?'

'Yes, it might be Lucy.' Charlotte rummaged around in the contents of her bag, looked at her phone and then put it straight back.

'Was it her?'

'No. It can wait. Tell me about the dragonfly.'

Peter began to recount his childhood tale, ending by waving his arms frantically and buzzing around like a human Spitfire. 'It was grateful for just being free. It didn't need anything else. That's always amazed me.'

'Well, I think you're amazing. You make me forget about all my troubles and see life from a completely new direction.'

'Did you know dragonflies have a voracious appetite for sex?' Peter said with a wink.

'I take back everything I've just said. You've lowered the tone completely.'

They both laughed, mounted their bikes, and headed further down the park. At the sound of music in the distance, Charlotte pulled alongside Peter and said, 'There's a band over there.'

He nodded. 'Yes, sounds good, doesn't it? Shall we stop for a while? I'll find us a good place to listen.' There was a grassy patch under a sprawling plane tree. 'There,' he said. They propped their bikes on the other side of the tree and Peter sat with his back to the trunk, Charlotte between his legs, leaning back into him, his arms around her. The band were playing various cover songs from the eighties and they knew all of them; it really was their era. When 'Eton Rifles', Peter's favourite Jam hit, came on, he said, 'I wanted this record so badly.' There was a lump in his throat.

'Didn't you get it?'

'No—I never did.' He paused and looked at her. 'Sometimes you don't get what you want, but I have this time.'

20

SCRATCHES

Peter picked up his phone.

'I wanted to call you and thank you for such an amazing time on our cycle ride.'

'It was good, wasn't it? So great to feel the wind in our hair.'

'I loved it. Hadn't been on a bike for years and I laughed so much. You really are a tonic.'

'My pleasure, lass. We should do it again.'

'Well, I was wondering if you would accompany me to the Rescue Centre's dinner. It's a thank you to all who've supported the new hospital wing and everyone involved in the building. It's tomorrow evening in London.'

'I'd love that. Will I have to lay a few bricks or tile a roof?'

'You are silly. No, just be mine for the evening. Show everyone I'm not a sad, lonely singleton and even fend off any unwanted advances.'

'So, it's not only the dogs who like you there, then?'

'Will you come?'

'I'll be your loyal companion and sit and roll over if you want me to.'

'I'll take that as a yes.'

'Does that mean I can kiss you in public?'

'No! Definitely not.'

'Well, that's a no, then.'

'What do you mean?'

'It will be hard resisting snogging you, and I don't think I'll be able to abstain.'

'That's a big word for you.'

'That's why I just stick to snogging.'

'You're so common!'

'And you love it.'

Charlotte didn't answer. Peter broke the silence. 'What time shall I see you there?'

'Seven-thirty, smart-casual. That doesn't mean a boiler suit and hobnail boots.'

'See you then, gorgeous girl.'

Peter wore the one of his three shirts that Charlotte hadn't seen before, and his chinos. He waited by the gate and watched the various other people arriving. Many of the men were in suits, and the ladies in summery dresses and heels. Moments later, he noticed the black Bentley draw up outside. The driver opened the door and out stepped Charlotte in her teal dress and heels. Peter couldn't believe his eyes. She looked incredible. He straightened his back and walked confidently towards her.

When she spotted him, she smiled. He smiled back. 'You look sensational.'

'Thanks. Nice shirt.' She put her hand on his chest. Peter put his arm around her waist, pulled her in tight, and kissed her. A dignified, but lingering, I-want-you kind of kiss. Then he took her arm with great pride, ready to escort her into the building. He couldn't help noticing some red scratches on her forearm. She'd tried to conceal them with make-up, but on closer inspection, he could see how they stood out.

He paused for a moment. 'What's with the scratches?'

'Not now, Peter. This isn't the time. It was the cat.'

'But you don't have a cat.'

Charlotte carried on up the stairs, and the conversation ended as she began to greet the fellow guests. They were all people who had a vested interest in the centre or who'd been specifically invited with a view to having them contribute. Charlotte was a past master at whipping up interest and encouraging others to become involved, and when she presented her speech to the audience, Peter was in awe. She held court and commanded their attention. Since her sizeable contribution to the new centenary wing, the centre was now able to undertake life-saving operations and offer more animals a safe haven and the possibility of a new and safer life.

Charlotte looked beautiful, confident and assured. Peter was transfixed. She had a positivity which seemed to lift the entire room, and at the same time she showed immense compassion to the cause and the animals.

Charlotte looked over at him a couple of times mid-speech and Peter smiled back.

After the event, he suggested they grab a drink at a little wine bar on the next street. They walked hand in hand along the pavement, Charlotte's heels click-clicking and Peter strutting like a peacock, with his feathers on full display.

'I can get Cartwright to pick us up and take us somewhere a little nicer?'

'No, let's find our own way. This is Battersea, not the Bronx.'

'I trust you, Peter, but remember, I can't walk miles in these shoes.'

'Look, there's the place.' He pointed to a bar which had tables outside, with small glass vases containing lavender.

They took one of the tables and Peter observed how Charlotte flicked her hair as she smiled, letting the evening sun catch every strand.

'My mum used to do that. I remember our holiday to Blackpool, just me and her. I'd ridden one of the donkeys on the beach.'

'What do you mean, "one of the donkeys"?'

Peter laughed. 'Have you never seen the donkeys? You can ride them along the beach. They have names. Mine was *Dandy*.'

'Are they wild?'

'No, no, you don't have to lasso them and ride them bareback. They arrive every day in a van and they're walked up and down the beach. For children to have fun. Anyway, we were sitting on the pier. I had a strawberry ice cream and mum had vanilla. The sun was just like it is now, showing off her hair, just like yours.'

'Was she beautiful?' Charlotte said, captivated by his story.

'She was the most beautiful woman, always smiling and incredible fun.'

'She sounds like an amazing woman.' Charlotte smiled the biggest smile and her eyes became full and bright. 'You're so incredibly in touch with your feelings. I like that.'

Peter smiled back, looking intently into Charlotte's eyes. 'We've both been through many things, and we're just finding out about each other. But I can tell you one thing.'

'What is it?'

'I like you. I like you a lot.'

'Oh, Peter.'

'You also need to tell me about those scratches.'

'Like I said, it was a cat. Anyway, it's a while ago, so nothing to worry about.'

Peter looked at her. 'Sure.'

Charlotte broke the uncomfortable silence. 'Peter, I'd really like to go away with you. Somewhere. Just the two of us.'

'That would be fabulous, but...'

'What is it? Don't you like the idea?'

Peter didn't know what to say.

'I thought we were, you know, getting close?' she said, welling up inside.

'We are. Don't you worry about that. It's just—I've had too many days off work and I can't really justify any more. Not at the moment, anyway.'

'Oh, I see. Well, I've sort of kind of booked it already.'

'Are you kidding?'

'Do you not like the idea?'

'Well... When is it?'

Charlotte kissed him. 'Next week!'

21

CHARLIE

The boutique hotel was nestled in the rolling countryside of the Cotswolds, next to a river and an arched stone bridge, where brown trout could easily be seen in the clear water. The banks were filled with yellow flag iris, offset by vivid green rushes and sweeping willow trees that dangled their leaf tips into the water.

After exploring their room, where they hugged each other intensely for the best part of ten minutes, Charlotte and Peter kissed before heading out of the door into the fresh air. It was one of those crisp, bright sunny days, cold to start, but dry and uplifting. Peter had worked out a route along the river within the Windrush Valley.

They walked along the bank and watched the various ducks dabbling and diving. Charlotte asked why many of the trees had been cut back so severely.

Peter loved that she was interested and explained how, traditionally, trees such as willow and hazel had been used for tools, weapons, fuel and to build houses and boats. Cutting them to the ground and allowing them to regrow was a sustainable way of making sure there would be plenty of their wood in the future.

'Coppicing was one of the first renewable energy sources, and completely environmentally friendly, since the dormouse makes use of this early growth for nesting and food. It's funny how Stone Age Man understood that, yet we're only just realising it now.' Peter chuckled to himself.

'Wow, that's interesting. I've seen similar trees in my woodland,' Charlotte replied. 'But why are these trees cut higher up?'

'It's simple. Deer will come and eat the new shoots, so cutting them above deer height combats that. It's called pollarding.'

Charlotte hooked her arm into his as they walked side by side and, with the sun on their faces, they watched the river flowing by.

'I can feel an incredible energy among these beech trees.'

'What can you feel?' asked Charlotte. Peter encouraged her to put her hands on the trunk of the largest one.

'There's something strong here. It's hard to explain, but I feel the trees want to give us their energy. It makes sense to me that they're the most grounded living thing. Their roots are deep in the earth and the energy they need to survive is immense.'

Charlotte pressed her body against the smooth silvery grey trunk. 'I know this tree. The roots of it form the staircase to my favourite place. Did you say beech?'

'Yes. *Fagus sylvatica* is the Latin name. Can you feel it?'

'I can feel something, but I'm not sure what. Do you think the energy comes into us?'

'Yes, of course. You're going to think I'm crazy, but I seem to breathe it in. It comes into my mouth and into my veins.'

Charlotte took a deep breath. 'I'm tingling and I can feel my heart racing. Is that it?'

Peter smiled. 'That's exactly it. Let it fill your body and mind.'

'Peter, I feel lightheaded, like I'm a little bit drunk.' She giggled and Peter noticed her eyes were open wide and bright.

'You're beautiful, you know that? So incredibly beautiful.'

'I don't know what's happening to me, Peter. I feel as though I have not a care in the world. That anything is possible. I feel fre-e-e-e...' She spun around and around. 'I'm free,' she shouted as she continued to spin wildly.

Peter grabbed her. 'Come on. I'll race you to the top.' He pointed to a grassy track leading up a steep hill in front of them. They raced to see who could get to the top first, playfully impeding each other and pulling each other back to gain an advantage. Peter took the lead and Charlotte threw a clump of grass at him; he pretended to fall over, giving her the lead. They laughed, and their minds and bodies became giddy with the fresh air and their new-found love.

Peter regained the lead and staggered to the top. Hands on knees, he caught his breath and then stood up straight.

'Hey, Charlie, come look at this.'

Charlotte came to his side and looked out across the magnificent countryside, stretching out before them as far as the eye could see.

'No one calls me Charlie.'

There was silence. The two of them stood rigid, looking out

across miles and miles of fields, forests and rivers to the distant dark silhouette of mountains beyond.

'No one calls me Charlie,' Charlotte repeated dogmatically.

Peter carried on, looking straight out at the view. 'I do,' he said. 'I do... I think I'm falling for you, Charlie. It's crazy. I don't really know who you are, but I'm hooked.'

Charlotte turned immediately to face him. 'I think I'm hooked too, Peter. It is crazy. But why not? We deserve it.'

Peter held out his arms and held her face with his hands. 'You're right, we do.'

She looked up into the sky and shouted, 'Crazy. We're both crazy!'

Peter laughed. 'What's wrong with the Charlie thing?'

Charlotte looked down at the ground. 'Nothing. It's just... you're the only person to see me for who I really am.'

With that, Peter grabbed her hand and started running down the hill.

'Come on, Charlie. Let's see who's quickest to the bottom.' Their feet barely kept up with their bodies as they ran hand in hand, laughing out loud, shouting their happiness to the whole world.

'Last one down is a big fat hairy goose,' Peter shouted, edging ahead.

Charlotte laughed. 'Wait! I don't want to be a hairy goose!'

Light was fading fast as they arrived back at the hotel. Peter gallantly tripped over a rock in order to gain the Hairy Goose title, and the dirt on his hands and knees was the reward for his bravery. The warm light in the leaded windows of the hotel was inviting. He opened the door, and they rushed into the lobby, where they were greeted by the hotel manager.

'Will you be joining us for dinner this evening, sir, madam?'

They were both starving after their walk and simultaneously answered, 'Yes, please!' then laughed like schoolchildren.

'Can we say 7.45? Give us a chance to shower and change,' Peter suggested.

'Change what?' Charlotte giggled. 'Partners?'

He smacked her on the bottom and chased her up the stairs to their room. Once there, he hurriedly tried to put the key in the lock and kept missing it. Charlotte started kissing his neck, which put him off even more.

'Just you wait till I get you inside, lass.' He finally unlocked the door, and they fell inside. It was warm and cosy; the maid had put the little lamp on, closed the curtains and sprinkled rose petals on the bed, but they didn't notice any of that. Peter unzipped Charlotte's coat, and she reciprocated.

'Well, Miss Charlie... what am I going to do with you, eh? Distracting me like that at the door.' He held her tight and kissed her gently on the lips. She responded passionately and began unbuttoning his checked shirt.

Peter pulled Charlotte's fleece and three other layers over her head to reveal her little lace bra. Her breasts were small and pert. Still in their walking boots and trousers, Peter pulled her close again and turned her around. He lifted her hair with one hand and kissed the back of her neck, working his way up, gently nibbling her ear, before running his tongue across her smooth skin to her shoulder.

Charlotte shuddered with pleasure as Peter touched her and teased her with his mouth. He moved across her back to her other shoulder, kissing and tasting her skin. Each time he touched a sensitive spot, her body, almost in shock, gave a jerk.

'Your skin is amazing and your shoulders so feminine,' he whispered as he kissed her neck and slowly undid her bra. The release of her breasts sent a shiver down her spine. She was starting to lose control, and she loved it.

He let her hair fall and, with his hand on her shoulder, turned her around. She felt vulnerable and powerless. So often she had to be sensible and 'proper' and 'in charge' of the household. Peter seemed to have the ability to take all that away. Her nipples touched his muscular chest; his hand supported her head and held her tight as they kissed frantically, lips wet, embroiled, immersed in a trance-like dance, their tongues entwined. He unbuttoned her trousers, still kissing, and their eyes met and held. Her trousers became loose. She loved that Peter seemed to know exactly what he was doing, skilful with his hands and not pausing with his kisses to undo a buckle or zip. He was confident, and she was happy to let him take control.

His hand was on her waist as her trousers fell away. He traced the lace of her black thong then moved his hand onto her bottom and pulled her in even tighter.

Relishing how hard he was against her, Charlotte continued their kiss. Their tongues tasted, licked and flicked. He occasionally bit her lip. She thought about how he instinctively knew how to touch her; he was strong but gentle, slow and respectful, not rushing, or heavy-handed, but purposeful and tender. Her heart raced with delight as she sensed herself becoming excited. She grabbed his belt and undid it, unbuttoning his jeans and letting them fall to the ground. Peter took her hair in one hand, lifted it off her skin and kissed her shoulder and neck again, while gently pulling. She gave a responsive gasp and felt his hardness trying to force itself out of his Calvins as she rubbed her hand against it. She'd wanted to know if he was as excited as she was, and he definitely was. The awkwardness of their trousers around their walking boots was swiftly dealt with as he sat her on the edge of the bed, kissed her, and gently pushed her back. He reassured her with kisses down her chest, running his tongue very close to her nipples, but just avoiding them. In so many of her previous encounters, the boys would just grab and suck like she was some sort of sex toy. Peter was different, so very different, and she craved more and more.

He ran his hands down each leg, kissing her skin at the same time; she hardly noticed that he'd taken off her boots and trousers. She lay down on the bed, vulnerable and available, and gazed at his broad chest and muscular arms as he removed his remaining outer clothes and positioned himself over her, his pants still constraining his eagerness.

He kissed her once on the lips and said softly, 'Are you OK?'

Charlotte looked deep into his eyes and nodded.

He wanted to be sure she was OK, and if she wasn't, he would stop. Charlotte knew this, and it made her even more hungry for his love. He had that perfect respect that enabled her to relax completely, and his tenderness and thoughtfulness were so very, very sexy.

Her entire body tingled as he picked her up and moved her into the middle of the bed. His eyes locked onto hers; he opened her legs with his hand, his gaze not flinching, pushed himself up and knelt between her in a press-up style. She felt the hairs on his forearms as she ran her hands up them to touch his muscles. She was in awe of his strength, and his manly body put all her senses on red alert. She felt he only had to kiss her one more time and she would orgasm.

Peter took one of her hands in his and their fingers locked together. He kissed each shoulder in turn. Her body shivered as he held her hand tightly. She could feel his breath as his little kisses moved down to her right nipple, his tongue and then his lips teasing around it, gently sucking; she gasped and gave a little squeal. Her left nipple was the more sensitive of the two and linked directly to her ultimate pleasure. It stood erect as she squirmed with intense pleasure; it began to verge on the uncomfortable, but he was able to ease off and then bring her back to the edge.

Wow. How he understood her body was beyond her. It was as if they'd known each other forever. Peter worked his tongue down further and further, her body twitching with delight as she anticipated the joy he was about to give her.

Their hands still interlocked, he kissed down to her hip and then lower, to the top of her leg. Breathing deeply, Charlotte let his fingers go and he used both hands to push her legs further apart, his kisses now gentle on her lace panties. Her heart seemed to skip a couple of beats as his tongue, barely touching her, ran up and down. She put her hands on his head to encourage him further, his curly black hair between her fingers intensifying her excitement.

He knelt on the floor, pulled her towards him with both arms and at the same time removed her thong. He repositioned his tongue and started stroking her gently down and up, barely touching, but she could feel everything intensely. He moved around, side to side, just occasionally flicking over her clit, then down again, pushing his tongue slightly into her. She gyrated her hips, synching with his movements, pushing his head into her with her hands.

His pace quickened, and the intensity drove a burning feeling inside her. She craved him on the button and angled herself so he couldn't avoid it. He gained momentum, down again and back up to break the agony. She could feel herself losing control and was completely at his mercy; she lay there with thoughts of blue eyes and the feel of his hair. She didn't know where to put her arms; her body writhed and bucked; his speed was perfect. His hand came up to her left nipple to stroke and toy with it. That was it.

That was it. She felt a rush of intensity; her blood seemed to boil inside her; he didn't stop, and then a calm came across her—the kind of calm you feel just before a storm, and then the release, like a bolt of lightning. She exploded with sheer ecstasy. Her body cramped and juddered; she let go of everything and gave herself to him; the sensation kept coming in waves of caramel, each one slightly less in intensity, but with each one a deeper love forming for him. He was perfect; he understood her body, and she wanted him inside her.

There was a beautiful calm as she lay there, unable to move —an inner peace, fulfilment and joy. Peter brought himself up so that their eyes met. He kissed her on the lips.

'I think we're late for dinner.' He laughed.

'I want you inside me,' she said impatiently.

'You'll have to wait, naughty girl. You can't have everything whenever you want.'

'You're driving me crazy.' She could have everything she wanted whenever she wanted, but for the first time, she was not in control, and she loved it.

'I want you inside me,' she said again.

Peter kissed her and then moved his hips into position. They kissed again, and he pushed inside. He felt solid and sure, and slowly he kept pushing and pushing until she could feel his entire length. He gently started to grind; she felt him on her G-spot and she started to well up inside. Her clit was stimulated, too. She touched the ridged muscles of his stomach with her hand. Hell, he was strong.

He pulled almost fully out and then in again and out, and

deep in and out and in and out... he was hitting every point spot on. 'Yes!' she cried. Utterly helpless, absorbed by his rhythm and ability, she felt the blood filling her chest, neck and head as exquisite feelings consumed her whole body.

He pushed in again, so deep, and moved his hips slowly and purposefully, stimulating everything, in particular the bit deep, deep inside, the holy grail. Most men she'd known went in like a steam train, in and out like a ramrod for their selfish needs, but Peter loved pleasing her; she could feel his sensitivity and his creative spirit, almost as though he was playing a delicate musical instrument—in tune with its body, skilful with his hands and committed to the music.

Charlotte wrapped her legs around him and he stayed deep inside, gyrating purposefully and slowly, but with a rhythm—a rhythm that seemed to open up so many hidden secrets from within her body and soul. He lowered his entire body onto her, his hands under her shoulders, supporting his weight on his elbows. He held her tight, and they were locked together in a bond which seemed to be nature itself.

He moved his head down to lick her left nipple and the molten lava within her started to build. This was it; she wanted to give him everything and she vocalised her intent. She tightened around his shaft and her chest and neck became red as the blood rushed from heart to brain and vice versa. She thought about his amazing control and stamina and she started to erupt. She wanted to be consumed by him; she wanted him, and then the point of no return—every nerve ending and every gorgeous feeling she had ever had all came together. Her mind seemed to explode as the volcano erupted. Her body jerked as he continued to hold her tight and jerked again as a second wave came through her. He seemed to be able to read her entire body and mind; still with the same movement, he thrust himself deeper and deeper. It was coming again; she couldn't control the ecstasy as a warm feeling of love and desire consumed her every thought and movement. She held on to him, signalling that she wanted him to come inside her, pulling the back of his curly hair as he reached a climax. His reaction seemed to trigger something else within her and she began once again to well up inside; her body jerked and writhed with complete fulfilment as he pushed one last time and released his love for her, his body twisting and bucking.

He kissed her as she held his face with her hand. She felt safe and reassured. He turned to lie on his back and held her tightly in his arms as she rested her head on his chest. 'Are you OK?' he said, in a gentle voice.

'Yes, in your arms.'

'You're safe and wanted,' he replied and squeezed her even tighter.

'What time is it?' Charlotte asked.

Peter looked at his phone. 'Flippin eck, it's nearly nine!'

The following morning, Charlotte awoke to nothing but the sound of Peter breathing quietly, close to her ear. It was one of the best nights' sleep she'd had in years.

'Peter, I've been thinking.'

'Mmm?'

'I'd really like you to come and visit me in Oxfordshire. At the family house. Loxley. I could show you the trees there.'

Without opening his eyes, Peter slurred his response. 'Yeah, sure. No problem.' Then, after a moment of silence, 'When?'

'The weekend after next?' she said optimistically.

Peter thought about it then turned to her. He examined her

face. 'How can I refuse?' he said, lifting his hand to her hair and running his fingers from front to back. Charlotte shuddered and moved her head away abruptly.

'What's wrong?'

'I don't know. Nothing.'

'You seem agitated.'

'It's the fingers in the hair thing. I'm not used to that. It feels strange.'

Peter rolled onto his back. 'God you're complex. I used to love Mum doing that to me.'

22

LOXLEY

It was the early evening when Peter drove up the grand drive, through the trees and out into the parkland. He was expecting to see a little cottage or gatehouse where Charlotte might live, but nothing materialised. The imposing stately home came into view as he crossed over the humpback bridge. It made Downton Abbey look like a three-bed semi.

'No way is this the place,' he thought. 'It must be a hotel.' As he approached, he was unsure where to park. There was none of the usual hotel parking/reception signage. But right on cue, Cartwright appeared and indicated he was to park right by the majestic front door.

He escorted Peter into the cavernous entrance hall. Peter gazed around at the huge paintings, tapestries and sword displays on the wall, and in particular the four olive trees positioned in gigantic earthenware pots. The air smelled of antique opulence with a hint of the Mediterranean. Charlotte appeared from a side door, dressed in skinny jeans and a jumper with a dragonfly across the front.

'Peter, come through. It's so good to see you.' She took his hand and led him into the sitting room, where a log fire was burning in the biggest fireplace Peter had ever seen. They passed an immaculately polished grand piano and Peter stopped to look at the photograph on top.

'Is that you?' he asked, peering at a young girl and a gentleman.

'Yes. With my father. It was taken here on his birthday. I was ten.'

'He looks like a nice guy,' Peter commented.

'His heart was in the right place,' she replied, with a hint of sourness in her expression.

They hugged in front of the fire.

Peter eyed the imposing portrait of her father above them. 'Is this your father's house?'

'No... As I said, I lost him a few years ago now. On my sixteenth birthday, to be exact.'

Peter held her tight. 'He died on your birthday? I lost my mum on my birthday too.'

'Really?'

'I was thirteen.'

'What about your father?'

'I never knew him.'

'I remember.'

There was a silence as they squeezed each other. Then Charlotte wiped a tear on Peter's shoulder.

'We are similar, aren't we? I mean, different, but similar.'

Peter took half a step back, breaking the hug, then lifted both his hands, brushed back Charlotte's hair and held her face. 'We deserve to be loved. Both of us. We've suffered the same loss, but the most important thing is, we know how to love.' With that, their lips came together, and they kissed with their hearts.

Charlotte was the first to break away. 'I've arranged for coffee on the veranda and then I thought we could take a walk.'

'That would be great. I saw some stunning old trees on my way in. Who owns the land? Is it National Trust?'

Charlotte giggled. 'No, Peter. I own it.'

'What! The parkland and the trees and…?'

'Yes, everything.'

Peter said nothing, just raised his eyebrows slightly.

The smell of fresh croissants and coffee beckoned them onto the veranda, where Charlotte chatted more about the house and showed Peter old and weathered maps from when Capability Brown had first conceived the design.

'Shall we walk together? You can teach me more about the trees.'

Peter peered over his map. 'I'd like that.'

The morning blue skies gave way to a blustery afternoon, with light clouds flitting fast across the sun and forming great shadows over the estate parkland as far as the eye could see. They walked arm in arm down to the river. The bullrushes waved in the breeze and a pair of great-crested grebe bobbed and dived together, just out from the bank. Peter picked up a flat stone from the little stony beach and skimmed it effortlessly on the top of the water, where it plopped into the depths.

Charlotte picked up a stone, too. 'Can you show me?'

'It's a bit too square, that one.' He scanned the beach for a more suitable skimmer. 'Here, try this.' He gave her a flattened, rounded pebble. 'Have you skimmed a stone before?'

She shook her head, then proceeded to try to throw it as

she would a frisbee. It plummeted immediately. Peter rooted around again to find another suitable projectile. He chose a stone which would fit perfectly into her hand and was heavy enough to provide speed, yet light enough to bounce. He put it into her hand, came behind her and guided her arm back and out to the side, his other arm around her waist to stabilise her. She twisted her head to look back at him. She could feel how strong and in control he was. She wasn't thinking about the stone. She was thinking about his groin pushing into her bottom.

'What you need to do is hold the stone firmly and curl this finger around the top, so you can release it spinning.' He positioned her finger on the stone. She wasn't listening. She was thinking how private it was down by the river, and how his control and strength made her feel entirely defenceless and vulnerable.

'Are you concentrating?'

'Oh, yes, sorry. I throw and spin, is that right?'

'Yes, and you need to get down almost level with the water, like this.' He held her tightly as he crouched down with her to get a good stance. Then he stepped back to let her throw. Charlotte put her finger exactly where he had said and spun the stone as she released it towards the water.

One skip, two skips, then three and a fourth.

'Yes,' she shouted. 'You're a brilliant teacher.' She flung her arms around him. 'Come on, I want to show you something.' She grabbed Peter by the hand and led him along the river. 'It's a bit of an adventure.'

'Where are we going?'

They ran along the water's edge, navigating the badger set.

'Hello, badgers,' Charlotte sang as she skipped along.

Together they negotiated the steep bank into the woods and down towards the lake.

'This is it,' she said proudly.

'Wow, that's a fabulous tree.'

'No one knows about this place. It's my special hideaway.'

'This is a very old tree, and in such good condition.'

Charlotte smiled. 'How old, do you think?'

'From the size of the trunk and the long, long branches, easily 300 years.' He stroked his chin. 'Maybe even older.'

'I measured it to be 290.'

'Well, I think you're a genius,' he said, poking the trunk with a stick.

'I always knew that,' she said, laughing, and grabbed hold of the rope to pull the swing towards her. 'It's a wise old tree, for sure.' She climbed onto the seat and pushed with her legs.

Peter stood, looking with wide eyes, taking in the picture postcard of a beautiful woman, in her favourite place, happy and carefree. He watched her swing back and forth and took a mental photograph of the whole scene. A snapshot he never wanted to forget.

He walked up to the swing, and as Charlotte swung back, he pushed her gently. She laughed as she felt him push.

'Faster!' she shouted. Her legs were flung up in the air and her hair flew in the swinging breeze as he pushed her harder and harder. She sang at the top of her voice and laughed and laughed.

Peter stood proudly behind her, his heart filled with warmth, his mind filled with desire. He held off the pushes and stepped back to run his hands over the trunk of the tree, feeling its rough, fissured bark, and came across an indentation. Examining further with his fingers, one by one, he found a set of carved letters. He smiled a huge smile.

Charlie.

He ran his finger across each letter. Charlotte hadn't seen him and was still swinging and singing, lost in her own world of joy and happiness. An overwhelming flush of something amazing filled his body from toe to head. She was Charlie—his Charlie. She was perfect, he knew. She obviously had an affinity with the tree, he could feel it, and seeing her so happy gave him a sense of belonging—and also a responsibility to keep her safe and well.

Suddenly Charlotte called out as something fell into her lap.

'It's a gnarl!' She stopped swinging. 'Peter, it's a gnarl. I call them gnarls. What on earth is it?' She showed him the deformed, weirdly shaped acorn, with spines and bumps in green and red.

Peter laughed. 'It's an oak gall, but I love the word gnarl.' He took it from her hand. 'The gall wasp buries inside to lay its eggs and a chemical reaction creates this amazing deformity. The incredible thing is that they were used in the making of ink for writing. In history, many manuscripts and books, like Shakespeare's plays, the Magna Carta and other important documents, were all written using gall ink.' He handed it back to Charlotte.

'God, you are so sexy,' she said.

'Have you ever climbed to the top of a tree like this?' Peter asked.

'I've always dreamt of climbing to the top,' she replied optimistically. 'To be able to feel the tree's movement and share the view it sees.' She jumped onto the swing and tried to clamber up one of the ropes.

'I have some climbing ropes and harnesses in the pickup.'

She gasped. 'Do you think we can get up to the top?'

He nodded. 'If you have the will, I can teach you.'

'You are amazing. Can we do it this afternoon?'

'Sure.'

～

Peter fastened Charlotte into a harness and pulled a long, brightly coloured rope out of a bag. It looked like the sort of rope a rock climber would use.

She stood admiring his manly physique and his capable hands as he manipulated the equipment.

'The first thing we have to do is get this rope over the first branch so we can climb to that one and then progress higher and higher. The important thing is to stay attached to the rope and the tree at all times. We have to trust the rope, but more importantly, we have to trust the tree. Nature is powerful. You just have to trust. OK?'

She nodded. 'OK.'

Peter gathered the end of the rope and began to tie a knot. 'The best way to throw the rope, so that it unfolds back to us after it's gone over the branch, is with this hangman's knot. It's almost identical to ones they would have used back in the day, but instead of thirteen wraps around itself followed by a loop, we just use eight or nine.'

Charlotte examined the rope. 'Why not the full thirteen?'

'So it's not too heavy to throw and, with nothing in the noose, so it will unravel and the end will fall back to us.'

'Do we attach ourselves to the end?'

Peter smiled. 'Exactly. You're a fast learner.'

Charlotte kissed him on his cheek.

Peter threw the knot over the lowest branch and, as planned, it unravelled back to him. He tugged down on the line. 'Remember, you have to trust the rope,' he said, pulling it off the branch. 'Here, you have a go.' He handed Charlotte the end.

She got to work forming the knot and, after a little assistance from Peter, she felt confident. 'So, this adds weight to the line so we can throw it?' she asked.

'One hundred per cent, and it's easy to tie when we need to do it further up, too. Tie it one more time, so I know you've got it, and then have a go at getting it over the branch.'

Charlotte assembled the rope with precision and, on the second attempt, managed to get it over the branch and the knot to unravel. She jumped up and down with joy.

'If you're that excited on the ground, wait till we get you to the top.' Peter chuckled as he tied the end to her harness and secured her for the climb.

Throw after throw, and thrust after thrust, the pair slowly worked their way up, one branch at a time. Peter made sure all Charlotte's knots were safe, and eventually they arrived among the highest tips of the tree. He installed a second safety line, just to make sure she was completely secure, and then pushed her up so she could put her foot on a sturdy branch and get a good view of the estate.

Charlotte could feel the tree moving back and forth beneath her in the breeze.

'It feels like it's twisting, Peter.' She held his arm.

'Yes. All trees are designed to flex and twist. It's their way of dealing with stress—high winds and snow, that kind of thing.'

Charlotte stood straight and looked around her. 'Wow, Peter, this is amazing. I think I can see my friend Emma's house over there on the hill—yes, I can see her horse in the field, and look, there's the church spire in the village.' They stood together, surveying the land and breathing in the feeling of great achievement.

She turned to Peter. 'You know, my shrink says there are five steps to well-being. One: be active. Two: learn something. Three: give something. Four: connect. And five: take notice.'

'Wise words.'

'You've given me all those, Peter. We've climbed a tree— God knows how you managed to get me up here. I've learned so much from you, I've given you my trust and possibly my heart.' She giggled. 'We've connected with this amazing piece of nature and being up here looking out at this bird's-eye view has shown me how to take notice.' She took in and relished the fresh air. 'Thanks, Peter. You've made me forget all my worries.'

He laughed. 'You don't need a shrink if you can climb trees.'

'You're right. Somehow, you've made me feel free again,' she said, smiling.

Peter smiled back. 'Well, I've learned something too, and if you don't kiss me right now, I'm not going to show you how to get down.'

23

YOU'RE A GRAND LASS

Peter received a call from Gran to say that Grandad had fallen off his bike. He'd had a 'minor' collision with the number 71 bus, and he was in the hospital. And that Peter 'really should see him.'

'I've had some bad news about my grandad. It sounds as if it could be quite serious.'

'Oh, dear. I hope he's alright. Where is he?'

'He's in Sheffield Royal Infirmary. The ambulance took him straight there. I really do have to see him.'

Charlotte held his hand. 'Of course. How long will it take you to get there?'

'About three hours. Do you want to come with me?'

Charlotte took a minute to think about it. 'Yes. Yes, I really do. I'll get Cartwright to drive us.'

'No. I'll drive,' said Peter urgently. 'Grab some things and let's get off as soon as possible.'

Peter's old Toyota pickup had seen better days. Arborists are not renowned for pristine vehicles. He gathered the empty crisp packets and water bottles from the footwell and attempted to brush the dust and bits of twig and leaves from the passenger seat with his hand.

'Fit for a queen,' he said.

Charlotte laid her shawl on the seat and immediately asked for the heating to be put on max.

'The heater doesn't work too well after I took it through a ford a few months ago. The water was almost up to the windows,' Peter added enthusiastically.

Charlotte attempted to smile and manoeuvred an empty Coke can which kept rolling out from under the seat.

'I'm glad you're coming with me.'

'It feels right somehow.' She put her hand on his knee. 'You supported me, I support you.'

'Yea. It feels right. You know, I'm glad I met you.'

Charlotte smiled.

'I guess I've done a lot of processing since Mum died. I felt abandoned and let down. Gran and Grandad have been amazing, but I think I shied away from relationships in the past because I was worried I'd be let down again.'

Charlotte squeezed his knee.

'The thing is... I'm having fun with you. I loved it when you were in the tree with me. To share things like that is... special.' He looked at her and smiled. 'I guess you've broken me out of my rut. Made me think I could share my life with someone. Someone who isn't going to... you know.'

'I could say the same thing about you. Do you think I haven't felt let down? You're different from most people. Grounded and in touch with your feelings. You say things as they are. And you're not a bad kisser, either.'

'That's the only reason you're with me, isn't it?' he said, laughing.

'I'm also having fun, and you let me be me. Charlie. I like that.'

He looked at her again. 'Maybe we're good for each other, then?'

'Maybe?'

On arriving at the hospital, they found Gran having a little nap in the chair beside Grandad's bed. Peter's heart sank when he saw Grandad hooked up to a bleeping monitor. He had huge bruises on his chin and right cheek, but at least he was alive.

Charlotte asked Peter if he wanted her to stay, and he nodded. He reached for two chairs and, as he did so, the nurse came over.

'Alreet, tha must be t'grandson?' she said, in her broad Yorkshire accent.

'Yes. How is he? It looks bad,' Peter asked.

'Well, e's 'ad a reet old shock and we think e's brocken his ip,' the nurse said, looking unsure. 'He'll 'ave X-ray later and we can 'ave a better look. Tha knows e's on t'morphine reet now and e's bin in a lot of pain.'

Peter leaned over the bed and had a closer look as the nurse disappeared.

Charlotte looked at his grandad, too, and said, 'What on earth did she say? I didn't understand a word of it.'

'She said he's had a right old shock and they think he's broken his hip. He's on morphine now and in a lot of pain. They're going to X-ray him later.'

'Oh!'

At that point, Gran woke from her doze. She must have been there all afternoon. 'Peter, am I glad to see you? Look what the old bugger has gone and done.' She gave him a hug.

'Gran, this is Charlotte.'

'Pleased to meet you, love. Is he treating you well?' Gran

was putting on her posh voice, like she always did on the telephone or with anyone new. 'He's told me a bit about you. Is this your first time to Yorkshire?'

'Erm, no. I came to the Barbara Hepworth exhibition in Wakefield last year.'

'Well, that's Peter's home town, Wakefield, and you can see why Barbara buggered off to Cornwall, can't you? The cathedral's nice, but that's about it.' She laughed. Gran had a wickedly sharp sense of humour, and it was welcome. They needed something to brighten the mood.

Charlotte tweaked Peter's arm. 'I'm just going to get some coffee. I'll give you a little time together. Do you want any?'

Gran smiled. 'No, I'm fine love. You know where you're going?'

'I'll follow the signs,' she said.

'She seems nice, Peter,' Gran said after she'd gone. 'All posh. She ever been in an NHS place before?'

Peter raised an eyebrow. 'I doubt it, Gran.' They both looked at the door she'd just walked through and had a chuckle.

Peter's grandad turned his head to look at him. 'Peter, my lad.' His voice was croaky and you could tell he was sedated. Peter took his hand and his grandad squeezed it.

'Hello, Grandad. Do you think it might be time to finally park the bike up now?'

Grandad sighed and closed his eyes. Peter knew he would be reluctant to give up his freedom.

Gran was rooting in her bag, and as Peter stepped back, she thrust a couple of £20 notes into his hand. 'That's for taking the trouble.'

'Gran!' said Peter. He stuffed them back into her hand. The

ward door opened and in walked Charlotte, looking a little shaken.

'It's like a war zone out there! People on stretchers in the corridor and in the lift, and most of the visitors look they need treatment too. And I can't understand a word anyone is saying.'

Peter and Gran looked at each other.

Gran broke the silence. 'Don't worry, love, they're all on the waiting list. Did you find a coffee? Because they say you're better off having the tea here.'

Charlotte looked puzzled. 'Well, I had to get it out of a machine.'

Grandad's monitor started to go crazy; the bleeping seemed to quicken as he turned his head to see who'd come in.

Peter held his hand again. 'Grandad, this is Charlotte.'

She tentatively leaned over. 'Hello. Pleased to meet you.'

Grandad smiled at her. His eyes were blue. There was a bit of Peter in his eyes and in his appearance. 'I do hope you're going to get better soon,' she said.

Grandad looked at her face, then at Peter, and then back at Charlotte. 'By all accounts, you're a grand lass. Look after him, won't you?'

24

007

'What's a grand lass?'

'It means they liked you. A good girl, you know?'

'Oh!' She placed her hand on his knee. 'You love them dearly, don't you?'

'I owe them everything,' he said, placing his hand on hers. 'I'm worried Grandad hasn't got long. He seems weak. They have nothing, really, but they're always the first to give. Their love, I mean.'

'They obviously have people to look after them at home?'

Peter huffed. 'Nope. They're proud people. They'd refuse it, anyway.'

'Why are they so stubborn?'

'They're not stubborn. It's the working-class way. You owe no one anything and you survive. That's it.'

Charlotte appeared puzzled. 'I don't understand why people just don't pay for someone to help them, and why so many people were queuing at the hospital.'

'You really are detached from reality, aren't you?'

Charlotte replied quickly, 'That's not fair. I know what it's like to suffer.'

'With all due respect, you don't have a clue what it's like to sleep in a cold bed shivering because you haven't the money for heating, or go without food so your children can eat.'

'It's not the 1800s, Peter.'

'Tell that to the people who work sixteen-hour days in a café, waiting tables for a pittance. You're way off here, Charlotte. Those people weren't queuing at the hospital because they wanted to. It's the National Health Service. They have no money to buy private.'

'Peter, everyone can heat their houses. It's a basic need.'

'The miners and their families used to get free coal and then they stopped it. Unemployment in some areas is massive. The steel industry, manufacturing, textiles, the things which have kept Yorkshire strong are virtually all gone, and you think people want to sit in the cold for the fun of it?'

Charlotte sat quietly and Peter could sense the air thickening. 'Look, I'm not trying to have a go, just saying it as it is. As I said, we're proud people.'

'You scare me a little when you talk like that. As if you're against me. Other people have problems too, you know. Like having parents who didn't love them and feeling lonely and trapped. Money can't help with that.'

'OK. I'm sorry. I don't want to upset you. It's just the truth. We all have issues. No one's better or worse than anyone else.'

'Do you really think I'm detached from reality?'

'Maybe we're good for each other. Maybe we both have skewed views of the world, because of what we've been through?'

'Stay at mine tonight, Peter. I'll feel lonely without you. We can hold each other tight. I'd like that very much.'

'I'd like that too.' He glanced over. 'I get lonely too, you know.'

'Losing Father was a tremendous shock and I'm worried about Mother, too. Some days I feel like I've lost her. She's not well at all.'

'That must be hard. But what about Lucy? I would imagine children are good company, aren't they?'

'She's at boarding school most of the time, but I do feel guilty sending her there and I'd love to have her around more.'

'Well, why don't you put her in a local school? Sounds like a no-brainer to me.'

Charlotte dabbed at her cheek with a handkerchief. 'It's not as simple as that, Peter. You don't understand.'

'Sounds simple to me. Is she happy there?'

'No, not really.'

'So she's not happy and you're not happy? I'm no brain surgeon, but you could change that and make things better for everyone.'

'Peter, please. My father wouldn't want it. It's a family tradition, and she's heading for Cambridge, like me.'

Peter shook his head. 'Maybe we really are from different worlds.'

The following morning, Peter was woken by a soft kiss on his shoulder as Charlotte pushed her naked body against him.

'You make me so happy,' she said. 'I was thinking about our chat last night. There are things you don't understand about my life, just like the things I don't understand about yours. But somehow, you seem brave and make sense of this crazy world.'

Peter smiled.

'I've waited a long time for a man like you. I've made up my mind. Come on, I have something to show you.'

'What time is it?'

'Six o'clock. Come on.'

'What's happened to you? What do you mean, you have something to show me? Have you booked it with Cartwright?' Peter added, with a deadpan expression.

'What do you mean?'

'Never mind. Come on, then. You've got me all excited now.' He rolled over and straddled Charlotte with his arms, his body hovering above hers, and kissed her smack on the lips. Charlotte smiled a big smile and gazed into his eyes.

Peter pushed himself into the air and jumped out of bed. He started running around the room naked, pretending to be a youthful and victorious track runner.

'Come on, then, what is it?' he cried. 'I can't stay lying in bed all day like you, you lazy thing.'

They both laughed. Charlotte looked at him, admiring his physique and smile. 'You're mad, you know that?'

'Yes, I am,' he said, doing naked star jumps and running vigorously on the spot.

'Mad... mad, mad, mad, *mad*!' She grinned from ear to ear.

They both slipped on their clothes and Charlotte headed down the grand wooden staircase, leading Peter by the hand. She led him out across the gravel yard to a half-timbered, double-fronted garage.

'Where are we going?' Peter asked.

Charlotte opened one of the large oak doors. It was dark inside, and it took a while for Peter's eyes to adjust to the light. Then Charlotte stood directly in front of him, blocking his view.

'I've waited a long time for this moment,' she said. 'I've had this a while and have saved it for a man who deserves it.'

She reached out and switched on the light, then stepped aside.

Peter stood rigidly on the spot. His eyes followed the classic curves of the car in front of him, all the way from the gleaming spoked wheels to the polished chrome lights. The huge silvery-blue bonnet protruded like a whale.

'Do you like it?' Charlotte stroked her hand elegantly along the vehicle.

Peter didn't say a word.

'You don't like it,' she said, with a hint of disappointment. 'You don't like it, do you?'

Peter was unable to move his feet. The confusion in his mind made him feel queasy and his breathing became rapid.

'It's lovely. A beautiful car.'

'Aston Martin DB5 1961. It needs insurance. I'll get Cartwright on it right now. It's yours. Peter?'

Peter's eyes narrowed. He looked at the immaculate body-work and inside at the perfect leatherwork. He'd never seen anything so masculine and yet so feminine, the perfect combi-nation of manly power and delicate refinement.

Charlotte leaned on the bonnet by the passenger door. 'You don't like it, do you?'

'It's stunning,' he replied. 'Do you not use her?'

'She's yours, Peter. I love her, but she's more of a man's car, and I have my little soft-top. Get in and get a feel for her.'

Peter hesitantly pulled the door handle. It felt solid in his hand. He slid into the driver's side, grasped the leather steering wheel and pushed his body back into the seat. It hugged him like it was made for him; no adjustments were needed, and he gently ran his fingers over the dash in front of him. Although the engine was off, he positioned his foot on the accelerator.

Charlotte jumped in excitedly beside him. 'She suits you, handsome man,' she said.

Peter turned his head towards her. 'She's beautiful. Really beautiful,' he said again.

He turned back to face the front, his eyes fixed ahead. In his mind he was driving the two of them around the hairpin bends of the Amalfi coast. He could picture the car holding tight into the corners as they sped effortlessly through the hills, the blue sky and sunlight accentuating every curve of the vehicle and the wind blowing Charlotte's hair and delicate dress high up her slender legs, her red stilettos contrasting with the car's trim.

He gripped the steering wheel tighter and, without looking at Charlotte, said, 'She's not for me.' His eyes stayed focused. 'I can't have this car... I'm not worthy of such an item.' He vigorously grabbed the door handle and in one move, pushed open the door, climbed out, and headed outside.

'Peter! Peter! What's wrong?' Charlotte cried. 'Peter, wait... What's wrong? Don't you like her?'

She tugged at his arm as he hastened his pace. She tugged again, and he pulled his arm forcefully away.

'Peter, you're scaring me. I've never seen you like this. Please... stop and tell me why you're being like this.'

He came to a sudden halt and turned to face her. 'I saved every penny I had, did two paper rounds and a milk round at the same time and worked twelve-hour days in my first proper job to buy my first car—a clapped-out green Fiesta with no radio or heating, and the rain leaked in through the door. I've never really had much better than that since, and here I am sitting in the driver's seat of a classic sports car, which I just don't deserve. I'm sorry, it doesn't fit well in my mind. You can't just give me something like that. I don't want to be bought like some sort of... commodity.'

Charlotte started to cry. 'Peter... I'm... I'm not trying to buy you... I thought we could have adventures together in the car, just you and me, adventures without a care. I always knew you were coming, and I saved her for you. Please... I want you to have her, with all my love.' She sobbed uncontrollably and put her hand on his chest.

'I'm sorry, Charlotte. I can't have the car and that's the end of it.'

25

DIAMONDS AND HANDBAGS

'I'm sorry, I have to go now,' Peter said. 'I have to do some work for a change.'

'Did I upset you about the car? I didn't mean to. I thought every man dreamed of being James Bond.'

'It's not you, Charlotte. It's... just the car. It brings back very unhappy memories. I'm sorry. I don't want to look ungrateful.'

They kissed and hugged.

At that moment, the Bentley entered the drive and began its approach.

'Sorry I didn't get to meet your mother.'

'She's ill, Peter. I'll know when the time is right. Anyway, it seems you're about to meet my daughter.'

'I thought we agreed at least six months before we meet?'

'It wasn't the plan, but here we are,' Charlotte said, with a raised eyebrow.

Cartwright opened the door and Lucy stepped out. 'I'll bring your bags through,' he said, in his usual reassuring voice.

'Thanks, Carters!'

On seeing her mother, Lucy ran up and flung her arms around her. 'Mummy, I've missed you so much. Where's Vincent? Can we go shopping? Can we, can we?'

She squeezed so tight, Charlotte squealed. 'Just slow down a minute. We have all weekend. No rush. Anyway, this is Peter.' She gestured with her hand towards him.

'Hello,' Lucy said with a polite smile. 'Can we go shopping now?'

'It's nice to meet you too. What are you wanting to buy?'

Lucy didn't reply, but instead looked at him with contempt.

'Let's have some lunch and see how we go. Peter, you'll stay, won't you?'

'No. I have things to take care of. You have a great shopping trip.'

The table was set in the conservatory. The silverware and crockery, with the family crest, formed a splendid sight as the midday sun warmed the room.

Cartwright entered with two bowls of soup and placed them on the table. 'Madam, I have a message from Mira. She's running a little late and will join you after lunch for "the girls' shopping trip".'

Charlotte nodded and thanked him, and Lucy began slurping her soup. 'Are we shopping for more puppies?'

'No, Lucy. Vincent is enough to handle as it is. I have other plans. I thought we'd go up to London. I feel like we all need a bit of cheering up.'

Mira eventually arrived and the three of them put on their coats and headed out to the car, where Cartwright was waiting. He drove into the centre of London and pulled up outside a place on New Bond Street. He opened the car door, and the head of sales, a smart, extremely thin Frenchwoman, was waiting. She invited them in and handed Charlotte and Mira glasses of champagne.

'Good afternoon, ladies. What are we looking for today? Anything special?'

Charlotte took a sip from her glass. 'Good afternoon, Monique. How are you?'

'I'm well, thank you. Point out anything that takes your fancy and we'll bring it to you. Bags, jewellery, perhaps?'

'Everything,' Charlotte replied. 'I'm particularly looking for a special necklace for an engagement I have coming up.'

Lucy and Mira immediately started examining the handbags.

The ladies spent three hours in the shop and had various items brought down for their perusal. Charlotte settled on a necklace with a round, five-carat diamond centrepiece and fifty-one other diamonds along its length.

'My treat to myself,' she said, smiling.

Lucy coveted a leather handbag with a hand-stitched flower motif and diamond earrings, and Mira was enquiring about a small clutch bag in green suede.

'Have them, girls, if you like them. I have the best daughter and friend anyone could wish for, and everything feels really good at the moment.' Charlotte gestured to Monique. '*Nous allons prendre les trois articles, merci.*'

The staff immediately set about wrapping their purchases, boxing them ready to be taken away there and then. All three women had smiles as big as the moon as they got into the car, where they collapsed on the rear seat with exhaustion.

'Everyone happy?' asked Charlotte.

'Yes,' they replied.

'So, I hear the new man has his feet under the table,' Mira said, after a brief silence. 'Are you picking up all the waifs and strays now?'

'What do you mean?'

'I mean, first the dog, and then a Yorkshireman. And by all accounts, they're both a little moth-eaten around the ears.'

Charlotte couldn't believe what she was hearing. 'Mira. How could you say such a thing? You haven't even met him.'

'I know. I wondered why you were hiding him. Anyway, rumour is, he's not the goody-two-shoes you think he is.'

'What do you mean?'

'It's nothing. Just some gossip about a criminal conviction.'

'I can't believe you're being so hurtful. You know I'm growing very fond of him. He's different, and he's thoughtful and... he makes me feel wanted and loved.'

Mira and Lucy looked at each other.

'Of course darling, of course. And I bet he doesn't need any money, either?'

26

I JUST SAW A RAT

Peter had still heard nothing from his landlord about the leaking skylight, and now there was a damp patch and a musty smell in the corner by the fridge. He was keen to get out and find somewhere with more than one room—a flat that wasn't north-facing and might allow the sunlight in. He'd neglected his work somewhat since meeting Charlotte and it was time to knuckle down and increase his potential to rent a new, healthier place.

Putting on a pair of freshly cleaned jeans and a casual sweater, he took his watch from the bedside table and noticed it was five minutes slow. He pulled out the tiny winding knob and set it to the correct time. At that moment, his phone suddenly started to ring, which startled him, and before he could get the watch on his wrist, it fell in slow motion to the hard floor. The glass face smashed and the tiny knob broke away. Peter then stepped back and accidentally bent the casing with his shoe.

'Shit!' He looked at the broken pieces on the floor.

'Peter.'

'Oh, is it you?'

'That's not a pleasant way to say hello.'

'Sorry. I just broke my watch.'

'Peter! I need to see you.'

'Really? What is it?' he said, picking up the pieces with his free hand.

'It's just a nagging query I have. What's the address?'

Peter continued to look at the broken pieces of the watch his grandad had given him. 'No need to come here. Just ask me.'

'No Peter. What's the address?'

'51b Park Square.'

'I'm on my way. I'll be twenty minutes.'

Peter immediately sprang into action. He bundled all his dirty washing and set the machine to 'get this done ASAP'. His bedding followed, and out came his box of dusters, cleaning cloths and bleach. Oh my god, the bathroom! Everything needed a good bottoming. He dumped the towels by the washing machine and then realised there wouldn't be time to wash and dry them, so instead he bundled them into a bin liner and stuffed them under the bed. The strategically placed books and pan, which were collecting the dripping water, would have to remain in place as long as possible. It had just stopped raining, so it would be unlikely to pour in when she arrived.

The twenty minutes seemed to disappear as quickly as the bleach down each plug hole, and just as he was fluffing some cushions and watering his pot plant, he received a call from Charlotte.

'Peter, I think I'm here, but can't work out where you are. Is it a flat? There are some very large bins and I'm sure I just saw a rat, and there's a dark set of steps.'

'Hi, gorgeous. Yes, I'm up those steps. Don't worry, I'll come down and meet you. Two minutes.' He quickly removed the pan from the floor and poured the contents into the sink, placed the books on the coffee table and did a final check of the room. Before he descended the stairs, he glanced at the pieces of broken watch. His heart sank. It looked unrepairable.

Charlotte walked into the flat and something crunched under her foot. 'What's that?'

'What's what?' Peter was hoping it wasn't a pair of stray pants from under his bed.

'Sounds like glass.' She looked down at the floor. 'What is it?'

'It's the watch I was telling you about. It was my grandad's. He gave it to me as a present on my twenty-first. I'm gutted. It meant a lot to me.'

Charlotte was distracted by something dripping on her head. 'What was that?'

Peter looked up at the botched skylight. 'It's just a bit of internal irrigation. It means I never have to water the plants,' he added, hoping she could see the funny side.

'And what's that on the wall?' She pointed to a rusty black metal box.

'That's the electric meter.'

'What do you mean?'

'Well, you put money in it and electricity comes out.'

'Really?'

'It's still rationed out here. Too many people stealing it.' He laughed.

'Peter, I don't know whether or not to believe you. Why do you stay here?'

He shoved the broken watch pieces into a drawer. 'It's just a stopgap. You know. While I get my business up and running.'

Charlotte felt another drip of water hit her shoe. 'Is there somewhere we can go to talk? A little café perhaps? Without internal irrigation?'

The walk to the café felt uneasy. But the café was cute and there was a leather sofa, which Charlotte bagged. Peter uncomfortably ordered two coffees and joined her.

'What is it?' he asked.

'I need to ask you something. It's been preying on my mind. Something Mira said to me.'

'Mira?'

'Yes. I don't know how to put this. I thought I was getting to know you and then...'

'What is it?'

'She said that you had a conviction. That you weren't an honest man. Please tell me this isn't true?'

Peter bowed his head. 'She's right.'

Charlotte stared at him in disbelief. 'So, you're a criminal?'

He looked up. 'Well, technically, yes. But it was a long time ago. Something I regret.'

'No shit!' Charlotte said, looking stern.

Peter quizzed her with raised eyebrows.

'They say that in Yorkshire. Don't you know?'

He squirmed in his seat. 'I was a boy. I didn't realise what I was doing. I punched another lad. He said my mum was a prostitute.'

'And was she?' Charlotte replied.

'Of course not. He taunted me. She was the kindest, loveliest, most warm-hearted woman in the world. There's one thing

I know for sure. He was evil. You could see it in his eyes. If it wasn't me he was picking on, it was some other poor soul. I reacted badly, but he needed putting in his place.'

'So that gave you a criminal record?'

'Well, that and stealing a rose for my mum's grave.'

'A rose?'

'I needed her. My mum. I was young.'

Charlotte put her hand on his shoulder. 'Oh, Peter. You have been silly.'

'I know that.'

'As long as there isn't anything else?'

He shook his head. They simultaneously sipped their coffees.

'That's a relief. I have to be able to trust everyone around me. Do you understand?'

'Of course I do. And likewise.'

'Can we get back to where we were?'

'Nothing's changed for me.'

'Good.'

They kissed and the tension in Charlotte's shoulders dropped.

'I have something else to ask you,' she said. 'I'm heading out to the Austrian Alps for a friend's birthday party and some skiing, and I would really love you to accompany me. I want you to be by my side. Show you off to all my friends. Have you skied before?'

'Skiing? No. I've seen it on TV, but I'm no Eddie the Eagle. I like the bobsleigh, though.'

'Don't worry. Perhaps you could just come out for the last four days? I'll have had enough of skiing by then. There's a bobsleigh track right in the town.'

'You're kidding.'

'No. I think it was the Olympic track years ago.'

'Look, it all sounds amazing, but I'm not sure I can afford it and I don't even have any kit.'

'You are silly. You'll stay with me. I'll book you a private jet. It's the easiest way to get there with no fuss.'

'A private jet?' Peter thought he'd misheard her.

'Yes. You'll have to get to the airfield, but you'll have it all to yourself.'

'Blimey!'

Charlotte felt pleased that she'd confronted Peter and found out the truth. It felt like she'd officially integrated Peter into her life. She could now have him by her side, and it made her feel more complete. As the car took her home, she grinned from ear to ear and relaxed back into the seat.

As they pulled in through the archway, Charlotte looked up at the sign above the arch: *Loxley*.

'I think the sign needs a new lick of paint, Cartwright. Could you flag that up with the estate manager as soon as possible?'

'Certainly, madam.'

'Thanks, Cartwright, I appreciate that. You know, I some-times feel I should call you by your first name. It's Terence, isn't it?'

'Yes, madam, but that won't be necessary.'

As the car went over the arched bridge, it was always the sign she was nearly home. She gazed out of the window and realised she was noticing much more about the trees now: the twisted bark of the sweet chestnut, the wrinkled stockings on the cherry trunk, the bright yellow of the chicken of the woods fungus on the oak, and the way the tips of the tree of heaven branches seem to point up to... well, heaven. She smiled. Peter had taught her things she never knew before. She'd always found solace within nature and in particular her oak tree by the lake, but Peter had enabled her to appreciate it so much more.

Cartwright stopped the car right outside the front door and, to Charlotte's complete surprise, she saw her mother on her knees, planting up red and white flowers in the soil beneath one of the turret windows. One side was already complete, and her mother was busy with her trowel on the other.

'Mother, they look absolutely lovely.'

'Hello, Charlotte. They do, don't they? I thought we needed a little more colour and some optimism around the house, and it's a beautiful day.'

Charlotte had to blink hard and then arrive at the scene again to feel that what she was seeing and hearing was real. Her mother appeared completely well. Bright and focused.

She knelt beside her. 'What are you planting?'

'Begonias, dear. I've always loved the smell of begonias. Reminds me of one of the few occasions your father took me to the Chelsea Flower Show. Although I do remember a wasp stung him right on the end of his nose and it flared up just like a clown. I did enjoy that day, though. It was the year before you were born.'

'Do you miss him?'

'Who?'

'Father.'

'He was a cantankerous old walrus, and he neglected me. Of course, I had everything I wanted, but I really wanted so much more from him.'

'What do you mean?'

'Love, Charlotte. Love. To feel cherished and adored. Someone to hold you tight and make you giggle with excitement. Don't trap yourself with a cold-hearted man who's more interested in business than in you, because one day you'll be watching the gardener raking the lawn, his bare shoulders and strong back working in the sun, all sweaty and manly, and you'll crave some attention from him. You'll want him to take you into the summerhouse and end all your frustrations. I was once a happy, carefree woman with a burning heart and could turn heads at the polo club, you know.'

Charlotte passed her a begonia. 'I'm sure you were. Did you ever... you know?'

'You mean take advantage of the summerhouse? No, never, but I often thought of it and I came very close once when I went in there to look for my still-life etchings and a very young and fit gardener helped me erect my easel.'

'There's a new man in my life,' Charlotte said, in a half-whisper.

'I thought I'd seen you looking a little giddy.'

'Have you noticed that?'

'Once or twice, or maybe more. The trouble is, I'm having trouble with my memory. I can't remember yesterday, but I can recall so many things from when I was a girl.'

'Like what?'

'We went for a day trip to the coast. I remember Mother and Caroline. She was a fun sister back then, and a few of the cousins rode donkeys on the beach and paddled in the sea.'

Charlotte smiled and helped firm in one of the plants. 'Donkeys! Sounds like fun.'

'So, who's the man? From good stock, is he?'

Charlotte paused, raised her eyes to the sky, and nodded. 'Yes, very good stock.'

'Which family?'

Charlotte paused again. 'Shall I fetch a watering can? The flowers look parched.'

'Yes, darling, that's a wonderful idea.'

Charlotte rose to her feet and started walking to the wooden gate in the perimeter wall. 'Love you, Mummy.'

On returning, she placed the watering can beside the flowers. Her mother had gone. She looked around and noticed she was sauntering up the drive, singing softly to herself.

Charlotte caught up with her. 'Mummy, where are you going?'

Her mother's face, which had been alive only two minutes before, was now blank and almost lifeless. 'I'm going home. I need to see my daughter and feed the cat.'

'Mummy, it's me. Charlotte. I am your daughter.'

Her mother suddenly stopped and looked at her. Her eyes were confused and distant.

'No, you're not, my dear.' And then she carried on shuffling along the gravel.

Charlotte took her mother's arm. 'Let's go back to the house.'

'Get off me. I'll call the police.'

Charlotte felt a tear in each eye and her heart seemingly shatter into a thousand pieces. 'Let's get you home.'

27

THE ALPENBLICK

Peter reclined in his executive leather chair and pushed the button to raise his legs. He tipped his ice-cold beer into a chilled glass and gazed out of the oval window at the clouds below, and the immaculate sunshine that streamed in to warm his face. If this was what air travel was all about, he was a convert. He drank half his beer and then had a little walk around the cabin. He couldn't stop running his hand along all the walnut and leather trim. He then attempted to lower the projector screen, until it jammed at a wonky angle and he gave up. He peered out of the window on the opposite side. The clouds below were parting, and he could see mountain tops covered in a pristine white carpet.

Charlotte was well known among the jet set. She regularly used private planes and didn't like mixing with the crowds at airports. She knew the places to be seen and the people to be seen with, and it seemed she did it effortlessly.

Peter's private chauffeur took him from the airport up the steep, winding mountain road. As they arrived at the hotel, he could see Charlotte by the front door, chatting to a crowd of people. Overly made-up women in fur coats and boots and men in cool sunglasses and the latest ski suits surrounded her. There was a sign above the door in large gold lettering: 'The Alpenblick Palace'. It was a palace alright. A monstrous black Rolls-Royce stood to attention at the door and men in matching top hats were ushering in people and bags, with the utmost courtesy.

Peter felt a little uneasy. These people were not his usual crowd. He didn't really care for all that fake double-kissing and the guys who only talked about their fathers' car collections and what was trading well globally. But there she was, holding court, and she looked like a film star: glamorous and dazzling in an all-in-one white ski suit and black boots, her hair up in a pink-and-white headband.

The car stopped in front of the hotel in a space cleared in the six-foot-high snow. Peter and the chauffeur tussled over the door. Peter was used to opening his own doors and hated the thought of someone being subordinate to him. It didn't feel right, and he was struggling to come to terms with it.

Was he meant to give a tip? He didn't know, so he didn't. He just smiled at the chauffeur and walked towards the group. They all turned simultaneously and looked at him, then parted as he focused on Charlotte. He walked up the snow-cleared steps, held her tight and kissed her long and hard on the lips.

A high-pitched plummy voice broke the embrace. 'We've heard so much about you, Peter. I'm Mira.' He turned to face a small brunette lady wearing far too much lipstick.

'All good, I hope,' he replied, trying not to give away his discomfort. He gave her the obligatory double kiss and soon realised you weren't actually meant to plant wet lips on the cheek each time. He did that with his grandma, but it wasn't the done thing in these social circles.

The rest of the group executed their *mwah, mwahs* eloquently, but Peter continued to plonk a juicy one, as it just didn't feel right not to. He hated the seeming superficiality. The men stood back, waiting their turn to greet him. The first was a stout Frenchman, Claude, with a political handshake. The second was Filipo, a trim, loud Italian with a flimsy handshake like a damp dishcloth, but he seemed friendly. Lastly, a huge hand reached from the back.

'I'm Charles. A pleasure to meet you,' said a deep, decidedly arrogant public-school voice.

Peter grasped his hand. 'And you, Charles. I'm Peter.'

Charles continued the handshake while looking Peter straight in the eye. 'I'm a very old friend of Charlotte's—a very old friend.'

The handshake continued and Peter cringed inside as he began to feel uncomfortable, but he remained composed and said confidently, 'That's nice. Good friends are hard to come by.'

'Yes,' replied Charles, as he gripped Peter's hand even tighter.

Charlotte broke the deadlock, grabbing Peter's other hand and dragging him away. 'See you guys later. Come on, Peter, I want to show you the apartment. You'll love it. There's a view over the lake and the mountains beyond. I need to get out of this ski suit, too. I've been skiing all morning—well, in between the *glühweins*.' She giggled. 'I've missed you. It seems like weeks and weeks.'

Peter tried to take in all the splendour as Charlotte dragged him by the hand. 'Are those bears' heads real? How thick is this carpet? It's like walking on clouds. Do you have a whole apartment here?'

Charlotte laughed and continued to pull him excitedly. 'You are silly. It's mine.'

'What is?'

'Come on, help me out of this ski suit.'

They ran to the apartment hand in hand like excited teenagers and by the time they reached the lift, they were kissing passionately.

'I've missed you so much, Peter,' Charlotte said, as the lift door opened.

He pushed her against the wall of the lift and kissed her intensely. He had missed her, too. He pushed himself against her and she lifted her leg and wrapped it around his, enabling the two of them to become even more entangled. He started grinding against her, longing for the lift to keep on going and going.

It stopped, but before the door opened, they pulled themselves together as best they could and, still kissing, managed to make their way to the apartment. Once they were through the door, Charlotte started stripping off her clothes.

'I'm going to have a shower. Fancy joining me, sexy man?' She winked and ran into the main bathroom, smacking her own bottom and looking back with the cheekiest of grins.

Peter didn't delay in ripping off his multiple layers and headed purposefully for the shower, where he could see her feminine curves behind the glass as the steam rose. He took his time removing his socks, leaning back against the wall, watching her rubbing soap into her breasts. She pretended not to see him as she pushed them up provocatively, allowing the water to run over them and make her nipples harden. He watched her, transfixed by every contour of her body, and although he was ready and eager to make his move, he held back to enjoy her beauty. The steam filled the room and gradually began to obscure his view.

He could just make out her figure beyond, and then, cheekily, her bottom came right up against the glass as she bent over. That was his moment to intervene. From his position, naked against the wall, he rose to his full height. His flat stomach and muscular legs tightened as he walked confidently around the glass and, in the steamy bathroom, he found her shoulder with his hand and proceeded to turn her around silently so that she was facing away. He gently but purposefully bent her over so that her hands were against the glass.

The powerful shower, thrusting warm water down her back and across her bottom, made Charlotte tingle with excitement. Peter had one intention, and he knew exactly what he wanted, and she loved that. She loved him to take control, and the thrill of him silently walking in and moving her into position was enough to make her orgasm, even though he'd barely touched her. She was ready for him and suggestively opened her legs wide. The warm water ran between them and she wanted him inside her. She felt his hand on her back. It ran down to her bottom and then—*smack*—playfully spanked her. She loved that, too.

She reached back to guide him in, but he grabbed her hand and placed it back on the glass. She felt both his hands on her hips. She knew what was coming and then, sure as anything, he was at her gate and pushing in deep, with no messing about. She gasped for breath, and gasped once more as he almost completely withdrew and then thrust in again. He was unbelievably turned on; she

233

could feel his every inch as he gained pace. She felt wanted. She'd often dreamed of being taken with such animal instinct and here he was, doing just that. His pace didn't slow and he became harder and harder. She wanted him to give her everything. A hot flush pulsed through her body and, without resisting, she let it build and build until she was on the brink. That fabulous point of no return. He then slowed right down and, with one last deep push, he twitched inside her and his body jerked as his hands grasped her hips. She felt herself let go and, with complete fulfilment, gave in to his masculinity and power. She felt a unique, incredible unity between them. When she felt him slowly pull out, she gasped; she would have loved for him to stay inside her forever.

Then his deep Yorkshire voice said, 'Where's the soap, then?'

Charlotte looked around to see him grinning, and he winked at her. She'd always hated a winking man, but Peter just had this thing about him which made it sexy. Her heart continued thumping as they playfully washed each other down, lathering the soap and exploring each other between kisses.

They dried each other with fluffy white towels and then donned dressing gowns, before Charlotte dragged Peter around the rest of the roof top apartment, showing him the five bedrooms, seven bathrooms, and the huge living area with rustic furniture, and then took him onto the split-level balcony overlooking the frozen lake, where people were skating. Beyond, what seemed like a thousand white-tipped peaks stretched as far as the eye could see.

'Do you like it?' She gripped his hand. 'I love it here. It's so magical. I feel alive.'

'It's beautiful. Like nothing I've ever seen before.' He took a great breath of the cold air, deep into his lungs.

'Come on, I'll take you to my favourite shop. We can have coffee and the most exquisite chocolates.'

They walked arm in arm along the snow-covered street and Charlotte pointed excitedly. The shop window was jam-packed with homemade chocolates in all shapes and sizes: tempting snowballs dusted with icing, trees, bears, logs, alpine cabins, buttons and large solid blocks, all made from continental chocolate. Charlotte especially loved the ornate ribboned boxes displaying different skiing characters, some with scarves, some flying off ski jumps, and some just looking cool, gliding down a slope—and all to be consumed, if she could get her hands on them quickly enough.

She led them through the shop and into a spacious café at the rear, with large wooden tables and antique ski memorabilia. The whole place had the romance of an Alpine chalet, with its exposed wooden beams, vaulted ceiling, shutters at the windows and raging log fire. Charlotte spoke to a waitress in German, who showed them to an impressive wooden table, which looked like half a tree.

'I'd like a coffee, and because of you, I'm feeling naughty. Can I have a mixture of my favourite skiers, too? I'm just popping to the bathroom. Will you order?' She disappeared down some steps and Peter was left without words.

As the waitress approached, Peter became a little uneasy. He didn't speak a word of German—well, other than words he'd heard in war films, but those weren't likely to go down well in an Austrian mountain café. The woman spoke and Peter looked puzzled.

'Do you speak English?' he asked, feeling ashamed that he

couldn't even order a couple of coffees.

'Nein,' she replied ironically, followed by more German. Peter searched every corner of his brain for something which would help him.

'*Zwei* coffee and a plate of chocolate skiers.' He did the usual British thing of shouting slowly and precisely in his broadest Yorkshire, so there was no doubt she would be able to understand. The woman looked at him with a stern face, and Peter smiled.

Help! was the only thing he could think as he pointed to the couple at the next table drinking coffee. '*La*... same as them. Coffee.' He was embarrassed now, but he had to get Charlotte what she wanted.

The waitress disappeared through a door and at the same time Charlotte appeared, all smiles and looking cute in her white ski pants and black headband. She sat down. 'Everything OK?' She kissed him on the cheek.

'I'm not entirely sure.' He screwed his face up and felt uncomfortable. 'We could get something, or we might get nothing. My German is a little rusty, to be honest.'

'Oh! Right. Sorry. I assumed everyone did languages at school.'

'Well, English is hard enough for some people when you're from Yorkshire, tha knows,' he replied.

There was an uncomfortable silence between them, and Peter hoped the lady would arrive with the coffees and cut through the silence, but she didn't. In fact, she walked past three times with drinks for other people, but not for them.

Charlotte seemed disheartened and stared silently out of the window. An uneasy Peter felt inadequate and useless. He attempted to summon the waitress, but she ignored him. Twice.

'Did you order the chocolate skiers, Peter? My father would always order the skiers.'

He squirmed in his seat. 'You might have to ask her, because I don't have a clue.'

'Oh, Peter, it's only some chocolate and coffee.' She seemed in a mood. He'd never seen Charlotte like this.

'Hey, are you OK?' he said, putting his hand on her shoulder. 'What's wrong? Were you so desperate for a coffee?' he joked.

'I'm OK. Suppose I'm used to my man being able to look after me without me having to do all the thinking. I'm used to men who can order drinks without me holding their hand.'

Peter stared at her. He felt lost. Their connection, to him, felt incredible, and this came as a colossal blow. An empty feeling grew inside him, like indigestion, from his feet up. He didn't like it, but he wasn't going to let it take over.

'You know, you're beautiful, even if you are in a mood.' He tried to make light of it all.

'I'm not in a *mood*, Peter. I'm just a little disappointed.'

Peter held his head high. 'Well, you're still beautiful, and you have to teach me some German pretty damn quick.'

She looked at him, smiled, and put her hand on his arm. 'I'm sorry. I miss my father dearly. He always brought me here.' She looked sad and helpless and came close to Peter for a squeeze.

'I understand. It can't be easy. I'm never going to be your father and would never want to be.'

'I always have to make the decisions at home and make sure everything is running well—the houses, the staff, Lucy. Even my ex-husband needed organising. Sometimes it's nice to let go and hand it over.'

'In that case, let's leave the choccy skiers for another time.

Let's explore more of the town. You said there's a bobsleigh run. Maybe I can zip down on this tea tray.' He grabbed the tray out of the woman's arms as she passed and gave her a wink. She wasn't amused, but Charlotte laughed. She gave the tray back to the lady and kissed Peter on the cheek.

'You are funny, Peter.'

The pair strode up the hill into the town, swinging their arms and holding each other's hands tight. 'I reckon that tea tray would have been perfect for my maiden voyage,' Peter said, in high spirits.

'Don't be silly. It's not even big enough for that big head of yours, let alone your cute bum.' She gave *him* a wink, and they both doubled over laughing.

They passed many chalet-style shops, restaurants, ski-hire places, high-end boutiques and branded jewellery emporiums. Then they turned a corner and Peter's eye was drawn to a shop selling skis, snowboards and every type of peripheral tech imaginable.

'Wow, there's some fabulous-looking gear. I think I might enjoy skiing.'

'Do you want to ski with me tomorrow? I didn't want to push it if you've never been before.'

'Well, it is a ski resort, and it doesn't look too hard.'

'Really? I'm so excited. You can use daddy's gear, he was about your height, and I'll ask the concierge to arrange skis and boots. What size feet are you?' she said, getting straight on her phone.

'Size 10.' Peter tried to imagine what her father looked like. He was glad he didn't have to buy anything, as he only had enough to stretch to a pair of gloves. It didn't stop him feeling a little uneasy about wearing a dead man's ski suit, though. 'It's not from the 1970s, is it?'

With one ear to her phone, Charlotte scrunched up her face as if to say, what are you talking about?

'The ski suit,' Peter explained. 'It's not bright red with a white stripe, like the General Lee, is it?'

'They will bring everything to the apartment first thing in the morning.' She stuffed her phone into her pocket. 'Oh! Yes, I get it. Don't worry, that style's back in this year.' She giggled.

They hurried back to the apartment, stripped off and cuddled in bed. Charlotte lay with her head on his chest and he wrapped his arms tightly around her.

'We can do this, you know. You and me,' he said.

'Do you think so? Sorry I have my little moments. I'm not always as strong as I make out. I was once fearless. Nothing stood in my way. But since Father died and Mother... you know, I've lost my courage somewhat, and sometimes I get scared. Do you know what I mean?'

'I know that feeling.'

'Do you?'

'Of course. When my mum died, I was waiting for her and she never came. I felt let down, angry and rejected. She was my everything and I still have an empty place in my heart which will never be filled. It taught me a great deal, though.'

'What?'

'No matter how low you find yourself, no matter how desperate you are, you have to fight for what is true. Never stop trying and never give up. It hurts. For sure. But never let it take you down.'

'I love that about you, Peter. You seem to have it all in perspective and under control.'

'Not really.' He laughed. 'You haven't seen me ski yet.'

'I can trust you, can't I?'

'Trust me? Do I look like a second-hand car salesman?'

'No. I mean, that you want me for me, even with my hang-ups, and not for my money. My ex-husband went for the kill when we divorced and I have to protect Lucy.'

'I'm not your ex-husband and wouldn't take anything away from Lucy. I'm with you for your body, that's all.'

'Peter, you're impossible. Some people are telling me to be careful.'

'Mira?'

'It doesn't matter who.'

'Charlotte, you work it out for yourself.'

They drifted off for a snooze before their dinner date with the rest of the ski crowd.

Peter woke suddenly. They'd been asleep in each other's arms for a good ninety minutes, and they were meeting the gang at 7pm for dinner at a restaurant in town. He kissed her gently on the forehead and hugged her.

'We need to get a move on, or we'll be late,' he whispered in her ear. She roused, smiled, and started running her leg suggestively against his. 'We haven't time for that. Honestly, what are you like? I think you're just with me for one thing. We'll never get out of here.'

She kissed him. They both laughed and sprang into action, searching for garments, and Charlotte had a quick shower. 'I won't be long. I don't want to get my hair wet, although I could do with a handsome man to dry me off.' She smiled, spanking her own bottom.

'You really are a naughty girl. Get on with it. We need to be out of here in ten minutes.'

While Charlotte showered, Peter took a jumper out of his bag and put on his jeans. He stood on the open-air balcony looking up into the cloudless night sky. 'You would have loved it here, Mum,' he said with a smile.

'Are you ready, then?' Charlotte shouted from inside.

He turned to look at her. She looked sensational in black ski-pants, fur-lined boots with fur around the top, and her ski jacket, which also had a mass of fur around the hood and cuffs. Peter felt good in jeans—a bit of a casual look, but his dark blue roll-neck jumper suited his physique and smartened his appearance.

'Have you seen my purse?' Charlotte rummaged in some bags on the floor.

Peter shook his head. 'Nope.'

'I'm sure I left it on the table.'

Peter took another deep breath of cold, Alpine air. It felt good.

'Peter! Have you seen my purse?'

'No. I haven't seen your purse.'

'Well, it's a mystery. I knew I had it when we got back last night and now it's missing. Someone must have it.'

'What are you saying?'

'I'm not saying anything, other than, it's strange, that's all.' She stood with her hands on her hips. 'Are you sure you don't know where it is?'

Peter shook his head. 'Did you check your bag?'

Charlotte snapped back immediately. 'Yes! Of course I checked my bag. Six times!'

He nodded. 'What about your coat?'

Charlotte paced to her coat hanging on a peg by the door.

Peter followed her with his eyes.

'Oh! Yes, it's here.'

~

The air was cold and silent as they crossed the road and climbed the hill.

Sitting on sheepskins around a gigantic wooden table, the others were waiting impatiently. Peter squeezed in and Charlotte followed. Lots of handshaking and double-kissing followed as they settled in. They then discussed the menu, finally agreeing on a cheese fondue accompanied by expensive wine.

'So, Peter, do you ski?' probed Mira, who was sitting directly opposite him. Everyone was quiet, awaiting an answer.

'No, to be honest, never, but I've been watching people today and I'm going to give it my best shot.'

'Everyone skis here, Peter. This isn't really a place for beginners.'

'Well, I'm not just here for the skiing.'

'You must be a bobsleigh expert then!' Mira laughed and the whole group followed.

Peter's insides churned like a washing machine about to end its cycle. He hadn't expected such questioning. Mira seemed a little aggressive and appeared to be testing him, and although he was squirming inside, he felt he had her sussed and would try to keep one step ahead.

'It's funny you should say that. I'm mentally prepared for all the twists and turns, Mira. I ran the coal bunker many times. Ever heard of that?'

Mira screwed up her face like she'd smelled a bad smell. 'No. Is it in Canada?'

'Somewhere equally wild.' He held his hands up like the paws of a bear.

'And where did you go to school?' piped up Charles from the end of the table.

'School?' Peter blurted out with a splutter. 'I, erm, went to my local school.'

'You sound northern. Was it Ampleforth?' Charles replied.

Peter looked at him and smiled. 'No... Grimestone. Think Ampleforth without the monks, and with bars at the windows.'

This was enough to stop Charles from probing further, and then the great steaming bowl of cheese was delivered to the centre of the table. What the hell was this? A steaming bowl of molten cheese? Where was the meat?

Peter watched the others tucking into the bowl and soon joined in, dipping pieces of bread into the hot cheese and pretending it was nice. Charlotte chatted with her friend Melissa and the others talked between themselves about high-brow things Peter knew nothing about. As he shoved one piece of molten-cheese-y bread into his mouth after another, he began to feel a little isolated. He tried to not let Charlotte down by staying dignified, but deep down he knew he was out of his depth, and certainly not in the inner circle. Yet.

After the fondue, the drinking continued, and people moved around the table. Mira had cornered Charlotte away from the group and they were in deep conversation about something. Charles was on his second bottle of wine mixed with copious whiskey chasers, and he latched onto Peter like a limpet. His eyeballs appeared to be swivelling in different directions.

'She's an incredible woman, is Charlotte.' He slurred his words. 'And I've known her a long time. We're very close, you understand me?'

Peter nodded

'I have to make sure no Tom, Dick or... or... mmm, what's his goddamn name?'

'Harry,' said Peter.

'Yes, that's right. I have to make sure Charlotte is safe and protected. Yes, *safe*!' he shouted inappropriately.

'So, were you once her boyfriend?' Peter asked.

'Yes... Well... erm... technically... no, but we used to study together at Cambridge, and I know everything about her private life.'

'Well, Charles, she's in good hands now. I'll make sure she's safe...' Peter turned. 'Right! I think we'll make a move. Are you ready, Charlotte?' He put his hand on her shoulder.

'Not yet, Peter. I'm talking with Mira.'

Mira looked at him with a solemn face.

'I'll just be getting some fresh air,' Peter said jovially. 'All that cheese has gone to my head.'

He shuffled away from the table and made his exit. He needed to clear his head and, as he walked up the street, the cold air felt like ice crystals on his face. The neon sign above the pharmacy displayed -23 °C. He rubbed his arms to keep warm and walked around for a couple of minutes, scuffing the heels of his boots as he went from one side of the street to the other. On hearing voices in a doorway, he spotted the group kissing each other goodnight. He felt he was on the outside somehow, but walked over to them and shook the hands which needed shaking. Charles was still in the restaurant being sick on the bathroom floor, and one of the other guys had stayed with him while they awaited a taxi. Peter kissed the ladies goodnight, and he and Charlotte made their way to the apartment. He held out his hand to Charlotte, which she declined.

'Are you alright?' Peter asked.

'I can't believe what you did in there.'

'What do you mean, what I did in there?'

'You walked out and left me.'

'You were with friends and I just needed to get some fresh

air.'

'Poor Charles was not happy because of something you said to him.'

'Me? You have to be kidding. I think he thinks he's your boyfriend.'

'He just wants the best for me, like everyone else in there.'

'What does that mean?'

Charlotte remained silent.

'Oh, I see—Mira,' Peter said with gritted teeth. 'What did she have to say for herself?'

They walked down the hill towards the apartment. Peter turned and stopped in front of Charlotte, who was huddled in her coat, her face just about visible through the fur.

'We are not going to let this fester, Charlotte,' he said firmly. 'Maybe we're all a bit tired.'

'I just get a little confused sometimes, Peter. There are so many people saying things to me. People I trust.'

'What things are they saying?'

'That you're a gold-digger, that I need to be careful.'

Peter stood proud. 'Well, what do you think?'

'I don't know. I have to listen to the people around me. I've known them a long time and they have my best interests at heart.'

'You really think that? You think Mira doesn't use you to buy her things and jet around the world?'

'That's a hurtful thing to say. I don't see you offering to pay for everything.'

Peter shook his head. 'I can't believe you just said that. I'm not here to use you. I'm here because I thought you wanted me here. I'll pay my fair share.'

They walked in silence to the hotel. At the door, Peter turned and faced Charlotte head on. 'Look, this is difficult for both of us. I didn't mean to be rude. I'm not here for your money or to take anything away from you. I'm here because I think a lot about you.'

Charlotte nodded. 'It's just that we are very different people, and my friends made that obvious tonight. I've known them a long time.'

The following day, they woke to a cloudless sky. The sunrise over the Alpine mountains gave the white peaks a hue of orange and the snow on the trees seemed to sparkle like delicate gemstones in their millions.

Peter took to his feet and, naked, opened the patio door and stood admiring the view. He was amazed at how the trees were able to survive such harsh temperatures and withstand the heavy weight of the snow on their limbs. Golden-coloured larch, dark green spruce and silver fir, all dusted with pristine snow, stretched from the shore of the frozen lake up to where the high exposed peaks of solid rock provided no favourable environment. Peter had never seen such natural beauty, and as he took the freezing cold air into his lungs, was grateful that he had the opportunity to experience such a fabulous landscape.

Charlotte stepped up to stand beside him.

'You alright?' he asked tentatively.

'Not really. I didn't sleep well.'

'Me neither. Look, I meant what I said last night. You must decide what you want. To be honest, I was hurt, and I still am. I'll give you some space. I understand about your friends, and I'm not surprised they're unsure about an interloper like me, but on the other hand, I don't want to throw away what we've built already.'

Charlotte took a deep breath. 'Thanks, Peter, you're right. Just give me an hour or two.'

'Don't think about it too long. I'll leave you in peace and I'll explore the town a bit more.'

'OK,' she said, with a grateful smile.

Within the grand lobby, numerous twinkling chandeliers led the way to the front door. Peter became aware of a young person coming towards him in a big fur coat. Her hood dropped, and she was instantly recognisable.

'Lucy! What are you doing here?'

'I could ask you the same question. I'm staying with friends at their chalet, but I need some money. Is Mummy in the apartment?'

'Yes, she's just out of bed. She might be in the shower. You might need to knock hard.'

'I have a key,' she said, rolling her eyes.

'See you later.'

Peter followed a narrow pathway up the hill and through the village, to where the tree cover became dense. Pine trees weighted heavily with snow lined the route, and he had to negotiate his way in places where the snow had drifted to beyond knee-deep. A three-way wooden sign pointed to the town, the station and the bobsleigh run.

Around the corner, he caught a glimpse of a white tower and the colourful flags on its roof. As he neared it, he could make out the word 'Finish' and then, to his delight, one of the corners of the bobsleigh run came into view. He was surprised by how big it was in reality. Sleek and steep. Very steep.

He entered the bridge over the course just as someone

came hurtling underneath at breakneck speed. 'Wow,' he said out loud. Another man was standing watching.

'You fancy a go?' he said to Peter in an English accent.

'I'd love to. I've always dreamt of it. Can you just pay and play, if you know what I mean?'

The man laughed. 'There's a three-week waiting list, but essentially, yes.'

Peter laughed too. 'I'm only here for another three days.' They both looked down at the track as another body hurtled by.

'I'm Peter.'

'Jez. Good to meet you.'

'Likewise.'

'Is it what you imagined?'

Peter kept looking at the icy track. 'It's amazing. Better than I imagined and steeper.'

'You don't look too sure.'

'There's a bitter-sweet feel to the whole trip to be honest. It's a long story.'

An icy silence anchored Peter to the spot. He carried on staring at the course as it disappeared into the distance, bend after bend after bend. He felt lonely.

The quiet was sliced in two by another bobsleigh hurtling down and then a blast of cold air followed, hitting Peter in the face.

'Are you alright, buddy?' Jez said.

'Yeah, I'm alright. Hold your nerve and keep your head strong. That's the secret, isn't it?'

Jez nodded. 'Do you want to come up top and see the sleds? I have a friend up there, should be able to get into the start compound.'

Peter's eyes opened wide. 'Are you serious? I'd love to.'

The jet-black body against the stark ice, sleek and polished, made Peter catch his breath. 'Can I touch it?'

'Sure. It's one of the practice sleds. You can sit in it if you want.'

Peter didn't hesitate. He placed his hand on the body, then ran his fingers over the large, embossed number on the front. 'No 1'.

He clambered inside and took his position, grasping the steering column and peering over the front as if ready to go.

Jez smiled. 'You look at home in there.'

'It feels really natural.'

'Well, I've just heard that there's a spare beginner's slot tomorrow afternoon. It's not from the top. You start three-quarters down, but it's a chance to see if you like it.'

Peter gripped the column tighter and stared out across the front. 'I'd like that. How much is it?'

'It won't cost you anything. It was a friend of mine and he's had to cancel because of an injury skiing. Maybe buy me a beer sometime.'

Peter smiled and started to climb out of the sled. 'It's a kind offer, but I have more important things to deal with.'

'That sounds like woman trouble,' Jez said, putting his hand on Peter's back.

'You're not wrong. I need to stop being an idiot and sort it out.'

'Is she that important to you?'

Peter nodded. 'Yes. Very important.'

28

RED FLAGS

'Mummy! Mummy, can I have some money? Where are you?'

'I'm on the balcony, Lucy.'

'I've just seen this divine necklace in the shop next to the café. Can I get it? Ple-e-e-ease.' She gave her mum a cuddle and then started hanging off her shoulders.

'How much is it?'

'It's a hundred, or two hundred maybe. No more than three hundred. Ple-e-e-ease.'

Charlotte took a deep breath. One that tasted of exasperation and disappointment. Then she let it out with fortitude. 'No, Lucy. It's not your birthday. It's the kind of thing you can save your pocket money for.'

'I have, I have. I just don't have it with me. Go on, Mummy, please.'

'No. I'm putting my foot down. I'm fed up with everyone just expecting. Just expecting everything from me.'

'Are you ill, Mummy? Why are you being so boring?'

Suddenly, the door burst open. 'Tell me everything, darling.

I saw him walking up to the bobsleigh track. Have you thrown him out?'

'Hello, Mira.'

'Come on, tell me. Have you come to your senses?'

Charlotte started to sob. 'I don't know what to think. My head's a jumble of different feelings.'

Mira pulled up a stool. 'Well, I don't think I'm talking out of school here, but you really could do better for yourself.'

'What do you mean?'

'You can have anyone you want, and you're settling for a working-class Yorkshireman, with nothing to his name?'

'She's right,' said Lucy, who was perched on the arm of a chair.

'Don't you start. I need support from you two, not the opposite.'

'I'm just saying, that's all,' said Mira. 'We're the ones you can trust. '

Lucy come over and gave Charlotte a hug.

'Thanks, darling.'

'Are you sure I can't have the necklace?'

Charlotte broke the hug. 'I don't think I can trust anyone anymore. Please leave me to think all of this through.'

Charlotte took a photo of her father from the table. She remembered him dropping her off at ski school when all she wanted was to ski with him. She threw the photo on the floor and the glass smashed into a thousand pieces.

'I have to be strong,' she said to herself. 'Trust my own judgement and try to go with my heart.' She walked onto the balcony and looked over the lake to the forest of trees beyond.

Peter had to apologise for his behaviour. That was simple. She deserved that. She had to be strict with Lucy. She was becoming a powerful young lady, and a little too powerful at times. And Mira was only trying to be a good friend.

'I have to believe in my own judgement,' she said out loud. 'Stop dwelling on the past and find my courage.'

Placing a blanket over her knees, Charlotte positioned herself on the bench seat at the centre of the balcony. With her phone in hand, she decided to ask the opinion of someone else.

'Sam, it's Charlotte.'

'How are you, gorgeous?'

'I'm in a bit of a state. So many thoughts buzzing around my head. I remember you saying one had to take notice of red flags, and there are plenty. It's just my heart says the opposite. What shall I do?'

'I know you, Charlotte. You've a good brain, but you've always been ruled by your heart. Try to put aside all those boring common-sense things which always seem to distract us.'

'That's easier said than done. I just keep thinking about what Father would think, and would he approve of a working-class man?'

Sam took a few seconds to reply. 'I'm going to say what I think and you might not like it. But we go back a long way and I love you dearly, so I think it's the best.'

Charlotte sighed. 'Go on then. Everyone else has had a say-so.'

'You loved your father, yes?'

'Of course.'

'But you didn't respect him. You opposed him every step of the way when you were younger. You were disappointed by him.' She paused, then added, 'I said you might not like it.'

'Go on.'

'He let you down so many times. Why do you want to please him now?'

'He's dead, Sam. He can't answer for himself.'

'Exactly. Look, no disrespect, but you're sailing the ship now. He entrusted you to do that and to make your own decisions. He wouldn't be happy with whoever you brought home. Listen to your heart, Charlotte. If Peter makes you feel happy, then some might say it's more than your father did.'

Silence followed, and it seemed Sam felt she'd said enough.

'You're right,' Charlotte said. 'Brutal, but right. I'm going to give him a second chance.'

'You do what's right for you, Charlotte. Work out what your priorities are and go for it.'

'Well, I guess my priority is Lucy. I want to be a good mum and I don't want her saying the same things about me when I'm gone.'

'No one will care when you're gone. You're living your life now. Not in the past or in the future, but right now. Be a good mum by being true to yourself.'

'You ever thought about becoming a shrink?'

'You must be kidding. I have my own issues to contend with.'

'I'm sorry, darling, it's all been about me. Do you want to tell me about your troubles?'

'Not really. Other than I'm realising that if you find a good one, then hang on to them. Let's catch up when you're back home, shall we?'

'I love you, Sam. Thanks for being honest with me. I'll meet you for supper somewhere lovely. I'll text you next week.'

Peter didn't stop to watch the bobsleigh hurtle beneath the bridge. His stride was long and his pace determined. He took a right at the wooden sign and headed to the town. He knew what he had to do, and there wasn't any time to waste. Turning the corner by the Breitling watch shop and up a set of steep steps, he turned again and stared into the window. Chocolate skiers performing back flips and one even waving from a bobsled. He took a deep breath and headed for the door. It flung open, and a large lady with at least three bags in each hand barged her way out, forcing Peter into a side passage.

'Ouch! You want to watch who you're barging into,' Peter said, before being instantly distracted by someone else. 'Lucy! What are you doing in here?'

Lucy's look of contempt could have lowered the –15 air temperature another ten degrees. She shrugged off the boy who was stuck to her like a limpet and straightened her top.

'A love bite. Nice.' Peter's irony made the red blemish on her neck stand out even more.

'Do we have to do the pleasantries every time?' Lucy said.

He smiled. 'No, but great timing. Looks like I saved you from being eaten alive.'

She pushed the boy away, put her hand on her hip and raised an eyebrow.

'Would you help me buy your mum's favourite chocolates?' Peter asked.

'What? Those stupid skiers?'

'Yes, those stupid skiers.'

She huffed and the air temperature felt like it had plummeted a further five degrees. 'Just point at the ones you want. It's not difficult,' she said, as if he were a six-year-old child.

'The problem is, your mother likes the ones behind the counter, in the special box. I'd really appreciate your help.'

'Why would I help you? Whenever I see Mummy, she always looks so unhappy.'

'Look, Lucy, I'm not here to make things difficult for anyone. I have your mum and your best interests at heart and, if anything, I want to make things better for all of us. You might even grow to like me.'

'I can't see that happening. I don't have time for losers.' She raised the other sluggy eyebrow.

'Come on, Lucy. Your mother loves you. I don't want to take that away from you. Give me a chance.'

Lucy huffed again. 'Alright. But I want you to promise something?'

'Sure.'

'Don't tell mother about what you've just seen.'

At that point the boy, in his dazzling white trainers and jeans almost around his ankles, shuffled to one side with a grunt.

'You have my word. One box with the full assortment and wrapped in a purple bow, please, and get yourself something.' He stuffed the money into her hand.

'No thanks,' she muttered under her breath. She grabbed the notes and entered the shop.

Peter waited impatiently in the passageway. 'I'd shove off if I were you,' he called to the boy, who was lurking in the darkness, his trainers the only noticeable sign of life. 'I'm on your case, lad,' he added in his deepest voice.

The door opened and out stepped Lucy, with a pink-and-white paper bag under her arm.

'Did you get them?'

Lucy tutted as the large woman from before tried to get back into the shop. She stepped aside to allow her in, and in doing so slipped on black ice at the top of the steep steps. She hit the ground hard and continued to fall backwards, tumbling in an ungainly way down the steps. Peter leaped into action, but there was little he could do as Lucy careered down several more steps to the bottom, and then came to an abrupt stop against a trash bin, where she lay motionless.

29

CHERRY TREE

'Oh my God! I came as soon as I could. How is she? What happened?'

Peter stood up from the plastic waiting room chair. 'I'm waiting for the doctor. He said he'd come out and explain everything. She's OK. Shocked, and a bit battered and bruised. Her arm didn't look too good, though.'

'Her arm? What the hell happened? And what were you doing with Lucy?'

A trolley with a patient attached to a drip and escorted by two porters rushed by.

'Sit down a minute. Do you want a coffee?'

'No, Peter, I don't want a coffee. What the hell happened?'

'We bumped into each other in town. She was... erm... shopping, I think. There was some ice, black ice, and she went hurtling down some steps.'

Charlotte stood and started pacing the corridor. 'I'm sick with worry, Peter. Can I see her?'

'The doctor said to wait here, and he'd be out as soon as he could. It's busy in there.'

The heavy-duty double doors swung open and a grey-haired man in a white coat approached. 'Are you Lucy's mother?' he asked, in perfect English.

'Yes. Is she alright?'

The doctor looked at both of them. 'She's suffering from shock and her body temperature is right down. She's broken her arm in two places. That's treatable and I'm sending her for a CT scan. She's also hit her head. The scan will give me more information.'

Charlotte broke down in tears and flung her arms around Peter.

'Thank you,' Peter said, acknowledging the doctor with a nod and a blink.

'Grab a drink in the family room and I'll have more information as soon as the scan results are back.'

'Any sugar?' Peter asked later, pouring boiling water into a municipal white mug.

'Yes, please.'

He handed her the coffee.

'I don't know what I'd do without you, Peter. Thanks for helping Lucy. I hope she'll be OK. I've heard horror stories about bangs to the head.'

'I think she'll be fine. It could have been a lot worse.'

'You saw it?'

'Her arm took the impact. I didn't see any blood when I checked her ears and nose. She was breathing and conscious when I carried her over here.'

'You carried her?'

'There wasn't time to mess around. She was cold.'

'Oh, Peter. She's my only child. I can't bear to... you know.'

He put his arms around her shoulders and hugged her

tight. 'It's going to be OK,' he said, cradling her head with his hand.

~

Charlotte's coffee sat cold on the table as they waited. They wanted to question every nurse and doctor who went by, and every time the door opened, they both looked like eager dogs awaiting their next command.

'She's in a private room on the top floor,' the doctor told them. 'We're still waiting for the scan results, but she's conscious and her arm is in a plaster. You can go up and see her.'

'Thank you, doctor. Will she be OK?'

He stroked his chin and smiled. 'It looks promising, but I will need to see the scan results to be certain. I think she'll be pleased to see you.'

Peter and Charlotte hurried up to the top floor, then hesitated outside the room. They could see Lucy through the thin vertical pane of glass in the door.

'I'll go in on my own, Peter. It might be too much if we both go in.'

Peter kissed her cheek. 'Absolutely. Send my regards and I'll be sitting out here if you need anything.'

'You're a love.' She repaid the kiss and slowly entered the room where Lucy was snoozing. Her heart sank as she came close and saw her beautiful daughter looking so pale, and connected to heart-monitoring equipment. She carefully placed her hand on her shoulder.

'Mummy's here. My beautiful baby. Are you in pain?'

Lucy opened her eyes and smiled, although she looked tired and her lips were pale.

'A little.'

'Is it your arm?'

'Yes.'

'I'll ask for more painkillers.'

At that moment, a nurse came hurrying in and gave Lucy some white pills and a cup of water. 'These should help to settle her down,' she said in German.

'Can you see me OK?' Charlotte asked. 'They said you might have bumped your head.'

'You're a little blurry, but my head feels OK.'

'Can you remember what happened?'

Lucy stared at the wall and nodded. 'Yes, of course. I was heading to meet Kyra, and I bumped into Peter. He seemed angry and I thought you two had been fighting. He was clenching his fist and shouting. I tried to ignore him, but he came closer and closer. That's when it happened.'

'What happened?'

Lucy took her gaze from the wall and looked Charlotte in the eyes. 'He pushed me. He pushed me so hard, I went hurtling down the steps. You know, near the chocolate shop.'

'Those are steep steps. Why on earth would he do that?'

There was a pause and Lucy winced as she touched her plaster cast.

'He said I was obstreperous and inconvenient. That I was causing problems for him and that I needed to be taught a lesson.'

'Are you sure the knock to your head hasn't made you imagine that?'

'It's as clear as anything, Mummy. He was so angry. I was scared and there was nothing I could do.'

Charlotte sat back in her chair and raised her head. 'Are you a hundred per cent sure?'

Lucy nodded and then winced again. Charlotte's breathing became rapid, and she started to shake. She stood and felt dizzy, then steadied herself on the back of the chair. Taking a deep breath, she approached the door and opened it.

Peter was eagerly waiting on the other side. 'How is she?' he asked.

'She's shaken and in some pain. I want you to go now, Peter.'

'No. I'm fine. I'll wait here until we know she's going to be OK. In fact, I was thinking of getting some food for you.'

'I want you to go, Peter. *Now!*'

'What's wrong? Is she bad?'

'I don't want to talk about it now. Go back to the apartment and I'll be back later. You'll have to walk or catch a cab. I'll get the hotel car to pick me up when I'm ready. I can't leave her.'

'I'm happy to stay. Do whatever I can do.'

'Leave me to sort my own daughter.'

'I don't understand.'

'She says you pushed her.'

'*What?*'

'That you were angry, saying she was trouble and needed to be taught a lesson.'

'That's not true. Why would I do that?'

'To get her out of the way, maybe?'

'Out of the way? That's ridiculous.'

'Peter, I'm not discussing it here. I need to look after my daughter. Leave us. Please.'

Peter trudged slowly back through town. He didn't feel like going back to the apartment alone. He spotted a bar with an open door, plonked himself on a stool inside and stared at the floor. His mind was numb. He felt confused and was unable to speak when the barman addressed him. Then, to his surprise, a beer appeared in front of him.

'The plan was for you to buy me a beer,' a voice said.

Peter looked up.

'Man, you look like you've just seen something horrific. The plan backfire?'

Peter exhaled and shook his head. 'It's worse than that, Jez.'

Jez sat beside him. 'Wanna talk?'

'No.'

'Drink that then.' Jez pushed the beer closer to him.

Peter drank it down in one, burped, and asked the barman to supply two more. 'I just don't understand life sometimes. Do you ever feel like no matter how hard you try, nothing seems to go right?'

Jez took a slug of beer and ordered two whiskey chasers. 'Life can be like that. My wife was killed when she rolled her toboggan in St. Moritz.'

'On the Cresta Run?'

'Yes. She was competing in the Skeleton and broke her neck.'

Peter took a slug of beer, followed by the whiskey in one. 'Shit. I'm sorry to hear that. You OK?'

'I'll never be OK. I just have to take each day as it comes and remember to stay strong.'

Peter finished his beer. 'Yes. Stay strong. Two more beers, and two whiskeys as well.'

The pair were joined by two other guys Jez knew, and the drinking continued.

∾

'So you think you can handle the course?' said Jez, barely able to stay on his stool.

'I'd like to think so,' Peter said, slurring his words. 'It's a sledge and a slope. I used to do that down our road outside the house in the snow when I was a kid.'

Jez slid onto the floor while trying to order some more whiskey. He clambered onto a table and lay face down, gripping the legs with both hands. 'I'll show you how it's done.' He summoned one of the lads to fetch another table.

Peter joined him face-down and followed Jez as they went through the many bends of the run, gripping the table legs as if they were hurtling down at eighty miles per hour. Nearing the finish line, they both fell off their respective tables and Jez threw up on the floor.

'Life can be really shit,' he said, wiping his mouth on his sleeve.

'I gotta go. Can someone call me a cab to the Alpenblick?'

A short while later, Peter staggered in through the door to their suite and, through bleary eyes, spotted Charlotte sitting by the window.

'You look drunk. Is that what I can expect of you in my hour of need?'

'I was just talking to some friends. How's Lucy?'

'You just don't understand, do you?'

'You're damn right I don't understand,' Peter muttered to himself, laughing.

'It's not a joke, Peter. She says, you came up behind her, and pushed her with all your might down the steps.'

'You don't believe her, do you?'

'Peter. Please don't insult me. She's my daughter, of course I believe her. Are you saying she's a liar?'

'*Yes.* I damn well am. Why would I do that?'

'To get your hands on my money. Do you think I'm stupid?'

'I can't believe this is happening.'

'Maybe Mira is right.'

'What do you mean, maybe Mira's right?'

'She said I shouldn't trust you, and she's right. I should have listened to her from the beginning.'

Peter was stunned. He tried to focus and to scrutinise Charlotte's face, while a hollowness consumed him like a full-on blow to the stomach.

'Is that what you think?'

'She's not the only one.' Charlotte turned and started walking away.

'You *can* trust me,' Peter said firmly, but in complete dismay. 'It's *that* bunch of toffee-nosed leeches you want to be concerned about.'

Charlotte stood firm and tried to stay composed. 'So it *is* all about the money! And I see your anger and your criminal conviction now. It's all making sense.'

Peter looked down at the floor and shook his head. 'That woman is a bitch. Your money, that's the last thing I'm interested in. I'm in love with you, you idiot.'

'I've known Mira a long time and I can trust her. And I don't doubt my own daughter either.'

Peter shook his head. 'I've watched you pay for everything for her,' he said, getting red in the face and stumbling. 'She uses you as her private piggy bank.'

'That's not fair. She's a friend, and she's going through a bad time at the moment. I have to believe what she's telling me. Anyway, Lucy could have died. This is serious, Peter.'

'She's using you and you're too blind to see it. I have a couple of beers with some guys and a bit of trouble when I was a kid and *I'm* the one you can't trust.' Peter squeezed his eyes shut for a moment. 'Your daughter is lying, and your mates are so stuck up their own arses, with their false smiles and hands in *your* pocket, they bore me senseless. Open your eyes, Miss Charlotte.'

'Listen to you. I can't trust you, Peter. I need someone I can trust a hundred per cent.'

Peter shook his head again. The empty void within him had crept up into his throat and was almost strangling him. 'You're the most incredible thing to have happened to me. What about our bond? Do you really think I would be stupid enough to throw all that away? Of course I'm concerned about Lucy, but I didn't do it, I swear.'

'Don't keep lying to me, Peter. I'm on to you now. I have to protect myself and my family, without having you treating me like an idiot.'

'It's all about you, isn't it? The bloody Miss Charlotte show. If you don't think you can trust me because of other people stirring the shit, then we have nothing.'

'Well, you said it, Peter. We have nothing.'

Peter took to a chair and put his head in his hands. 'Look, Charlie, let's just calm down and make sure Lucy is OK and let's try to find a way through this.'

'Don't call me Charlie. I'll arrange for the jet to take you home tomorrow, Peter.'

Charlotte stormed into the bedroom and slammed the door. Peter took a blanket off the chair and collapsed on the sofa.

Charlotte sat up in bed and sobbed. Mira was her closest friend, and Peter's comments about her being a leech were unfounded. Charles was a good judge of character too, and she always trusted him. And she had to protect Lucy.

She continued to sob, wiping her eyes on a silk handkerchief she'd pushed up her sleeve.

She looked out of the window across the frozen lake. The trees on the shore were lit up by twinkling fairy lights which glistened against the night sky.

She turned and looked at Peter's scruffy old duffel bag on the floor. One pocket was hanging off, and it had a stain in the bottom corner where a pen had leaked. He couldn't even afford a new bag. He was using her, and she knew it, deep down. She looked through the gap in the door at Peter sleeping on the sofa. Beside him was her father's chair: grey, stiff, upright and classic. She imagined him sitting there and meeting Peter. It wouldn't work; her dad wouldn't approve. Above all, she had to trust Peter, and something fundamental had changed.

She sat with a huge fleece blanket around her, looking out across the mountains, unable to sleep, just staring, contemplating her feelings, and rocking back and forth.

The morning light woke Peter. He opened his eyes, aware he was being watched. His sore head was soon forgotten, with the sight of Charlotte in the chair beside him.

'We need to talk.' She seemed stern and cold.

Peter wrapped the blanket around him as he sat up.

'We sure do. Did you mean what you said last night?'

Charlotte took a deep breath. 'Look, Peter, I need to be able to trust the people closest to me. I have too many red flags and yesterday was a step too far.'

Peter sat with his shoulders rounded, slumped forward. His

hair and stubble were rough from the night on the sofa. 'It just doesn't make any sense,' he said. 'One minute we're the happiest couple alive and the next it's all over. It's crazy. I'll say it one last time, and if you don't believe me, then so be it. I can't keep banging my head against a brick wall.'

Charlotte said nothing and kept looking at him.

'I didn't push Lucy. I'm telling the truth and I wish no one any harm.'

'I have to go with my gut feeling, Peter. I always promised myself I wouldn't ignore too many red flags, and Lucy is my top priority.'

Peter stood up, thrust both arms towards her and raised his voice. 'Red flags? What are you on about, red bloody flags? I've done nothing wrong, other than be myself. I don't understand.'

'Peter, you're scaring me,' Charlotte replied, in a quivering voice.

He walked across the room and slammed his hand against the wall. 'Is there someone else? Is that what this is all about? Has old friend Charles been giving you some attention?'

The sarcasm hit Charlotte full-on, which made her tense. 'You're way off, Peter. That's not fair.'

Peter punched the wall with his fist. 'Not fair? *Not fair?* 'What's not fair is that your so-called friends and your devious daughter have managed to poison you against me and convince you I'm some kind of con-man.' He lowered his voice and knelt down close to Charlotte. 'Just look at me and think about all the things we've done together—the feelings, the way we can't bear to be without each other, our kisses—and tell me it's over.'

Charlotte paused. Peter stared into her eyes. She'd seemed about to speak, but held back and looked away. The silence said it all.

'I see,' said Peter.

'I've booked the jet for later this morning.'

'No way am I taking your charity. I'd rather walk home than have you spending a penny on me, thank you. I need to get some air and think about things.'

Peter slammed the door behind him.

Charlotte sat in silence on the sofa. Her phone began to ring. 'Doctor. That's good news, so the scan revealed nothing. When can she come out of the hospital? Just another day. That's fine. I'll call by shortly to see her. Thank you, doctor.'

She quickly texted Mira, who amazingly appeared five minutes later.

'Are you alright, my darling?' Mira wrapped her arms around her. 'You've done the right thing. He's not a nice man. I've just seen him heading to the bobsleigh! First thing on his mind.'

Charlotte burst into tears and the two of them held each other tightly. 'I don't know what I'd do without you, Mira. I'm so upset. As if I don't have enough to cope with.'

'I called in on Lucy and she seems fine. She told me all about it. He's not one of us, Charlotte. He's cruel and would never fit in. There are plenty of other eligible chaps just waiting to sweep you off your feet. Did I mention, Bertie Forbes-Hatherington has just arrived in town?' Mira gave her a knowing look. 'You know how much he likes you.'

Charlotte burst into uncontrollable tears and started wailing.

Peter scuffed around in the cold, working out his exit strategy. He hesitated at the three-way sign. Straight on to the village centre, right to the bobsleigh and left to the train station. He took in a deep breath and headed back to the apartment with a heavy heart.

He knocked on the door. Mira answered.

'I'll see you later, darling.' She gave Peter a sneer and skipped off down the steps.

Charlotte was standing at the window with her arms folded and her back to the door. 'I've booked you a place on the jet.'

Peter walked in, grabbed his bag, and continued to pack. 'No, thanks. I'll make my own way.'

'Don't be stupid, Peter. You're in Austria,' she said, continuing to look out of the window.

'Like I said, I'd rather walk.' He zipped up his pen-stained bag.

'Well, how are you going to get home?'

Peter threw the bag over his shoulder. 'Don't worry about me. You just think about Lucy. How is she?'

'What do you care?'

'I care very much. But I can't stand this injustice.'

Charlotte didn't reply.

'Bye, then,' he said.

She turned around and looked at him with disdain, as if he were a complete stranger.

'Bye, then,' he said one more time. He knew that if he went, there would be no going back. He couldn't procrastinate any more. Slowly, he turned to the door. The pain in his heart filtered through to his legs, each step hurting, killing him, stripping him of all the beautiful thoughts and the warmth which had occupied his being since they'd been together. He reached for the door and looked back one more time.

'I hope Lucy will be OK.'

Charlotte stood upright and dignified, staring at him, watching his every painful step

Peter opened the door. He paused for a moment, still hoping for a change of plan, but there was silence. The cold hit him square on as he took the first step down, and then the next, and, without looking back, allowed the door to close behind him.

He walked to the three-way sign and looked up at the three destinations. *Centre.* He hadn't particularly gelled with the place; he'd found it unwelcoming and harsh. *Bobsleigh.* A dream which had vanished. *Station.* The only place left.

'Excuse me, sir,' a voice said behind him. It was the hotel concierge, looking puzzled. 'I didn't realise you were leaving today. Can we assist with the car, sir?' The man gestured to the elegant black-and-chrome Rolls-Royce waiting in front of the grand doors of the hotel. Peter looked at it, its immaculately polished bodywork reflecting his image like a mirror.

'The car?' he said hesitantly.

'Yes, sir. Where are you heading?'

'Erm, well, the station, I guess.'

The driver opened the door and Peter climbed into the rear seat with its overwhelming smell of leather and cigar smoke. The driver took his scruffy bag and placed it in the cavernous boot. *Boom*, *boom*, went the boot and rear door, and the vehicle floated out onto the street like a luxury liner leaving port.

'The station, sir?' asked the driver.

'Yes, please.' Peter ran his hand over the plush interior, picked up a miniature bottle of whiskey, and promptly returned it to the central console mini-bar.

'What time is your train, sir?' asked the driver.

'I don't know,' replied Peter. 'I don't know.' The station was

900 metres down the road; it was hardly a car journey, but Peter sat back and breathed deeply. He kept his eyes forward and didn't look back.

The train journey was spectacular, traversing steep mountains, crossing dangerous-looking viaducts and disappearing into tunnels drilled straight into the mountainside. Peter was spellbound by the sheer magnificent beauty of the landscape, the snow-covered peaks and the expanse of trees and forest, and wondered how it was possible to engineer such a route. It was a journey he'd rather not have been doing on his own; it was the sort of experience which should be shared and savoured. But it gave Peter time to contemplate and, somehow, try to piece together the events of the last few days and make some sort of sense of it all.

The train stopped at a station in a picture-postcard village. The timber chalets had thick snow on their roofs and logs piled by the doors. People were going about their daily business, and skiers and people on sledges hurtled past as though it was the norm.

Peter gazed out of the window and focused on a cherry tree standing on its own in a field, its trunk disappearing into the immaculate carpet of snow. He could recognise a cherry easily by the orange speckled rings around the silvery grey trunk—a bit like wrinkled stockings, he always thought. He remembered the cherry tree outside his school classroom window. Sometimes he would stare at it and wonder how it changed to match the seasons, and he would always get himself into trouble with the teacher for daydreaming.

The train loaded and unloaded passengers, and Peter

continued to focus on the tree. How did she survive such harsh conditions and then every spring blossom and flourish into such a beautiful specimen, with white or pink flowers and vibrant green leaves? A true miracle of nature. The train pulled away, and the tree stayed in his mind as she slowly disappeared from sight, alone, strong and resilient, waiting for the warmth of spring to show her beauty.

He took the leaky pen out of his bag and from somewhere, God knows where, started to pen some poetry. All he could think about was Charlotte in the mountains, and the solitary cherry tree, so vivid in his mind.

Cherry Tree

Standing proud within winter's deep white carpet,
the robin's song should not wake her from her slumber.
She awaits that shaft of light to stir her earthy optimism,
the power and energy, erect to touch the sky.
Tender to the touch, her buds begin to swell,
the new birth concealed, but not for long.
Her beauty, she will tell.
Glorious the robin's breast, perched on her slender arbour.
He feels her love, her fragile core, but knows the power within
her,
the veins of life in vibrant green, enough to stop the heart.
Her youth and beauty on display, but this is just the start.
Nature's scars, and battle wounds inflicted by deer's antler,
are not enough to stop her growth and blossom year on after.

The words seemed to flow. He'd never written poetry before, but his emotions were running high and his mind was working overtime. Of course, he was hurting—hurting badly. His body was numb, but his eyes were alive, and the vision of the cherry tree, alone in the snow, naturally made him think about what could have been. As the train continued its winding downhill route through the mountains, he became increasingly weak and spent an hour or so staring out of the window, watching spruce tree after spruce tree after spruce tree pass by. It had a hypnotic effect on him.

The train left the mountains and ran along the shore of a splendid lake and towards the city. The change in scenery jolted Peter's brain back to reality. All that dominated his mind was how much he loved Charlotte and how, the further he was from her, the more likely it was that they wouldn't recover from this tragic episode. He took out his phone and pasted the poem into a text to her. His finger hovered briefly over the send button. He thought about how she would react to it and then sent it.

Charlotte headed up to the hospital. She was anxious to make sure Lucy was in full recovery and to get her out as soon as possible. Her phone beeped continuously with messages from Mira and the crowd wanting to know how things were. They had no idea that Peter had gone, but nevertheless, they were concerned at the lack of response from her. Charlotte just ignored them. She felt numb—at times desperately upset, but above all disappointed in Peter, in his behaviour and his total lack of honesty, integrity and responsibility. She was angry that he had turned out to be the man she had feared he was— fickle, spineless and selfish.

~

Charlotte, Lucy and Mira reclined in their leather upholstered seats as the jet took them UK-bound.

Charlotte put her hand on Mira's arm and looked at her for an uncomfortable few seconds. 'I love him. I guess I always will, but I have to let him go.'

'You need a gin and tonic, darling, to get your head straight.' Mira broke physical contact and walked over to the drinks' cabinet.

Charlotte wrapped a blanket tightly around her and said nothing.

By the time their jet had touched down at the private airport just outside London, the one the Queen uses for her trips abroad, Peter had been back in his flat for a week, mopping the rainwater which had come through the leaking roof light and had accumulated in a puddle by the fridge. There was a smell of damp throughout the place, so after he'd tidied up the half-drunk mugs of tea and the abandoned plate from his last meal, he sprayed deodorant into the air to mask the unpleasant, fusty, depressing atmosphere which was his home.

Cartwright was waiting for Charlotte on the runway with the car engine running and the door open. Firm and reassuring, he gestured to the rear seats, took their bags, placed them in the boot and slid into the driver's seat.

'Home, madam,' he said calmly. Charlotte didn't have to say anything as the car purred along the edge of the runway and out through the security gate. She reached in her clutch bag for her phone, opened the text from Peter and read the poem, word by word. She reached the last line and started to sob uncontrollably, the tears rolling down her cheeks and dripping onto her lap, her hand shaking as she tried to stem her outpouring with a tissue from her pocket.

'Lucy?'

'Yes?'

'When Peter pushed you?'

'Yes.'

'What did he say again?'

'Mother! I have a serious head injury here. Do you expect me to remember every detail?'

'You said, "You are obstreperous and inconvenient." Is that correct?'

'Yes! I told you, he was angry. Can we leave it now?'

'Those exact words?'

'*Yes.*'

'That's all I needed to know.'

30

THE ROBIN

Peter paced up and down in the flat and then trudged to the shop to buy some floor cloths and bleach. He felt as though he suddenly had no purpose. Empty, like he'd run out of fuel. The flat was damp and the black mould on the ceiling was spreading wider and wider. He walked back through the park, but not even the trees were of interest.

Perched on a bench, he noticed a plane high in the sky, its white vapour trail billowing. He laughed. Jets, Rolls-Royce, anything you want for breakfast. It wasn't reality. He was kidding himself if he thought he belonged in that world. And it wasn't as if he even craved it. Far from it.

Back at the flat, he put on the radio and embarked on trying to clean the mould off the roof. Elvis came on and he sang away to the words of 'I'm All Shook Up', smiling as he remembered helping his mum and singing along, all those years ago.

$\sim$

There was only one place Peter wanted to go. He walked past the door to the church, where the vicar was pinning up notices in the porch. They acknowledged each other with a nod. Peter approached the grave and looked at the restored headstone, which he'd managed to repair after it had been knocked over thirty years previously. He knelt in front of it and placed the bunch of flowers he'd bought.

'If there's one thing you taught me, Mum,' he said, 'it's to go with your heart, because the heart never lies... and I've done that. You'd think your heart would be tough because of that, but it's not. It's soft and vulnerable. I remember the day I punched Scott Moorfield. I did it because he was being unfair and I had no other way of dealing with him. Today is a bit like that. I gave my heart, and now it's breaking, and it's breaking so badly. What do I do, Mum? My heart says stay and my pride says go.'

Peter couldn't hold in his pain. The tears and the lump in his throat were almost the same as on the day he'd lost her.

'What do I do, Mum? You showed me what true love is, and I found in in the most beautiful woman, but I can't stand the pain again. I lost you and, Mum, the pain has never left me. If you walked up here right now, I'd have you back and the pain would go.' He sank to his elbows and looked at her headstone. 'I wish you were here, Mum. What do I do?'

He felt the vicar's hand on his shoulder. 'She loved you, Peter, and she knew you loved her. Life sometimes isn't fair, and we have to grow strong in order to move on. Where the seed of love has been sown, it will grow, and at the right time and with the right person. She gave that to you.'

Peter nodded and the two of them looked at the grave in silence.

A robin flew onto the headstone from the yew tree and

looked at Peter. She began singing the most beautiful song and flapping her wings, occasionally rising a few inches off the stone and then landing again. Peter held out his hand. The robin stood still, looked at his hand and then at him. He kept his hand still and felt the vicar squeeze his shoulder. The robin flapped her wings again and jumped onto his fingers.

The vicar, Peter, and the robin remained perfectly still. Even the air was still, and there was no sound. The robin seemed to trigger something in Peter's subconscious, almost hypnotising him and pulling at his inner thoughts. She sang her beautiful song one more time, turned away from him, hopped towards his fingertips, then looked back and was gone. Peter looked about him. She wasn't in the tree or on the head-stone. She'd gone, but she'd left him with something. Peter wasn't sure exactly what it was, but his heart seemed to heal slightly; the pain seemed a little less intense, and he smiled. He glanced around for the vicar, but he was also nowhere to be seen. He was alone once again.

31

OBLIGATION OR LOVE?

Charlotte chose the couch instead of the cream leather chair. Mr Shorofski sat back in the opposite chair and looked at her over the top of his wire-rimmed spectacles, as he always did.

'How are you today?' he asked, in his usual calm, liquid voice.

Charlotte adjusted her skirt neatly over her knees and sat up straight. 'I've had a bit of a shock. A man I thought I was in love with cannot be trusted.'

Mr Shorofski, thumb on chin, stroked his lips with the back of his index finger and said nothing.

'For the first time in a long while, I've been happy. Floating on a cloud of intense joy. I couldn't have dreamed of such a connection, yet I've been betrayed.'

He stopped her with his finger. 'And?' he said, looking straight at her.

'I am the head of the family and there's a great deal at stake here. I have to trust my family and closest friends.' She paused and Mr Shorofski let the pause continue, without interrupting.

'But I'm confused. What I feel and what I see and hear are complete opposites. I've put all my faith into my relationships with people who I thought had my best interests at heart, and now I doubt them. Above all, and most worryingly, I feel I've failed as a mother. The two most important people in my life are vying for my attention and I feel I can't have both. If I take one route, I will be a better mother, but will betray myself. The other, I will betray my daughter, but I will be free. Free to love and free to be loved.' She pushed herself out of the chair.

Mr Shorofski nodded. 'A life without choice is a life without meaning. There are many crossroads we encounter in life, and choosing the way ahead can often be painful. You have to decide which is more important. Your head or your heart.'

Charlotte listened intently.

'Which is more important to you, obligation or love?' His calm voice brought her back to her seat. 'Head or heart?' he said, one more time.

She didn't know what to reply and sat still. Dead still.

'Would you be prepared to give up everything for love?' he asked calmly. 'Sometimes we have to value our lives by the warmth and love we find within us and ask ourselves what is most important to us in life.'

Charlotte sat in complete silence. Her counsellor had the unique ability to make her brain do the opposite of what she was expecting. She sat for a good three minutes, thinking, then opened her mouth to speak and nothing came out. She stood up, collected her coat from the stand herself—something she would normally never do—and turned to Mr Shorofski.

'Thank you. I've made up my mind.'

~

The car drew up in front of the house and, on entering, Charlotte could see Lucy on the sofa in the lounge, with her arm, rigid in plaster, resting her legs on a Terence Conran pouffe.

'Mummy, could you fetch my notepaper and a pen?' she called. 'You know, the paper with the family crest? I want to thank my friends for a fabulous ski trip.'

Charlotte didn't reply. She just observed for a moment and then took off her coat and disappeared into the library. She sat motionless at her desk and stared out of the window. A robin flew down from a branch, its red breast distracting her. It stopped and looked directly at her and then, in a blink of an eye, flew onto an adjacent tree and out of sight.

Lucy called out to her again, and so she rose from her seat and entered the lounge.

'How is your arm?' she asked. 'Is it painful? Here, the notepaper. Will you write to all your friends?'

'Yes, it was such a fab holiday.'

'Despite a horrific accident?'

'The doctor said bones heal twice as strong, and I'll be out of this cast in no time. Come and sit with me. You can help me with ideas of what to write.'

'You seem happy.'

'It takes something like this to make you appreciate what's important in life.'

'Is that right?' Charlotte said. She made her excuses and took to her room. She caught a glimpse of her tarot cards and picked them up from the shelf. She hadn't looked at them in quite a while and perhaps they would help her? She sat on the floor, cleared her mind as best she could, took a deep breath and opened the box.

Shuffling them in her usual way, she tried to think positively and asked the deck for guidance. She stopped shuffling and dealt the first three cards from the top onto a pristine slab of Blue John stone.

Now the three cards lay in front of her as though on a mystical altar.

Soulmate

It was unusual for a card to reveal itself twice in a row.

Release and Surrender

The picture showed an angel with open arms, with brilliant light radiating behind it, and the words: 'Open your arms and release the challenges you have held. Open your heart to love and happiness.'

Charlotte's breathing was deep and her hand was shaking.

Deception

The picture was of a seated man wearing a mask. A woman with a painted face stood over him, her hand on his shoulder. His hand was raised in defence.

Charlotte looked at each card, studied the pictures, ran her finger over each one, read the words out loud and pondered the significance.

Soulmate

He'd connected with her like no other human being had ever done. They were completely different people, from different backgrounds and with different beliefs. There were so many red flags, mostly to do with trust. How could he be her soulmate?

Release and surrender

She had done exactly that. She'd put her vulnerable heart right at his feet and he'd tossed it around like a die on a game board. There was no doubt he was a fantastic lover, but how did he know all those moves and lines? He must have been with hundreds of women to fine-tune his art.

Deception

She had to trust the people around her, and they were right. Peter was an outsider.

And he'd crossed a boundary for which there was no excuse. Her friends had told her from the start, but she hadn't listened. How foolish.

She put the cards down and, legs crossed, started to meditate to try to clear her mind, but she couldn't seem to settle. There was something nagging her.

She noticed a fourth card on the floor beside her. It must have been with the original three and had dropped out without her noticing. Should it have been one of the three? Did she fumble the cards and not notice this card was meant to be read with the others? It was face down. She peered at it, wondering whether to turn it over or not. Slowly, she reached for it and picked it up. She took a deep breath and her leg started to shake. What if it was one of the original cards, and she should have looked at it, instead of one of the others?

Her breathing became rapid as she slowly began to turn the card over. She wanted to see its face, but at the same time, didn't. If it wasn't the card she wanted to see, and if she didn't reveal much of it, she could always not have seen it.

She tilted the corner and then, without hesitation, flipped it completely over. Her heart stopped, and she gasped. She turned her head away, so she didn't have to look at it, and threw it onto the floor. Then she stood and made a dash for the door, her body rigid but shaking as she slammed it behind her.

32

THE WRONG TROUSERS

Chris and Anna greeted Peter at the door.

'Come in. Fancy a beer?'

'Sure.'

'Hi, Anna. The dolls been on any skiing adventures recently?'

'I don't really play with dolls much now.' She rolled her eyes with the look of an eight-year-old going on eighteen.

Peter gave up trying to sound cool.

Chris handed Peter a beer. 'Cheers. Well, there's nothing more obvious than a man who wants to talk,' he boomed. He plonked his rotund posterior on a stool while simultaneously taking a huge swig of his beer. 'So... she's dumped you.'

'How do you know?'

'Pete, I've known you long enough to know you're not here to discuss how well your homegrown tomato plants are getting on.'

'Well... yes, she's dumped me. Well... I dumped her. Well... yes, she dumped me.'

Chris stroked his chin. 'Nice and clear-cut then. Do you

want her back?'

'Well... I'm not sure.'

'Well, that's a yes then.' Chris swallowed the last gulp of his beer. 'There's the answer. Right, another one?'

'I mean... no. You just can't treat people like that. One minute you're in love, the next she can't trust me. It's not right. My self-respect won't let me be treated like a piece of dirt. No. I need to move on.'

Chris put both hands on the table and leaned forward. 'Jesus, man! You don't know what you want. Look, it's simple.' He took a crafty look towards the kitchen to make sure no one was listening. He didn't see Anna hiding just around the corner. 'Boy meets girl, girl meets boy. Boy fucks up, and she ditches him. She holds strong, he holds strong, then he has to do all the crawling. That's how it always is. What's your plan? You having another beer, or are you going to sip that all night like an old man?'

'I'm OK. You have another.'

'You need a plan, mate, if you want her back. Pull yourself together, put on your best shirt and get around there to win her over. Or move on, take it on the chin and forget her. It's your choice.'

Peter sat back in the hard wooden chair, looked at the ceiling, and sighed. 'The thing is, the daughter hates me and so do pretty much all her friends. I feel uncomfortable having staff run around after me and, to be honest, I'm struggling to keep up financially.'

'But you love her? Yeah,' Chris said, knocking back his beer.

'Like never before. She has this earthiness, like a tomboy. Fun, yet beautiful too. I just don't seem to fit into her world, though, and I can't seem to do anything right.'

'Pete! I thought you would have worked women out by now after everything you've been through.' He took another look towards the kitchen. 'They're looking for their Prince Charming. The bar is set unrealistically high. One false move and she's already settling for second best. You can't win. I spend most of my married life on bended knee. It's the secret to a hap... happy—well, a marriage.'

Peter pushed his drink away from him. 'Great advice, thanks! Where's the optimism there? I've been done an injustice and of course she had to go with the daughter. Blood is thicker than water, but where's the truth? I need to stick up for myself and make sure honesty wins.'

'Mate, is it just about the game? Or is something greater at stake here?'

'I love her. I can't imagine life without her. I'm not interested in the private jets or the—'

Chris interrupted him. 'Private jets! Listen, mate, I'd eat some humble pie for the sake of a private jet.'

'Seriously, what are you like? I don't know why I even thought you might help.'

'Go and win her back, Pete. Go and win her back.'

Two months passed, and not a day went by when Peter didn't think about her. There were many instances where he was poised to send a text but backed out at the last minute. He figured that if she worked out the truth, she would be in touch. But nothing materialised. He concentrated on his work and managed to get a small deposit down on a little cottage. It wasn't anything flamboyant, but it was something he could call his own and hopefully get away from the ever-encroaching black mould.

One morning, Peter's phone woke him with a jolt. He reached for it. A text message from Charlotte. It was empty. A message with no content. He lay back and pondered what it could mean, and then replied.

'*Did you mean to send that?*'

She replied instantly. '*So sorry Peter, I pressed on you by mistake. x*'

Well! Not only was it a complete surprise to get a response, but it had one thing, and one thing only, which Peter couldn't take his eyes off, and that was the small but very obvious x.

He read it a thousand times, and still didn't know what to do.

Reply and look desperate?

Not reply and look like he didn't care?

Reply and take it too far?

Not reply and lose her forever?

Reply and look stupid?

Not reply and never have the chance again?

He looked at the text again, then up through the roof light far into the sky. 'Mum, what would you do?' he asked.

The clouds parted slowly to reveal the sun. There was a shaft of light which shone straight into his eyes, blinding him temporarily. 'Blimey, that was quick!' He squared his shoulders. 'You only live once, and sometimes that's not for long,' he said to himself. With a determined look on his face, he started to reply, but not before thanking his mum.

'*It's great to hear from you. Look, I'll come straight out with it. I have something for you. I can't really say, but it's important. Can we meet up?*'

He pressed send and instantly regretted sending it. 'Shit,

she's not going to like that.' He backed away from his phone like it was suddenly radioactive. He waited. Waited some more and waited again and nothing. He put the kettle on as a distraction but kept glancing... and... nothing. He poured the water into the mug and stirred the tea bag. 'You've gone and blown it, you idiot,' he said out loud. Then—ping—his phone lit up. He tentatively peered at it, and it was indeed a text from Charlotte. His heart thumped, one big thump, like eight or ten of them had all been squeezed together.

'I don't think it's a good idea to meet up. It's not been an easy time and I don't want to get upset again. Lovely hearing from you x'

Peter's head slumped down and his whole body cramped.

'I understand. I don't want to open up any old wounds, but I really have to get this to you and has to be done in person. Px'

He knew he was pushing his luck and started hopping around the floor like it was on fire. 'Damn, that's going to look really obvious.'

Then—ping—a reply.

'If it's that important, can you just drop it at the house?'

'It's something I'd prefer to give you in person.'

'I guess I could do Wednesday. I can only manage 3pm. Let's say the Adelphi Hotel. I won't have much time. I do hope it's important. Cx'

That was it, that was it! He jumped in the air and ran around the room, knocking over piles of clothes and books.

'Yes!' he cried.

Reply, reply, reply—yes, don't forget to reply.

'That's great, see you at 3pm Pxx'

He tried to act cool and pushed his luck with the extra kiss, but there was a plan and there was a chance. Tomorrow it was.

Wednesday morning came, and after breakfast Peter

dressed in a pair of grey trousers, a blue shirt and a jacket which he felt fit for the Adelphi. He'd promised to pop in on Chris before the date. He was helping him lift some heavy furniture upstairs, but he thought he would also run the situation by him to see whether he was doing the right thing.

'Is this solid oak or is there gold bullion in these drawers?' Peter said later, wiping the sweat from his forehead.

'Hey, if you're not up for the job, I can get Anna in to replace you.'

'Yeah, yeah, fatso, it's actually me that's doing all the lifting here.'

'So, you going to win Miss Charlotte back, then?'

'That's the plan. Do you think I'm doing the right thing?'

'Depends on whether you think she's the right one for you. I mean, is she one of us? Could you bring her around here for a drink and a laugh? Anyway, look, you always said it's better to live your life than to hold back and regret it. Why don't you take a leaf out of your own book?'

Peter nodded.

'Do you still love her?' Chris asked.

'Yes, I really do, from the bottom of my heart. She's amazing.'

'Well, there you are, then. You don't need me to tell you to go for it.'

Peter stood in the doorway to the hall and took in a deep breath. 'You're right. I don't want to lose her.'

Anna came in from the kitchen and handed him a glass of cold water. 'I thought you'd better know something, uncle Pete,' she said.

'What is it?'

'If you're going to win back the girl of your dreams, don't do it in those trousers.'

Peter glanced down. 'What's wrong with these trousers?'

'You look like a 1980s geography teacher, and they're a bit tight.' She wagged a finger and twirled away like a catwalk model.

Chris shook his head. 'Kids, eh?'

Peter didn't have time to go back to the flat and change. And what did an eight-year-old girl know about dating, anyway?

He thought he'd get a small bunch of flowers and after leaving Chris's he headed to a flower stall by the tube station. He rounded a corner, caught a glimpse of himself in a shop window and did a double-take. Damn it, she was right! The trousers looked a little half-mast and were a bit too tight on the bum, too. Oh, no! He wanted to feel confident and look like a man who deserved a woman of Charlotte's class. He had twelve minutes.

Spotting a menswear shop on the opposite side of the street, he dashed in and started browsing the smart-casual trousers. He took a pair into the changing room and put them on. Perfect—the right length and not too teacher-ish this time. He strutted to the cash desk, told the man he wanted to buy them and offered his hip (where the tag was) for him to scan. The man was a little bemused, but blipped the scanner and took his money.

Peter calmly walked out of the shop with his old trousers under his arm. He saw a bin, dumped the old trousers straight into it and scanned the street for a flower stall. A tramp who'd been walking past pulled out the trousers, said, 'Cheers, Mister,' and immediately shoved them into a bag. Peter chuckled. The tramp obviously didn't mind looking like Magnus Pyke, and Peter was happy his old trousers had gone to a good home.

'OK, five minutes,' he said under his breath. He dashed to the flower stand, bought a small but tasteful bunch of blue and white flowers with some green fern, and legged it to the hotel. The trousers felt good, and he felt confident.

Charlotte was already there, waiting. She was wearing a red skirt, black heels and a cream jacket, and she looked incredible. Peter suddenly felt a tad nervous as she noticed him entering the room.

'I've ordered some green tea,' she said. 'How are you?'

'I'm good, really good, thanks. You look absolutely stunning.'

'Thanks, Peter.' She gave him the once-over. 'You look like you've lost a bit of weight.'

'A bit.' He smiled.

'So, what is it?'

Peter took a seat and, after a little hesitation, started to speak. 'Well. First of all, thank you for agreeing to meet. Oh, yes, here are some flowers.'

'They're lovely. Is that it?'

'No. No, not at all. I have something else, but I need to get a few things off my chest first.'

Charlotte didn't move a muscle, just listened intently.

'There are some things that need explaining. You hurt me. Yes, I'm sticking my neck out here. You hurt me because you said you couldn't trust me. For you, it must have seemed straightforward, but for me, it was a shock—no justification and all completely wrong. Yes, I did get into trouble when I was a boy, but I did that for my mum, you know that... and he bloody well deserved it. Even the policeman and vicar said that. It's all water under the bridge, and you know me. I'm not a violent man. Anyway, please let's draw a line under that.'

Charlotte still didn't move. She looked him straight in the

eye and continued to listen.

'I also never touched Lucy that day. You know I wouldn't do that.'

'Peter, look—'

'Hang on a minute, there's more. Nature is at my core, you know that too. The simple things in life are what matter to me, not money, cars or things. Just you and me cycling with the wind in our hair—remember that? Hearts. Hearts is what this is all about; our hearts combined against the world, strong together and saying to everyone, you carry on with your petty lives, because we have it and we have it deep in our souls. I know you feel that too. I've felt it when we make love and you look at me. It's simple, and it's as honest and as clear as day.' Peter took a breath. 'I love you. No, not just three words—I truly, truly love you, and we had it all, and I can't sit back and let it go. You mean the world to me. Your whole being is etched on my heart. I understand your fears, and what happened with Lucy was fake. I didn't go anywhere near her. She was obviously trying to forge a wedge between us, and it worked, but surely we're stronger than that.' He took another breath. 'I don't want anyone else. All I want is you, and that's Charlie I'm talking about. I don't care if you're rich or poor. I can keep you safe, and if we have to live in a cave and eat berries, that would be enough for me. There's nothing more I can say. I know deep down you feel the same, too. I know it, and we shouldn't waste our time with any other thoughts. Come on, Charlie, let's do it—for the rest of our lives. Come on, you and me!'

'Did you have something for me?'

'Oh, yes. Here.' He handed her a neatly presented box, tied with a purple bow.

Charlotte tentatively untied it and opened the lid.

'I hope they're the ones you like.'

'Oh, Peter. What can I say? You know they're my favourites. How clever.' She mused through the contents, deciding whether to partake or save until later. 'OK, look. I heard everything you said and strangely, I believe you. I had my doubts about Lucy that day, but there are other things I need to consider too.'

'Come on, Charlie. You and me. We can beat this.'

Charlotte paused. 'I'm not sure, Peter.'

'One thing I've learned is that you have to be bold and seize every opportunity. If you feel something's good in your heart, then you should fight for it with all your might. Forget about the hearsay and the doubters and listen to your own heart.'

'You make it sound so easy.'

'That's because it is. Think about all the incredible things we have in common. Nature, trees, laughing, kissing, freedom, passion, resilience and defiance against all the things that have tried to keep us down. We're strong because we've grown strong. Now let's grow stronger together.'

Charlotte looked deep into his blue eyes. 'And we could be dead tomorrow.'

'Exactly.'

'I must be out of my head! Don't let me down, Peter.'

Peter nodded and gave her a gentle kiss on the cheek. 'Shall we have a choccy skier to celebrate?'

Charlotte rolled her eyes. 'I thought they were for me.'

Peter smiled.

'You know, you still have the tag on those trousers,' she said, without smiling back.

Peter started to laugh. 'You see. It's right there. I'm an idiot. An idiot who can't even dress himself properly.' He laughed out loud. 'I need a woman just for that, if nothing else.'

Charlotte finally smiled. 'I admire your courage, and I know you meant that from the bottom of your heart.'

He nodded.

'I've had time to think about a lot of things, and it hasn't been easy. I told you I have to listen to my red flags.'

Peter butted in. 'It was never going to be easy with a man like me, but life isn't easy. You have to listen to your heart.'

'But I have listened to you,' she went on, 'and there's no doubt we have a connection like no other. I was happy. Happier than ever. Can I ask you something?'

'Yes, sure.'

'Do you know what obstreperous is?'

'What is this, an entrance exam? Erm, is it something you'd find in a steel foundry?'

'Not quite.'

'Well, why do you ask?'

'It doesn't matter,' she said smiling.

'Is that the exam over?' He just wanted to jump through the roof with excitement, but calmly rose to his feet and touched Charlotte's elbow. She stood up, and he put his muscular arms around her and held her tight. 'I'm going to make sure you're safe and cared for,' he whispered into her ear. 'Let's have some fun, eh? We need some fun; we deserve it. Oh, and don't forget the label while you're there.' They both laughed and squeezed each other tight.

'Peter, there's one more thing.'

'What is it?'

'Thank you for coming today. I gave a lot of thought to what you said about Lucy. I've decided I'm going to pull her out of the school at the end of this year. You were right. I can make that decision, and you helped me make it.'

Peter smiled, then kissed her.

33

THE ELVES ARE COMING

'Hello, badgers,' shouted Peter. He gave a wave, to Charlotte's delight.

'Come on, there's something new I want to show you.'

They approached the place where the fallen tree had once created the secret river crossing, but as Peter grew nearer, he could see a new pristine bridge with a handrail, and steps made from solid timber.

'I had it made,' she said proudly. 'Access for the game-keepers but also... you know where.'

Peter ran his hand over the smooth grain. 'It's stunning. Like the old tree that had fallen.'

'Yes. I asked them to use it to make the planks.'

'You're a genius.'

'I know... and look what I have.'

Charlotte produced her father's hunting knife. 'Let's carve our names on it.'

'You could have had a bespoke sign made with your name on.'

'Peter! Let me tell you something. It's the simple things in life which are important.' She giggled. 'And not the things you can "just have". I can't remember who told me that.' She was laughing so much, she nearly fell into the river.

Peter shook his head and started laughing, too. 'Well, get carving then, know-it-all.' He offered his strong arm and pulled her close. They stood completely still, saying nothing, just looking deep into each other's eyes. It was a look that registered in their stomachs and, as their pupils dilated, entered each other's souls. Peter squeezed her tight to his chest. His heart beat against her. Boom, it went. Boom. Resonating with strength and courage.

The swing hung motionless, as if waiting patiently for Charlotte to take her position and bring it to life.

'I'm home, Peter. Call me by my name. My real name.'

'You're home, Charlie.' He grabbed the ropes and began to push.

'Yes. Push me hard. I want to fly.'

She flew higher and higher, her legs flailing in the air as Peter pushed and pushed. She giggled loudly and as the swing drew back, Peter jumped, clasped the ropes with both hands and clambered onto the seat, so that he was standing on either side of Charlotte as they swung together.

'Yee-ha,' he shouted, like a flying cowboy.

The afternoon raced along and, after more swing acrobatics and stone-skimming practice, they eventually collapsed on the stony beach, Peter reclining on his elbows while Charlotte rested on his chest.

'I've never shared this with anyone. Just didn't seem right, before. The thing is, when I'm with you, I forget about the world. I forget about everything, and just be in the now. I feel free and relaxed and honest. Do you know what I mean?'

'Of course. It's the same for me.'

'But you don't have the same worries as me.'

'We all have worries, Charlotte. The biggest thing I've learned is not to dwell on the past. There's nothing we can do about it. What's the point? It's difficult, I know. I'm not saying I don't get dragged back occasionally, but the here and now is where we are.'

'You make it all sound so easy and simple.'

'Well, it is. Follow your heart and everything will be OK, Mum used to say.'

'Will you help me?'

'Depends.'

'Don't let me lose sight of all that. Pull me into line when I'm getting confused.'

'You don't need me to do that. You already know it. Just be true to yourself. It's your stone-skimming which needs real attention.' They laughed and Charlotte lobbed a large stone into the water, which plopped and disappeared instantly.

'Can we forget what happened between us?'

'Of course we can. It's all part of our individual growth, but more importantly our growth together. We're learning all the time.'

'I know you're right. I'm getting hungry,' Charlotte said, pretending to munch on a handful of acorns. 'Let's go back and have some lunch, and I want to show you around the house.'

They entered the arched wooden door and kicked off their shoes. 'If you're going to be the man of this house, you'd better know your way around.'

'But I'm not...'

Charlotte put her finger on his lips. 'I know. Shhh. I have things I want to share with you.'

She led Peter to a stout wooden door off the grand hall and opened it wide. There was a huge table in the middle of the room, strewn with paper of every colour, paints and brushes, handwritten manuscripts and half-finished patchwork blankets.

'It used to be the hunting room,' Charlotte said. 'Full of guns, and gross heads of all the poor beasts who dared to roam the estate. I made it into an art room. Well, a creative room. I'd like to spend more time in here, when I can.'

Peter walked up to the desk. 'My mum used to write poetry and paint sometimes. I like to make things from wood. Is there a workshop?'

'That must be where you get your poetry skills?'

Peter blushed.

'No, but there could be. The old stable could quite easily be converted into a woodwork shop. Would you teach me how to make things from wood?'

Peter laughed and nodded.

The next room felt chilly and smelled of mothballs. Peter couldn't believe his eyes as he scanned painting after painting stacked side by side on the floor, stretching from one wall to the other. Some were so huge, they almost touched the ceiling, and there were others piled on top of each other. Charlotte grabbed one and pulled it out.

'It's a small Renoir,' she said, while carrying on rummaging. 'There's a Constable in here somewhere, too. I've been planning to put it up in the dining room. I must get Cartwright to sort it.'

Peter was gobsmacked and shook his head in disbelief.

'Come on, I want to show you the secret passage.'

They entered a wood-panelled corridor, and Charlotte leaned back. 'You see that candlestick?' she said, pointing.

Peter nodded.

'Pull it toward you.'

'This is like something from a movie,' he said, tentatively pulling it. The wooden panel beside the candlestick began to move, revealing a small passageway beyond. Charlotte entered and Peter followed, bowing his head in the narrow space that seemed to run between the walls, before a small flight of wooden steps brought them to a dead end. Charlotte stopped, smiled a huge smile, and then pushed hard with both hands against what looked like a solid wall. Suddenly, Peter could see a chink of daylight, and as the wall moved it revealed a room beyond, with solid oak carved panelling, and an ornate painted ceiling. The oak floor was partially covered by an immense tiger skin, which on closer inspection had the paws and head still attached. Peter turned away. He didn't like to see that a wild animal had been made into something you walked over. He tiptoed around it and stood looking at a large wooden desk with a reading lamp. There was a blotting-paper writing pad with an inkwell beside it holding a pen.

'Wow. This looks like somewhere the Queen would write letters or stamp official documents.'

'It's Father's office. It was always private when I was young, but I come in here secretly and occasionally and sit in his chair. I haven't moved anything. It's the same as it was when he was alive.' She opened a drawer in the vast desk and slid in the hunting knife.

'It looks like a shrine in here. The portrait on the wall and the slippers under the desk.'

'I guess so. All his personal items are in here. I didn't know what to do with them. It seemed wrong to throw it all away.' She shrugged and pushed herself out of the chair. 'I loved him, but I hated him too, so I can just shut the door on him and have my peace.'

'Sounds like the opposite to me.'

'Come on, let me show you the King's room.'

Further along the corridor was another stout solid-wooden door. Charlotte twisted the golden knob and, as Peter saw inside, he gasped. A four-poster bed stood majestic in the centre of the room, with blue-and-gold drapes hanging in folds to form a shelter above. This room was carpeted again in deep blue and with the royal crest in gold.

'Henry VIII reportedly slept here, and so did Princess Margaret. We really hope, one day, it might see another royal visitor.'

Peter sat on it and bounced up and down. 'It's not very comfortable.'

'I know! It's like concrete.'

They both laughed, and Peter pulled Charlotte on top of him. 'Fancy being my queen?'

Charlotte looked deep into his eyes. 'Maybe.'

They left the room and walked a little further to yet another intimidating door. When Charlotte opened it, Peter saw a blaze of pink and make-up and clothes all over the floor.

'This is Lucy's room.'

'Jeez! That's a man's idea of hell.'

'It's my idea of hell. She insists on not having it tidied.'

They moved on swiftly and, at the very end, Charlotte slowly opened another door and peered in. 'Mother? Mother?' She smiled and closed the door again. 'She's sleeping. We'd better not disturb her.'

Peter grimaced and put his finger over his lips, and exaggerated a tiptoed escape.

They then descended a black wrought-iron spiral staircase to the lower floor.

'Let's have some lunch. I'll show you my room later.' Charlotte smiled and started to race Peter to the dining room, where canapés awaited them.

Peter poured water into crystal glasses and handed one to Charlotte.

'I do hope I haven't exhausted you, showing you the house?' she asked politely.

Peter gulped some water. 'Seeing that room of your father's made me think about how nice it would be to have had the same for my mother, but she had nothing. Well, apart from her clothes, shoes and some trinket jewellery. There's nothing left. Just memories.'

'I'm sorry, Peter, she was obviously a wonderful woman.'

Peter nodded and scrunched his lips, holding back a tear. 'I do have her chair. I forgot. Her little leather chair. I have that.'

'Look, I've been thinking about how you make me feel and everything you've said about realising what's important in life and learning to trust. Why don't you bring your mum's chair here and we can set up a room for her? We could get some paintings of Yorkshire and fill it with flowers every day.'

'What? And put sheepskins and coal dust on the floor? No, thanks.'

'I was only trying to help.'

'I know. I'm sorry, but she's gone now. I don't really need some fancy shrine.'

'I'm sorry too. I didn't mean to put pressure on you.'

'Do you mean what you say about us having a proper relationship?'

'Yes, Peter. I do. It feels funny saying it, but I mean it. You've made me wake up and realise how stupid I've been.'

'Are you sure you can trust me? I'm a known criminal.'

'Please. Don't rub it in. I'm learning to overcome that. I've had some issues with money going missing in the past and I'm just scared I'm not up to the job and might lose everything, and then Lucy will have nothing and be homeless.'

'I can't see that happening, really. You're a very capable woman. Just believe in yourself and believe in us.'

'I'll try, Peter. You make it all seem so easy.'

Suddenly an almighty crash followed by a heavy thud could be heard within the house.

'What was that?' Peter asked.

'I think it could be Mother. I'd better go and check.'

'I'll come too. It sounded bad.'

'No, Peter. She hasn't met you yet. She might get spooked.'

Charlotte disappeared, and Peter took the opportunity to nibble on crudités and bread. He wanted to go up and help, but after a few minutes, Charlotte was back at her seat and looking a little forlorn.

'Was it her? How is she?'

Charlotte burst into tears and tried to prevent her mascara running down her cheek with the cotton napkin. 'I'm losing her, Peter. She's ill, so very ill, and it breaks my heart to see her like that. If only there was a cure, I'd buy it, no matter what the cost.' She shivered. 'It's so sad. I don't know what to do. She hardly recognises me these days.'

Peter rose to his feet and put his arms around her. 'Hugs always made things better when Mum was around. Hugs are the greatest thing in the whole world.'

'You're so right, Peter. You make me feel safe when I'm in your arms. I feel fragile sometimes. I know I don't always show it, but I do. That's what I admire about you. When you're here, I feel invincible. My tarot cards said I would meet my soul-mate, and that I had to release and surrender. I'm doing that right now, Peter. I can do this, but I want you by my side.' She lifted her head and stared into his eyes, as though she wanted to say something else, but couldn't.

'What is it?' he said, holding her hand tight.

'You won't let me down, will you? Please don't let me down.'

'I won't. I'm here for you, for us. I'm so madly in love with you, nothing is going to stand in my way.'

'You promise?'

'Of course.'

Suddenly, Vincent barked loudly, and the door burst open. 'Mummy, I've missed you so much. I hate that school.'

'What on earth are you doing here? Did Cartwright fetch you?'

'No, they sent us home early for the weekend because of a leaking water boiler which flooded the whole upper school. I got a cab and put it on the account. Hello, Vincent, my only friend,' she said, ruffling him behind the ears.

'I wish you'd called.'

'I did, but you didn't answer. Anyway, what's *he* doing here?'

Peter jumped straight in. 'Hi, Lucy, how's the arm?'

'It hurts, thanks to you.'

'*Lucy.*'

'It's alright, Charlotte. Maybe this is a good time to put things to rest and move on, for the good of us all.'

Lucy chomped her chewing gum loudly and gave him an indignant look.

'Maybe it's time to forget about the past,' Peter went on. 'Your mum and I have been talking and we're going to make a go of things. I want you to know I'm not here to push you away. In fact, the complete opposite. If your mum has less to worry about, then she has more time for you. I'm here to make things better. We draw a line under what happened in Austria. As far as I'm concerned, it never happened. And maybe now we can become friends.'

Lucy looked at Peter with daggers in her eyes.

Charlotte put her hand on his knee. 'Thank you, Peter, that sounds like a good compromise. Lucy?'

'Well, you would want it to "just go away", wouldn't you?' she said, with her head cocked to one side.

Charlotte stepped straight in. 'Lucy. We're drawing a line under this now.'

'OK, in that case I want you and me to go pony-trekking this weekend. To the place you've been promising to take me—just the two of us.'

Charlotte sighed. 'You can't just storm in like that and demand a weekend away. Peter is here for the weekend. He's our guest.'

'See! Just as I thought. He comes first, and I have to look after myself. It's just not fair.'

'Lucy, you're over reacting. It's not possible to go trekking this weekend. You have to book these things.'

Lucy stamped her feet. 'I hate you, I don't want you in this house. I hate you. I hate you both.' She stormed out of the room.

Charlotte shook her head and looked at Peter. 'What are we going to do?'

'She'll come around. Let's give her time,' said Peter, giving her a reassuring hug.

'It's beautiful, isn't it?'

'Yes, it really is,' the old lady said, without turning her head.

She was sitting in the dappled shade of a tree with far-stretching lateral branches. The morning sun was warm and her footprints were still visible in the dew on the lawn. A delicate bone-china cup and saucer lay beside a teapot and a small glass vase, randomly stuffed with handpicked forget-me-nots, herb robert and green fern.

Peter calmly rested his hand upon the back of the intricate white metal seat. 'It's one of my all-time favourites,' he said.

Continuing to look forward, she sipped her tea. 'And mine. But do you know her secret?'

Peter smiled. 'Yes, I do.'

She turned her head and looked at him. 'Come. Sit beside me.' She unfolded her shawl and placed it over both their knees, and smiled.

'I must introduce myself. I'm Peter.'

'I know who you are. The accent of a northern miner and one who knows the secret of the walnut. You're "the new man".'

'Have there been many?'

'No. My daughter may be somewhat flaky, but she is discerning. Anyway, tell me the secret of the walnut.'

Peter smiled 'You mean the ladder?'

'Go on.'

Peter reached for a sizeable twig from the lawn, snapped it in two and peeled it into separate halves, revealing an intricate ladder running throughout the core. 'This is the ladder,' he said, showing it to her.

She smiled and took his hand, gently examining his palm and fingers with her thumb.

'Rough and practical hands,' she said. She continued to explore the contours of his hand and then looked out beyond the walnut tree. 'When I was a young girl, I had a walnut tree in my garden. I used to dream about climbing down the ladder into the heart of the tree. Through the roots and deep into another world. A world where I was free to explore, climb and run without a care. I had friends among the roots—pixies and fairies who I would laugh with and who would play tricks on each other. I'm glad you know the secret.' She paused. 'Rough hands,' she said, slowly turning her head. 'Honest hands.' She paused again. 'You're here for a reason. I can feel it.' She looked straight into Peter's eyes. 'Things are going to change. Unrest. Yes, unrest in the house.' Her brow narrowed and creased. 'But peace will follow.'

Her gaze seemed to penetrate Peter's mind and, although he didn't understand what she was saying, he felt a tingle in his hand and a warmth within his heart.

'You're a beautiful woman. It's a privilege to get to know you, Lady Winterbourne.'

'Look after her, Peter. Look after her. The elves are coming. The elves. I can see them hiding in the bushes. They're coming for us. Is it summer or winter? The elves are coming.'

Peter took her hand and held it tight. 'It's going to be alright,' he said. 'It's going to be alright.'

34

THE STORM

'Thank you.'

'Thanks for what?' Peter replied.

'There's a new warmth in the house. I know it's silly, but the whole place feels warmer and brighter when you're here. Even Lucy seems different. Must have been your chat with her a few weeks ago when you were last here.'

'That's my bubbly personality and sharp wit you're talking about, and my ability to deal with troublesome teenagers.'

'Mmmm, well, whatever it is, I'm liking it. And you haven't kissed me in at least two hours. You're neglecting your duties.'

'Well, let me put that right.' He walked towards her with a swagger, put one arm under her legs and the other behind her back, and picked her up in one clean lift. She couldn't take her eyes off his. They seemed purposeful and just as she remembered from their early dates. He definitely had the look of the wolf in him, which made her quiver. Peter carried her over to the window seat and laid her down gently. Then, as if with wolf blood running through his veins, he unbuttoned his shirt and threw it onto the floor. Charlotte bit her lip with anticipation. He then dropped down beside her, took her head in his hand and caressed her ear lobe. Again, she quivered and her breathing quickened. His hands started to explore her neck, then shoulders, and occasionally his forearm brushed her nipple, which increased her delight. Then it came. The most beautiful kiss, tender and soft, yet confident and, oh my, a one-way ticket to surrender. She touched his hair and ran her hand down to the back of his head, and then along his bare and bulging bicep.

'Tea, madam?' Cartwright's voice stopped them in their tracks and Peter scrambled for his shirt.

'Oh, no thanks, Cartwright.' Charlotte's out-of-breath voice somehow made Peter's bare chest even more obvious.

'No, not right now.'

'Right you are, madam,' he said with a courteous nod and then vanished into the hallway.

'Jeez! He scared the living daylights out of me. Talk about bad timing,' Peter said in a huff. 'Was he watching through the keyhole for his moment?'

'Sometimes I wonder,' Charlotte replied, adjusting her blouse and sitting upright.

A large tree branch suddenly hit the window, startling the two of them.

'There's a storm coming,' Peter said. 'I heard it on the radio. A big one—high winds and rain. Must be brewing out there.'

'I must get the estate staff to batten down the hatches.' With that, Charlotte picked up her phone to call the estate yard and put the wheels in motion. She looked out of the window, where torrential rain had already begun battering the glass.

'Is that your new car outside?' she said, while waiting for them to answer.

'Oh, erm, yes. The old one was on its last legs and I've had some good jobs come in lately.'

'Looks nice.'

'It's a pickup but with heated seats and a satnav.'

'The Aston Martin is still waiting for you in the garage, you know.'

'Please, Charlotte, not now.'

'You didn't have to get yourself one. It's yours. I told you that. Why are you so against it?'

Peter started to speak, but then the estate yard answered. Charlotte instructed them to fasten down anything which could potentially move, and to close the sluice-gate to the upper pond so that the water would be diverted into the river and not overspill towards the house.

Vincent, who had been snoozing in his bed by the fire, became anxious as the wind whistled down the chimney, causing a backdraught into his face. He made a whimpering sound and kept looking at them for reassurance.

Peter stroked him. 'It's going to be OK, Vinny. Just some wind. It'll be all over in a day or two.'

Vincent didn't seem to understand and kept close to Peter's legs.

'So, you never really said why the DB5 wasn't good enough,' Charlotte said stubbornly.

Peter sighed, turned his eyes to the ground and then back to meet hers. 'It's the car that killed my mum. An Aston DB5. Some idiot, over the alcohol limit, thinking he was some kind of hero. A selfish bastard who didn't care about anyone else and was in a car that made him feel invincible. I just can't face taking that out onto the road, let alone having it as mine. I'm meant to have old crappy second-hand cars and cheap pickups.'

'I understand about your mum, but I can assure you that it wasn't this car. I knew the previous owner.'

'Thanks for understanding. You're helping me too. Challenging my thoughts and trying to make sure I follow some of my own rules, like not living in the past.'

Charlotte nodded. 'You can't have double standards, Peter.'

'You're so right. At least I'll think about the car.'

'I'd like that.'

Another sizeable branch crashed against the glass, making all three of them jump. The wind was whistling through every gap and crevice of the old building. Vincent cowered under the coffee table and Peter suggested they all congregate in the study in the centre of the house, prepare everything and hunker down for the night. Charlotte called Lucy, who was listening to music with her headphones on and hadn't noticed anything. Peter and the staff ran around making sure all was secure, while Charlotte and Lucy cuddled up together on the sofa, wrapped in a huge blanket.

Peter checked outside while he was letting Vincent out of the front door and noticed the heavy topiary pots were already lying on the ground. Within one minute, Vincent was back in and shaking off the water on his back.

The vicious wind whipped the building and tested the trees, and the rain didn't stop all night or the following day. The government declared a national emergency as vast areas of countryside, villages and some towns were deluged and cut off by floodwater.

The next day, they woke to silence. No wind and no rain battering the windows.

'I feel uneasy,' Charlotte said, pulling up the bedsheets around her shoulders.

'I'll get up and see what the damage is.' Peter gave her a

kiss and then leaped into his jeans. He met Cartwright in the hall, who told him it appeared they'd got away virtually unscathed, apart from the topiary and other various pots strewn all over, a mature tree down in the parkland, which was nowhere near the drive, and a smashed window in the orangery. Peter ventured outside, where there were various utility vehicles and the staff were remedying the damage.

Charlotte was watching from the window, with Lucy and Vincent by her side.

Peter rolled his sleeves up and gave a helping hand to right the huge earthenware pots and gather up stray tree branches to load into the back of a truck.

Charlotte had arranged for breakfast to be served in the pantry, where the Aga constantly warmed the air and the large oak table could accommodate everyone.

'It looks like only superficial damage,' Peter said, on entering the room. He washed his hands in the white Belfast sink and stood in front of the Aga to warm his core. 'There's the odd roof tile down and a few smashed windows, but we're dry and warm, and there's nothing that can't be fixed.'

Charlotte poured Peter some tea and took it to him. 'You're my hero.' She handed him the mug. 'It was a vicious storm. I'm glad we're all safe.'

Lucy rolled her eyes and coughed in order to prevent any kind of embrace from anyone. Stuffing a triangle of buttered toast into her mouth, she stood and walked to the door, while encouraging Vincent. 'I'm taking him out for a walk. I'll assess the damage and probably go and look at the fallen tree in the parkland.'

'Be careful of that tree,' Peter urged. 'It might be on the ground, but could twist and roll, so don't go underneath it. It's best I come with you.'

'No, thanks. We know what we're doing. It's our house. Come on, Vincent.'

'Leave her, Peter. She knows the estate well. Let them have some freedom.'

Peter plonked himself at the table and started eying up the cinnamon rolls.

'I think Vincent's lead is broken,' Charlotte called through the open door. 'The clasp is damaged.'

Lucy shouted back from halfway along the hall. 'I've tied it directly to the collar. It'll be fine.'

As she left, Peter said, 'I asked Cartwright to organise the window and roof repairs. Most of the minor jobs I can probably do myself.'

'Thanks, Peter.'

Peter nodded and proceeded to stuff pastry into his smiling mouth. 'I'll go round the rest of the house after breakfast and get the wider picture for you, if you want?' he said, after swallowing his mouthful. 'Has anyone checked on your mother?'

'Thanks, Peter, that's very kind. Yes, I saw her earlier. She's fine. I had breakfast sent up to her.'

Peter looked at Charlotte. He liked how she wore her hair up, just simply tied back with a band. It was her 'I don't have time to do anything with this' look. He studied how naturally beautiful she was with no make-up, and his eyes fell on the freckle on her ear.

'You're the most beautiful woman I've ever seen. You know that?'

Charlotte pretended to go all coy on him. 'Really?'

'Yes,' he said, and carried on staring at her.

Charlotte looked at him and smiled.

When Peter had finished his breakfast, he headed out around the house to establish if there was any more damage.

Charlotte had decided to check on her mother again and to chat with Mrs Hathersage about provisions for the next few days. Given the circumstances, she wanted to offer the possibility of hiring some temporary help, if it were required.

Peter surveyed every room in the house, checking the windows and for any water ingress. There were rooms which looked like they'd never been entered before, stale-smelling and cobwebby. Some were like museum pieces, some seemed like storage rooms for antiques and paintings, and some were lived-in and loved spaces like in any house. He exited via the courtyard door and surveyed the outer perimeter of the house. A gnarly old willow tree had had a huge branch shed and was now lying on the ground. A small table was wedged behind a drainpipe, which he promptly dealt with, noting the bracket needed replacing. Turning the corner, he approached the service yard area. This was effectively the back door to the main kitchen, the delivery yard and bin store—a place well hidden from the grandeur of the frontage and never to be seen by any guests or royalty. Cartwright was loading items into the rear of his car. He walked by and noticed silverware, and what appeared to be a painting or two wrapped in hessian.

'Are there many damaged items?' Peter enquired.

'A few, sir,' he replied. 'I'll drop them at the repairer's later this morning.'

Peter carried on his surveillance and then returned, to catch Charlotte singing to herself in front of the Aga.

'The snow is snowing, the wind is blowing, but I can weather the storm,' she sang. 'Peter, how is everything?'

At that moment, the door flung open and was nearly detached from its hinges. In burst Lucy, covered in mud and screaming.

'Come quickly. Vincent is trapped under the water. Come quickly, he's going to die.'

Peter and Charlotte followed her without hesitation as she ran out across the garden and over towards the upper pond.

'Please hurry,' she cried.

The sturdy and imposing sluice-gate was capable of diverting vast amounts of water into the upper and lower ponds. They were called 'the ponds', but in any other situation, lakes would probably be a better description. Peter peered down into the deep gully that funnelled the torrent of water which was forcing itself through the sluice and down into the pond below. He could just make out the top of Vincent's head as he tried to keep afloat.

'He's down there!' Lucy shouted and pointed. 'He's going to die!'

Peter flung off his jacket and immediately dived into the fast-flowing water. The current dragged him under, and he struggled to breathe. With all his might, he surfaced, took a life-saving breath and dived again, to a position where he could wedge his leg against the wooden sluice and push the dog out of the water. Frantically, he tried to force Vincent out, but he soon realised his lead was trapped in the sluice. He grabbed the lead with one hand and held Vincent's head above the water with the other, and plunged under. He tugged the lead, but it was jammed. He pulled and pulled, but the harder he tried, the more it seemed to bite. Eventually, he resurfaced and gasped for air.

'Lucy,' he shouted. 'You need to open the sluice. Do it!'

Lucy panicked. Peter recalled opening the lock gate on the canal when he was a boy. It was the same principal.

'Rotate the wheel in front of you anti-clockwise,' he shouted, before going under again. He tried to force the lead again, but it was stuck solid. Releasing his own breath, he held the dog once again so that it was partially out of the water, in the hope he might survive. Lucy put her hands on the large metal wheel and tried to turn it. Charlotte tried too, but the force of the water was making the gate impossible to move. Peter came to the surface once more and with his eyes looking straight into Lucy's, he shouted, 'Do it! Do it now, for both of us.' He then disappeared beneath the torrent.

Lucy and Charlotte gave all their strength against the wheel and suddenly it moved, not much, but enough to give them confidence they could do it. Peter emerged again, but this time he couldn't shout. They moved the wheel a little more. Peter was struggling to hold on to Vincent. His strength was waning as his body demanded oxygen. They moved the wheel a little more, but it wasn't sufficient to dislodge the trapped lead or release the force of the water. They moved it again, but both Peter's and Vincent's heads were now completely submerged. Together, they forced the wheel.

Charlotte cried out, 'Peter, Peter!'

'No, don't do it,' Lucy said, grabbing her arm, as Charlotte abandoned the wheel to jump in after them.

Peter felt dizzy and disorientated. His vision under the water was increasingly blurry as he searched with his hand for the clasp on the collar. He fumbled with his fingers and remembered the lead had been tied to it. There was nothing he could do. He felt the overwhelming urge to take a breath, but resisted and felt his stomach buck. He kicked with his leg and forced his head out of the water, enough to take in a breath and then sink again. He tugged violently at the lead, angry that he couldn't dislodge it.

Charlotte crouched overlooking the water and shouted at the top of her voice for Peter to come back to the surface. Tears poured down her face as she wrung her hands. Lucy tried with everything she had to turn the wheel, but it was rusty, and the force of the water impeded any further movement.

The torrent of water and lack of oxygen had depleted Peter's strength, but not his determination. He forced his foot against the sluice, gritted his teeth as water filled his mouth and gave the lead one final pull. It came loose. He closed his eyes and grabbed Vincent tight into his body and then felt the power of the water expel them downstream. He was powerless to resist the force and went with it, tumbling in the turbulent flow like a piece of driftwood.

Charlotte ran down the bank, not taking her eye off them, tracking them until they became grounded on the pebbled shore. She grabbed Peter's shirt and turned him over. Still clutching the dog, he lay still, not moving.

'*Peter*,' she wailed.

She knelt in the water and pushed his back to try to get him on his side. His body was like a dead weight. She pushed his shoulder, and he flopped with his face down into the dirt and stones. She thumped him in the back with her fist.

'Peter! Peter!'

35

MIRA'S HUNCH

'He's dead!' they both shouted simultaneously.

Lucy copied Charlotte, opening Vincent's mouth and thumping her hand between his shoulders.

'He's not breathing. Please do something.'

Charlotte looked at Lucy. Their desperate silence hindered any further action.

Peter suddenly coughed and vomited. His breathing shallow and rapid, he lay motionless.

'Peter, thank god you're alright.' Charlotte grabbed his jacket and placed it over his wet back. 'I thought I'd lost you.'

'He's dead. He's dead. You didn't save him. He's dead.' Lucy collapsed in a heap beside Vincent. He was cold and lifeless.

Charlotte looked at her. 'There's nothing more we can do. Let's get Peter back to the house.'

Lucy took no notice. She flailed her arms and wailed in agony, her whole body tense with anguish and frustration. 'You didn't save him.'

~

The bedroom door opened and out came Charlotte's doctor. 'He'll be fine. I recommend rest for a day or so and keeping him warm, but he's been lucky. Maybe some soup or warm tea would help.'

'Thank you, doctor. I appreciate you coming out so quickly.'

The doctor nodded and closed the door behind him.

Lucy confined herself to her bed for the following two days. She nibbled on cheese and declined anything else. She couldn't imagine life without Vincent. She'd loved him. He'd always been excited to see her, and when she was at home, he'd routinely slept at the foot of her bed. The pain in her heart wouldn't subside, and she cried for him.

Charlotte popped in with glasses of water and even chocolate, but Lucy didn't want to talk.

Charlotte had loved Vincent too. She recalled the day she took him home from the rescue centre and sighed. 'I have to head to London to sort a few things. I suggest you come with me. Take your mind off things?'

Lucy shook her head. 'No. I'll stay, but don't be away long, will you?'

'I won't. Just a day. Cartwright and Mrs Hathersage are on duty, and Mother is in her room. Are you sure you won't come with me?'

'I'm sure. I'll talk to the gamekeepers about a burial for Vincent. Can we do that when you return?'

'Of course we can,'

Charlotte took tea in for Peter. 'I'm heading into London. I have an important meeting, but I'll be back tomorrow evening. I would suggest your coming with me, but I think it's best you rest. I'll get a cab and see you tomorrow.'

Peter sat up in bed and nodded. 'I won't argue. Let me

know when you get there safely.'

She kissed him on the forehead and headed out the door.

The following day, Peter took a stroll around the garden. He took the air deep into his lungs and felt thankful he was able to breathe and walk around. Some roses had become detached from their stakes, and there were one or two storm-damaged climbers and precarious trellis panels. He set to re-tying the roses and adjusting the trellis. The wisteria needed some remedial pruning. Peter considered for a moment that there might be a disgruntled gardener who he could be rubbing up the wrong way. Perhaps he might even be doing them out of a job. But Peter felt capable; he wanted to do it and it seemed like the household needed all the help it could get, so he set out looking for some secateurs or a knife. He kept quiet about his search because he didn't want to put anyone out, but working in the garden felt like a bit of therapy after his ordeal in the sluice. He tried the door of a locked shed, but to no avail. He searched the drawers in the kitchen, but other than various kitchen knives and some scissors which weren't large enough to cut through the substantial stems, he drew a blank. He then remembered Charlotte's father's hunting knife. Perfect, he thought. He dashed upstairs, pulled the candlestick and crept along the secret passage, and into his study, where the right-hand drawer contained the knife within its leather sheath. He only needed it for a few minutes and would restore it to its position when he was finished.

The knife sliced perfectly through the climber stems, producing the clean cut he was intending. Peter removed the torn-out sections, reattached the rambling stems to the trellis and trailed them back along the top of the veranda. He was impressed at how sharp the knife was and how easily it had done its work. He smiled as the sun caught the silver blade and, with a bit of spit and a careful rub on his shirt, it gleamed as good as new. He slid it back into the sheath, promptly returned it to its place within the drawer and closed it. He was just righting the candlestick when Lucy came around the corner.

'Sorry, I didn't see you there,' he said, nearly bumping into her.

'You're alive, then?'

'Thankfully. Yes. How are you? It was quite an ordeal up there.'

'No thanks to you.'

Peter held his tongue and made a thin-lipped smile.

'I loved him,' she said, wiping a tear from her cheek.

'I know that. He loved you, too. He was a brave dog. I'm sorry... sorry I couldn't do more.'

'Me too,' she said, turning her back and continuing to her room.

Peter watched her disappear, then headed for the orangery, where he apologised to Mrs Hathersage profusely about being late for lunch.

'It's not a problem, Peter. It's just a stew chef made earlier. It can wait until you're ready. I saw that you were busy repairing the wisteria and knew you might be delayed.'

'What would Charlotte do without you?' Peter said, placing his napkin on his knee.

'I was thinking exactly the same myself,' she said, then disappeared into the kitchen. Moments later, she reappeared with a steaming bowl of stew and potatoes.

'I'll make tracks after lunch,' Peter said. 'I have things to catch up on at home and it seems a bit strange being here without Charlotte.'

'I'm sure she would want you to stay, Peter. You're no burden to us.'

'That's kind, but I've neglected my own life recently.'

'Right you are,' she said, with a warm smile,

Charlotte had neglected a number of her commitments too and, although sad to leave Peter and Lucy, she had meetings she couldn't put off anymore. No sooner was she back at the London house, than there was a knock at the door. Mira marched in with gusto.

'I was just passing and heard you were in town.'

'Mira, how lovely to see you.' *Mwah, mwah.* They kissed, and Charlotte took her coat.

'So... long time no see. I thought he'd chopped you up with a chainsaw and buried you under the Venetian paving.'

'I assume you're talking about Peter.'

'Who else, darling?'

'Sometimes, Mira, you are totally out of order. Why on earth would he want to do that?'

'Maybe to move someone else into your home once you're gone?'

'Mira, have you had a shock to the head?'

'No. But it looks like you have. I heard about Vincent's death. Unavoidable, by all accounts.'

'You've been talking to Lucy?'

'She filled me in on the whole charade.'

'I can tell you, he did everything he could, and I don't doubt that.'

'Just be careful. I told you I have a hunch about that man. Anyway, I haven't been to Loxley in what seems an age. Do you still have the lemon tree I gave you for your fortieth?'

Charlotte poured two glasses of chilled white wine and handed one to Mira. 'What kind of hunch?'

'Darling. It's nothing really.'

'Go on?'

'Well, you did ask. Everyone but you can see he's just after you for your money.'

'Mira, with all due respect, we've been down this road before and I can tell you, hand on heart, he loves me. Not for convenience or money, I can tell. I feel it.'

'Well, I think you need to have a word with Lucy.'

'Mira, please. We seem to be going over old ground here.'

'With all due respect, Charlotte, I think it's you who is out of the loop here. If no one else is going to say it, I am.'

'Are you jealous, Mira? I didn't want to say that, but you forced me.'

'I'm not jealous of your father's things, which have gone missing.'

'What on earth are you talking about? This is ridiculous.'

'Lucy doesn't seem to think so. Apparently, she saw Peter coming out of your father's office and it appears a lot of his personal items are missing.'

'What?'

'His watch and gold cigar lighter, among others,' Mira said confidently.

Charlotte shook her head and tapped an impatient foot.

'I just want you to be happy, Charlotte. This is not about me, I'm just the messenger. My guess is that he's probably disappeared by now. Fled to cash in his stash and buy himself a new pair of scruffy trainers.'

36

DEAR ME

On returning to Loxley, Charlotte went immediately to her father's study. The items were indeed missing. His pocket watch, solid gold cigar lighter and, on discussion with Mrs Hathersage, it seemed some other items too: a couple of paintings and some antique silverware.

Devastation hit Charlotte right in her gut, as though deception and anger were wrenching her vital organs. How could he let her down like this? After everything he'd said? She had to speak to him. It was strange, but now obvious, that he hadn't contacted her. Mira's hunch appeared to be good.

Charlotte sent a text.

'*Peter, how could you? You deceived me like a true professional. Took me for a ride and used me. Took my heart and threw it in the bin, like it was worth nothing. I want to speak to you and to see if you have the courage to meet me. C.*'

Peter replied, '*I have no idea what you are talking about. Is this a joke?*'

'*I want to meet you. Somewhere neutral. How about the bar*

where we had our second date? 8pm this evening? I need some explanations.'

Charlotte arrived early, wearing all black and boots. She thought about taking the same booth as before, but instead chose a table in the centre of the room. She didn't want to feel cornered and wanted a quick escape once she'd said what she needed to say. She took her seat and ordered two glasses of water.

'Hi,' Peter said, pulling out the chair opposite and taking his place.

'Hi. Thanks for coming, Peter. I appreciate it.'

'What choice did I have?'

'Look, I'll get straight to the point. I've made up my mind and there's no turning back. I don't want a fuss and please don't make a scene in here, OK?'

'OK. Go on then.'

'Good. I think it's best we split up. You know I have to have trust and respect in my relationships and this time, you've gone a step too far.'

'What are you talking about?'

'Peter, please don't humiliate me. You know perfectly well what I'm talking about.'

'No, I don't. Is this the scaremongers again? The jealous ones?'

'I can't trust you, Peter. I wish you would just come clean and then you can walk away with some pride and dignity.'

'This is ridiculous. Whatever this is, you've got it all wrong. I've done nothing to cause this. Are you saying I'm not honest and reliable?'

'I'm saying I can't trust you and that's vitally important. Don't you understand?'

'No. It makes no sense at all. I think you need to look a

little closer to home to find the truth. Remember last time? I might be from a different class than you, but that doesn't make me dishonest. I might have a different accent than yours, but that doesn't make me a liar. I might not have as much money as you—because let's face it, this is what this is really about—but I wanted nothing from you. Well, that's actually a lie. Because all I wanted was *you*. You are my everything, my soulmate, my true love. Why would I want to ruin that? It just doesn't make any sense.'

'I know you stole those items of father's. I have proof.'

'You what? What do you think I am? Desperate?'

'Lucy saw you taking them.'

'Taking what?'

'Peter, please don't make this any harder than it is. You know what you took, and I'd appreciate having them back. Didn't you break your grandfather's watch some time ago?'

'Well, yes, but what's that got to do with anything?'

'It's just too much of a coincidence.'

'What is?'

'No one else would have taken those things, Peter. I'm not going to the police. Yet. I'll spare you that, but they are things which belonged to father and they should be returned. Including the paintings.'

'I don't know what you're talking about.'

'Peter, please. Like I said, I won't press charges if you just hand them back. Drop them by the house, any time. I won't be able to forgive you, but at least we'll be able to draw a line under this.'

Peter shook his head. 'Look, I don't have the things, whatever they are, and I'm hurt by the accusation. Think long and hard about what you're saying here, because this is very destructive. You're breaking my heart, Charlotte.'

'It's over, Peter. I'm going to leave now and, like I say, I don't want a fuss. Just please return the items and let us both move on. And the paintings, please.'

'I don't have any paintings.'

'How many other people have you conned like this? Stolen their trust and their hearts? You let me down and you promised you wouldn't.' Charlotte stood and started walking for the door.

'Wait!' Peter said. 'You've got this all wrong, Charlotte. All wrong. Think about Lucy's track record. She's done everything to make this hard for us.'

Charlotte started to sob. 'I feel such a fool, Peter. Everyone was right. You're just a common thief.'

'Just do me one favour. Go to your tree. Go to that wise old tree and ask it where the truth lies, because I know the truth and I think you do too, really. Ask yourself about all the great times we've had together and how we thought we were invincible. If you still come to the same conclusion, I will respect that. I'll be devastated, but I will never contact you again. Never. I can't see myself ever loving again, but I will try my damnedest to try to erase you from my memory.' He stood up. 'You think you've been hard done to here, but I can hold my head high and be proud to be me. It's you who will be burdened with this for a very long time.'

'I'm leaving now, Peter.'

'So that's it, then? Guilty without trial? We leave it in this dreadful state and just walk away?'

Charlotte didn't reply. She took the door handle, opened the door, and left without looking back.

~

On returning home, Charlotte took a bath and, after cleaning herself scrupulously and washing her hair, lay back and held her head under the water, with her eyes open. As she gasped for breath, her arms automatically pushed her up and she sat bolt upright, coughing and gasping. Her eyes filled with tears and she felt as though she emptied her soul into the dirty bathwater. She began to shiver as the water became cold.

She climbed out and dried herself and then sat on the edge of the bed. They were there. The four tarot cards prominently staring at her. She reached over and picked them up.

Peter had given her something she'd never had previously —the feeling of true, deep, passionate love, a love that brought out the real Charlie. No other man had ever unlocked that in her. It was something that felt a little unreal, like a fantasy, but it also had a very real connective side which filled her soul with light and warmth and optimism.

Peter was nothing like her father, who was honourable and honest, dependable, generous, and benevolent. He did have a touch and a look that no other man had blessed her with, but her father's strict code and ruthless leadership were what got things done, and what she ultimately respected. Peter had made her forget that. Even the tyrannical school she'd hated so much had given her structure and discipline and order, and that was ingrained in her. In reality, she craved it.

Peter was naughty, funny and playful, but that was all short-lived. She needed someone dependable and trustworthy, not a conman and a liar. With that she turned all four cards over and stared at the fourth. Then picked it up.

They were always right. Proven. Reliable and true.

New Birth

The picture showed a newborn child held lovingly in its mother's arms.

The words read, 'The birth of new life is the greatest gift. Cherish it and nurture your lifelong bond.'

Charlotte didn't know what to think. What did it mean? It had no relevance, no purpose. She let go of the card and it fell like a stone onto the rest of the deck. She collapsed on the floor and stared at the ceiling. She let her mind drift and then remembered a tarot card book she had somewhere in the library. Maybe it could reveal more about the combination of cards.

She ventured down to the library. The room was as big as most people's entire house, on two levels, with a black wrought-iron spiral staircase leading up to a mezzanine level filled with the classics, huge encyclopaedias and atlases. But it was the lower floor Charlotte wanted, where she kept the books on popular culture, autobiographies, novels and a whole five shelves dedicated to self-help and psychology.

Where was that book? She ran her finger along the shelves, doing that looking sideways and upside-down thing you have to do when searching the spines.

She came to the last book on the third shelf. It wasn't the one she'd been looking for, but it had a striking scarlet-and-black cover, and so, intrigued, she started to pull it out. A piece of paper fell out and floated to the ground like a feather. It was folded in half and had been placed between the last book and the bookend. The paper looked a little familiar.

She picked it up and carried it to the little reading table, switched on the lamp and sat down. It read:

Dear me,
You know why I am writing this.

You are so very lonely in this world. All your attempts to make a success of life are futile. You strive to succeed, and all you do is fail. You are worthless and insignificant. People know you are a failure, and they mock you.

Rejection is what you are most frightened of, and yet you crave it. Rejection is you; rejection is your soul.

You despise your mother, but you cannot show it; you adore your father, but really you hate him. You hate him in the pit of your stomach. You cry for him, yet you do not know why.

You have no trust in people, but you have no trust in yourself.

Life is not worth living, and it's going to end; yes, it's going to end and now is the time. Thank you to all my "family", thank you for bringing me into this "incredible life", and to show you how thankful I am, I will leave you.

Cry for me now; I am gone. I am no one.

Bye.

Charlie, age 13

Charlotte let her head fall backward and closed her eyes. She'd come full circle, from the time when she attempted to take her life all those years before. She cried and cried. Her world had truly fallen apart. She'd once again been abandoned and abused and enough was enough.

~

The following four weeks were spent with no direction or purpose whatsoever. There were invitations to parties, presentations, award ceremonies and even shopping trips with Mira, which Charlotte turned down. She even terminated her support for the animal shelter. She felt she had to withdraw from public life, from further humiliation and judgement. She couldn't face having to explain, justify and talk about things she simply didn't have the answers to. It was easier to hide away.

Peter never delivered the items, and she resented him even more. No one had ever treated her so badly. She definitely was the fool—taken in by his charm and romance, and then spat out like a sour gooseberry.

She squirrelled herself away in her room and had food sporadically delivered, and then would leave most of. She periodically heard her mother on the floor above, crashing around or shouting in the middle of the night, but she didn't have the energy to investigate. Lucy was home fewer and fewer weekends as she became more independent, and Charlotte tried to put on a brave face.

Cartwright moved around quietly, like an old pair of reliable slippers, and was always there should she need anything. He fully understood what to do and what not to do. In many ways, he'd become her male rock, and Charlotte trusted him to make decisions on her behalf and manage the household in her absence.

'Do you want me to arrange for the stonemason to repair the entrance archway, madam? A car ran into it last week and there is some damage to the main structure.'

'Yes, please, Cartwright. Just organise the quote, and if you think it's reasonable, access the maintenance account and deal with it directly. I don't want to have to think about those sorts of issues for a while.'

'What about the replacement garden furniture we talked about? And the Bentley is beginning to have mechanical issues on a regular basis. Shall I organise a replacement?'

'Yes, go ahead. I can't think about these things right now. If you identify a need, then please just go straight ahead.'

'No problem, madam. Can I get you some tea? Or maybe something a little stronger, perhaps?'

'Yes. Gin.'

'Right away, madam.'

37

MACKEREL AND CAPERS

Strolling around the parkland was soon becoming Charlotte's sole venture out of doors. Contact with nature seemed to be her only saviour. The flipside was it sometimes reminded her of Peter. She'd hear him in the back of her mind talking about how trees store their energy in their roots over winter, ready to burst into life in the spring, or else she'd hold a vision of him prodding the bark with a stick.

It was early and the air fresh. Charlotte had been up for some hours, and it was just becoming light. She helped herself to some toast and tea and then mooched around the garden aimlessly as the morning mist slowly began to lift. Her stomach ached and, although the fresh air was helping, the cramps began to worsen. She fell to her knees and vomited into the tree Mira had gifted her. She felt lightheaded and weak. Maybe it was something she'd eaten the previous evening. She'd have a word with Cartwright later. She regained her feet and caught sight of him polishing what looked like a new Bentley. It was parked by the front door, right beside the old one. She thought it was strange to have both of them. She only needed one. She decided to go over and query the situation and then promptly vomited again into a stone water trough. She then abandoned the idea and, using her hands along the wall, navigated to the wooden door and collapsed on the floor. Mrs Hathersage found her in a crumpled heap.

'Come on, Miss Charlotte, let's get you upstairs and into bed. Are you not feeling well?'

'I don't know what came over me. I thought maybe last night's soup?'

'It was fresh, and I had it too, so I don't think so.' She helped Charlotte up the stairs.

'Something doesn't feel right,' she said, holding her stomach.

Instead of heading for a lie-down, Charlotte ran herself a hot bath, added natural lavender oil and lit a sandalwood candle. She felt she needed a soothing influence and time to breathe and relax.

Time seemed to stand still. She'd shocked herself by finding the old suicide note and it felt as though she'd been emptied inside, as though she was just a shell. No emotion, no feeling anymore.

Later, she sat in the cold window seat, looking aimlessly across the estate.

'I'd like to have dinner later this evening, Cartwright. Would you see if Mother would like to join me too? We've both been too isolated lately and I think it will do us good to eat together.'

'Certainly, madam. In the dining room?'

'No, in the orangery for a change. Please set up in the orangery. Nothing too fancy, just simple china and cutlery.'

'Certainly, madam. One more thing, if you have a minute?'

'Yes, what is it?'

'I wanted to book a little time off, if that's OK? A holiday.'

'Oh! A holiday. I mean, of course. You know I need you around the house. I can't do without you these days, but... yes, of course. How long?'

'Five weeks, madam. I'm planning to go and stay with my sister in South Africa.'

'South Africa? Five weeks? That's a very long time to not have you around. Have you checked with Mrs Hathersage?'

'Yes, madam.'

'Good. In that case, can you submit in writing the dates and I'll schedule that in to the diary.'

'It's next week, madam,' he said, with a courteous smile. 'When would you like dinner this evening?'

'Oh. I see. Well, I guess you haven't had much time off this year.'

'None, madam.'

'Then it's granted, but I'll need to find a stand-in for the time you're away.'

'I'll look into it, madam.'

'Check with Mother regarding dinner, but 7pm is perfect for me.'

Cartwright nodded and left the room.

Charlotte busied herself with a crochet blanket pattern she'd started months ago and hadn't felt up to finishing. Over-whelmingly, she felt the urge to make her home cosy and safe and, well... homely. She smiled to herself. Something she hadn't done for quite some time.

'I haven't eaten in the orangery since Princess Margaret came to stay. It was quite an event,' came her mother's frail voice.

'Good evening, Mother. When did Princess Margaret stay here?'

'Oh, it was many years ago. She liked it here. Said it was one of her favourite places to hide away and let her hair down. She was quite a woman.'

'I heard. Did she sleep in the King's room?'

'Yes, I think she did. I seem to remember you were only a baby, and we didn't want her disturbed by your crying. Yes, the King's room. Or maybe the east wing? I can't remember. What's for dinner?'

'I wasn't feeling so well this morning, but I've been craving mackerel and, for some reason, capers. Come and sit with me. You seem well?'

'Are you still with that man? Lovely eyes. Such a lovely man.'

Charlotte looked away at the window and the huge cedar tree on the lawn. 'No, Mother.'

'Shame. I could feel he loved you. He liked Eccles cakes, too. We had Eccles cakes when Princess Margaret came, you know.'

'Did you?'

'Honest, hardworking hands, those.'

'Dinner is served, madam,' Cartwright broke in, as he opened the door carefully.

'Wonderful, thank you.'

'Mackerel for you, madam and salmon for you, Lady Winterbourne.'

'Thank you, Cartwright. I don't know what we would have done without you recently.'

Cartwright disappeared and then returned with a silver tray upon which was the salmon and side dishes containing Hollandaise sauce and capers. He removed the plate from the tray and placed it on the table. Charlotte watched her mother smile and felt a warm feeling inside. She hoped for more times like this.

'Is there any pepper?' Charlotte's mother asked.

Cartwright nodded and, as he reached to retrieve the condiments, he exposed his breast pocket. Charlotte noticed a glint from a pocket-watch chain as the candlelight caught it. She'd seen that glint before, and she noticed it had a damaged link. A shiver went through her entire body, and she felt the urge to vomit again. She swiftly reached for a glass of water and sipped it, the water noticeably rippling as her hand began to shake.

Father's watch!

38

TWO TINY PHOTOGRAPHS

Peter positioned himself in his mum's old brown leather chair, the armrests weathered like a beloved pair of walking boots, the springs under the worn and sunken cushion no longer offering much support. He looked around the room and chuckled to himself at the botched roof light which had never been fixed, and the brown stain now covering half the ceiling. It was time for a new start. Time to move on. The offer of a new job managing wildlife conservation in the wilds of Scotland was too good to reject, and the distance away from the past few years would be what he needed to clear his head and have a fresh start. He drew in a deep breath, then slowly exhaled and took out the two tiny photographs he'd slotted into the 'secret' compartment of his wallet.

The first was a picture of his dear mum helping him to build a sandcastle on holiday, patting a sand-filled bucket to create the ultimate centrepiece for the castle and looking happy and proud.

'I love you, Mum,' he said, trying to hold back a tear.

The second was a photo of Charlotte and Peter taken in a

photo booth, during their trip to the Cotswolds. Charlotte was sitting on Peter's knee and they were both pulling funny faces, with their tongues sticking out. She looked happy, her eyes bright with joy and her smile wide and full of life. It was a moment in time when she'd looked carefree and effortlessly beautiful—the most beautiful woman he'd ever seen, in fact. He stared at the photo and couldn't take his eyes off her. He moved his thumb over her face as a tear slowly trickled down his cheek.

He placed the photo of his mum back in his wallet, took another breath and wiped the tear from his face, then ripped the other photo in two and threw it into a black bin liner, along with some old socks and the potato peelings and other food waste from dinner. He would get the chair sent up later, but for now, he placed the keys on the table, took one last look at the room, and closed the door behind him.

The train trundled through into the night and Peter slept intermittently as the constant and monotonous clickety-clack, clickety-clack became ingrained in his brain. He slumped in his seat, thinking about eagles, otters and pine marten, how much more straightforward animals were than humans, and how proud he was to be privileged to be protecting and working with them.

On arrival, they put Peter in the bothy, a kind of small, thatched cottage within the nature reserve. It was a quaint and rustic hideaway, with leaded windows and curly metal latches, secured slightly open when he arrived to allow the warm after-noon breeze to pass through the open plan lounge and into the bedroom, with its crisp white linen and blue tartan curtains. Peter put down his bag and instantly looked up at the ceiling. It was clean. No damp patches, and it smelled of pine forest and heather. He smiled. This was his new home now. It came with the job and it was perfect.

A robin was in full song as the breeze gently rustled the leaves of the mature oak trees outside, and Peter ventured out to explore what lay beyond. He followed a small path through the trees and noticed the robin was following him. He held out his hand, in the hope the friendly bird would hop on and introduce itself. It hesitated, bobbed up and down twice and then flew onto his fingers. It stood there and looked at him.

'Hi, Mum,' he said, feeling choked.

They continued their walk. Ahead, through the trees, the sunlight was shimmering on what appeared to be water. Peter persevered and eventually arrived at the edge of a vast lake surrounded by forest, with a backdrop of snow-peaked hills and the biggest sky he'd ever seen. A breath filled his lungs that was pure, fresh and tasted of home. He held out his hand, and the robin just carried on looking at him.

'It's going to be alright, isn't it, Mum?'

The robin continued to look straight into his eyes, then brushed its head up against his fingers. Its black eyes again focused on him, then it bobbed once, then again, and then flew off, disappearing into the lush green undergrowth.

Peter had stopped by a rocky outcrop. A pair of hen harriers were soaring on a thermal just above him. Their huge spreading wingspans and effortless flight made Peter gasp.

'Why didn't I come here earlier?' he thought to himself.

'I've just taken tea up for Miss Lucy. Would you like some too, Miss Charlotte?' Mrs Hathersage asked in a soft tone.

Charlotte said nothing. She continued to gaze out of the window with her chin in her hand. A robin landed on the ledge and began tilting its head, bobbing up and down as if trying to gain her attention, but she didn't pay it any notice and continued to stare aimlessly out into space. Mrs Hathersage put down a tray of tea next to the one she'd placed there an hour before.

'You have to drink and eat something,' she said, urging Charlotte to come out of her daze. Charlotte remained silent. Mrs Hathersage turned to leave. 'I'll bring some fruit a little later.'

'I need to see Cartwright.'

'He's on leave, Miss Charlotte. He left early and said you'd approved it.'

Charlotte gritted her teeth and thumped her fist on the table. 'I need to speak to him right now.'

Mrs Hathersage became flustered and toyed with her apron. 'I don't think that will be possible. Is it something to do with the car?'

'The car?'

'He said that you gave him the Bentley as a thank you for dedicated service.'

Charlotte was dumbstruck.

'I thought it a little strange, but he has been here a very long time,' Mrs Hathersage said. By now her apron was almost completely wrapped around her hand.

Charlotte leaped up. 'And so have you, Mrs Hathersage, but one thing you've never done is betray me,' she cried. She strode across the room, out of the door and over the lawn into the walled garden.

A few moments later Charlotte heard footsteps, and Lucy came running into the walled garden. Charlotte stood wielding an axe she had taken from the tool store and was offering it up to her father's tree.

'Don't do that, Mummy, don't do that! Just think about what you're doing,' Lucy said, holding up her hands.

'I'll do whatever I want. I'm not trapped by anyone or anything. I've had enough. Father left me with this burden, Mother is crazy, you have no respect for me or anyone else and I've been lied to and taken for a fool, so what have I to lose? My dignity as a daughter, a mother, a woman. I can chop down this tree if I want to. I hate him, this place, the responsibility of this life.' She drew back the axe.

'No!' shouted Lucy.

The axe hit the tree and made a cut. Charlotte drew it back and chopped it into the stem again.

'Mummy, please. I'm scared. Stop that.'

But Charlotte continued chopping. Sap oozed out of the scars and ran fast down the stem. Then, with one final blow, the tree toppled and crashed to the floor. Charlotte stood looking at the hacked stump and threw the axe over her shoulder with a sense of accomplishment.

Lucy ran back to the house. Scared of what her mother would do next, she flung open the door and fell straight into the arms of Mrs Hathersage.

'I'm scared,' she said. 'I've never seen her like this before. What do we do?'

'Don't worry, it will all be OK. She's been a little low recently and I'm sure it will pass. We have to stay calm.'

'But she's like a wild animal. I'm worried she might do something awful.'

'She obviously needs to get a few things out of her system.

We just let it happen. I'll keep my eye on you, Miss Lucy, don't you worry about that.'

'Do you think it's anything to do with me?'

'No,' she said reassuringly.

'She was hacking Grandpa's tree. Was it his fault?'

'Sometimes our parents frustrate us, and even let us down. It might be that.'

Lucy buried her head in Mrs Hathersage's chest. 'It could be Peter. She hasn't been normal since he went.'

Mrs Hathersage continued to hold her safe. 'That might be part of it too.'

'And what about Cartwright? Why did he leave?'

Mrs Hathersage sighed. 'I think he made a very big mistake.'

The evening came and Charlotte still hadn't been back inside. A chill in the air accompanied the disappearance of the sun and Lucy looked out of her bedroom window, but it was too dark to see anything.

'It's bedtime now, Miss Lucy,' Mrs Hathersage said, clutching a mug of warm milk.

'Will we be OK?' Lucy asked.

'Of course we will. Your mother is upset, but she'll come around. She always does.'

'OK.' Lucy clambered into bed, pulling her duvet tight to her chin and wishing that everything really was going to be fine.

A short while later she heard the creaking of a door and footsteps along the corridor.

'Mrs Hathersage... is that you?' There was no reply. 'Mummy? Is that you?' Again, there was no reply. Lucy crept to the door and opened it slightly to see down the hall. The candlestick was down and the door to the secret passage, wide open. She put on her dressing gown and, slowly and tentatively, went to investigate. The door was open and the room lit only by the reading lamp on the desk. Lucy entered.

'Mummy?' she said nervously. She scoured the room and noticed the right-hand drawer of the desk was fully open. She peered in. The hunting knife sheath was lying there, but the knife was missing. Beside the sheath was a pregnancy test strip alongside a letter.

Dear Peter

Wherever you are, I hope this finds you.

I write from the deepest corner of my heart, in the hope you may forgive me.

Words might seem cheap now, but I had to declare my true feelings.

I have come to realise many things since I met you and I've been foolish and hurtful in my actions. You grounded me, showed me genuine love and made me appreciate the important things in life. Walking in the rain together, looking out on life from the top of my beautiful tree, a single kiss on the forehead and your strong hands guiding me along the riverbank.

I once had the courage to jump the weir and hoped as a young girl I could banish my anxieties. I've been spoiled, I know that, but none of it is worth anything without you. I wasted my trust on others and deeply regret my conceited and ugly treatment of you—the man I love.

Without you, I am nothing. Without you, I can see no future, and without you, I am empty.

I should have stood up to others around me. I was weak, arrogant and judgemental. With you around, I felt safe, secure and loved, and I took it all for granted. I was wasteful with my gratitude, malicious in my condemnation and careless with your heart.

I realise it may all be too late and that I may never see you again. I wish that not to be the case. Deep down, I want to walk with you as an equal and love you in the same way you loved me. I admire you for standing up to me. I needed that. In many ways, you are the most courageous man I have ever met, and I look up to you from my position of shame.

Please forgive me.

My deepest love to you.

Your forever
  Charlie

39

THE SWING

Peter continued through the forest to observe a group of red deer cross in front of him. He was surprised at the size of them. Much bigger than he'd thought, and the stag that led the group was huge, with impressive antlers and his head held high, as if he owned the world. Confident, bold and with purpose, the stag took the group over the road. Peter hung back to let them cross and not spook them. His phone, on silent, was buzzing with an incoming call. He ignored it. Who would be calling at this time of night?

The deer went on their way and Peter returned to the bothy to finish his unpacking and make some supper. His phone started buzzing again.

'Hello?'

'Peter?'

'Yes. Who is it?'

'It's Lucy.'

'Lucy? Lucy who?'

'Lucy. Charlotte's daughter.'

'Lucy! I didn't expect to hear from you.'

'Peter. You need to come quickly. We need you. I need you.'

'Is this some sort of trick? Because if it is—'

Lucy cut him short. 'No, Peter, I'm serious. I'm so sorry for what I've done.'

'What's wrong?'

'It's Mummy. I'm worried she's going to do something stupid. Grandpa's knife is missing, and she's nowhere to be found.'

Peter struggled to respond.

'Please, Peter. I'm sorry for everything, but you were the only person Mummy truly loved and... please come quickly. The country house.'

'Lucy, it's nothing to do with me now. I have a new life in Scotland. There's nothing I can do. Is Cartwright on duty tonight?'

'No, he's gone. It's you I need. Mummy needs you. Please, I'm scared.'

Peter looked out into the darkness of the night and shook his head.

'Lucy, look. I'm a long way away... Lucy? Are you there?'

The phone was dead, out of battery. He threw it onto the floor. 'Damn!'

Lucy headed downstairs and found Mrs Hathersage pacing the kitchen. 'Where is she?'

'I don't know. I've scoured the house and gardens and there's no sign.'

'The knife is missing. Grandpa's knife. She has it, I'm sure.' They looked at each other and Mrs Hathersage put her hand on Lucy's shoulder.

Lucy thrust the letter into her hand. 'Look at this.'

'Oh, Lord!'

'I'll call the gamekeepers and get them on the job.' Lucy put her hand on hers. 'I'm calling the police.'

'You must find her. You must!'

The head gamekeeper responded with haste. 'I'll get the boys on it, don't worry. Any ideas where she might be?'

'We have no idea. She could be anywhere. She might have left the estate even.'

'Have you called the police?'

'No, not yet.'

'Do it now. You keep the house safe and I'll mobilise the lads to scour the park.'

Search lights, Land Rovers and hunting dogs set out into the parkland in military order. They searched the grounds, under bridges, the redundant cottage and the back road, with no sign. Lucy and Mrs Hathersage checked every room in the house, the cellar and even the boiler room, but she was nowhere to be seen.

'Any luck, lads?' Mrs Hathersage called to the game-keepers.

'No. She's not in the park.'

Minutes later, blue flashing lights could be seen speeding along the drive and then illuminating the house as the car came to a halt and two officers stepped out. Lucy and Mrs Hathersage greeted them and filled them in on the details so far.

'So, she went missing around 9.30pm, is that correct?' the sergeant asked.

'Yes. She has a knife and we're worried she might get herself into trouble.'

'Is there anywhere she could be? A friend's house, a pub maybe?'

'No. Definitely not,' Lucy said. 'We checked the London house, but she's not there.'

Mrs Hathersage was beginning to look dizzy and she was clutching her chest.

'I think you need some tea and a sit-down for a moment,' Lucy told her. She turned to the police. 'Please help us.'

'I can't get a dog search team out until the morning and the helicopter is currently out on another job, so I'll have to call for backup and see what we can do.'

Another couple of officers arrived within ten minutes and began combing the hedgerows, nearby lanes and outbuildings as the night closed in.

The noise of a police radio and a flashlight startled Lucy. She and Mrs Hathersage had drifted off to sleep side by side in the chair, wrapped in a blanket.

'Have you found her?' Lucy asked. 'What time is it?'

'It's 2.30am. I don't think there is anything else we can do until I get the dog team here, ETA 5.30am. Are you sure there isn't an obvious place she could be?'

'No.'

Suddenly, the headlights of a vehicle lit up their room as it raced down the drive.

'This could be the dog team,' the sergeant said. 'They're early, though.'

Mrs Hathersage peered through the window at the speeding vehicle. 'It's probably the gamekeepers,' she said with some optimism as it came closer. 'They've been out all night looking. Yes, it's a pickup. It's the gamekeepers. Oh, I do hope it's good news.'

The truck came to a crunching halt on the gravel and out stepped the dark silhouette of a man carrying a torch. Lucy and Mrs Hathersage rushed to the door.

'Where is she?' the voice said.

'We don't know,' they said, looking at each other.

It was Jim Armitage, the local butcher.

'I heard she was missing and wanted to let you know I saw someone walking down Quarry Lane by the old malt mill when I was coming back from a delivery. I think it could have been her. It was getting dark and I couldn't see her face, but thought you needed to know.'

'Thank you, Jim. We need all the information we can get. Let the police sergeant know.'

'OK, will do. And I'll go and search out towards the mill and the quarry.'

Mrs Hathersage smiled at Lucy. It was the best news yet of her mother's whereabouts and Jim had brought some optimism into the cold, bleak feeling within the house.

Mrs Hathersage took to the kitchen to make some tea and hot chocolate for them both. The sergeant raced to and from his car. His radio was constantly busy with the voices of seemingly calm operatives mobilising units and reporting back. Lucy huddled on the window seat in a stiff wool blanket as Mrs Hathersage brought through the drinks.

'I've mobilised everyone to the quarry,' the sergeant said with kind authority. 'The gamekeepers and an additional officer, and the news from the dog search team is their ETA is one hour.'

'Will they find her?' Lucy said, clutching her blanket tight to her chest.

'They're doing their very best. I'm sure they will.' Mrs Hathersage was desperately trying to remain calm for Lucy, but there was a distinct hint of uncertainty in her voice.

'I'm heading up to the quarry now to co-ordinate the search. Will you hold the fort here, Mrs Hathersage?' The sergeant wrote down his phone number and laid it on the table.

'Of course. We're tired, but we can't rest until she is found.'

'Please, just find her. I'm worried and scared,' said Lucy, wiping tears from her eyes.

'We'll find her. Don't you worry about that,' the sergeant said, before striding out of the door.

'You left your—' Mrs Hathersage stopped. She wasn't able to tell him he'd left his hat and torch on the table. Seconds later, they heard the car on the gravel, and he was gone. She put her arm around Lucy, and they huddled together, Lucy in floods of tears and Mrs Hathersage trying to be strong.

'They will find her, won't they?'

'Of course, my child. They know what they're doing. Don't you worry.'

Moments later, they heard the car returning. It skidded to a halt on the gravel.

'He's realised he's forgotten his things,' Mrs Hathersage said, raising her eyebrows and grabbing the items.

The door flung open, and she nearly dropped the torch.

'Where is she?'

'Peter! I knew you would come,' Lucy shouted.

'She's been missing for a long time now. We're worried sick and have no idea where she is, but the police are searching up by the quarry.' Mrs Hathersage placed the hat and torch on the table.

'I know where she is,' said Peter. 'Let's hope it's not too late.

I'd have been here an hour ago if it wasn't for a puncture and three petrol stops.'

'Where?' asked Mrs Hathersage and Lucy simultaneously.

'The lake. The oak tree by the lake.'

Lucy shook her head. 'The lake? No one goes down there.'

'Exactly.' Peter checked his head torch and ran down the steps.

Lucy chased after him. 'Wait. I'm coming with you.'

'No! No, Lucy. I need to be fast.'

'We're a team now. I'm coming,' Lucy insisted. She followed Peter across the lawn and down through the parkland.

'We need to be quick.'

'I know. Come on,' she said.

They raced through the trees, jumping over roots, fallen branches and the badger holes. The moonlight highlighting the many obstacles was a welcome help, and the two of them galloped along the riverbank towards the bridge.

'Where is it, Peter?'

'It's gone. Looks like it's been washed away in the storm. I can see remnants of it over there.' He pointed to a pile of timber smashed against the rocks and some beneath his feet. He looked down, and the head torch picked out the etching in the wood. 'Peter & Charlie.'

'There's another way. Come on.'

Peter used the moonlight to pick his way through the undergrowth and shone the torch for Lucy so she could navigate the undulating ground.

'Ouch!' Lucy fell, twisting her ankle in a badger hole.

'You alright?' Peter shouted, frustrated at the slow pace and damaged bridge.

'Yes. I'm fine. I'm with you.' She took to her feet and limped along cautiously.

Peter heard the rushing of water and knew they were on the right path. He jumped over a log and then down into the shallows at the top of the weir. He walked purposefully to the middle, to where the fast-flowing funnel of water looked like a torrential oil slick moving in the eerie, dark silence before erupting over the top with all the noise of an alpine avalanche. He'd jumped it before, so it was possible, but he hesitated.

'Lucy?'

'Yes?'

'This is where I leave you.'

'No way, mister. Nothing's stopping me.'

Peter sighed. He took one look at Lucy quivering on the bank and one look at the terrifying leap, then walked back through the water, grabbed her, and put her over his shoulder.

'Hang on tight.' He started to run, his feet occasionally slipping on the wet stone. He gathered pace, reached the edge and... Lucy screamed, and Peter felt the rush of the air and the water below them as they jumped.

He tried to grab onto Lucy as he felt her slipping away, then his foot hit something hard and his knee took the full load of both of them.

They collapsed in a heap, Lucy still clinging to Peter.

'You OK?' he asked, catching his breath.

'Yes.'

'We made it.'

He scaled the bank onto the grassy slope and Lucy jumped free.

'Thanks.'

Peter looked her in the eye and said nothing, then took her hand. 'Come on, we need to hurry.'

A hanging mist along the shoreline made it difficult to see more than a couple of strides ahead and they stumbled their way along, ducking under the low branches of a majestic chestnut tree, which looked dark and mysterious in the mist, like a witch with her arms long and open, guiding them in the right direction. Peter knew the oak wasn't far away, but he couldn't see it. Suddenly, he spooked a blackbird. *Chip, chip, chip*—the bird sounded its alarm, breaking the silence of the calm, melancholy air. The screech of an owl could also be heard through the mist ahead. The eerie sound made Peter and Lucy stop and look at each other.

'It's not far now. Hurry.' Peter scrambled up a slope, grabbing hold of a sturdy protruding root to pull himself up. The owl broke the silence again and he shone his torch to see. The light instantly picked up the body of Charlotte, hanging from the tree like a discarded rag, her grubby cream dress and legs gently blowing in the breeze. He scrambled with his hands on the floor to get to his feet and came across the discarded seat of the swing, the rope ends severed brutally and the knife lying beside it.

Charlotte's ghostly figure hung limp and motionless, the rope around her neck with the hangman's knot, just like he'd shown her, with its thirteen wraps above the noose. Peter took the knife and, rising up on his feet, grabbed Charlotte around the waist and cut the rope with one stroke.

Her body fell like a rag doll against his chest, and the two of them collapsed onto the floor. Lucy watched from a distance. She couldn't believe what she was seeing. It didn't look like her mum hanging there. None of it seemed real.

Peter laid Charlotte on the ground, draped his jacket over her and started to resuscitate, tilting her head back and breathing his air into her lungs. One breath and then another, followed by another and another. There was no response. Her face was pale.

'Come on, you stupid girl!' he cried, and started another breath.

'Mummy!' Lucy shouted.

'Lucy, call the house and tell them to get an ambulance here as quick as possible. A helicopter. Whatever! Quickly!'

Peter's hoarse but commanding voice jolted Lucy into action. He continued the breathing, but Charlotte's body lay completely still and lifeless. He relentlessly forced his life breath into her, unable to stop, willing her to recover.

He struggled for his own breath and took a second to fill his lungs and feel Charlotte's hand for a pulse. She was almost completely cold. Her face looked at peace. Her mouth had a slight hint of a smile and she looked calm. He put his hand on her cheek and a tear dripped onto her face.

'You stupid bitch,' he said, losing control. 'You stupid, stupid, beautiful woman.'

'Look!' Lucy shouted.

Peter turned to see. 'What is it?'

Lucy showed him the stark white pregnancy test stick she'd found on the ground by the swing. It was identical to the one in the drawer.

'She must have got a second opinion. It's positive,' she said, looking into Peter's eyes.

Peter looked at the test stick and gave her one last breath, a deep one, with everything he had to give, put one hand on her cheek and the other on her stomach, then broke down. She was gone. Silent. Unresponsive.

He gave another breath, knowing it was futile and knowing he had failed her. Her body was motionless and drained of life. Free from all those worries and anxieties.

'There's nothing else we can do. We're too late.'

Lucy looked at Peter in disbelief as he held Charlotte's cold and defenceless body.

'You have to try again, Peter.'

Peter shook his head.

'Please!'

Suddenly, there was a small cough. Peter immediately noticed a twitch in Charlotte's arm. He put his cheek by her mouth and sensed her faint breath. His heart racing, he shouted, 'Charlie...!' He put his hand against her face again. 'Charlie, can you hear me?'

He ran his fingers repeatedly through her hair. Slowly, one eye opened and then the other. She looked at him, her face peaceful and calm, and mouthed, 'Peter'.

There was no sound, but he heard her loud and clear.

'Charlie... I love you, Charlie.'

The End

ABOUT THE AUTHOR

J A Crawshaw was born in Yorkshire, England, in 1969. He is
the father to two grown up sons and a passionate
environmentalist and tree lover. This story was greatly inspired
by nature and its ability to influence our lives and hopes the
natural energy came through while reading this book.
He is currently working on other contemporary fiction titles
including an exciting trilogy.
Sneak previews, cover reveals and insider information can be
found by joining his 'Keep in Touch' group via the website,
where you will receive your free book as a thank you.

More information can be found at
www.jacrawshaw.com

ALSO BY J A CRAWSHAW

The second book in this series THE VIEW BEYOND follows straight on from where this book finishes. Find out what happens to Charlotte and Peter in this bitter sweet continuation of their journey.

Charlotte's return to a normal life, full of happiness and love, is turned upside down when an unscrupulous man leaves her destitute.

Will she crumble under the harsh reality of heartbreak, loneliness, and despair? Or earn the acceptance of the new people around her, confront her adversaries and look beyond her old life to seek a second chance of fulfilment and true love?

Her quest for the truth reveals shock results and in challenging her own beliefs and capabilities, establishes a true resilience and discovers that happiness might just be where you least expect it.

A life worth living might seem out of reach, but opening your mind to the view beyond, could be utterly life changing.

REVIEWS

We all value reviews, but seldom leave them.

Less than 1% of readers leave a review, so when I receive one, I'm thrilled. I mean, really thrilled, to the point, I leap around the room.

I would be incredibly grateful and honoured to receive feedback on any store, platform or social media site.

Here are reasons why it's so important to me.

1. I can improve my writing, so you enjoy it more.
2. I know if I'm on the right track in terms of what you like to read.
3. It gives me confidence to carry on writing.
4. It makes the book more visible to other readers.
5. It makes us writers feel loved and I'd like to share that love with you.

Scan To Review

FREE BOOK

Claim your free book when you join many others in my Keep in touch group www.jacrawshaw.com/freebook

Find your creative passion. Join the Art Group today!

Printed in Great Britain
by Amazon

44301161R00212